ALL RIGHT HERE

All Right Here

a Darling Family novel

CARRE ARMSTRONG GARDNER

Tyndale House Publishers, Inc.
Carol Stream, Illinois

Visit Tyndale online at www.tyndale.com.

Visit Carre Armstrong Gardner's website at www.carregardner.com.

TYNDALE and Tyndale's quill logo are registered trademarks of Tyndale House Publishers, Inc.

All Right Here

Designed by Jennifer Ghionzoli

Edited by Sarah Mason

Published in association with literary agent Blair Jacobson of D.C. Jacobson & Associates LLC, an Author Management Company. www.dcjacobson.com.

All Right Here is a work of fiction. Where real people, events, establishments, organizations, or locales appear, they are used fictitiously. All other elements of the novel are drawn from the author's imagination.

Library of Congress Cataloging-in-Publication Data
Gardner, Carre Armstrong.
   All right here / Carre Armstrong Gardner.
      pages cm. — (Darling family)
   ISBN 978-1-4143-8814-4 (sc)
1. Families—Maine—Fiction. 2. Foster parents—Maine—Fiction. 3. Marriage—Fiction. 4. Christian fiction. I. Title.
   PS3607.A7267A79 2014
   813'.6—dc23   2014002915

Printed in the United States of America

20   19   18   17   16   15   14
7   6   5   4   3   2   1

To Tim:

I have you fast in my fortress,
And will not let you depart,
But put you down into the dungeon
In the round-tower of my heart.

And there will I keep you forever,
Yes, forever and a day,
Till the walls shall crumble to ruin,
And moulder in dust away!

H. W. LONGFELLOW, "THE CHILDREN'S HOUR"

CHAPTER

1

NICK WAS GOING TO HATE his birthday gift. Even as she taped down the ribbon and set the wrapped package on the kitchen table, Ivy Darling was already sure of this. It was a book of Mark Strand's poetry, and although she had gotten her husband a book of poetry every birthday for the six years they had been married, he had yet to open the front cover of one of them. That did not stop her from hoping, nor from appropriating the books for her own collection after a decent waiting period. Gifts, she thought, sometimes said more about the giver than the receiver. When you gave something you loved and thought beautiful, you were inviting another person into your world. You were saying, *Here is*

something that brings me joy. I want to share that joy with you.
She couldn't help it if her husband had never been all that
much into joy sharing.

To be fair, it was also important to give something the
other person actually wanted. With this in mind, Ivy had
bought Nick a year's membership to the Copper Cove
Racquet and Fitness Club, which he would love, as well as a
bathrobe, which he needed.

She would give him all three gifts when he got home
from work, before they went to his parents' house for dinner. She did not want him to unwrap the things she had
chosen in front of his mother, who would be hurt if her own
gifts were upstaged. Nor did she want to give them in front
of Nick's sisters, who would diminish them by being bored
with everything.

She found the broom and swept up the scraps of wrapping paper, then emptied the dustpan into a plastic shopping
bag and carried it to the back porch. The five o'clock sunlight flashed off the windows of the vacant house next door,
making her squint. The place had been empty as long as
she and Nick had lived here. It was a depressing sore on the
pretty neighborhood: the house bleached and shabby in the
summer sunshine; the grass growing high against the warped
and splintered front steps, unstirred by human movement.
A faded For Rent sign sagged in one window. She turned her
back on it and went inside.

Ivy was sprinkling chopped nuts on top of the iced birthday cake when she heard Nick's car in the driveway. She met
him at the door with the remains of the frosting and a kiss.

"What's this?" he said, frowning at the sticky bowl.

"It's your birthday icing. Did you have a good day?"

He stepped around her and set his briefcase under the hall table. "It was all right. What are you doing?"

"Making your cake. We're going to your parents' for dinner, remember?"

He ran a hand through his thick hair. "I forgot. I was hoping to go for a run. What time do we have to be there?"

"Six o'clock. I wanted you to open your presents here first."

He went through to the kitchen and began washing his hands, eyeing her over the top of his glasses. "You're not wearing that to my parents' house, are you?"

Ivy looked down at her T-shirt. It was yellow, with a picture of half a cup of coffee over the words *Half Full.* Below that, her faded cutoff shorts ended in ragged hems. "What's wrong with what I'm wearing?"

"You look like a slob."

She gave him a gritty smile. "You say the nicest things."

"I'm only saying it for your own sake. Don't you have anything with a little shape to it?"

"Yes, but it wouldn't be nearly as comfortable."

"Come on, Ivy."

"All *right,* I'll change before we go. But if we're going to be on time, you have to open your presents now."

He dried his hands and turned to survey the packages on the table. "What'd you get me?"

"A present you'll love, a present you need, and a present you'll learn to love."

"Hmmm . . . ," he said, pretending to think. "A Porsche, a Porsche, and a book of poetry."

"Close. Come on, you have to open them to find out."

She sat down across from him while he opened the packages. She had been right on all scores. He was indifferent to the poetry, satisfied with the bathrobe, and pleased with the gym membership.

"There's no excuse for me now," he said, pulling his wallet from his back pocket and tucking the envelope into it. "I'll be in shape before you know it." Nick, who was already in great shape, was the only person Ivy knew who thrilled to the prospect of more self-discipline.

"You look great just the way you are," she said, standing and kissing him on the top of his head. "But if you want to half kill yourself in the gym five days a week, knock yourself out. We should probably leave in fifteen minutes, unless we want to give your mother an ulcer."

"Okay. Just . . . don't forget to change your clothes."

Her smile felt grittier this time but she did as he said, reminding herself that he was only trying to protect her from his mother, who had a finely tuned radar for her daughter-in-law's every shortcoming, fashion or otherwise.

❧

Nick's parents lived across town, never a long drive even at the time of day considered rush hour in bigger cities. For three-quarters of the year, Copper Cove was small even by Maine standards so that now, in June, when the tourist season had filled the beach houses and hotels along the water, the town still did not feel crowded. Cars moved lazily along High Street, pulling in at Cumberland Farms for gas and at Blue Yew Pizza or Salt Flats Seafood for supper. Traffic, Ivy was sometimes surprised to realize, was just not something you ever thought about here.

At Nick's parents' house, his sister Tiffany met them at the door. "Oh, it's you."

"We thought we might show up," Ivy said. "You know, since it's Nick's birthday party and all."

"Happy birthday," Tiffany said grudgingly. "Everyone else is already here. The guys are watching the Red Sox game with Daddy." She aimed this bit of news at Nick. "And Mumma's in the kitchen," she added, a clear hint that Ivy should join her mother-in-law there and *not* join her sisters-in-law at whatever they were doing.

They followed Tiffany through to the kitchen, where Nick's mother, Ruby, was emptying fish market bags into the sink.

"Oh, wow, lobster," Ivy said. "Thanks for having a birthday, Nick."

"Nicholas!" cried his mother, turning from the sink and drying her hands on a towel. "Happy birthday, sweetheart. Thirty-two years old!" She tipped her cheek up for a kiss, smoothed down the sleeves of his shirt, and straightened his collar. Ivy had an image of a plump, pretty wasp buzzing around a pie at a picnic.

She set her cake carrier on the sideboard. "I brought the cake."

"Wonderful." Ruby brushed imaginary lint from Nick's shirtfront. "What kind is it?"

"Carrot cake with cream cheese frosting."

Ruby turned from Nick and eyed the cake as though Ivy had said it was made of sand and seaweed. "Oh . . . ," she faltered. "I *was* afraid one cake wouldn't be enough for all of us, so I *did* ask Jessica to make a cheesecake to go along with it." She smiled damply at her son. "You know how Nick loves cheesecake."

Ivy felt her nostrils flare. As a matter of fact, Nick did *not* love cheesecake. He preferred *carrot* cake. It had been one of life's long lessons, however, that objection was always futile with her mother-in-law. She felt her mouth twitch in a rictus grin. "Can I help with dinner?" she managed to choke out.

"You might set the table. We'll use the good china. The cloth is on the ironing board in the laundry room. You'll have to put the leaves in the table, but Nick can do that for you."

Nick trotted off to find the extra leaves and Ivy, having retrieved the tablecloth, began counting out forks and knives from the sideboard. The familiar task calmed her. "It's quiet around here," she observed as her mother-in-law added salt to two enormous canners full of hot water on the stove. "Where is everyone?"

"The men are watching television, and the girls are looking at Jessica's new scrapbook."

Nick had three sisters. His family, the Masons, and hers, the Darlings, had always belonged to the same church. In her growing-up years, none of Nick's sisters had seemed to object to Ivy as long as she had been just another girl in youth group. But from the moment Nick had brought her home as his girlfriend, Jessica, Angela, and Tiffany had circled like a pack of she-wolves guarding their kill. Together, they presented a solid, hostile wall designed to keep Ivy on the outside. They whispered with their heads together when she was in the house and stopped talking when she came into a room. They planned sisters' shopping trips in front of Ivy and did not invite her to come along. When Nick and Ivy were engaged and a family friend hinted that the groom's sisters might want to throw the bride a shower, they'd been offended and told Ivy so, with the greatest of umbrage.

Ivy liked people—all kinds of people—and in general, people liked her back. She was unused to having her friendliness met with such stubborn, protracted rejection, and at first she had been bewildered by Nick's sisters' antagonism. "They hate me for no reason," she had once wailed to her own twin sister, Laura. "I can't understand it. It's like being in eighth grade all over again." By the time she and Nick had been married a year, however, she was wiser. Nick's mother doted on him, and this was at the root of her daughters' treatment of Ivy. Nick's sisters were not horrible to her because of anything she personally had done; they simply resented Nick for being their mother's favorite and were punishing Ivy for being his wife. It was a situation Ivy had gotten used to.

More or less.

When the lobsters were ready, Ruby sent her to call the family to the table. She found Jessica, Angela, and Tiffany upstairs, in Angela's old bedroom, looking at what appeared to be paint chips from a hardware store. When they saw Ivy, they stopped talking.

"Yes?" said Angela, who was Nick's middle sister, tucking the paint chips under one leg.

"Your mother says come to the table." She would not give them the satisfaction of being asked what they were doing.

"Thank you, Ivy. Tell Mother we'll be there in a moment." Angela stared at her until she took the hint and went back downstairs to the kitchen.

Nick's father, Harry, had muttered a long, rambling grace and they were all cracking their lobster claws when Angela rapped her fork against her water goblet. "Everybody! Everybody," she called, half-rising from her chair. "Vincent and I have an announcement to make."

"Angela, that goblet is *crystal*," her mother protested.

"Well, it's an *important* announcement, Mother."

Some blessed instinct of self-preservation warned Ivy of what Angela was about to say and gave her a heartbeat of time to compose herself for it.

"Vincent and I—" Angela looked around the table in delight—"are *pregnant*!"

It was evident that Jessica and Tiffany already knew, but that to the rest of them, it was a complete surprise.

"And here's the best part," Angela said, looking at Vincent and gripping his hand atop the tablecloth. "We're having the baby at *Christmas*! My due date is the twenty-fourth, but the doctor says if I haven't had it by then, he'll induce me so the baby can be born on Christmas Day. Won't that be so much *fun*?"

"Tell them how you planned it, Ange!" Tiffany said.

Angela looked around, ready to implode with pride. "Okay, ready for this? We knew we wanted to have the baby at Christmas, right? Because . . . *so* meaningful. Like Jesus. And obviously that meant we would need to get pregnant in March. But I didn't want to get really gross and fat while I was pregnant. So last January I went on this diet—"

"I remember," said Ruby, frowning. "I didn't approve. You're thin enough as it is."

"Right." Angela snorted. "I thought so too, because that's what everybody tells me? But then I thought, *Just wait until nine months from now.* So I went on this diet and got down to a size four, which was my goal, and *then* we got pregnant. Now it's just gotten warm enough to go to the beach, and . . . look!" She stood up and turned sideways, smoothing her T-shirt down over her stomach, and Ivy saw what she had missed before. A small but very definite baby bump.

"So . . . showing, right? But still cute!" Angela beamed around at them.

Ivy stared back. She felt powerless over her own facial expression and could only hope she didn't actually look as though she wanted to vomit all over her lobster tail.

Angela was impervious to disapproval. She bubbled on. "You should see my maternity swimsuit. It's *so* cute! And by having the baby in December, I'll totally have time to get back in shape by next beach season!"

Her husband, Vincent, a caustic CPA who sipped black coffee as incessantly as most people breathe oxygen, said, "Tell them about the nursery." It turned out that the paint chips Angela and her sisters had been looking at were for the nursery, which would be done in a Beatrix Potter theme. . . .

It went on and on. The problem with Angela and Vincent reproducing, Ivy thought bitterly, was that they would create another person every bit as narrow and self-absorbed as themselves. Sometimes the world—or at least Nick's family—did not seem large enough to hold another person like that.

Nick had little to say on the drive home.

"The woman from Family Makers e-mailed me yesterday," Ivy said at last, breaking the silence. "She asked if we would consider foreign adoption." She looked at her hands but watched Nick from the corner of her eye.

He kept his own eyes on the road and did not answer her.

Which, she reflected, her heart lying in her chest as cold and heavy as one of Ruby's lobsters, was more or less an answer in itself.

✧

It had been an especially good summer so far, with hot blue days subsiding to brief rain showers nearly every evening, and the garden showed it. The colors were reaching toward their peak, an untidy riot of blossom, which was how Ivy loved it. Along the split-rail fence, the red bee balm and pink tall phlox clashed in a kind of reckless ecstasy. Black-eyed Susans nodded in some faint, unfelt breeze—rogue wildflowers among the more genteel daylilies, gayfeather, and baby's breath. In front of these, the cheery yellow cinquefoil bush rustled and the hostas waved their pale-purple arms in greeting.

The afternoon was alive with the hum and drone of insects

hidden in the tall grasses beyond the flower bed. In the clean, baking heat, the brilliance of her garden was as refreshing as a glass of cold water. Ivy had planted all of it and knew each of the flowers by heart, like old and well-loved friends.

Her sister Sephy was finally home from college and had called to say she was coming over in the afternoon. Sephy had stayed on in Ohio an extra month to take a summer school course and to babysit some professor's kids, and Ivy had missed her.

Ivy was up to her elbows in an azalea bush when the familiar dark-green Corolla pulled into the driveway. She shaded her eyes with a gloved hand, extracted herself from the bush, and hurried over.

"Sephy! How was the babysitting?"

Her red-haired younger sister got out of the car with some difficulty and hugged her—a soft, comforting hug with no thought of the dirt Ivy was undoubtedly leaving on her clothes. "Fine, thanks. And it was *nannying*, if you please, not babysitting."

"Oh, excuse me. What's the difference?"

"You get paid more for nannying. And you get to go to Cedar Point with the family."

"Sounds like a good gig. How about an iced coffee?"

"It's the only reason I came over."

They went into the house, and Sephy found the pitcher of coffee in the refrigerator while Ivy washed her hands. "Are you exhausted?" Ivy asked over the sound of the running water.

"Completely. I worked on Tuesday and took my last

exam. On Wednesday I drove halfway home and spent the night with a friend in Rochester. I drove the rest of the way yesterday. Kids, exams, then eight hours in the car each day. It's been a long week." She yawned. "Are those brownies?"

"Help yourself." Ivy opened the plastic container and handed it to her. "What are your summer plans?"

Sephy ticked them off on her fingers: "I'm taking two classes online—statistics and nursing management; I'm working as a CNA at the hospital; and for the next four weeks, I'm giving piano and voice lessons for the youth program in Quahog."

"Wow, no rest for the wicked. Why are you taking summer classes?"

Sephy bit into a brownie and rolled her eyes in bliss. "They're about half the price if I take them online, for one thing," she said around a mouthful of chocolate. "For another, it'll loosen up my schedule next year. Not much, but a little. They say the two years of clinicals are brutal, so I may as well get ahead if I can."

"Any thoughts about what you want to do after graduation? I mean, I know it's still two years off. . . ."

"I'll come back here and work at Coastal, I hope." Coastal Maine Regional Health Care Center was the hospital in nearby Quahog, the closest thing there was to a city in this part of the state.

Ivy was surprised. "You could work anywhere, be a traveling nurse, make a lot of money, see the world. Why would you want to come back here?"

Sephy took tall glasses from the cupboard and ice from the freezer, considering the question. "I love home. I don't want to see the world."

"Good. Call me selfish, but I like the thought of you living nearby."

Sephy handed Ivy's coffee to her black and added cream and sugar to her own.

"Sit down," said Ivy, pulling out a chair at the small kitchen table. "I'll tell you all the gossip. What do you want to know first?"

Sephy pulled out a chair for herself and, settling into it, asked, "Has Amy started her job yet? She was still out when I went to bed last night, and she was gone by the time I got up this morning. But she e-mailed me that she's working at the music store for the summer."

"And giving drum lessons on the side."

"She's manic."

"In a way she is, really. Or maybe she's just too brilliant to be satisfied with a normal pace of life like the rest of us." In the spring, their youngest sister had earned her associate's degree in theater and fine arts—this after finishing high school in three years. "Did she tell you she's starting at UMO in the fall for her bachelor's degree? With a full academic scholarship, mind you."

"Amy's smarter sound asleep than the rest of us are wide awake." Sephy took a sip of her coffee. "What about Laura? I don't hear from her much."

"Same," said Ivy. "Still working for the door company. We're going to the mall tomorrow night. Want to come?"

"Let me see how tired I am by then. How's David? Does he have a girlfriend yet?"

"Ha! Mom wishes. He goes on the odd date here and there, but there doesn't seem to be anyone in particular."

"I hope Mom's not breathing down his neck about it. He's only thirty."

"Practically past his expiration date."

"Poor David!"

Ivy shrugged. "It doesn't seem to bother him. He just rolls with it."

They sipped their coffee in companionable silence.

At last, Sephy ventured, "Any news on the adoption front?"

Ivy shook her head. "The waiting list for newborns is miles long. They suggested we start thinking about international adoption."

"And are you going to?"

"Not yet. Nick's nervous about adopting a baby who looks different from us. He's afraid he wouldn't be able to love it."

"Are you serious?"

Ivy looked into her coffee. "I suppose it would be a constant reminder that it's not his."

"And that matters to him?"

"I guess so."

Sephy digested this in silence. She was the most restful of Ivy's sisters because she knew when to keep her opinions to herself, which was more than could be said for Amy or Laura. Just now, Ivy was more grateful than ever for this quality.

After a bit, Sephy said, "And it has to be a newborn?"

"Yes. Same reason."

"But if it were up to you—completely up to you—what would you do?" her sister asked gently.

Ivy looked up from her glass. "I'd take the first child that came along—any age, any race, any sex—and I'd take as many of them as they'd let me have."

❧

Ivy set her purse and a shopping bag down on the table and scanned the mall food court. Her twin sister was late, as usual, and Ivy was irritated. She hated sitting by herself at a table. Besides being a waste of time, it made her look lonely and pitiful, as though she had no friends. Luckily she had reading material.

She groped in one of her shopping bags and pulled out a tiny book, three inches square, that she had bought on impulse in the register line at T.J.Maxx: *God's Little Book of Promises*. She had picked it up thinking her mother-in-law might like it. Since Nick's birthday, she had been feeling guilty about her attitude toward Ruby, who was always much more likable from a distance than she was when you were actually having dinner at her house. The book consisted of a short Bible verse and a one-sentence homily on each miniature page. It was fairly pedestrian reading—exactly the kind of thing her mother-in-law would love—and she was halfway through it when she heard Laura say, "Hey, you."

Her sister slid into the chair across from her, cool and slim and smelling like a bouquet of freesia. "Have you been here long?"

"Ten minutes. Where have *you* been?"

"Having my eyebrows threaded and getting a manicure." Laura stretched out a hand and wiggled her French-tipped fingers. "What are you reading?"

Ivy showed her the tiny book and explained.

"How is old Ruby?" Laura wanted to know. "Still nagging you to change your name?" She pursed her lips up at the corners and spoke in a fussy voice. "Come now, dear, why do you insist on keeping your maiden name? It's so *worldly*."

"I kept the name Darling because I like it so much," recited Ivy, playing along.

"But I'm sure it makes poor Nick feel like you're ashamed of being married to him." Laura's imitation of Ruby was uncanny.

"Nick and I discussed it before we got married. He's perfectly fine with it."

"But what do *other* people think?" Laura leaned forward and pointed a finger in Ivy's face. "And there *is* that verse in the Bible, you know, about a wife leaving her parents to cleave to her husband."

"Actually, it's the other way around. It says the husband should leave his parents and cleave to his wife."

Laura snorted and spoke in her normal voice. "You didn't really say that to her, did you?"

"No, because it hasn't ever come up. I mean, she's never played the Bible card on the subject before. But I would if I had to."

"Well, let's hope you have to someday. I'd love to see her face. Old cow." Laura turned her attention to the ring of restaurants surrounding them. "What are you having? Sushi?"

"Mall sushi, are you kidding? I'm having an eggplant par-migiana sandwich from Amato's. How about you?"

"Something from Fresh Express. I need to drop a few pounds."

Ivy rolled her eyes. "From where?" She and Laura were fraternal twins and hardly even looked like sisters. Of the two, it was always Ivy who needed to drop a few pounds, but always Laura who was trying.

Laura shrugged. "Meet you back here in ten minutes?"

They got their food and met accordingly. "Sephy's home from college," Ivy informed her, blowing on her sandwich to cool it off. "She stopped by yesterday."

"How does she look?" Laura pried the plastic lid off her very small salad. "Still as fat as ever?"

"Laura! That's *mean*."

Her sister raised a perfectly shaped eyebrow. "It's true. She's what, five foot four? And she has to weigh over 250 pounds. What else am I supposed to call that?"

Ivy put down her sandwich. "But it's *Sephy*. Our sister. Surely that's not the first thing that comes to mind when you think of her."

"Of course it is. It's the first thing everybody thinks of." Laura watched Ivy's face and said, "Isn't it the first thing *you* think of?"

"No. Never. I mean, obviously it's . . . obvious. But when I think of Sephy, I think of her kindness. Her beautiful sing-ing voice. Her generosity. She's the sweetest person I know in the whole world."

Laura reached for her Diet Coke. "She may be sweet, but

she's still fat, and I think I'm doing her a kindness by calling a spade a spade. The rest of you tiptoe around the fact and pretend it's not there, but in the end you're not doing her any favors." She paused to take a bite of salad, bare of dressing, and chew it before going on. "For instance, how many dates do you think Sephy has been on during the two years she's been away at college?"

"I have no idea. She hasn't told me."

"She hasn't told you because there's nothing to tell. And don't get me started on the health problems she's going to have." Laura punctuated her words by jabbing her fork in the air. "Diabetes, heart disease, high blood pressure . . . it's disgraceful for a nurse."

Ivy very much wanted to end the conversation. What Laura was saying was true; there was no denying it. But she was making it sound so ugly, and Sephy was . . . *Sephy*, after all. Their sweet younger sister would never think of talking about either of them—or anyone else, for that matter—in this way.

"I think I'll get some frozen yogurt for dessert," Ivy said pointedly.

"Go ahead and change the subject, Ivy, but it's not going to change the truth. I love Sephy as much as you do, but protecting her is never going to help her. And yes, I'll have some yogurt with you. As long as they have something fat-free."

❧

Jane Darling was tearing lettuce for a salad when Amy stalked into the kitchen and collapsed onto a stool. Slumping forward, she lay sprawled across the counter, her head on her arms, and let out an agonized groan.

"Bad news?" Jane said mildly. She was used to her youngest child's mode of expressing herself, and it did not worry her.

"College," said Amy, without looking up.

"What's wrong with college?"

"They've changed my room assignment *again*."

"Ah. And what did they say this time?"

"Nothing! Just . . . 'Your room assignment has changed. Name and contact information for new roommate listed below.' This is the *third* time." Amy whimpered and knocked her forehead on the countertop.

"It will all work itself out." Jane began to peel a cucumber.

"How much confidence am I supposed to have in a university that can't even get its student housing act together?"

"They're only human, just like you. I'm sure that with all the incoming students, there are a lot of logistics to sort out."

"Oh, please. If I were in charge, I would *so* have the housing problem solved by now."

"I don't doubt it," said Jane, who rather shuddered at the notion of the University of Maine, Orono, housing office with Amy at its head. The image of an Army boot camp sprang to mind. She instantly, and guiltily, quelled it.

Amy sat up and pulled a letter from the pocket of her shorts. "'Heather Vonderheide-Smythe,'" she read. "What kind of name is that? She sounds rich. She sounds like a *prom* queen."

She would have wilted against the countertop again, but Jane, having covered the salad with plastic wrap, handed the bowl to her. "Find a place for that in the fridge, will you?"

"Guess where Miss Heather Vonderheide-Smythe's from?" Amy took the bowl and went to the refrigerator. "And there is no room for *anything* in this refrigerator." She set the salad bowl on the counter and began to rummage through the shelves, rearranging things. "Falmouth!" came her voice from within the fridge. "Falmouth, *Maine*."

"So?" said Jane. "What does it matter where she's from?"

"*Mo*-ther!" Amy emerged from the refrigerator, set the salad inside, and closed the door. "It's one of the most afflu-ent towns in the *state*."

"It doesn't follow that she's a snob." Jane dampened a sponge and began to wipe the counters. "Listen to yourself, Amy. You know nothing about this girl, yet you've already labeled her. Boxed her up and written her off. That's not like you."

Amy was silent, and Jane went on. "Think about this: maybe Heather what's-her-name of Falmouth has just gotten her letter saying she's to be the roommate of Amy Darling of Copper Cove. What do you suppose is going through *her* mind right now?"

Amy resumed her seat on the barstool and laid her cheek against the granite countertop.

"You two may end up being the best of friends."

Amy snorted. Then, very quietly, "I wish I didn't have to go away to college."

"Oh, my dear." Jane came and sat at the bar across from her. "You don't *have* to do anything you don't want to do. Least of all go away to college."

Amy raised her head and glared at her mother. "Well,

what other choice do I have? I've exhausted all the opportunities here in Copper Cove." With the grace of a dancer, she unfolded herself once more from the stool and stood up. "How else am I supposed to get a good education? On a *full scholarship*? It's this or nothing." She stalked from the kitchen much as she had entered it.

Alone, Jane Darling retrieved a jar of sun tea from the reorganized fridge and poured herself a glass. She raised her eyes ceilingward. *Would You mind soothing her nerves a little? I mean . . . so the rest of us can bear her for the next few weeks?* She sipped her tea. *Just asking. That's what You tell us to do, after all.*

CHAPTER

2

PARCHMENTS BOOKSTORE, where Ivy worked, was on the corner of Seacrest and Gull Streets, on the waterfront. Wednesdays were Ivy's half day to work, and on this particular Wednesday morning, she and Esme, the college-student manager, were alone in the store, stocking shelves with the latest James Patterson and talking.

She had told Esme all about Angela's pregnancy. Esme, who was well acquainted with and frequently entertained by the Saga of Nick's Family, had commiserated, though Ivy could tell she hadn't really understood. But then, Esme did not want children of her own so badly that just the thought of a baby made it hurt to breathe.

They had moved on to the subject of hair. Ivy's hair was a sensitive issue with her. It was thin and fine, the color of a field mouse. In her whole family, she was the only one who had terrible hair. Her mother and Sephy were both stunning Irish redheads. Her father's hair, and Amy's and their brother David's, were a glossy chestnut. Even Laura, who had hers colored professionally, managed to look as though she were a natural, sparkling blonde. But then Laura pulled off everything she did with a sophistication that utterly eluded Ivy.

"You should go auburn," Esme told her. "That's not red or brown exactly, so the color would be unique. And I think it would look very natural on you."

"To be honest, I don't want to spend the money at the salon every eight weeks," Ivy said.

Esme made a dismissive gesture. "Do it yourself. That's what I do. The brand I use is great. Gives you all-over color *and* highlights at one time."

Ivy considered the younger girl's hair. It was pretty: the blackest of blacks, with bluish tints. It wasn't Ivy's style exactly, but she had to admit it looked good on Esme. "You don't have to do a cap or anything?"

"Nah. Just mix up the little packets of color in the kit, work it into your hair, wait twenty minutes, and wash it out again. It's the easiest thing in the world."

Ivy made up her mind. "I have to stop by the drugstore after work anyway. I used the last of the shampoo this morning, and Nick needs a new toothbrush."

"Again? You're always buying that man a new toothbrush."

Ivy considered this. There was some truth to it. "How do you know that?"

"You always tell me."

"He gets a new one every three weeks," she told Esme. "He heard on NPR that if you change your toothbrush that often, you're less likely to catch a virus."

Esme stopped rearranging shelves and stared at her. "You're joking, right?"

Ivy shrugged. "That's Nick for you."

After work she stopped by Rite Aid and headed straight for the hair-color section. She found the NaturaLites display, which was Esme's brand, and after some contemplation chose a shade called "Sugar and Spice." There were precious few directions written on the outside of the box. The model on the front looked half-asleep, one hooded eyelid showing, a shock of gleaming hair blown carelessly over the other. In flaring gold script the box promised to imbue her plain brown hair with "rich, coppery highlights." It sounded close enough to auburn for her. She took the box, grabbed a two-pack of Nick's favorite toothbrush, and headed for the checkout.

An hour later Ivy stood in her bare feet on the bathroom tile and stared at her reflection in horror. Her hair hung in damp strands around her face, and the color could not be described as anything but a dark, sullen *pink*. She switched on the light over the sink and turned her head from side to side. No, there was no making it auburn, or even burgundy or plum. It was just . . . pink.

She snatched up the instruction sheet, which, unlike the outside of the box, was so crammed with directions in three languages that she lost her place every time she looked away from the paper. She searched it, hoping there was a step she'd forgotten that would magically change the way her hair looked.

There! There it was: *Shampoo solution from hair, rinsing thoroughly until water runs clear.* She hadn't done that part. Ivy reached inside the shower curtain, then stopped and let out a little whimper. In her excitement over the prospect of "rich, coppery highlights," she had forgotten to buy shampoo.

She looked at her reflection again. Was the pink getting worse? It seemed to be. What could she wash it out with? A bar of soap? Her brother, David, had gone through a phase, when he was nine years old, of washing his hair with Zest because he liked the smell of it. Also, he had considered regular shampoo to be makeup and therefore only for girls. Ivy remembered how dull and tacky his hair had looked during that phase. No, definitely not bar soap. Dish detergent?

Dashing to the kitchen, she squirted a generous amount of Dawn Fresh Apple scent into her hand and leaned her head over the sink. Unfortunately, once it was lathered into her hair, she found that the dish soap was impossible to get out. She scrubbed and rinsed until the water ran clear, and still when she rubbed her head, she could hear the little crackling sounds that meant there was soap in her hair. She groped for a dish towel and, holding it around her sopping head, stumbled back to the bathroom, where she unearthed half a bottle of conditioner. She worked a handful of it into her scalp and knelt by the tub. For several more minutes she rinsed under the bathtub tap. At last she wrapped the whole mess up in a towel and went to the bedroom to assess the damage with the help of a blow-dryer.

Once dry, the pink was, if possible, even more lurid. On top of that, her once-soft hair was now the consistency of straw. Pink straw—it wasn't pretty. Surrendering any remaining hope, she called the salon.

Her regular hairdresser was named Nora. Every eight weeks for the last six years, as regularly as clockwork, Nora had been trimming half an inch off Ivy's chin-length bob. Ivy was loyal, a regular. And now, when it was an emergency, Nora could not make time to fit her in. Ivy tried not to feel betrayed. Nora said she was sorry but added that the other stylist, Cricket, was free. If Ivy could be there in five minutes, Cricket could squeeze her in. Nearly sobbing with relief, Ivy stuffed her head of pink straw under a ball cap, found her car keys, and was on her way.

Actually, she reflected as she pulled her little white Jetta out of the driveway, she was glad. Cricket was cute and trendy, and just a little outrageous, and Ivy had always secretly wished to have her as a hairdresser instead of the more staid and practical Nora. When Ivy had first walked into New Waves Hair Solutions six years ago, sight unseen, Cricket had been with a customer, while Nora was free. Nora had been the first one to cut her hair, which marked Ivy as her territory forever. She and Cricket were the only two stylists in the salon. It would have been too awkward to abandon Nora—safe, predictable, and consistent—for all the fashionable flair of Cricket. Instinctively, Ivy knew this much about beauty salon politics.

The salon smelled, as it always did, of fruity hair spray, suntan lotion, and perm solution. Nora, busy painting a teenager's head with a caustic-looking paste, waved her little finger at Ivy and threw her a sympathetic look. Ivy pulled off her hat and did not miss the customer's expression of horrified fascination. That sealed it. Teenage faces didn't lie: she was a freak.

Cricket, chic in a 1970s-style microskirt with high, fringed suede boots and long pigtails, took her in hand at once. She led Ivy to her station and pushed her gently into the chair before snapping open a plastic cape and fastening it around Ivy's neck. "What happened?"

"The directions said to leave the stuff on my hair for twenty minutes. I thought if twenty minutes was good, maybe thirty minutes would be better," Ivy confessed.

In the mirror, the stylist gave her a look both shrewd and stern.

". . . and maybe forty minutes would be even *better?*" Ivy said meekly.

Cricket shook her head. "I won't lecture you this time, but I hope you've learned your lesson." She fingered the brittle hair. "We can't color it again; it's too damaged."

"Can you do *anything?*"

"The only thing we can do is cut it as short as possible."

Ivy tried to suppress an image of herself as a twenty-seven-year-old rock band groupie. "Go ahead," she said, squeezing her eyes shut. "Do whatever you think is best."

But half an hour later, Ivy considered her reflection and smiled. It was a startling change. Her hair was close-cropped all over and stuck up in soft spikes around her face. It made her dark eyes look huge. There was no disguising the fact that it was still pink, but the hairdresser had worked a mahogany-colored mousse through it that toned the color down to something even better than fashionable.

"It really shows off your heart-shaped face," Cricket told her with satisfaction.

Ivy turned her head from side to side. "I didn't know I had a heart-shaped face."

"Well, you do. And you look like a new person."

That was an understatement. Still, it was . . . cute. And daring. Ivy hadn't felt cute *or* daring in a long time. She wrote a check for the haircut, two bottles of mahogany mousse and one of hideously expensive salon shampoo, and a tip, then left the salon feeling lighter than she'd felt in weeks.

It was five o'clock when she pulled the Jetta into the garage, keeping as far to the right as she could so Nick would have room to back his Volvo in, and walked back down the driveway to check the mail. There were three envelopes: a quarterly statement from Nick's retirement fund; a packet of coupons from a target-marketing company; and something from Home Circle, the latest adoption agency they were trying. At the sight of it, her pulse picked up the pace. She trotted back to the house and let herself in the side door. Collapsing into a kitchen chair, she tore open the letter from the agency, ripping the envelope in her haste, and skimmed the page inside.

Dear Ms. Darling and Mr. Mason . . . Blah, blah, blah . . . There it was: . . . *names have been added to our waiting list.*

Ivy made a noise of disgust. Her nose began to prickle, and her vision swam with hot tears. Another waiting list. How long this time? She scanned the letter again. *Projected wait of four years.* And after one or two of those years, they'd just be moved to another waiting list. By now she knew how it worked. This was the sixth list they had been on since they had started this process three years ago. It was a miracle, she thought bitterly, that anyone got to the point of adopting a baby in this country before they died of old age.

She blinked away the tears. There was no point crying about it again. It was only one more in what was likely to be a long string of these letters. She tore it up, along with the envelope, and hid it at the bottom of the trash can. She'd tell Nick about it eventually, but not tonight. His opinion of her hair was going to be enough to cope with; she didn't think she could face his reaction to the letter on top of that. It was not that he would be disappointed. She wished he *would* be. He would go through the motions of disappointment for her sake, but Ivy knew he would secretly be relieved. Nick did not really want to adopt a baby; what he wanted was to have one of their own.

She ran a hand through her spiky hair. Her former brief optimism had evaporated. She felt inadequate, embarrassed of herself. She was an almost-thirty fashion disaster who could not remember to do something as simple as buying shampoo. It was no wonder her husband was perpetually irritated by her and she'd been wait-listed by adoption agencies across the state. Maybe she didn't deserve to have children of her own. Maybe God knew that people like Vincent and Angela would somehow make better parents.

Part of her knew she was being unreasonable. What did the adoption agency know about her hair color? What did they care? She tried to tell herself that it had just been a bad day. Things would look better by tomorrow. She tried to believe it, and failed.

She tore up the coupon packet and put the retirement fund statement on the hall table for Nick to find. Now *that* was something he would care about.

Nick stared at his wife. "Your hair!"

Ivy began to rub at her chin, a nervous habit he despised. "I didn't mean to do it," she said in a rush. "I was just going to, you know, highlight it a little bit. Only I didn't follow the directions quite right, and I left it on too long, and . . ." She flapped a hand at her head. "This happened. It was worse before, actually, but Cricket at the salon fixed it for me."

He went to the sink and washed his hands, then sat on a chair to loosen his tie and take off his shoes. He didn't know what to say; he really didn't. Ivy was always "not following the directions quite right" and getting herself into trouble. She couldn't tell north from south and got lost every time she drove someplace new; she never paid attention to where she parked her car and spent hours searching for it in mall lots or parking garages; she misplaced her cell phone and her keys at least once a week. She had once ruined the vacuum cleaner by sucking up water with it ("It was just a *small* puddle!"), and two winters ago, her car had to be repaired to the tune of $1,200 when she accidentally pumped diesel fuel into the tank instead of gasoline ("I *wondered* why the nozzle didn't fit right. . . .").

Nick sighed. "You can be such an airhead."

"I know." She rubbed harder at her chin. "But do you like it?"

"Of *course* I don't like it. You look like something that fell off the stage at a . . . a Boy George concert."

She bit her lip, and he realized she was trying not to laugh. "Nick, that's so eighties."

Her levity irked him. "Stop doing that to your chin."

She put her hand behind her back. "At least it's unique, right?"

As if that were a good thing. Trust Ivy to try to turn a catastrophic mistake into a virtue. "I liked you better when you weren't unique," he snapped.

"Oh, Nick! *Everyone's* unique."

"At least it's short. It'll grow out fast, and you can get back to looking the way you did before."

Her hand strayed to her chin again before she remembered and dropped it. She spoke quietly. "You've never been happy with that either."

Nick picked up his shoes and stood. He didn't have time for this. If Ivy was about to start making unfounded, sweeping statements about their entire marriage, there would be no reasoning with her. "Don't make this my fault," he said. "I'm not the one who couldn't follow directions and ended up looking like a freak show." He went to the bedroom, put his shoes on the shoe tree in his closet, changed into shorts and a T-shirt, tied his sneakers, then went back to the kitchen.

Ivy was still standing in the same place, and he did not meet her eyes. If she was crying, he didn't want to see it. He wanted to go for his run without being slowed by the weight of guilt over the fact that he was less than happy to come home to a wife who had accidentally colored her hair pink.

Leaving the driveway at a jog, Nick started on his four-mile loop, picking up the pace as the houses of the town thinned out and fell behind him. His route followed the bike path that ran along the Little Caribou River, shaded by maples but always hot at this time of day in the summer. He nearly always had it to himself. Nick loved running in the heat. Pushing himself through the discomfort, the blood boiling to the surface of his skin, his throat dry and his breath ragged, gave him a sense of self-mastery and reminded him that there were still some things in his life within his control. His wife not being one of them.

It wasn't as if Ivy's scatterbrained ways had come as any surprise to him. She had been exactly the same when they were dating and then engaged, right up to the day of their wedding, when she had lost her white satin shoes and ended up wearing sneakers under her wedding dress—which, fortunately, had been floor length. It was just that this particular quality, which had somehow seemed quirky and charming in his twenty-year-old girlfriend, was irritating and childish in his twenty-seven-year-old wife. Because it was always he, Nick, who had to follow behind and clean up her messes: find a way to get into the car when she locked her keys inside, pump out the water when she left the utility sink running for three hours and flooded the basement . . . and on and on. He had long ago ceased to find her mistakes amusing.

As he passed the three-mile mark and turned for home, his thoughts loosened along with his limbs, and he felt some of his irritation with Ivy begin to unspool and drop away. He supposed calling her a freak show had been a little harsh. He knew how he would find her when he got home. Red-eyed and silent for the rest of the evening. Or she would call one or all three of her sisters and they would talk for hours while he sat in the living room and read the paper and felt like an outsider in his own house.

He rounded the last corner, and as his front yard came into sight, he automatically slowed. There was nothing to do but apologize to her. He would say he was sorry for the freak show comment, and he really was, but that was all he would say. He didn't like her hair and wasn't going to pretend he did. If it continued to cause tension between them, so be it. There was nothing new about that.

❧

Over supper later that week, Nick told Ivy, "The For Rent sign is gone from the house next door."

"I didn't notice. I wonder who's rented it."

"It can't be anyone too promising. The front steps are about to fall off, and the grass hasn't been mowed all summer. It must be up to my waist by now."

"Maybe the landlord will fix it up before the new people move in," Ivy said.

Nick snorted. "I wouldn't count on it. Walt Michaud owns it."

"He was just in the news, wasn't he? He owned those awful apartments down by the river that ended up being condemned. And . . ." She paused, trying to remember the story. "He went to prison. One of his buildings was full of prostitutes, right?"

"That's him. Slumlord, pimp, and all-around dirtbag. He has a prison record as long as this table. If he mows the grass, fixes the porch, and paints the place before his tenants move in, I'll *eat* the grass."

"Maybe a nice family's rented it, and they'll fix it up."

Nick raised an eyebrow. "I don't know who's rented it, but I can promise you one thing: it's not going to be a nice family."

"Well, that's too bad." Ivy stood and began to clear the table. "Did you remember that we're going to Mom and Dad's for supper tomorrow night?"

"I have a deacons' meeting," Nick said, as she had known he would.

"That's not until seven thirty. You could stop by Mom and Dad's for an hour after work, couldn't you?"

"And drive all the way across town and back with gas prices the way they are?" He shook his head. "It doesn't make sense. I'll just stay at the office and catch up with some work until it's time for the meeting."

"You're going to have to eat sometime," she reminded him.

"I'll grab a sandwich at Amato's."

She could have pointed out that he would spend more

money on a sandwich shop meal than he would on gas, but she said nothing. Gas prices weren't the real issue; Nick simply didn't like to spend time with her family. They were too loud and kissy, and could never seem to be *serious* about anything, he often said. Which were exactly all the things Ivy loved most about them.

So Ivy went alone, as she usually did, bearing a lemon cake and a package of portobello mushroom caps for Amy, who did not eat hamburgers. She was the last to arrive.

"Hello, sweetie," said her mother, relieving her of the cake carrier and kissing her on the cheek. "Look at your *hair!*" An instant clamor arose as each Darling examined and exclaimed about her mahogany-pink spikes.

"*Very* chic," said Laura, who would know.

"Beautiful!" said Sephy, who thought everyone was beautiful.

"Striking," said Amy, to whom this was the ultimate compliment. Amy wore her own hair in long, matted dreadlocks that, tonight, were coiled atop her head in a heavy bun that somehow managed to look elegant.

"It's all right, considering whose face is under it," said David. But he knocked Ivy on the shoulder and kissed the top of her head when he said it.

Ivy handed the mushroom caps to Amy, who seized them. "You're the best, Ivy. Mom always forgets!" She skipped off to the grill, where their father was turning hamburgers and chicken pieces.

"I don't forget," their mother whispered. "I just like to see her suffer."

Laura Darling stood behind her desk at Jade River Doors, sorting a sheaf of papers for filing. She wore an ivory linen pantsuit that she knew showed off the narrowness of her waist and did something amazing for her hips. The last time she had worn it, Max, her boss, had given her an appreciative glance on his way into his office. "You're a sight for sore eyes," he'd said.

Since then, the suit had hung in the closet while she had counted the days until she could wear it again without appearing too obvious. Two weeks had seemed about right, so today she had pulled it out and paired it with a periwinkle shell that brought out the blue of her eyes. She liked the fresh, cool look of linen but hated the way it wrinkled as soon as she sat in a chair. It had already sustained some damage from the drive to work in the wilting heat. Resigned to a day of mostly standing, she had worn flat, comfortable shoes. She was tall even without heels—five feet, ten inches—but she usually wore them anyway. Her height never bothered her. On the contrary, she was proud of the way it emphasized her slenderness. A literature professor in college had once called her "willowy."

She was bent over the filing cabinet when Max breezed through. "Morning, Laura," he murmured, his eyes fixed on a report in his hand. "Hold my calls this morning, unless it's my wife; I have a lot to do before the meeting with Kaiser. What time is Plummer coming?"

The last thing Laura did every evening before leaving the

office was to look over the next day's schedule and commit it to memory. "The meeting's at ten thirty," she told him.

"I'll need you to be there," Max told her, "but you'd better come to my office at ten so I can give you a heads-up on a few things first." He looked up for the first time from the papers he was holding. Laura did not miss the flash of appreciation in his dark eyes. "You look nice today."

"Thank you."

He gave her a second, more appraising look but said only, "Forward the phones to Diana before you come" and shut himself into his office.

Kaiser Door was a small New Hampshire company that Max had been trying for two years to buy. This last round of negotiations had been the most promising as Kaiser's founder and CEO, Don Plummer, began to voice a longing for retirement. Their meeting lasted an hour in the boardroom, developed into an impromptu tour of the Jade River Doors factory and warehouse, and ended with lunch at Nonna Mia's, a tiny Italian restaurant on the other side of town. Plummer left them at the restaurant with the promise of another meeting the following week.

When he had gone, Max turned to Laura, his face glowing. "I think he's going to sell."

"I think you're right." They raised their water goblets and clinked them together. "I'll get today's notes sorted out and have them on your desk first thing in the morning."

"Listen, Laura . . ." He hesitated. "I know it's asking a lot, but I'd really like to look over those notes tonight and start working out a proposal for Plummer while today is still fresh in my mind."

"I'll see what I can clear from my desk after lunch and get right on it."

"Actually, I have a pretty full afternoon myself. You wouldn't be willing to stay after work just an hour or two so we could look over the notes together? You were here for the meeting; I'd like to hear your impressions." He smiled at her—not his quick, confident boardroom flash, but a half smile. A secret smile. "Would you mind?"

Mind? Laura sipped at her water. No, she wouldn't mind at all.

❧

At ten o'clock on a Saturday morning, Ivy saw a small orange-and-white U-Haul truck pull into the driveway of the house next door. Not a big family, then, Ivy concluded, watching from behind her kitchen curtains. To her surprise, the woman who emerged from the driver's seat and opened the back of the truck was black. Ivy tried to think if she knew of any other African American people in Copper Cove, but she came up blank. She didn't know any non-Caucasians at all. She didn't think there were any. That might be unusual for most towns in America these days, but then this was down east Maine. She shuddered to think of what Nick's family would have to say about their son's new neighbors. His parents were the type who still called black people "coloreds."

She watched with interest as three children climbed out

of the back of the truck and began to help unload. There was a very small boy, a boy in his teens, and a girl somewhere in between them whose head bristled with colorful, bobble-wrapped pigtails. It would be fun to have kids next door. Ivy went to the fridge and began to pull out the ingredients for banana bread.

No one answered the door later that afternoon when she brought over the banana bread, two loaves of it wrapped in a new dish towel. The U-Haul had disappeared shortly after noon, with the woman driving. She had not returned.

Ivy stood on the small, square porch and knocked several times, taking in the colorless sheets and towels that had been hung over all the windows in the house. She knocked twice more, but the house was as silent as it had been the day before, when it stood empty. Finally she went home and, finding a plastic container big enough to protect both loaves from squirrels and stray cats, sealed the bread inside and carried it back to the little house, where she left it on the porch. Back in her own kitchen five minutes later, she happened to glance through the window in time to see the neighbors' front door open. The container disappeared, and the door closed again.

"Huh," she said aloud to the empty kitchen. "Very friendly people."

On Monday, Ivy got up an hour early, pulled on her sneakers, and let herself out the front door. She set a good pace and, turning left, headed toward the cove half a mile away. If she hurried, she could walk there, do the length of the beach and back, and be home before Nick was up.

The tide was out, and after her walk she sat on a worn piling and stripped off her shoes and socks. A seagull pecked at a sand dollar nearby. She hadn't collected sand dollars since she was a kid. Barefoot, she wandered down to the water's edge. This far north, the Atlantic never got very warm, and even now, in midsummer, the damp-packed sand was cold. She walked a little way, letting the small waves rush up and swirl around her ankles before they ran backward again, tickling as they sucked the sand from underfoot. Gulls the size of chickens eyed her resentfully as she passed. They stood in her path until she was almost upon them before taking a few swaggering steps away, feigning indifference. The trick to finding sand dollars, she remembered, was to come at low tide while it was still dark. The minute dawn began to lighten the sky, the seagulls would come and snatch them all. One early morning soon, she would bring a bucket and a flashlight and come sand-dollar hunting. She pulled out her phone and glanced at the time. She needed to head back.

The exercise left her with a buoyancy that lasted through breakfast. Nick noticed it over his black coffee, scrambled egg whites, and whole-wheat toast. "You're humming. It must have been a good walk."

"It was," she said. She put a bowl of leftover macaroni and cheese in the microwave for her own breakfast and, when it was warm, shook on some hot sauce and joined him at the table.

Nick frowned at her bowl. "That's not breakfast."

"It is to me." She stirred the hot sauce into the cheese. "I want to go sand-dollar hunting one of these mornings. And sea glass—I love sea glass! My sisters and I used to collect it all the time. I'll fill a little mason jar with it and put it on the windowsill. It'll look like jewels when the sun shines through."

"It'll just be another thing to collect dust."

"I could use it as a bookend. That way it'd be utilitarian too."

"You can't keep books on the windowsill. They'd get faded."

"It would be beautiful, though. Isn't that worth something?"

"I'm just pointing out that it's not very practical."

"Well, practicality isn't exactly my strong suit."

He stood and carried his dishes to the sink. "You can say that again."

All at once, she felt tired. What was a jar of sea glass, after all, or books on the windowsill? He was right; there was no point, really.

Later, at the bookstore, Ivy and Esme worked together to set up a new display called *Maine Writers: Past, Present, and Future*.

"I had a great walk this morning," Ivy told her.

"Good for you! How far did you go?"

Ivy placed a stack of *The Best of Longfellow* beside *Edna St. Vincent Millay, The Collected Works* and considered it. "A couple of miles. Can we put two poets side by side?"

Esme tapped her chin. "Here, better put Harriet Beecher Stowe between them." She arranged a stack of Carolyn Chute novels in the *Present* section beside a selection of Stephen King. *Future Writers* featured a display of short stories written and illustrated by the Copper Cove Elementary School fourth graders. "Two miles is great. I hate walking. I hate any exercise, actually. Here, can you find a place for that on the *Future* table?" She handed Ivy a stack of red flyers.

"'The Art of Short Story,'" Ivy read aloud. "What's this?"

"Adult ed," said Esme. "You know, evening classes over at the technical college. They teach things like pottery and yoga and soap making. This month they have this writing class, so I thought we could advertise it on our display."

Ivy skimmed the advertisement.

The Art of Short Story.
Cover the fundamentals of developing character,
plot, theme, and setting. Learn to structure your
short story and begin to find your own voice as you
read the stories of accomplished authors and write
your own.
   T, Th, 6–9 p.m. 8 weeks.

Ivy folded one of the papers into eighths and slipped it into her back pocket.

Esme saw her do it. "Are you a writer?" she said in pleased surprise.

"Not really."

"Then why are you keeping the flyer?"

"I don't know—as a reminder, maybe. I might take some other kind of class one of these days. Maybe soap making." Ivy spoke lightly, but the truth was, the line *begin to find your own voice* had sounded a chord inside her. She liked the idea that she might have her own voice. If she did, it was buried so deep that she wouldn't recognize it if it shouted out loud to her. But reading that one little line, she had suddenly felt that if she didn't find that voice and learn how to use it soon, it would fade like the binding of a book kept on the windowsill too long. It would grow dry and cracked until it withered up and became unfindable. The impression was a brief one, but strong.

CHAPTER

3

"Jane! Jane Darling!" Hailed from behind, Jane stopped and turned. The sanctuary was crowded, and at first she couldn't tell who had called to her.

"Jane!" Ah, Jeff Willette, Grace Chapel's music director. He was several people back in the crowd that was milling its way, without hurry, toward the doors.

"Hi, Jeff!" She raised a hand and waved to show him she'd seen him, then waited at the end of the pew.

"Whew," he said, mopping his forehead with a tissue, "it's hot enough in here."

"Quite a crowd out this morning."

"Jenny Harriman's wedding yesterday," Jeff said. "They have family here from all over New England."

"Oh yes." Jane looked at the throng around them. "I wondered why there were so many old familiar faces."

"Nice to know you can always come home, isn't it?"

"There's nothing sweeter."

"I don't want to keep you, Jane, but I was wondering if you and some of your crew might be up for doing special music next Sunday. Scott Adams was going to play his trumpet, but he's broken a finger."

"What a shame. Summer is the worst time for a child to have a broken bone. Think of all the swimming he'll miss."

"Oh, it's not so bad. It's just taped, but it's one of his valve fingers, so he's out of commission for a while."

"Well, I'm sure it's no picnic for him in any case. I'll send him a card."

"So . . . special music, then?"

"I can't speak for the rest of them, but I'll ask around and give you a buzz this afternoon."

"That would be great." The music director wiped his forehead again. "Even if it's only Ivy on the violin with Sephy on the piano."

"Well, Sephy goes back to Ohio the day before, and Amy will be off to Orono by then too. Maybe I can talk Laura and Ivy into it. I'll let you know, Jeff."

❧

Ivy had always liked Sundays. As children, Laura and David had hated them. For starters, they resented being dragged out of bed at eight o'clock in the morning, although it was two hours later than they got up on school mornings and at least an hour more than they slept on Saturdays. It was different, they argued. School was just school—you had to get up for it. And nobody in their right mind would waste a Saturday morning lying around in bed, not when there were cartoons to be watched, bicycles to be ridden with the neighborhood pack, and in later years, basketball and cheerleading practices and weekend jobs. Sunday, as everyone knew, was the only *real* day off. The only day to sleep in. Unless you had cruel parents who made you go to church every single weekend of your life. It was like not having a day off at all, really. It was like being a slave.

Then there were the quarrels over what to wear to church. For David, jeans had been outlawed on Sunday mornings, and he had to wear a collared shirt. The girls had it much worse: they had to wear skirts, even in winter, and always with the hems below the knees. "Church," Laura had stormed at their mother one time, when she had been sent back up to her room to change into *something more appropriate*, "is nothing more than a place to sit in a pew for two hours and be pinched and itchy!"

Though Ivy hadn't liked wearing skirts, hose, and dress shoes any more than Laura, it hadn't stopped her from enjoying the rest of the day. Blueberry muffins for breakfast. The Sunday school teacher who gave you a colored pencil or a scratch-'n'-sniff sticker if you knew your memory verse. People invited over for lunch afterward, different ones every week. Vacation Bible school in the summers. The pastor's sermon was always boring, of course, but before and after it there was the singing.

Ivy—along with the whole Darling family—loved to sing. Five or six times every year, they sang special music in church as a family. When they were young, their mother would arrange them all from oldest to youngest on the stage, and they would sing a spiritual or a hymn in five-part harmony. Sometimes their mother would play along on the piano, or their father on the guitar, but mostly the Darling children sang a cappella. When she was younger, Ivy hadn't understood the import of the absolute attention that would be fixed on them at such times—the long, profound moment of silence when they had finished, and why the congregation clapped afterward, which hardly ever happened when other people did special music. But it had all contributed to the feeling she had about church—that here was family beyond her circle of seven, people she had known all her life who loved her. Who would, in fact, love her even if she couldn't sing a note.

Along the way, what she had once called "that Sunday feeling" had become a personal faith. As a child, she had been drawn to church by the sure and certain knowledge that she was loved by God and by His people. Now it was the other way around. She was drawn here not only because God loved her, but also because she loved Him in return. And wasn't that the very heart of worship, the point of being here in the first place: to pour back out to God some of the love that He, in every circumstance, was continually pouring into you?

She was thinking these things as she left her violin in the church's offstage music room and went back to the sanctuary to sit with her husband. Before she reached the pew, she saw her mother-in-law's head bent together with Nick's.

Ivy slid into the seat beside Ruby. "Good morning."

"Oh, Ivy." Ruby had a church bulletin in her hand. "I was just reading here that you're doing special music today."

"My mother and I are, yes."

"Wonderful, dear," Ruby said in a clipped voice. "Only, it's a little confusing as to *who* exactly is performing."

Ivy felt suddenly weary. "Is that so. How?"

Ruby thrust the bulletin at her and glanced around to be sure they weren't overheard. "It says here, *Jane Darling and Ivy Darling*."

"That's us."

"But you are Nick *Mason's* wife. By printing your maiden name in the bulletin, it sounds as if you're not even married to him! How will people know who you are?"

"Darling is not my *maiden name*, Ruby. It's my *last name*." She was saved from defending herself further by the opening chords from the piano, where her mother was hammering out the prelude—a double-time arrangement of "When the Saints Go Marching In."

She wanted to be merely irritated by Ruby's comments. Irritation tempered by detached amusement would have been the perfect frame of mind, she thought. But she could not attain it. Instead she felt like she had failed Nick. Was, in fact, failing him every day.

When it was time for her to play, she botched the opening notes of "What Wondrous Love Is This?" and played the whole piece badly. Looking into the congregation midway through to see her sister-in-law Tiffany filing her nails with an air of greatest boredom did not help. She was grateful that her mother was an accomplished enough pianist to cover for her.

❧

Heat beat up from the asphalt in shimmering waves, and the air was a sticky, suffocating quilt. It was Ivy's half day at work, and the mercury was still on the upswing when she left the bookstore at noon. In the car, the air-conditioning blew a thin, lukewarm wind that did nothing to cool her. She was as thirsty for the salt breeze of the ocean as she was for a glass of water.

When she pulled into the drive, she was surprised and pleased to see all three of the children next door sitting on their little porch. In the month they had lived there, she had often seen them playing outside in the evenings, but they had never spoken to her, nor she to them. Now she waved as she got out of the car. Neither boy responded, but the little girl's hand went up a fraction, in the tiniest return wave. Ivy thought of walking over to ask if they had liked the banana bread. They certainly seemed to like her plastic container. She had never seen it again. But she decided it was too hot to bother. She needed the beach more than she needed her container back.

Inside the house, she threw a few things into her beach bag and spent two blissful hours alternately soaking herself in the ocean and drying out on a blanket in the breeze, reading a borrowed novel from the bookstore. At a quarter to four, with the sand disappearing under the incoming tide, she packed up and headed for the car. There was supper to think about, and she had never felt less like cooking. As she drove the half mile home, she mentally rehearsed the contents of the refrigerator and decided she had everything she needed to make a chicken Caesar salad. It was one of Nick's favorites, and she could grill the chicken outside instead of in the beastly hot kitchen.

The three children were still sitting on their front porch, where they had been when she left. Ivy set her bag down in the driveway and walked over.

"Hi," she said, shading her eyes against the glaring sun. "I'm your neighbor. My name's Ivy."

The children looked at her solemnly. At last, the oldest boy said, "I'm DeShaun. This is Jada, and this here's Hammer." His voice was deep and quiet and held the trace of an inner-city accent.

"Nice to meet you all." She looked around at their shadeless, scorched yard. "It's kind of a hot day to be sitting outside for so long, isn't it?"

The girl answered her this time. "Our mama's not home, and Hammer peed hisself."

"Shut up, Jada," said the oldest boy. The little boy, Hammer, clutched self-consciously at the front of his shorts, where a lighter-colored perimeter around the crotch proved Jada's story.

"Can't you go inside and get him a pair of clean shorts?"

"Door's locked."

A sick chill broke over Ivy. Had their mother actually

locked them outside in this heat? "Where's your mom?" she asked the oldest boy. Already she'd forgotten his name.

He shrugged. "Don' know."

"How long has she been gone?" In an instant the boy's face changed, became shuttered, wary. "Because," Ivy added quickly, "it might give you an idea of when to expect her back."

He lifted one shoulder. "Not that long."

"She left right after *The Price Is Right*," Jada piped up.

If that old game show was still on from eleven o'clock until noon, these kids had been outside far too many hours. Ivy took her time, treading lightly. "Well, it seems like you've been waiting here a long time. Would you like to come to my house and use my bathroom? And maybe have something cold to drink?"

"No," the oldest boy said. "We'll wait right here. She'll be home before long."

"DeShaaaaaun," Jada wailed, "I have to *go*. I can't hold it." She grabbed at the front of her own grimy pink shorts.

DeShaun. That was his name.

"I want a drink!" This from the little boy. DeShaun rolled his eyes, but Ivy saw that he, too, was tempted by the thought of getting inside, where it was cooler.

"I'll tell you what," she said. "We can leave a note for your mom on the door, so when she gets home, she'll know right where you are. She won't have to worry for a minute."

DeShaun considered this. "A'ight," he said, standing up. The other two jumped off the side of the porch—first the girl, then the little boy—and raced ahead of Ivy to her driveway. There, she retrieved her bag and collected her mail from the box before leading the way into the kitchen.

Inside, the three children stopped as though they had walked into a wall.

"Come on in," Ivy said, glancing through the envelopes in her hand.

They stayed where they were.

"What? You can come in; it's okay."

"You have a pretty house," Jada whispered.

Ivy looked around the kitchen in surprise. It was clean, but certainly nothing spectacular. The appliances were old, the cupboards a dark, unappealing wood. She and Nick had been talking about renovating it sometime in the next year or two. She glanced at DeShaun and saw an odd, fleeting expression there. It was replaced at once by something hard, but she recognized what she had seen. Shame.

The children all smelled very ripe, an unpleasant combination of unwashed bodies and urine that was magnified inside the stuffy house. Like almost everyone else in this part of Maine, Ivy and Nick did not have air-conditioning since it only got hot enough to need it for a week or two out of the year. This happened to be one of those weeks, and Ivy lost no time in throwing open the windows and sliding-glass door.

"You boys can follow me," she said. In the downstairs bathroom, she showed them where the washcloths, soap, and towels were. "Maybe Hammer would feel better if you helped him clean up," she said to DeShaun before closing the door and leaving them to it. She took Jada to the upstairs bathroom and waited outside the door while the girl took care of business. "Don't forget to wash your hands," she said when Jada came out, and the little girl obediently trotted back inside.

When she emerged, a single glance at her wet, grimy fingernails told Ivy that the child had never been taught to do this basic task properly.

"I think you missed one or two spots," she said, making a show of inspecting the ragged, dirt-encrusted knuckles. "Let's do it together, because I need to wash mine anyway."

They stood at the narrow sink, crowding each other, while Ivy showed her how to wet the bar of soap and rub her hands together until they were coated in lather, like white gloves. "Now fingernails, thumbnail too. Backs of your hands— good job. Now between your fingers, knuckles, and wrists. Got it all? Great! Rinse them all over again under running water. Always warm, because cold water doesn't get your hands clean. Then dry them; the job's not done until they're dry. Now we're ready for a snack, right?" She left the bathroom feeling that she'd worked harder in those three minutes at the sink than she had all morning at Parchments.

In the kitchen she chose not to look too closely at the boys' hands. Hammer's shorts, although reeking of urine, seemed to be more or less dry. For lack of anything to replace them with, Ivy decided her only course was to try to ignore the odor and hope their mother would get home soon. She directed the children to sit at the kitchen table while she filled glasses with ice, then found a package of Oreos in the cupboard and arranged a dozen of them on a plate. She set the cookies in the middle of the table and turned to mix a pitcher of instant lemonade.

When she turned back to pass the children their drinks, she blinked at the empty cookie plate. Surely they had not eaten a dozen cookies in the ninety seconds it had taken her to make the lemonade. Had they pocketed them for later? Crumbs around Hammer's and Jada's mouths suggested that they had eaten at least some of them. She removed the plate and replaced it with the entire package of Oreos. "Have some more cookies," she said.

They ate and drank with a speed that astonished her, and the package of cookies was nearly empty when she realized they were not even beginning to slow down. "How about some sandwiches?" she asked, opening the door to the refrigerator and pulling out cheese, sliced ham, mayonnaise, and mustard. They ate sandwiches as fast as she could slap them together, but when Jada and Hammer had each eaten two, they showed signs of lagging. DeShaun ate six altogether, switching uncomplainingly to tuna salad when Ivy ran out of ham and cheese.

As they ate, they talked, answering her questions without hesitation, their reticence melting away with their hunger. DeShaun Johnson was fourteen, she learned; Jada Lovett was nine, and Hammer Hernandez was six. A discreet probe revealed that none of them knew their fathers, nor did they seem to think there was anything unusual about this. Their mother's name was Lily Allen, and she worked as a waitress at the Platinum Palace in Quahog. Ivy knew the place by reputation and was fairly certain it wasn't only food and drinks Lily Allen was serving her customers from eight to four every night. The motley family had moved to Maine from Detroit, but none of the children was sure why. They could only tell her that it had all happened very suddenly. They had a grandmother in Michigan, and their mother had a sister somewhere—DeShaun thought it was in Texas—but that was all they could tell her about their roots.

While the children finished eating, Ivy called Nick to ask how soon he'd be home.

"I have a deacons' meeting at seven thirty, remember? I told you this morning I was going to stay late at the office." He sounded irritated.

She noticed DeShaun casting nervous glances through the window at the empty driveway next door.

"Oh, that's right," she told her husband. "Never mind. See you when you get home then." Nick hung up before she did.

"Should we see what's on TV?" she said to Hammer and Jada.

"Yeah!"

"Cartoons?"

Ivy turned the station to Nickelodeon and left the two of them on the couch, Hammer sitting on several thicknesses of clean towels, both of them absorbed, slack-mouthed, in an episode of *SpongeBob SquarePants*.

"Now," she said to DeShaun when she returned to the kitchen, "why don't you and I run over and leave that note for your mother on the door?" She gave him paper and a pen, and he wrote the note while she searched out a roll of Scotch tape. Once they were outdoors, she asked, "When do you really think she'll get home?"

He lifted one shoulder in a shrug. "I don' know. She usually works nights, but today she left early and didn't say where she was going. I don't think it was to work, because her restaurant's not open during the day."

"Has she ever gone off and left you locked out of the house before?"

"Yeah, once or twice in Detroit she did."

"How long was she gone when she did that?"

He hesitated, then lifted his shoulder again. "Four, five days."

Ivy felt her breath leave her. For a moment she could not speak. Then, "If she doesn't come back tonight, is there anyone we can call? Do you have friends here in town?"

"Not really."

They had reached the gray, sagging porch, and Ivy saw with new eyes the bags of garbage stuffed underneath the three front steps and piled against the windows inside. She waited at the bottom while DeShaun taped the note to the door, making sure it was sealed down on all four sides.

When he rejoined her, she said gently, "I think you should plan on spending the night at my house. Just in case." He looked at the ground and gave a small nod.

Back at her house, Ivy sent DeShaun into the living room, took the phone into her bedroom, and shut the door. She dialed her cousin's work number and tapped her fingers on the top of the dresser as she listened to it ring. Four, five, six times. "Come on, come on," she muttered. The clock on the dresser said three minutes past five. *Please, God, let her not have left work on time today.* Seven times; eight. And then the blessed relief of hearing her cousin Bailey's voice on the other end, irritated and impatient, but the real, live Bailey all the same. The person who would have the answers.

"Child Protective Services of Maine."

Several exhausting hours later, the three children, bathed and wearing odds and ends of clean clothes scrounged from Ivy's and Nick's closets, were sleeping in the two upstairs bedrooms. The three-man Copper Cove police force had shown up at the darkened house next door and broken in. The officer who eventually took Ivy's statement refused to describe to her the condition of the house, saying only that it would have given her nightmares. Later, he had taken DeShaun back to the house in order to find clothes and other things the children might need to spend a night or two with the neighbors. The things DeShaun had brought back were now cycling through the washer in Ivy's laundry room, and Bailey had arranged for Ivy and Nick to have temporary, emergency custody of the children. The authorities were looking for Lily Allen.

In the morning, Ivy called Esme and told her she wouldn't be in to work, explaining why. Hammer awoke with his clothes and bed saturated with urine. Ivy put him in the bathtub, then dumped the mattress pad, sheets, and one blanket that had been affected into the washing machine and scrubbed the mattress with Febreze and Spic and Span. When she finished, she and DeShaun dragged the mattress down the stairs and outdoors to air in the sunshine of the backyard.

"Does he often wet the bed?" she asked the older boy.

"Yeah. He pees his pants all the time too."

"All the time? Like, every day?"

"Yeah. He never learned to use the to'let. I tried to teach him a coupla times, but it didn't really work."

That turned out to be the understatement of the year. Not only had Hammer never been toilet trained, but the urine seemed to flow from him in a steady stream that he never even heeded. By ten o'clock that first morning, he had wet through the extra pair of shorts DeShaun had brought over from next door and a pair of Nick's boxers and was wearing a second pair of boxers nipped in at the waist with a clothespin while Ivy laundered his clothes again. As the washer was filling, she called her mother.

Jane Darling, who had heard the whole story of the children next door during an eleven o'clock phone call the night before, had the answer. "They have these wonderful things called Pull-Ups now," she told her daughter. "Like diapers, but the child can pull them up and down like underwear while he potty trains." She gave Ivy some tips on the finer points of toilet training and ended the call by saying, "I'll pray for you, my dear. You're doing a wonderful thing here. Keep fighting the good fight."

Since her mother was on her way out the door to a garden club meeting and Ivy did not trust Hammer to stay dry long enough for a trip to the supermarket, she called Laura. "Are you busy?" she asked the moment her sister answered her phone.

"Of course I'm busy. I'm at work."

"You wouldn't go to Hannaford on your lunch hour and pick me up a package—two packages—of these things called Pull-Ups?"

Laura had already been put into the picture by their mother. "Oh, good, this means I get to meet the kids. I'll take an early lunch and be at your house in half an hour. No, give me forty minutes. What size Pull-Ups?"

"They come in sizes?"

❧

In those forty minutes, Ivy realized that she could not go anywhere without Jada following at her heels. The little girl wanted to be everywhere she was and to help with everything she did. This turned out to have its uses when it came to clearing the breakfast table and washing the dishes; however, Jada augmented her presence by a constant stream of chatter that Ivy, used to a quiet house, was soon forced to tune out from sheer auditory exhaustion.

DeShaun was as taciturn as his sister was loquacious. As soon as he had eaten breakfast and helped Ivy deal with the mattress, he asked if he could watch television and disappeared into the living room with the remote control. Ivy did not hear from him again until it occurred to her to call him to the kitchen for lunch. He ate three grilled cheese sandwiches, then watched TV again until supper. Later, he joined Nick in watching the news and a PBS documentary until Ivy sent him to bed at ten o'clock.

Nick was being surprisingly good about the upheaval in his home. He made no effort to befriend the children, but nor did he object to their presence. "What else were you supposed to do?" he had said rhetorically when he came home from his deacons' meeting. "You couldn't just put them out in the street."

With Hammer in Pull-Ups, the second day was easier.

Still, the kitchen sink had become a self-perpetuating fount of dirty dishes, and Ivy had extra laundry to do since the children only had one spare set of clothes apiece. As well, they were constantly hungry. After she called Esme to cry off work for the second day in a row, and when breakfast and a mid-morning snack had been consumed, she loaded them all into the car and made an impromptu trip to the grocery store. The children were full of opinions about what she should buy. Not knowing how long they might be with her, she figured it wouldn't hurt to spoil them a little. She followed their advice, stocking up on chips, cookies, and ice cream, although she drew the line at soda, which she was pretty sure would only compound Hammer's problem and make Jada more garrulous than ever. Thinking guiltily of what Amy would have to say about the nutritional train wreck in her grocery cart, she also bought three loaves of whole-grain bread, several pounds of cheese, a jar of peanut butter, and enough fruit, chicken, and eggs to last several days.

The third day, Bailey called to tell her they were having no luck locating Lily. How did Ivy and Nick feel about keeping the children a few more days, while they continued to search? "Of course, we hope we'll be able to find the mother and that she'll be fit to take care of them," Bailey explained. "At this point, we're not assuming she abandoned them. She may have had a car accident and be lying in a hospital somewhere. It does happen from time to time. But just in case she has left intentionally—and don't suggest that to the children, for heaven's sake—it's easier for us if we have a plan in place."

"What kind of plan?"

"Well, if their mother really has abandoned them, they'll have to go into foster care."

"What, all three of them together?"

"We'll do everything we can to keep them together, yes."

"What do you mean *everything you can*? What if you can't?"

"Don't worry about that. I'm sure we'll find someone who's willing to take the three of them."

But Ivy had spotted the crack in the mortar and couldn't let it go. "Okay, but what if you *can't*? I mean, just for the sake of argument. What would happen then?"

"Well, for the sake of argument, if we can't find a home for all three of them together, they'd go to different homes. To be honest, the teenager will probably be the hardest to place, but if no one will take him, there are group homes and shelters where we might find him a bed. We'll do our best, Ivy."

"Group home? Shelter? *Bed?*" Ivy was appalled. "I've never heard of anything so awful. Bailey, tell me what to do here."

"You're doing enough by helping out for the time being."

"But how can we keep them from being separated, if their mother really has left them?"

Bailey sighed. "Sometimes we can't. That's the bald truth of it. We do our best, and often that's good enough, but remember you asked about the worst-case scenario. I'm only telling you the facts of what would happen then."

"Bailey, these are real, live kids we're talking about, not case numbers. And they're very sweet, although they run me ragged. How can we keep them from being scattered like a litter of puppies?"

Her cousin was silent for a moment. Then, "There's another option, but I'm hesitant to say it—"

"Say it."

"If you don't want those kids scattered like a litter of puppies, as you put it, then you and Nick *could* consider becoming their foster parents."

"And what does that entail?"

"You'd have to take a few classes—just eighteen hours; don't worry—and fill out enough paperwork to decimate a small forest, agree to a background check, and go through a home visit by a state worker who will make sure your house is physically safe for the children to live in. Things like that. But mostly, Ivy, it means you should be prepared to commit yourself to these kids for as long as it takes. And it often takes a very long time. Sometimes forever."

"Oh, dear."

"Yeah. I mean, you want to think about all the possibilities. You don't know who these kids are, where they come from, or what kind of baggage they bring with them. Foster kids can upset a household, ruin a marriage. It might not be fun for you. On the other hand, being a foster parent can be a wonderful, rewarding, life-changing experience. To be honest, it would probably be some of both. For better or worse, are you ready for your lives to be turned upside down? You have to ask yourself that."

Ivy was silent for several moments, thinking, as Bailey waited. At last, she said, "Okay, I'll talk Nick into it tonight."

"No, Ivy. Talk to Nick *about* it tonight."

"Same thing."

"Don't be stupid. This is a serious commitment. Don't take these kids in and offer them hope, only to find you have to give up on them because of some problem you can't possibly foresee right now."

"Right. I'll talk to Nick."

"Ivy . . ."

"Meanwhile, where do we sign up for these classes and the home visit and all that?"

Bailey sighed, but she knew her cousin well. "Got a pencil?"

That evening, Ivy called Esme at home. "I need to take some time off." She told her why and Esme, being Esme, was sympathetic and even cried a little, but in the end she could only promise that if Ivy's job was still vacant when she was ready to work again, she could have it back.

"I can't hold it for you," Esme warned her, "although I'll try my best. I don't want to work with anyone but you, Ivy, but I don't own the store. With the summer people in town, I'll have to hire someone else."

Ivy assured her she was forgiven this involuntary disloyalty and that everything would work out exactly right in the end.

She hung up the phone. "I can do all things through Christ, who gives me strength!" she announced bravely to the empty kitchen. No one answered her back, but she felt better all the same.

CHAPTER

4

FOR THE THIRTIETH TIME in as many minutes, Laura glanced at the clock on the wall of Max's office. Six twenty. A flush of anticipation went through her, as warming as a glass of wine. This was the third time she and Max had stayed after office hours to work on the Kaiser deal. In two days Jade River Doors would sign the contract to buy Don Plummer's company. Max was about to become a very rich man. Tonight he and Laura were going over the contract in minutest detail. She had realized that Max was mostly just nervous, needed to talk it all through again with someone. She was glad she could be there for him.

But he was a man used to compartmentalizing his life.

He claimed that he never mixed business with pleasure, and during these after-hours meetings, Laura had seen that this was true. Each time, he had wound up business matters at six thirty, never looking at his watch, seeming to possess instead an instinctive sense of exactly how many minutes had ticked away since she had locked the front doors and sat down across the desk from him, her files neatly stacked at her right hand, her arsenal of notebook, minirecorder, and laptop primed to catch his every word.

Both other times, he had taken her out to dinner afterward, driving the half hour across the bridge to good restaurants in Quahog instead of staying in Copper Cove, which would have been quicker and easier for both of them. She had to believe this was significant. Max and his wife, Carol, lived in Copper Cove, in a newer development called Presidential Heights. Laura had driven by their house twice before. Once, she had seen Carol out working in the flower beds, and her heart had jolted into a double-time tattoo that had not slowed down until she was nearly a mile away. She knew Max's wife from company Christmas parties—a shapeless woman who looked sixty, though she was ten years younger than that.

Laura had spent many hours lying in bed, alone in her apartment, dissecting the meaning of these dinners with Max outside the bounds of the town they both lived in. Knowing they were important. Counting on it.

Tonight, at exactly six thirty, she was unsurprised to see Max sit forward, loosen his tie, and say as he always did, "I think that about covers it. And now I owe you dinner for staying so late." What did surprise her was when he added, "Why don't we order in tonight and eat right here, in the office?" And while they waited for their lamb vindaloo and tandoori chicken to arrive, he went to a cupboard in the wall and flipped a hidden switch that filled the room with the sounds of Natalie Cole singing "Unforgettable."

They sat on opposite ends of the sofa, which before, Laura had always thought an odd piece of furniture for an office, but which now made perfect sense. He asked her questions about herself, really *listening* to her answers, in a way no one had ever listened to her before. But their curries arrived at exactly the wrong moment, and by the time they finished eating, the music had ended and it seemed awkward to do anything but go their separate ways home.

Laura didn't sleep at all that night.

Nick lay awake, looking up at the dark ceiling. The clock across the room told him it was after midnight, and he was no closer to sleep than he had been two hours ago when he went to bed. Beside him, Ivy slept the deep, profound slumber of a child. In the two spare bedrooms above him, the three neighbor kids presumably also slept.

Somehow they were still here, in his house. He had thought they were only staying one night. He had agreed to that. Of course they could stay one night. You didn't turn abandoned children out in the street, even if they were strangers. But that had been days ago, and somehow they were still here. And now Ivy was talking about letting them stay for a while. Nick knew his wife well enough to interpret that. *For a while* meant there was no end in sight.

When she had first brought up the subject, it had knocked him for a loop. He had opened his mouth to say, "Of course we're not going to keep three strange kids. What are you thinking?" And then the oddest thing had happened. He had been unable to actually say the words out loud. It wasn't a matter of not wanting to disappoint Ivy; he had plenty of experience with vetoing her crazier ideas. The many puppies she had wanted to take in over the years, for instance. Spending their vacation panning for gold in Alaska. He was practiced at saying no when he had to. But when Ivy had said, "Nick, could we consider being DeShaun, Jada, and Hammer's temporary guardians?" he had physically, in that moment, been struck speechless.

And then, as he had struggled to formulate the words, he had been overcome by the sense that taking care of these children was exactly what he should do. Didn't his faith demand it of him? Didn't the Bible say that looking after widows and orphans was the very definition of true religion? He wouldn't have chosen to do it, took no pleasure in the prospect of it, but it seemed somehow to be a fact he had always known. He, Nick Mason, was to take care of three strange children for a little while, and that was that. He had opened his mouth again, and the word had come out effortlessly: "Okay."

But now what? he wondered, staring at the ceiling, above which the two boys were sleeping. Weren't kids supposed to need love as much as they needed house space? He could give them the latter, but how did you just will yourself to love someone you felt no affection for? Should he pretend? Would he be expected to hug and kiss them like a real father would? Even as he examined the idea, he shrank from it. He could not pretend something he didn't feel. He wouldn't even know how to go about it. So house space it would have to be for now. If this was what God wanted him to do, he would do it. He hoped it wouldn't be for long, though. It had been four days, and he was ready to have his home to himself again.

One of the first and most evident needs the children had was for something to wear, so one morning Ivy—who hated buying clothes for herself, much less for three other people—bit the bullet and took them shopping. She was soon exhausted. Jada wanted to try on everything on the racks; DeShaun balked at trying on anything at all, and Hammer seemed physically incapable of keeping his hands to himself. In Target, the little boy raced from shelf to shelf, touching anything that interested him. He ignored Ivy's exasperated instructions to "leave that alone" and continued to pick up, shake, squeeze, push buttons, and turn upside down until at last he knocked a ceramic picture frame to the floor, where it shattered.

Ivy had a steadfast rule of never employing sarcasm with children, but now she snapped, "Thanks, Hammer. I had nothing better to do with twelve dollars than to pay for that frame."

"Hey, he's just a kid," said DeShaun, putting an arm around his brother and pulling him close.

"Come on, mister; you're riding in the cart," Ivy told the younger boy.

"He doesn't have to. I'll hold his hand," DeShaun said. "He won't do it again, will you, Hammer?"

Hammer shook his head and burrowed into his brother's side. He looked at Ivy, and it seemed to her that his wide eyes held a touch of slyness.

Ivy raised her eyebrows. "I would like him to ride in the cart, DeShaun. When he learns to keep his hands off things in a store, he can walk, but until then, I can't afford to pay for this to happen." She nodded at the broken shards of ceramic that were being swept up by a disapproving man in a red polo shirt.

"I said I'll hold his hand."

"And as the adult in charge here, I would like him to ride in the cart instead."

The older boy glared at her. "You can't make him. You're not our mother."

Ivy sighed. She had been waiting for the other shoe to drop. She only wished it had happened at home instead of in public, and preferably at a moment when her patience was not worn quite so thin. "Look, I know you would all rather be with your mom right now, but you can't be. The court says that Nick and I are in charge for the time being, so for Hammer's own good, and for mine, I would like him to ride in the cart, please."

She gently pulled the smaller boy from DeShaun's side

and picked him up. Hammer arched his back and shrieked as though she had touched him with a live wire.

Oh, God, not this. Not now, please. . . .

She wrestled him into the cart on top of the shorts and shirts they had already picked out, wondering if it was even legal to do what she was doing. She didn't see any other option, though: there were some battles you just had to win.

In the cart, a screaming Hammer popped back up and tried to launch himself at DeShaun. Ivy's heart pounded. All at once, every eye in the store seemed to be turned on them, every child services worker in the state to be lurking behind the nearest racks of clothing. "Hammer, sit down."

Jada had both hands clamped over her ears. "Hammer, shut up!"

Hammer bellowed and stomped, his sneakers ripping open a package of underwear in the cart.

"DeShaun," Ivy said in desperation, "help me out here!"

The older boy hesitated, then stepped in and picked up his brother. "You gotta ride in the cart, buddy, okay?"

Hammer clung on like a monkey and thrashed his head in a fierce no, his face wet with tears and mucus.

DeShaun tried to lower him back into the cart.

Hammer howled.

With his brother hanging off his neck, DeShaun looked helplessly at Ivy.

"Hammer!" she cried above his din. "Get in the cart and I'll take you to McDonald's."

The little boy shook his head and continued to scream, but it seemed to Ivy that his cries had lost a modicum of conviction.

"We're going to buy shoes, and then we'll go to McDonald's, but you have to get in the cart first." She felt a creeping shame that she had been reduced to bribery, a tactic to which she had sworn she would never stoop.

But her shame was eclipsed by pure relief when Hammer's cries subsided to wet snuffles and he allowed DeShaun to lower him into the cart.

"Let me wipe your nose," she said. She found a tissue in her purse, and Hammer submitted to the nose wiping.

Ivy straightened and stuffed the tissue into her pocket. "Shoes first, then McDonald's," she repeated. "Let's go." She turned the cart in the direction of the shoe department, feeling like a wrung-out washcloth. So much for winning battles. Maybe there were times when survival was the better part of valor.

୨

The last week of August, Ivy registered the children for school. She produced the papers showing herself and Nick as their temporary guardians. No, she did not have immunization records for them, nor did she have any standardized test scores. Yes, one of them had some special needs.

"Hammer—he'll be in kindergarten—still wets his pants. Is that going to be a problem?"

The secretary, a grayish, middle-aged woman, drew her eyebrows down in a concerned little V. "That all depends," she said. "Do you mean he still wets the bed at night?"

"Yes. No. Night, morning, midday. He was never taught

to use the bathroom. We're trying, but not making much progress." She bleated out a nervous laugh.

The secretary's eyebrows reshaped themselves into upside-down U's of delicate surprise. "Oh, dear," she said.

"He's only been with us a few weeks," Ivy told her, feeling apologetic and about ten years old. "And to tell the truth, I'm not sure how to solve . . . this issue."

The woman, flagged by her nameplate as Mrs. Newman, shook her head. "Miss Cooper will be his teacher, and she'll have to make the final decision. It's not very regular; I can tell you that. But you're in luck—Miss Cooper happens to be here setting up her classroom today. Let me call her room and see if she'll agree to see you."

Miss Cooper evidently agreed, because Ivy was soon following Mrs. Newman's gray head and gray T-shirt down the hall, with the sense that she was being granted all the favor of an audience with the queen. She gritted her teeth. Schoolteachers had always rubbed her the wrong way. There was something so officious about them, as though they believed they held a secret key to knowledge that no one else had access to. They were invariably bossy. She braced herself to dislike the lofty Miss Cooper.

But kindergarten teachers, it turned out, had changed since her day. Miss Cooper was slim and blonde, dressed in khaki shorts and a polo shirt, with the stance and voice of a girl jock. She looked like she ought to be running for senior-class president instead of teaching a classroom full of five-year-olds how to count and spell their names.

The three women sat in miniature chairs at a table

covered with stencils and sheets of construction paper, and Ivy explained the problem. "He's been living with us just a few weeks, since his mother abandoned him and his brother and sister. Apparently he was never potty trained, because he hardly ever uses the toilet. Well," she amended, "he does use it for, uh . . . number two. But he wets his pants at least four or five times a day. We have him in Pull-Ups." She hesitated, checking to see if Miss Cooper knew what Pull-Ups were, but the teacher appeared to be up on the jargon. "We have him in Pull-Ups, but he's almost too big for the largest size. I've never potty trained a child before. I'm probably doing it all wrong."

"Tell me how you're going about it." The fact that Miss Cooper sounded unbothered by what was, to Ivy, a crisis of gargantuan proportions began to make her feel a little better. She told Miss Cooper the things they were trying: regularly timed trips to the bathroom, a sticker chart, M&M's for a job well done.

"It sounds like you're right on track," said the competent Miss Cooper. "Since Hammer—is that his *real* name, by the way?"

"His brother and sister think so. They say it's all he's ever been called."

"Well, since he doesn't have any immunization records, he'll have to get his shots before school starts. While you're at it, you can have the doctor make sure there's nothing physically wrong with Hammer first. If everything checks out, then keep on doing what you're doing at home. We'll reinforce it at school. In fact, I'll see if we can get an ed tech assigned to him for the first quarter, just to work with him on using the bathroom."

"Pardon me." Mrs. Newman had her hand raised. "I just want to remind Mrs. Darling that Hammer will have to wear Pull-Ups while he's here at school. There are infection control issues, you know."

Ivy had the strong impression that Mrs. Newman had been the class tattletale during her own school years.

"Nonsense," said Miss Cooper briskly. "Pull-Ups can be counterproductive because they keep the child feeling dry. No, just send him in with some extra clean clothes and a packet of wipes so he can change if he has an accident. As long as the problem's not physical, I have a feeling that some healthy peer pressure will do the trick. When he sees that everyone else his age knows how to keep their pants dry, he'll learn quickly enough."

Ivy wanted to fall on the neck of this capable, comforting girl and weep with gratitude, but she settled for thanking her in a rational manner and promising to send enough clean clothes to school so Hammer would always have a supply on hand.

After that, she followed Mrs. Newman back to the office, where she arranged for Jada and DeShaun to take placement tests the next day. On the way home, she stopped at Marden's to pick up two extra packs of underwear and four pairs of discount sweatpants for Hammer. She had taken the children school shopping the week before, but it sounded as though the two pairs of jeans, two pairs of corduroys, and ten pairs of underwear she had already bought

Hammer weren't going to be nearly enough for what the efficient Miss Cooper had planned.

Jane Darling stood in the shadows on the porch, a bowl of coleslaw in her hands, and watched them through the screen windows. They were all on the side lawn of her home, as they often were on Thursday nights, and though the sight of her family gathered together was a familiar one, it never grew old or lost the glow of wonder it had always held for her.

There had been a time when Jane was considered a gifted musician. She had gone to a conservatory, majoring in piano performance, and had done one season of concerts with the Portland Symphony. It didn't pay much, but the schedule had allowed her to go back to school and earn her teaching certificate, and during a freak decade of teacher shortages, she had found a job teaching music at a Portland elementary school. She found a church as well, and a widow named Lola who owned a shabby house in a sketchy neighborhood on Munjoy Hill and rented her a room for twenty-five dollars a week. Kitchen privileges were included, but Jane had to pay fifty cents extra to do a load of laundry.

Lola had turned out to be as nutty as a Snickers bar, but she had a kindhearted grandson who often looked in on her on his way home from his own job as a school music teacher and band director.

The first time Leander had stopped by, Jane had just finished washing her hair and setting it in rollers.

"Get the door, Jane!" Lola had barked, snapping her fingers without looking away from the television. She was rooted deeply in a shabby recliner, watching a game show with a glass of Moxie on the end table beside her. Three days' experience of living in the house had already taught Jane that it would take a hand grenade and a crowbar to roust Lola from that chair before eleven o'clock, which signaled the end of prime time and thus Lola's bedtime. It had also taught her that there was probably as much gin in the glass at Lola's elbow as there was Moxie, and therefore the old woman might have been more incapable of getting up to answer the door than actually unwilling.

So Jane had opened the door to a tall, thin young man with large glasses and a long, serious face. He was startled by the sight of her and at first was so shy he could hardly string together a complete sentence. He had been lucky enough to greet his grandmother during a commercial break, but as soon as her show came back on, Lola had waved him away and ignored him as completely as she ignored her boarder. Jane had felt terrible for the nice young man and invited him to come into the kitchen for coffee. Only later, after they'd spent hours talking about Handel and faith and O. Henry over cups of instant Sanka, had she realized with horror that she still had her hair bound up in those enormous pink rollers. But he had come back again the next night, and the next. And nine months later, he had asked her to marry him, before he'd even so much as tried to kiss her. She said yes, and there was kissing aplenty from that point on. Saying yes to Leander was the first really perfect decision Jane had ever made.

David had been the second. Thirty years ago, on the day her son was born, a tangible sense of blessing had settled on Jane like a great mantle of warmth, and it had never dissipated. That day, it was as though a divine hand had descended upon the soft clay shape of her life, flattened it, and during the fourteen hours and thirty-two minutes of her labor, rebuilt it into something that was at once an unfamiliar mess and a flawless work of art. In an instant, she had changed, had become a different person from the self-absorbed girl she was before. She had embraced motherhood and a life of sacrifice and small services with an alacrity that left her more-ambitious girlfriends baffled, even concerned about her. But to Jane, even the meanest jobs—changing a diaper, cooking a meal, running the vacuum—had seemed hallowed. She always understood that she could have been slogging away teaching somewhere, as a working mother like her friend Peg, or she could have been a childless career woman like her sister, Ellen, who worked for L.L.Bean. Whenever Jane could muster the courage to imagine such a life, she shuddered.

Even two years after David, when life got busier with the arrival of the twins, Ivy and Laura, and after them Sephy and then Amy, the wonder of it all, of her family, had always been there. It wasn't often anymore that she had time to observe them unnoticed. Right now, she was meant to be bringing out the coleslaw and calling them all to the picnic tables. But she paused for a moment and watched her family, cherishing this splinter of sun-washed time and tucking it away in her heart, where it rested with a thousand other moments like it.

It hadn't been easy, of course. The children had all had their growing pains and their personal hardships.

Sephy's, perhaps, were the most readily apparent. Her fourth child had always had friends, but starting in high school, her weight had been a barrier to the kind of social life the rest of them had. As a size twenty-two, she could never dress like them or borrow and lend clothes like other girls did. People were often cruel. To Jane's knowledge, Sephy had never been asked out on a date. Libby Hale, Sephy's childhood friend from next door, had been her staunchest ally and had always seen to it that Sephy was included when other girls at school planned sleepovers or trips to the mall. There was very little Libby could do about the boys, though.

Once, when Sephy was at the mall with a group of girls, a boy walking by with his friends had made a long, low mooing sound. Libby Hale had grabbed him by the shirtsleeve, jerked him around, and punched him hard in the stomach. "Do that again, idiot," she'd snapped as the boy had doubled over, gasping for breath. The group of girls had broken up, laughing as Sephy blinked back tears of mortification. Jane and Libby's mother, Abigail, discussing the matter later, had thanked God in heaven that the boy had been too embarrassed to press charges against Libby for assault.

Sephy was at college now, and by all reports, doing well and having a marvelous time, but Jane's heart, which was always a little broken for her sweet, red-haired daughter, cried out again that it was not right for such a pretty girl with such a lovely, generous spirit to be so limited by her own body. She had learned, though, that there was nothing she could do about it, except to love Sephy the way she was and to pray for her. She did it now. *Help her to be all she can be, Lord. To discover all the best things You have planned for her life.*

Her eyes went to the propane burner by the grill, where Laura was pulling steaming ears of corn from a pot and laying them on a platter. This daughter was a different story altogether: tall, slim, blonde, and every inch aware of her own beauty. Too aware of it. She went out with the kind of men who made Jane uncomfortable. They were either too old or too rich or too . . . slippery. Laura was never forthcoming about her love life, although she seemed to be between boyfriends at the moment. Instead of being relieved by this, Jane was worried. She couldn't pin down her reasons for it. *Give her wisdom,* she prayed silently, there on the porch. *Make her want* wisdom. *Keep her safe; don't let her do anything stupid.*

Ivy was perhaps as different from her twin as two sisters could be. Where Laura's instincts for self-preservation were highly developed, Ivy had always been far too compelled to sacrifice herself for everyone. Jane understood her desire to rescue these neighbor children but feared she might have gotten herself in over her head. The little girl, Jada, was at Ivy's elbow now, setting napkins under the forks at the picnic table. The littlest boy was shrieking with joy as David pushed him back and forth on the tire swing at the edge of the lawn. The older one was holding a plate for Leander, who was loading it with hamburgers from the grill.

Nick, as usual, had not come. All was not right there. Jane knew it, though Ivy never breathed a word against her husband. Never even hinted that anything was wrong. Jane did not know what the problem between them was, nor how deep it ran. She wanted to believe it was nothing more than friction between two unlike personalities. Certainly she had seen how Ivy's bright carelessness irritated her methodical husband. She hoped that was all it was and that they would learn to work it out. She always hoped this, but she never quite convinced herself that it would happen.

David, her firstborn, and Amy, her last, were the two hardest workers in the family, she thought, watching her son through the screen. But David's consistent, nine-to-five work ethic, which had made him a partner in a landscaping business by the time he was twenty-five, had nothing in common with Amy's compulsive bursts of workaholic furor. Amy's frenetic creativity had gotten her far, but she was too thin and didn't get enough sleep. Her mother had learned to keep these concerns to herself, though. Amy was eighteen and did not appreciate interference. And now she was gone away to college. Like all of them, she would have to work out who she was and what was important in her own way and time. Meanwhile, Jane would stock the refrigerator with nutritious foods when her youngest was home and pray that Amy would learn balance before she had some kind of breakdown.

David. Her only son. To Jane's mother eye, there was no brighter, handsomer young man on the planet. But he was thirty and still unmarried, and this worried her. From time to time he took girls out, although Jane usually heard about it secondhand and weeks after the fact from one of his sisters. His apartment, decorated like a college dorm room, was no kind of home for a man his age, and she *knew* he didn't eat right. She wished he would hurry up and find someone before all the best girls were taken. Any girl would be lucky to have him. On the other hand, she didn't want him settling for just anyone. *Send him the right one,* she prayed as she watched him. *And I don't want to be bossy, but if You could hurry up about it, I would appreciate it very much.*

Then there was Leander, her husband, the cornerstone of their lives. He taught music at the local school and ran a small business out of his home workshop, cleaning and repairing the band instruments he loved so much. She and Leander had had their rough patches, but they had been married for thirty-five years, and he was still the best man she'd ever known.

The teenage boy, DeShaun, was coming toward her now and caught sight of her through the screen windows. "Uh, excuse me," he said. "Mr. Darling says to tell you it's time to bless the food and eat."

Bless the food, bless my family. "I'm coming," Jane told the boy and pushed open the door.

CHAPTER
5

❧

Ivy and Laura's twenty-eighth birthday happened to fall on Labor Day, and Ivy intended to make the most of it.

"What are we doing to celebrate?" Nick asked her on one of the last days of August.

"I want to go to Piper Point Beach for a picnic with my whole family. Sephy won't be there, of course, but Amy's coming home for the weekend."

"You have a picnic with your whole family every other Thursday. Are you sure that's all you want to do?"

"I have *dinner* with them every other week, not a *picnic*. The beach is different. A special occasion. And I want to rent a metal detector."

"A *metal* detector."

"You know, to search for coins, buried jewelry, that kind of thing."

"I don't remember any stories about buried treasure on Piper Point."

"No, but it's something I've always wanted to do. When I was a kid, I'd see the tourists combing the sand with them, and I'd be so jealous. I just *knew* I could find something valuable, if I only had the chance. Mom never let us, though, because they were too expensive."

"Ivy, be real. You'd probably find about fifty cents' worth of nickels."

"True, but have you ever noticed that the fifty cents you find on the ground always makes you happier than the fifty cents you find in your pocket?"

He considered this. "Not really."

"That, Nick, is because you have no sense of magic about you."

"There's no such thing as magic."

"How wrong you are, sir."

"Hmmmm. So a picnic on the beach with your family and a rented metal detector is all it will take to satisfy your sense of magic?"

"As long as you're there too. It's my birthday *and* Labor Day, so no excuses."

"I wouldn't make excuses on your birthday. Of course I'll be there. What do you want for a gift?"

Ivy considered this all-important question. She and Nick had certain gift-giving rules. Appliances and other things that could be considered needs were strictly off-limits for birthdays, anniversaries, and Christmas, not to mention Valentine's Day. Socks, underwear, deodorant, and maps were also nonstarters. The bathrobe she had given Nick on his birthday had been legitimate because although he had been wanting one, he had refused to spend the money on himself. It had cost her $135 at Macy's, so it was technically a luxury item.

"I want you to take me out for breakfast," she decided. "Just the two of us, and we can spend some time talking and catching up with each other before my family descends for the day."

"That's all?"

"These days, it's a lot."

"I think I can manage that."

He took her to the Silver Star Diner, the only place in Copper Cove that served breakfast, and after omelets and corned-beef hash and too many cups of black coffee, they left the car in the public lot and went for a stroll along the board-walk. There was a contentious chill in the early morning September air, and the slant of the sunlight was already hinting at autumn. The shop owners were just opening their doors for the last really good day of the season. Most would do business until Columbus Day, but between now and then the summer flood of tourists would slow to a thin stream and then to a trickle, and after that, there would be no profit in staying open any longer.

It was incredible that the summer could have flown so fast. August had been a blur to Ivy, the days dropping from the calendar with a speed that sometimes left her disoriented. She had never been so busy before, even in college, and the thought that summer had slipped by like water through her fingers, never to be retrieved again, made her sad.

They stepped into a used-book store that Ivy hadn't visited since June, although in other, less busy years, it had been one of her favorite haunts. She found a beautiful leatherbound copy of Elizabeth Barrett Browning's *Sonnets from the Portuguese* and a dog-eared collection of Emily Dickinson's works that smelled of must and actually had mites crawling in the pages but only cost $1.50. She searched out Nick among the stacks and showed them to him.

"The sonnets are love poems Elizabeth Barrett wrote to Robert Browning before she married him. In fact, they're so personal that she didn't want to publish them under her own name at first, so she gave the book this title to throw people off her trail. It was sort of a joke between her and Robert; he called her his 'little Portuguese' because she was dark."

"Dark? What the heck does that mean?"

"I don't know, dark-skinned? Dark-haired? Portugueselooking, at any rate. There were rumors that one of her ancestors had children by a black slave. Emily's father was utterly ashamed of it. Refused to let any of his children marry, in case the secret should rear its ugly head farther down the bloodline."

"Ah."

"Isn't that horrible? She married Robert Browning anyway and ran away to Italy." As an afterthought, Ivy added, "She was a laudanum addict."

"How romantic," Nick said dryly.

"Isn't it? And Emily Dickinson—" she waved the second book in front of him—"her poems are simple at first read, but very complex once you start paying attention. I've heard that you can sing all of them to the tune of 'The Yellow Rose of Texas.'"

"Is that true?"

"I don't know; let's try." She opened up the book at random and began to sing.

> "A bird came down the walk:
> He did not know I saw;
> He bit an angle-worm in halves
> And ate the fellow, raw.
>
> And then he drank a dew
> From a convenient grass,
> and then hopped sidewise to the wall
> To let a beetle pass."

She was delighted. "It seems to work!"

Nick took the book from her and flipped through the pages. "That's supposed to be great poetry? It's kind of disgusting, actually. Mundane at best."

She took the book back from him. "That's what I mean when I say her poetry's deceptively simple at first. Actually, you'd have to read the rest of that poem to get the whole meaning. The last lines are just gorgeous." She clutched the book to her chest and, from memory, said:

"And he unrolled his feathers
And rowed him softer home

Than oars divide the ocean,
Too silver for a seam,
Or butterflies, off banks of noon,
Leap, plashless, as they swim."

"That doesn't make sense," Nick said. "Butterflies don't swim. They drown in water."

She stared at him, startled. "I never thought of that. Maybe old Emily wasn't such a genius after all."

"This is why I don't read poetry." He took the books from her hands and bought them both for her.

They stepped outside as if surfacing from a dream and had to blink in the brightness of the morning.

"I suppose we should head home," Ivy said regretfully. "I still have food to get ready for the picnic."

When they got to the car, Nick pulled a small, wrapped gift from under his seat and handed it to her.

"What's this?"

He rolled his eyes. "Do you really want me to tell you? Should I say, 'It's a—dot, dot, dot'?"

"It was merely a culturally acceptable expression of surprise," she told him loftily. "I shall now open it and find out for myself what it is."

"Good idea."

It was a painting—a watercolor framed in driftwood—of

a great blue heron standing in a marsh. She loved it instantly. "Oh, Nick! Where did you get it?"

"Seascapes Gallery."

"It must have cost a fortune."

"That's none of your business."

"What did you do, cash in your retirement fund?"

"Ha. As if."

"Well, I really, really love it, and I know just where I'm going to hang it."

"Where?"

"On the wall beside the couch. It's just the right size."

"It's not just the right size. It's too small."

"I knew you would say that. You argue with me about everything."

"I'm right about this," he said, starting the car and backing out of the parking space. "Your spatial sense is nil. Worse than nil. If it were up to you, we'd be trying to squeeze the refrigerator into the counter space the microwave takes up. You have *negative* spatial sense."

"That might be true," she was willing to concede, "but think of all the kinds of sense I *do* have."

"Like what?"

"Like . . . people sense. I never met a person I couldn't make a friend of. . . . Well," she amended after a moment's thought, "except your sisters. They continue to elude me."

"You don't really want to ruin your birthday by talking about my family."

"You're right." As he maneuvered the car onto the main

road, she leaned over and kissed him on the cheek. "Thank you for breakfast, and the books, and the watercolor."

He looked pleased. "You're welcome. Happy birthday."

"I love you."

"I know."

❧

When they got to the beach later that afternoon, Ivy's parents were already there with Amy. They had claimed two picnic tables and had charcoal burning in two of the bolted-down iron grills provided by the park. It was a good thing, Nick observed to her as he pulled his Volvo into one of the few remaining parking spaces, that someone in the family had thought to arrive early. The beach was full of residents and late-season tourists taking advantage of the last day of their vacation. The morning chill had burned off, and the air was flawless: warm and dry, with just enough of a breeze to save everyone from being too hot.

The metal detector was a great hit with the children. They dogged Ivy's steps, digging with alacrity each time it beeped. Together, they found three quarters, six pennies, a rusty barrette, and a tiny silver ring that perfectly fit Jada's middle finger, before Ivy's wrists gave out. She handed the machine over to DeShaun. "It's too heavy for you, Jada," she said when the little girl protested. "You and Hammer and DeShaun can take turns. The first thing you find will be DeShaun's, the second thing is yours, the third thing is Hammer's, and so on, okay?" She looked at DeShaun. "Okay?"

"Yeah. Come on, Jada, quit whining. We're gonna find us some money, right?"

She brightened. "You have to give me whatever you find when it's my turn, DeShaun. Even if it's a million dollars."

"A'ight, sure. Even a million dollars."

They moved off down the beach together, and Ivy, watching them, thought not for the first time that much of the scant happiness in Jada's and Hammer's lives had been thanks to their big brother. He seemed to have an unconscious instinct for filling in many of the gaps left by the absence of both mother and father. She was sure he did not know he had such an instinct; he simply did what he felt, and the result was love. She wished better things in life for him than those that were most likely in store.

David materialized at her side and put an arm around her shoulders. "Happy birthday, little brat. Where's your other half?"

"Does that mean Nick or Laura?"

"Since it's your birthday, Laura."

"She's late, as usual. Where have you been?"

"Washing and waxing my truck. And wrapping your birthday present."

"Ooh, what did you get me?"

"I made you a mix tape of my favorite eighties bands: Duran Duran, Air Supply . . ."

She punched him in the shoulder. "What did you *really* get me?"

"You'll have to wait till present time to see. What are the

kids doing?" he added, shading his eyes to look down the beach after them.

"Nick rented me a metal detector for the day. They're using it."

"Oh, excellent! I've always wanted to try one of those." With a shout, he jogged off down the beach toward the children.

"You have to take turns!" Ivy called after him feebly.

Laura still had not arrived by the time the food was ready. They sat down without her to Leander's maple-grilled salmon and Jane's red, white, and bleu potato salad. Amy had made a salad of black beans and rice with a lime-cilantro dressing that turned out to be surprisingly good. Ivy, suspecting the children would turn up their noses at the salmon, had contributed hamburgers and a salad of roasted corn and red peppers.

"How are you liking college?" she asked Amy as they ate.

"Hate it." Amy stabbed at her corn salad and looked miserable. "My roommate's a *cheer*leader."

Ivy, who was acquainted with Amy's views on cheerleaders, said, "That's too bad. What about classes? Don't you like them?"

"They're all right." To Ivy's surprise, her little sister had tears in her eyes. She looked to her mother, alarmed.

"It's an adjustment period," Jane said firmly, reaching across the table and squeezing Amy's hand. "Things will get better. You just need to give it time." Over Amy's bent head, she mouthed the word *homesick* at Ivy.

Amy raised her head. "And Mom thinks I'm *homesick*, which is ridiculous."

They had given up on Laura and unanimously agreed to cut the cake without her, when she arrived at last—breathless, yellow scarf blowing in the breeze, and bearing a store-bought pound cake.

"Sorry I'm late," she gasped, sliding onto the end of the bench beside her mother. "The dry cleaner didn't have my order ready. I had to wait."

Amy, whose tears had dried, frowned at Ivy and mouthed, *Dry cleaner?*

Ivy frowned back. *No idea.* But she intended to find out.

She got her chance later, after the presents had been opened and the picnic cleared away and Nick was pitching horseshoes on the grass with DeShaun, Leander, and David. The tide was out, and far down the beach, Jane and Amy searched for sea glass and shells with the two younger children. Ivy and Laura sat at the table picking at the remains of the birthday cake, surrounded by their unwrapped gifts.

"So why were you really late?" Ivy asked.

"I told you. I was picking up my dry cleaning."

"It's Labor Day, Laura. The dry cleaner's closed."

Her sister rolled her eyes and said nothing.

"So . . . ? Tell me! It's not a man, is it?"

Laura examined one shell-pink fingernail. "Why would you jump to that conclusion?"

"Ummm . . . because with you, it's usually a man?"

Laura threw her a disgusted look. "You are so judgmental."

"I'm not being judgmental; I'm just saying you've had a lot of boyfriends. Ask Amy or Sephy."

"Oh, so you three have been discussing me behind my back? That must be amusing for you."

Ivy gaped at her. "What's gotten into you? Nobody's discussing you behind your back. I was just *asking* if it was a man."

Laura did not answer right away but stretched out one hand, admiring her rings and twisting them around her fingers. At last, she said, "It might be a man. But I don't think you'd approve."

"Oh. And why wouldn't I approve?"

"Tell me when anyone in this family has ever approved of one of my boyfriends."

"Um . . . okay. I'll admit we may not *like* all the men you choose to date, but that's not the same thing."

"You *never* like the men I go out with."

"Not true."

"Name one of my boyfriends in the last three years that you and the rest of them—" Laura waved a hand down the beach—"have liked."

Ivy considered this. "It's true that we didn't like Ike the Bike—"

"His name was *Dwight*, thank you very much," Laura snapped, "and it humiliated him that you and Sephy and Amy and David insisted on calling him Ike."

"No . . . it was just . . . Ike, like *Eisenhower!*" Ivy protested, struggling to keep a straight face. "It was a very patriotic nickname."

When Laura didn't laugh, Ivy said feebly, "It was a *joke*."

"He knew you were laughing at him. He knew you didn't like him. Who could blame him for leaving town?"

"We didn't like him because he *hit* you, Laura."

"He only hit me once, and that's none of your business."

"Do you even *hear* yourself?" She stared at her twin, but Laura continued to examine her fingernails and would not look at her.

"Okay," Ivy said, "how about Juan the Con? We had a good reason not to like him, either."

Laura's lips thinned. "His name was *Carlos*, and he did *not* rob that gas station. He was proven innocent."

"Actually, he plea-bargained and had his sentence reduced and suspended. That's not the same thing."

"Oh, excuse me. I thought I was in *America*, where a person is innocent until proven guilty."

"All I'm saying is that the whole family knows you have a history of choosing men who are . . . not always necessarily good for you."

"And since when are *you* the spokesperson for the entire Darling family?"

"I'm not! I'm just saying—"

"Well, as a matter of fact I *was* with a man today, but it's not what you think."

Ivy broke off a large crumb of cake and put it in her mouth. "What is it then?"

"It was just a friend who wanted to take me out for lunch on my birthday."

"So why are you keeping it a secret from the family?"

Laura hesitated.

Ivy was puzzled, and then the obvious truth dawned. "Oh no. Laura, he's not . . . Is he *married*?"

Her sister looked away. "It was just a friendly lunch."

"Laura! You know better than that."

"Did I ask for your advice?"

A small, sick curl of dread began to blossom in Ivy's stomach. She knew from experience that disagreeing with Laura would only alienate her. She reached out a conciliatory hand and forced herself to say, "Calm down and tell me about him, then. Come on," she added when Laura tightened her mouth. "I want to hear about your lunch. What's his name?"

Laura hesitated another moment, but the desire to talk trumped her pride. "It's Max," she said, still sounding miffed.

"Max, your *boss*? And it was really just lunch?"

Her twin shrugged her slim shoulders. "We've gone out a few times. Work-related stuff. We just finished a big project, and he wanted to thank me."

"And his wife's okay with this?"

"How am I supposed to know? It was just lunch between friends. Colleagues. That's all."

They heard a shout from down the beach. "Look at all my shells!" Jada was running toward them, struggling against the soft sand, her T-shirt pulled up to form a pouch that was bulging with the sharp edges of shells. Hammer was close behind her, with Jane and Amy walking more slowly, deep in conversation.

"Don't say a *word* to Mom and Dad," Laura hissed. "Not a word. Mom's on the library board with Carol, and she wouldn't understand."

Jada reached the table just then and, standing on her

tiptoes, spilled her cache of shells and sea glass and broken sand dollars across the table, squealing with joy.

"They're beautiful, Jada!" Ivy exclaimed. Over the little girl's head, her eyes met her twin's.

Laura lifted a perfectly manicured finger to her lips. *Shhhh.*

Uneasy, but feeling she had no choice, Ivy nodded and lifted a finger to her own lips in reply.

School was scheduled to start on the Wednesday after Labor Day, and by Tuesday night, the police still had no news of Lily Allen's whereabouts.

"How hard can they be trying?" Ivy wondered aloud to Nick. They were in the living room, she doing a crossword puzzle while he watched the Red Sox trounce the Twins on ESPN. "I mean, how many places can a person hide?"

"A lot," he said, not taking his eyes from the screen. "People disappear all the time. It's a big country. It's an even bigger world."

"If she defaulted on her student loans, they'd find her fast enough."

"I doubt she even finished high school, Ivy, to say nothing of going to college."

"I know that. I'm just saying that when you owe people money, they seem to be able to find you wherever you are."

"I'm sure Lily owes plenty of people money. What— *strike?* Get your eyes examined, ump! That was way outside the strike zone." He made a disgusted sound.

"Not the right people, apparently."

"What?"

"I said Lily apparently doesn't owe the right people money, since no one can find her. Anyway, tomorrow's the first day of school, and I'm going to take plenty of pictures in case she wants them someday."

"Don't kid yourself. She doesn't even want her children; why would she want pictures of them?"

"Maybe one of the kids will want them one day, then. And every child should have a start-of-school picture taken. Hammer especially, since it's his first day of kindergarten. He's so excited, Nick. It's really cute."

Nick grunted and yelled at the umpire again.

"I talked to him about staying dry all day, and I think he's really enthusiastic about trying. He knows that none of the other kids in his class will be wetting their pants. I think kindergarten could be the solution to his problem. Positive peer pressure, Miss Cooper calls it."

"Good. Good. *Safe!* He's safe! Yes!" Nick leaned forward, squinting at the TV screen.

"You're not even listening to me."

"What?"

"Oh, never mind." She watched with him for a few minutes and on the next commercial break said, "My hair's growing out. I need to get something done to it."

"Really?" Nick's eyes were glued to a commercial for a sports drink.

"I've kind of gotten used to having it pink like this. I was thinking I might just have Cricket do the same thing to it again."

Nick turned his face toward her, but his eyes were still on the TV. "Same thing?"

"You know, short. Spiky. Pink."

A low, sleek car appeared on-screen, zipping along the edge of a winding cliff. "Great, whatever you want," said her husband vaguely.

She tucked the crossword under her arm and the pencil behind one ear, standing up. "Good night, Nick."

"Night," he said to her back.

In the kitchen, Ivy measured coffee and water into the pot and set the timer for 6 a.m. The easy camaraderie she and Nick had shared on her birthday had evaporated as though it had never happened. When Ivy had awoken this morning, she had hoped it would continue, but Nick, with his customary workday tunnel vision, had spoken to her only abstractedly over breakfast, except to become irritated when she had spilled orange juice all over his newspaper.

What does he want from me, God? She waited, but God did not answer.

Ivy put the coffee away, gave the counters one more wipe, and hung the dishcloth up to dry. She went to the bedroom and began to change into her pajamas, wishing Nick would call her back to him, knowing he wouldn't, the old familiar sadness heavy in her chest.

DeShaun picked up his tray and turned to survey the crowded cafeteria. Nobody looked up and said, "Hey, dude, come sit over here," and he wasn't about to invite himself to a table full of jocks or larpers or nerds who were actually doing their homework at the lunch table or giggling blonde girls. The other option was a half-empty table in the corner. At one end of it, a kid in a wheelchair was parked. He had a big bib tied around his neck, and his head hung over to one side like it was too heavy for him to hold up. An aide was feeding him. There was a fat boy. A girl with thick glasses and greasy hair. Someone else—he couldn't tell male or female—wearing a too-small plaid jacket was hunched over a sandwich, with a stocking cap pulled down around . . . its . . . ears. One boy had a *Star Trek* lunch box. In ninth grade, a *Star Trek* lunch box.

Well, DeShaun was the only black kid in the whole high school and he had spent the morning being stared at and whispered about, so he figured he belonged at that table better than he belonged anywhere else. He went over, set his tray down on the end opposite the wheelchair kid and as far away from the rest of them as he could get, slung himself into a chair, and began to pick at his fries. They were half-cold and soft, but he had gone hungry too many times in his life to ever turn down food when it was available. He ate them all.

He had started on a thin, lukewarm cheeseburger when the kid next to him said, "Hey." At first, DeShaun didn't realize the kid was talking to him. It was loud in the cafeteria, and besides, nobody else had said a word to him all day. He had begun to think he was invisible. How you could stick out like a sore thumb in the hallways and in every single classroom and still be invisible, he didn't know, but apparently it was possible.

The kid reached across the two empty places between them and rapped his knuckles on the table beside DeShaun's tray. "Hey," he said again.

DeShaun looked up. Great. The kid with the lunch box. He was one of the skinniest people DeShaun had ever seen. His hair was short all over, except in front of his ears, where it hung down in long curls past his chin. On the back of his head, he wore a miniature black hat.

"What?" DeShaun said.

"What's your name?"

"DeShaun."

"Pleased to meet you, DeShaun." The kid stuck out a bony hand as if he expected DeShaun to shake it. "Milo Rosenberg at your service."

DeShaun glanced around the cafeteria uneasily. It would not do him any favors to be seen shaking hands with this weirdo. Ignoring the hand, he jerked his chin at the food in front of the kid. "Why you eatin' out of a lunch box?"

"I can't eat the cafeteria food. I'm kosher."

DeShaun had no idea what that was supposed to mean. He had only ever seen the word in one place before. "What, like a pickle?"

"Sort of. I'm a Hasid, so I can only eat things that are prepared in certain ways. Like, I don't eat meat and dairy together, so I couldn't eat that cheeseburger."

DeShaun looked at the cheeseburger in his hands. "Is it like an allergy or something?"

"It's a religion. Jewish. I wasn't always Jewish, though. I converted two years ago. My parents are Catholic, but I already had the name, so I thought, why not? I figured it was a sign."

"Oh." DeShaun returned to his cheeseburger, which was nearly cold by now.

"What religion are you?" Milo was not going to leave him alone.

"None."

"Ah, an atheist!" Milo said it with satisfaction, as though he had discovered a great secret.

"I'm not an atheist."

"No? An agnostic, perhaps?"

DeShaun swallowed the last bite of his cheeseburger and stared at the kid. He had never heard someone his own age actually use the word *perhaps*. "No, man. I told you, I'm not anything."

"Well, if you're not an atheist and you're not an agnostic, you must believe *something* about God."

DeShaun shrugged. "Never thought about it," he muttered. His social life, he reflected, would probably never get much worse than this. The lone black kid in a white high school, and the only person who would give him the time of day was a Jewish boy with a lunch box who wanted to talk about religion. He hunched his shoulders and peeled the foil lid off a pudding cup.

Someone passing by with a tray knocked into DeShaun's shoulder, hard, shifting his chair sideways. He looked up. A kid from the jock table was standing there with a tray, smirking at him.

"Hey, *boy*. You made me drop my fork. Pick it up for me," the jock said.

DeShaun looked at the fork on the floor and back up at the kid. He looked muscular, but DeShaun was a lot bigger. He'd never been much of a fighter, but he could probably take him if he had to.

The kid snapped his fingers. "I said, pick my fork up, *boy*."

DeShaun's heart was pounding hard, but he figured it was better to let people know early on not to mess with him. He put his pudding cup down and stood up, wider than the other kid and almost a head taller. He clenched his abs, in case the kid decided to drop his tray and hit him. "I'm not pickin' up your fork," he said.

A muscle in the other kid's face jerked, but he turned away at last. "You better watch yourself here," he said. "We don't like people from away."

DeShaun watched the kid walk away with a sense of relief. He had a feeling he hadn't seen the last of trouble with him.

Milo slid his lunch box across the table and moved into the chair beside DeShaun. "That's Josh Goodall," he said. "He talks like that, but he doesn't really mean any harm."

DeShaun picked up his pudding cup and began eating.

"Where are you from?" Milo asked.

Well, at least he wasn't talking about God anymore. "Detroit."

"I've never been to Detroit."

DeShaun could have guessed that.

"Were you in a gang there?"

DeShaun shot him a disgusted look. You didn't just ask somebody questions like that. "Why? Because I'm black?"

"Right."

This kid was clueless. Worse than clueless. Well, he was asking for it.

"Yep," said DeShaun, scraping out the bottom of his pudding cup. "I was in a gang. Worst gang in the city. The . . . the Pit Vipers, we were called."

Milo's eyes were wide behind his glasses. "Wow. Did you, like, carry a gun or a knife or a shiv or anything?"

"Oh yeah. Everywhere I went."

"Ever use them?"

"Only if I had to."

Milo lowered his voice. "Did you ever kill anyone?"

DeShaun held up two fingers.

Soundlessly, Milo's lips moved in the word *two*.

DeShaun leaned toward him. "Did hard time for it too." He stood and picked up his tray. "Don't tell anyone." He walked away.

"I won't!" Milo called after him. "I won't say anything!"

DeShaun shook his head. What an idiot.

The afternoon went like the morning had gone. Nobody talked to him, except teachers. He didn't understand a thing his math teacher said, and he almost fell asleep in world civ. His last class, earth science, was okay, but only because the teacher showed them how to hold fire in their hands without getting burned. You did it by lighting a puddle of hand sanitizer, then swiping your hand through it. He figured that class was going to be okay, except it was the only class without assigned seats, and Milo sat next to him. DeShaun spent the whole block ignoring him.

The high schoolers were in one building, while the little kids had a separate building next door, so he didn't see Jada or Hammer until he got on the bus to go home. Hammer was in the front seat, talking the driver's ear off. Jada was crammed into a seat halfway back, giggling with two little white girls. When she saw him, she waved and called, "Hi, DeShaun!"

"Hi, DeShaaaaauuun!" chorused the girls she was sitting with, and all three of them burst into giggles.

"DeShaun, sit with me!" Hammer cried. "That's my big brother," he informed the bus driver.

"Is that right?" said the driver. She looked like she was trying not to laugh. "Well, it's nice to meet you, DeShaun."

DeShaun jerked his chin at her and hurried past. He did not want to be seen talking to the bus driver. "I'm gonna sit back here, buddy," he muttered to Hammer and made his way to the back of the bus.

The only empty seats were beside a kid who looked like a senior and Milo. He sat with Milo.

"I didn't tell anyone about the gang," Milo whispered, shifting his lunch box so he could lean closer.

DeShaun sighed. It was shaping up to be a long year.

CHAPTER

6

WITH THE CHILDREN well settled into their school routine, Ivy went back to work part-time. Esme had agreed that she could work Tuesdays, Thursdays, and every other Saturday morning, which suited Ivy just fine.

One afternoon, Ivy's daily trip to the mailbox yielded a stiff parchment envelope. It was an invitation from Angela and Vincent, embossed in gold script with pink bunnies and blue ducks frolicking around the border.

It's a Gender Reveal Party!
Sweet little girl or busy little boy?
Find out on Friday and share our joy!

"I have a late meeting with a client that night," Nick said immediately, when Ivy showed him the invitation.

She narrowed her eyes at him. "Sometimes I think you schedule these meetings to avoid unpleasant things."

"Just one of the perks of the job, babe," he said, pulling on his running shoes.

Having no such convenient excuse herself, Ivy prepared to go to the party on the following Friday night, but to her guilty relief, the school nurse called that day to say that Hammer had a sore throat and a fever, and would Ivy please come pick him up? She missed the party, but she wasn't kept in suspense for long. Ruby called at seven thirty the next morning to deliver the postmortem.

"When Angela had the ultrasound over the summer," said her mother-in-law, "she told the technician, 'Do *not* tell me what sex the baby is.' She and Vincent wanted to be surprised, you see."

"Oh, really? Wow." Stifling a yawn, Ivy shuffled from the kitchen with a cup of coffee and settled into a corner of the couch.

"So Angela told the woman to just write *boy* or *girl* on a slip of paper and seal it in an envelope. Then she took the envelope to a bakery, gave it to the baker, and ordered three dozen cupcakes filled with the right color frosting—pink or blue. But she told the baker not to tell her which color he was using. Wasn't that clever?"

"So clever," Ivy murmured.

"Then, at the party last night, we all watched as Angela bit into the first cupcake and discovered . . ." Ruby waited.

Ivy realized something was expected of her. "What? What is it?" she asked, trying to sound breathless.

"It's a girl!" crowed Ruby. "But they're not telling anyone the name until she's born. They don't want to give away all the secrets at once."

"Of course not."

"Well, I can't talk all day—I have other people to call. Be sure and tell Nick the good news, won't you, dear? And give him my love."

"Of course, Ruby. Thanks for calling." Ivy hung up, went back to bed, and pulled a pillow over her head.

The first week in October, Dr. Payne's office left a voice mail to remind Ivy that she was due for her semiannual teeth cleaning. "It can't possibly have been six months already!" she wailed to Laura over the phone.

"Dentists run on a different calendar than we do," Laura assured her. "What they mean is that it's been six months, dental time. That's only two or three months to you and me."

"Well, I can't go. I'm busy."

"You haven't even scheduled it yet."

"No, but I'm sure I don't have a single day free for the next six months."

"Oh, Ivy, don't be stupid. It's just a cleaning."

"He'll tell me I need my wisdom teeth pulled. And what kind of dentist calls himself Dr. *Payne*, anyway? That hardly inspires confidence."

Her sister ignored this last and homed in on the real issue. "What do you mean he'll say you need your wisdom teeth pulled?"

"He's been saying it for years."

"Ivy! Why haven't you had them pulled, then?"

"I haven't gotten around to it."

"Liar. You're a chicken. You're afraid to have your wisdom teeth out. *Bawwwwk, buck buck bawwwwk,*" Laura clucked into the phone.

"Okay," Ivy snapped, "so I'm afraid. It's supposed to be really—*stop clucking at me*. Really painful. And it's dangerous, too. What if I get dry socket? Sephy had a patient once, at the hospital, who got dry socket after they pulled her wisdom teeth. Then the dry socket turned into a bone infection and she died."

"Bawwwk," said Laura. "All right, you big chicken. How about if I promise to go with you to your cleaning and take you out to lunch afterward?"

"Really? You'd do that?"

"Sure."

"For sushi?"

"Anything you want."

"I want sushi. And not from the mall."

"Done. Just make the appointment for an afternoon. And not a Friday. Call me back and let me know the date so I can arrange the time off."

"Okay."

"Call the dentist now. Don't put it off."

"All right, all right. But I think you're all using me extremely ill."

"I know," said Laura soothingly. "You have a hard life. Call the dentist."

True to Ivy's prediction, the dentist did remind her that it was high time she had her wisdom teeth pulled. He showed her on the X-rays, not for the first time, how they were crowding her other teeth, pushing the front ones out of shape. With Laura beside her, Ivy had very little choice but to let them schedule the surgery. The soonest she could get in was Columbus Day, which the oral surgeon's office apparently did not observe. Ivy remarked to Laura that this seemed unpatriotic of him but made the appointment, feeling sulky and victimized.

It was not until later in the week that she remembered Columbus Day was a school holiday. She called Laura again.

"I can't have my wisdom teeth out."

"Oh, really? Why not?" Laura sounded very patient.

"School holiday. Who'll be here to watch the kids?"

"Nick will. Columbus Day is a bank holiday too."

"Nope," Ivy crowed. "He has to go with me so he can drive me home. Apparently I'm not to be trusted behind the wheel after anesthesia."

"Ask Mom to watch them."

"It's their anniversary. They're going to New Hampshire for the weekend."

"Won't Amy be home from school that weekend?"

"She's staying on campus. It's homecoming."

"Really? Does she have a date?"

"Laura, we all know better than to ask Amy questions like that."

"Fair enough. How about your mother-in-law?"

"No way. Who knows what damage Ruby would inflict? Last time we were there, she asked Jada if 'colored hair' is hard to comb because it's so frizzy."

"Poor kid!"

"Fortunately, Jada's too young to get it. You know what she told Ruby? She said, 'Ask Ivy. She's the one got pink-colored hair!'"

Laura laughed but was not to be distracted. "I have Columbus Day off," she told her twin briskly, "so *I* shall come over and watch the children for you."

"Oh, you don't need to do that."

"Yes, I think I do. I want to. I haven't seen them in so long."

"Oh. Well . . . thanks, I guess."

"There's no need to overwhelm me with gratitude. But guess what? I'll even make supper for you all."

"You will? Will you make me soup? I'm sure I won't be able to eat anything but soup afterward."

"That's so sad. Of course I'll make you soup. What kind do you want?"

"Chicken noodle?"

"Chicken noodle soup it will be."

❧

On the Monday morning of her surgery, Ivy was not allowed to eat or drink, but because it was a holiday, she made pancakes for the rest of the family anyway, feeling a little martyred as she watched the rest of them eat with obvious enjoyment. Laura arrived to take over at seven thirty, and Ivy and Nick left, pulling into the parking lot of the oral surgeon's office just before eight o'clock. Time seemed to have sped up, as though this were some kind of bad dream. Ivy was unconscious by eight fifteen and discharged home by ten thirty.

"That wasn't so bad, was it?" Nick asked when they pulled into the pharmacy to fill her prescriptions on the way home.

"Not bad for you, maybe," she retorted, her face feeling thick and foreign as she spoke. Although she had to admit her jaw was more numb than painful.

At home, Laura met them at the door looking very pretty and domestic in an apron that said *King Arthur Flour*. "Now that wasn't so bad, was it?" she said, smiling.

"Why does everyone keep telling me it wasn't bad?" Ivy grumbled. "I assure you it was all very horrible. Or it will be as soon as the anesthesia wears off." They tactfully ignored her bad mood. Jada and Hammer presented her with get-well cards they'd made, pointing out that Laura had made DeShaun rake the fallen leaves from the lawn for her while she'd been gone.

"We didn't want to make you cards, but Laura said we had to," Jada informed her.

"Well, it was nice of you all to do it," said Ivy, "and aren't they beautiful? Thank you *very* much." She let Nick tuck her into bed for a nap while Laura went back to the kitchen to turn off the heat under the promised soup and to write out instructions for baking the lasagna she'd made the rest of the family for supper.

By the time Ivy awoke, Laura was gone, the family was eating supper, and there was a screaming pain ripping through both sides of her lower jaw. She shuffled out to the kitchen and poured herself a glass of water. "Where are those pain pills?" she mumbled to Nick, around what felt like a jaw full of broken glass.

"In the bathroom medicine cabinet. Sit down; I'll get you one." He brought it to her, and Ivy looked at it with distaste.

"It's huge. I'll never be able to swallow the whole thing."

"Try," said Nick heartlessly.

She got the pill down but lived to regret it. Within half an hour, her head felt so disembodied from the rest of her that she actually bumped into the refrigerator when she was aiming for the doorway to the living room. She made it to the couch and lay down, the room spinning around her. "Make it stop," she whimpered.

The doctor's office was long closed, so Nick called Sephy, who said it was just because Ivy wasn't used to taking pain medication. She assured him that one Vicodin had never killed anyone and said that Ivy would just have to wait it out. Once it wore off, she should switch to Tylenol and call the doctor in the morning.

Ivy spent most of the next day sleeping, and by the third day felt well enough to dust and vacuum the house and make an enormous pot of chili, although she went to bed at seven o'clock and slept for twelve hours straight. On Thursday, she went back to work. When Esme asked her how the surgery had gone, she automatically answered, "Oh, it wasn't that bad." And to her surprise, she realized she meant it.

⁊

"Ivy, have you thought this through, really? It seems like a very dangerous idea to me, taking in these three children from nobody-knows-where and letting them live right in the house with you."

Ivy shifted the phone to her other ear and schooled patience into her voice. "It might be a lot of things, Ruby, but how is it dangerous?"

Her mother-in-law spoke with urgency. "That oldest boy is nearly as big as you are. What if Nick's not home one day, and he tries something? Pulls a knife on you or . . . or sets the house on fire? You hear of things like that all the time in the news."

"I have no fear that anything of the sort will happen. They're basically good kids. A little rowdy, maybe, but certainly not dangerous."

Ruby changed tack. "And it's very good of you to want to help them. But you've done your part. Don't you think it's time for them to move on to a place where they can be more . . . permanent?"

"I think the best thing for them is to stay right where they are for the time being."

"How does Nick feel about all of this?" her mother-in-law said, attacking on yet another front.

Ivy gritted her teeth. She had never purposely been rude

to Ruby, but oh, it was tempting sometimes. "Nick and I are on the same page." She didn't add, *Not that it's any of your business, you interfering old cow.*

To her immense relief, the front door opened at that moment and she heard her brother's voice. "Hello?"

"I have to go, Ruby; someone's at the door. Give my best to Harry." Ivy hung up without waiting for a reply.

"Come in!" she called in the direction of the front door as she took several deep, calming breaths and tried to shake Ruby out of her head.

David came into the kitchen with a pencil behind one ear. "Special delivery for the Darling-Mason family."

"Special delivery?"

"Out in the truck." He jerked his head in the direction of the driveway. "Come and see."

Ivy followed him outside. His blue Chevy pickup was parked in the driveway, its bed filled with long, flat cardboard boxes.

The passenger door opened and out jumped her father. He turned to help her mother step down from the cab. "Morning, Ivy!" he called.

Her mother waved gaily at her. "Surprise!"

Ivy was bewildered. "What are you two doing here?"

"We have a gift for the children," said Jane. "David came along to help your father set it up."

Leander, meanwhile, had gone to let down the tailgate. He and David began unloading the long boxes and carrying them around to the back of the house.

"Is Nick home?" David asked as he passed. "He could give us a hand here."

"A hand with what? What is this?"

"It's a swing set!" Jane crowed, clasping her hands under her chin with the excitement of a child. "It's to welcome the kids into the family!"

Ivy stared at her mother, and what came out of her mouth had nothing at all to do with the thoughts that were churning through her mind. "DeShaun might be too old for a swing set."

"That's what Amy said. So we got him this." Jane took a small, brightly wrapped package from her purse and, linking her arm through Ivy's, pulled her back toward the house.

"What is it?"

"It's an iPod. All the kids have them."

And this did what all of Ruby's unkindness had not: Ivy's eyes welled up with tears, and she sat down right there on the front steps and cried on her mother's shoulder until she had no more tears left.

❧

It was six weeks into the school year, and DeShaun was no closer to having friends than he had been that first day. It was true that people said hi to him now in his classes, and he was almost always picked first for team sports in gym because he was good at them, but he still sat at the freak table for lunch and with Milo on the bus. There was a big difference between people saying hi to you and actually wanting to hang out with you.

Milo was turning out to be not so bad. He had laughed when DeShaun finally told him that no, he hadn't really been in a gang in Detroit. And DeShaun had been able to convince him to stop carrying that stupid *Star Trek* lunch box to school, which had made him mildly less embarrassing to be seen with. But he was still a nerd, and there was no denying that, of all the kids who got bullied in school, Milo got bullied the most. The soccer players shoved him up against lockers as they walked past, they snatched his glasses off his face and threw them down the hall at least once a day, and if he was bent over a water fountain getting a drink, it was a near certainty that one of them would come along and shove his face into the stream of water. Milo bore it all with a cheerfulness that infuriated DeShaun.

"Stand up for yourself, man!" he was constantly telling the smaller boy. "You don't have to take that from them."

"They're just having fun," Milo would protest. "They don't mean anything by it."

But one day Milo cracked, and when it happened, DeShaun cracked too. They were in gym class, playing dodgeball because it was raining out, and Josh Goodall wouldn't leave Milo alone. Josh wasn't big, but he was mean. He picked on all the kids from the freak table, even the wheelchair kid. Since that first day in the cafeteria, he had taken to snapping his fingers at DeShaun and calling him *boy* whenever he saw him.

"Boy," he would say in math class, snapping, "pick my pencil up off the floor for me."

DeShaun always ignored him, but it got under his skin anyway.

On this particular day, Josh and Milo were on the same team. Milo, who was enthusiastic about dodgeball even though he was terrible at it, held a ball in both hands. He was at the line, aiming the ball at the other team, when Josh ran up behind him and pulled his shorts down to his ankles. Milo's underwear went with them, and as he dropped the ball and scrambled to pull them back up, he tripped and fell, cracking his head hard on the floor. The gym went silent, except for Josh, who gave a loud whoop and cracked up laughing. Milo scrabbled around on the floor, his face the color of the scarlet banners on the wall, until he got his pants pulled up, then got to his feet and ran to the locker room. As he passed, DeShaun saw that his face was wet with tears.

Something inside of DeShaun erupted. He didn't even remember crossing the gym floor to where Josh stood, still laughing amid his statue-like classmates. When forced to tell the principal about it later, DeShaun would say the first thing he remembered was that his hand was around Josh's neck and Josh was up against the wall, his feet dangling several inches off the floor. "You little piece of—"

"DeShaun, put him down!" barked Mr. Sullivan, the gym teacher.

DeShaun ignored him and gave Josh a shake. Above his hand, Josh's red face was turning purple.

"Caitlyn, go get the principal," he dimly heard Mr. Sullivan say over his right shoulder. "Tell her it's an emergency.

DeShaun, put him down *now*!" He felt the gym teacher's hands on his arm.

Josh made a gurgling noise and tried to squirm. DeShaun tightened his grip and leaned in close. "You listen to me, *boy*," he said. "If you ever do something like that to Milo or anyone else in this school again, I promise you that this here—" he gave the boy another shake—"will be one of the best things that happens to you all year." He dropped him. Josh fell to his knees, clutching his throat and wheezing. DeShaun shrugged Mr. Sullivan's hand off his arm and went to the locker room to check on Milo.

Of course, there was a long talk with Ivy and Nick and Mr. Sullivan and the principal, Mrs. Kelley. They wanted him to apologize to Josh.

"I'll apologize to Josh when he apologizes to Milo," he told them, his arms folded. In the end, they couldn't make him, and since Josh also refused to apologize to Milo, the school suspended both of them for three days. It didn't even seem like a punishment at first. Three days off from school? DeShaun figured he should have beat up Josh long ago, if that was his reward.

Ivy soon taught him differently. For three days, he raked leaves and pulled weeds, cleaned old trash out of the basement and hauled it to the curb, then had to scrub the walls and cement floor on his hands and knees. After that, he painted the basement walls with two coats of paint and the floor with three. He scrubbed both bathrooms, vacuumed the entire house, and washed the windows, inside and out.

Half the time, he hated that Ivy was working him like a

dog. Who was she anyway, to make him clean out her basement and wash the toilets? But Ivy's lunches were way better than the school lunches, and along with teaching him how to wash windows, paint, and clean bathtubs, she also taught him to make a grilled cheese sandwich.

Once, when he was little, one of his mother's boyfriends had taken him out to the movies. They had seen *Charlie and the Chocolate Factory*. Afterward, the man had bought him a chocolate milk shake and a Hot Wheels car at the mall. It had been the happiest day of DeShaun's life. Lunchtimes with Ivy felt that same way. It was more than just half an hour to rest his arms and legs from the housework. Sitting there at the table, eating grilled cheese sandwiches that he had made himself and tomato soup that she had warmed up from a can, with the sun from the windows spilling across the kitchen floor, it was kind of like the inside of him could rest for a while too.

There was no break in the evenings. Jada brought a bag full of his schoolwork home with her each night, lugging both her own backpack and his off the bus as if the weight of them both together would kill her. In those three days, he worked harder than he had ever worked in his life, and at the end of the last day, he went to bed actually happy to be going back to school in the morning.

To his surprise, he discovered that he was something of a hero. Guys who had never talked to him before came up to him in the hallways, thumped him on the shoulder, and said, "Good work with Josh, man." Girls at their lockers called, "Hi, DeShaun," and fluttered their fingers at him.

At lunchtime, though, when more than one table called out, "DeShaun, over here, dude!" he shook his head and went to sit with Milo as usual. "Nah, this is my table," he called back.

❧

Halloween was fast approaching, and when she had finished at the bookstore one Saturday, Ivy stopped off at the farmers' market to pick up three large pumpkins. She pulled into the driveway to see Nick and the three children raking leaves and cleaning out the flower beds under a blue sky as crisp and clean as a new sheet.

"Oh, thank you for doing that," she called as she hauled the first of the pumpkins to the front steps. "I keep meaning to get around to it." Not for the first time, she realized how often she had said that since the neighbor children had moved in. Buying winter coats, cleaning the shower, ordering new checks—she was forever meaning to do something and just not getting around to it.

Nick put down his rake and came to help her unload the car. He lifted a pumpkin in each arm. "What are these for?"

"Jack-o'-lanterns."

"And exactly which one of us is going to be carving jack-o'-lanterns?"

She shot him a shifty glance. "Oh, come on, Nick, it'll be fun! If you save me the seeds, I'll roast them for you."

Hammer and Jada heard her and, dropping their rakes, ran to her, shouting. "Jack-o'-lanterns! We're gonna carve jack-o'-lanterns!"

A brief squabble ensued as they both tried to claim the biggest pumpkin, but Ivy said firmly, "The biggest one is DeShaun's because he's the oldest. Jada, this is yours; Hammer, yours." DeShaun sauntered over and laid a hand on his pumpkin, trying to look as though he didn't care much about jack-o'-lanterns either way.

"What kind of face do you want, DeShaun?" she asked him. "Funny or scary?"

He shrugged. "I don't know. Funny, I guess."

"Well, come on and help me carry in the groceries. I've got some apple pies to make while the rest of you finish the yard work. Do you like apple pie, Hammer?"

"I don't know. Ain't never had it."

"I almost promise you're going to love it. Meanwhile, you can each be thinking about the kind of face you want on your pumpkin. We'll carve them after supper."

The children had been living with them nearly three months, Ivy thought as she peeled apples over the sink, and she was still continually surprised at how many things they were doing for the first time ever. Their first apple pie, and although DeShaun had not said as much, she had seen it on his face: their first jack-o'-lanterns. Tears of gratitude blurred her eyes, and she had to put down her peeler and blow her nose. The hunt was still on for Lily and for relatives in Detroit who might be willing to take the children in, but just for now, for the hundredth time, she told God thank You. *Thank You for letting me have them, even if it's just for a little while.*

Later, as they carved the pumpkins, a project Nick

refused to help with, she broached the all-important subject of Halloween costumes. She could tell it was another first. Creative sewing not being her strong suit, and high-priced costumes not being in the budget, she hastened to add a few suggestions in order to steer their thinking. Jada wanted to be Lady Gaga. When Ivy vetoed this idea, Jada said, "Well, a princess, then," which was just fine by Ivy. Hammer was undecided between a pirate and a ninja but settled on the ninja when Ivy told him he definitely could not pierce his ear just to dress up like a pirate for one night.

"Are you going trick-or-treating?" she asked DeShaun, who had been silent throughout the discussion.

He shrugged. "Maybe. If the other guys in my class are going."

She heard the uncertainty. "Well, if they're not planning on going out, maybe you'd like to invite a few of them over here. You could watch scary movies and help Nick hand out candy to trick-or-treaters." She pictured Nick in the living room, raising his eyebrows behind the newspaper.

"Zach's got an Xbox. Maybe he could bring it over?"

"Maybe he could. I'll tell you what—you talk to the guys at school about it and let me know by the end of the week, okay? If that's what you want to do, I'll have to know how many pizzas to order, won't I?"

For just a second, a shining, hopeful look flashed across his face. It made the tears spring to her eyes all over again. The look was gone in an instant, but it had been there all the same. She would talk to Nick later and make sure he agreed to do whatever it took to make DeShaun's first party a success.

On a rainy afternoon, Ivy took Jada to the attic of the Darling house, where they spent a happy hour rummaging through four boxes of costumes. "Remember the plays you children used to put on for us?" said Jane, who had joined them. She pulled out three tatty wigs and examined them. "It's lucky I never throw anything away."

"Ooh, I remember this thing!" Ivy untangled a long dress of iridescent green lamé. "We dressed David up in it once and made him walk to the end of the driveway to get the mail." There followed a pink feather boa, a filmy white nightgown, a bowler hat, a tuxedo jacket with tails, and several pairs of shoes. When Jane unearthed a beaver cape in the second box, she said, "I think we could cut this down to Jada's size; the edges are moth-eaten anyway. And the green dress could be altered—nipped here and tucked there—to fit her. With the cape over it, it would be a lovely princess costume."

Ivy eyed it doubtfully. "It's not exactly Disney princess garb."

"I want to wear it!" said Jada. She picked up a pair of battered silver slippers and hugged them to herself. "And these. Can I wear them, Ivy?"

"We could stuff the toes with newspaper," said Jane.

"She'll be quite the ragtag princess."

"Well, sometimes ragtag princesses are the most beautiful kind," said her mother, bending to kiss Jada on the top of her head.

Amy, who was a better seamstress than her mother, came

home from college for the weekend just to do the alterations. Not only did she transform the green dress, decking it out with yards of plastic pearls and a sash of plum-colored satin, but she also found a rhinestone tiara at a thrift shop to complete the outfit. When she had finished that, a voluminous black magician's cape was reincarnated, by her needle and scissors, into a miniature ninja costume. She also fashioned Hammer an array of fearful-looking weapons out of cardboard and silver spray paint.

"You missed your calling, Amy," Ivy told her, full of admiration.

"Maybe I could find a nice job in a sweatshop instead of going to college," said Amy. It was clear that she was still not settling into university life as easily as they had hoped.

Jada and Hammer, giddy with joy, were allowed to wear their costumes around the house after school—until Hammer leveled a karate chop at his sister's stomach, starting an unholy brawl in which one of Ivy's lamps got broken. After that, Nick made them put the costumes away until it was time to trick-or-treat.

At five thirty on Halloween, dusk was falling over the bare tree branches of Copper Cove, and Ivy was about to set out with the two younger children, when the doorbell rang.

"Our first trick-or-treaters!" she said. But when she opened the front door, she got one of the bigger surprises of the year. A boy was standing there, a pale, slender, teenage boy wearing a yarmulke and a black frock coat. At first she thought it was a costume, but the long, curly earlocks of an Orthodox Jew hung down the sides of his face, and the beginnings of a scruffy beard sprang from his cheeks and chin, both clearly the work of long months, even years. His stature was the only small thing about him. A big nose and enormous glasses magnified his pale eyes and made them appear far too large for his thin face.

He stuck out an oversize hand. "Milo Rosenberg, at your service. Mrs. Mason, I presume?"

"Ah . . . it's Ms. Darling, actually, but you can call me Ivy if you want." She shook his hand gingerly, a little afraid the weight of it might snap the thin wrist right in two.

"Hey, Milo," said DeShaun, behind her, and suddenly illuminated, Ivy stepped aside to let in the boy who had been her foster son's first friend.

He was, she thought, one of the nicest-looking boys she had ever seen.

❧

By the time Ivy left, Nick was in charge of five noisy teenage boys, six pizzas, several liters of Mountain Dew, an Xbox, and five dozen pumpkin-chocolate-chip cookies. He made her take her cell phone and checked twice to make sure she had it turned on before she left the house.

"I won't be gone that long," she told him, laughing. "The boys will be fine. All they'll want to do is play video games and eat."

"They're just so *loud*."

"Plug your headphones into your laptop and watch a movie until I get back," she said, pecking him on the cheek. "They'll behave themselves well enough as long as you're in the room with them."

Nick stood at the front door, watching them go, then closed it and stood in the front hall, listening to the sounds from the living room, where DeShaun and his friends were playing video games. There were long, intense silences, punctuated by roars of explosive laughter and cries of what sounded like "Dude!" and "Dog!" Then someone cursed—at the top of his voice and with great relish. Nick frowned. It was time for him to make an appearance.

He sat in his chair with his laptop, as Ivy had suggested. There was no real hope of hearing his movie, though, even with his headphones plugged in. He made a show of being absorbed in it anyway, all the while shooting sideways glances at the boys. Two of them were eating pizza on the couch, and a half-empty pizza box lay open on the floor between two others. Red Solo cups of Mountain Dew sat on the floor, the coffee table, and the end table. He tried not to think of the potential damage to the furniture and the braided rug, which was from L.L.Bean and had cost over five hundred dollars.

He was so absorbed in his thoughts that a tap on his shoulder made him jump. He looked up to see the skinny boy with glasses and the long ringlets hanging down in front of his ears.

The boy's mouth moved. *Pardon me.*

Nick pulled his headphones out of his ears. At once, the

volume of the room shot up from too loud to unbearable. "Yes?" he shouted above the din.

The thin boy held up one of Ivy's cookies. "Are these kosher?"

"Are they *what*?"

"Kosher."

Nick stared at him. "I doubt it."

The boy gazed at the cookie with a bereaved expression and shook his head. Then, holding up one finger, he said, "But does not Yahweh require that we fulfill the spirit of the law, and not merely the letter?" He stuffed the cookie, whole, into his mouth, nodded his thanks to Nick, and went to sit next to DeShaun on the floor.

Nick thought the evening would never end, but at last parents arrived to take their teenage sons away, and after that, Ivy and the younger children came home. As Jada and Hammer sat at the dining room table and sorted through their pillowcases of candy, Ivy said, "Come on, DeShaun, let's get this place cleaned up."

They left him in the living room, collecting dirty cups, paper plates, and napkins, and together Nick and Ivy went to the kitchen to put away the cookies and leftover pizza. As they worked, Ivy asked him, "How'd it go?"

"Just like I told you it would: loud and messy."

"But did they have a good time?"

"They seemed to."

"How about DeShaun? Did he have fun?"

"Seemed to."

DeShaun came in with his hands full of sticky cups. "I need a trash bag or something."

Ivy opened a cupboard and held one out to him. "Make sure you dump all the leftover soda into the sink first." As he obeyed, she asked, "How was it?"

"Good."

In vain, she waited for him to offer more information. "Well . . . great. I'm glad," she said at last.

DeShaun said nothing and went back to the living room for another load.

Nick followed him. "DeShaun."

"What?"

"Ivy went to a lot of trouble to make this a good party for you. I think you need to thank her."

The boy lifted his shoulder in a half shrug. "Yeah, okay."

He cleared his throat. "And I gave up the TV for the evening and stayed here to . . . uh . . . chaperone." He felt foolish, demanding to be thanked, but how else did you teach a kid gratitude and good manners? He had no idea.

DeShaun looked at him. "Oh yeah. Thanks."

"You're welcome." He nodded toward the kitchen. "Ivy's in there."

Heaving a sigh, DeShaun turned, a stack of empty pizza boxes in his arms, and went back to the kitchen. Nick followed in time to hear him mutter to Ivy, "Thanks."

It seemed enough for her. "You're welcome," she chirped. "I'm glad it was fun for you."

DeShaun only said, "I'm done in there. Can I go to my room?"

"Sure. Good night."

He slouched from the room without answering.

"DeShaun," Nick called. Might as well do this thing thoroughly.

"What?"

"Ivy said good night. Come on back and say good night to her."

He dragged himself back into the kitchen. "Night."

"Now you can go." Nick watched the boy retreat. Ivy was wiping counters, telling him something about her mother taking pictures of the kids in their costumes, but he was only half-listening. Instead, he was reflecting that he had always found teenagers in general to be rather unlikable, and that having one living with them now was not doing much to alter this long-held opinion.

CHAPTER

7

FOSTER PARENTING CLASSES began on a damp, chilly night. To Ivy's surprise, Nick had agreed to go through with them.

"The kids seem to like it here," he had said. "They might as well stay for now."

Ivy launched herself at him. "Nick, you wonderful man!"

"All right, all right," he said. "Don't get your hopes up too much. They can stay as long as they don't give us any problems."

Ivy had hung on and silently prayed against problems of any kind.

The Department of Health and Human Services office in Rockland was overbright with fluorescent lights and warm with the smell of coffee. Ivy felt jittery, as though she'd already had too much caffeine. She reached for Nick's hand and found it as cold as her own.

In their classroom, a young woman was riffling through stacks of papers at the front of the room. "Hello, welcome," she said, leaving the papers and coming toward them, her hand outstretched. "I'm Melinda, and you are . . . ?"

They told her their names, which Melinda recognized from the registration forms they had sent in. "You're the first ones here; we'll be eight in all. Help yourselves to coffee and something to eat and have a seat."

Ivy claimed seats at one of the two tables in the room, while Nick got them both paper cups of coffee from a table at the back. "There are donuts if you want one," he said, putting the coffee down in front of her.

She shook her head. "I couldn't eat anything right now." To still her nerves, she flipped through the folder on the table in front of her, although she couldn't concentrate on any of the forms or packets inside.

The others arrived. A very large woman and a very small man with a thin mustache and slicked-back hair sat at their table. They pretended not to see Nick and Ivy sitting there until Ivy leaned forward into their field of vision and said, "Hi, I'm Ivy and this is my husband, Nick."

The woman said, "Pam and Rick."

Rick nodded to Ivy, raking her from head to waist with a leer. "Pleased to *meet* you."

"Charmed," Ivy said coldly and turned her back on him. A young, earnest-looking couple and a single middle-aged woman took seats at the other table, and the class began. They talked about health and safety for an hour before they took a break, during which Ivy saw Rick trying to chat up the young blonde from the other table.

"I hope all the classes aren't going to be like that," Nick said on the way home. "She almost put me to sleep a couple of times."

"I'm glad they'll up our reimbursement rate after we're licensed," Ivy confessed. "I don't want to sound like a money-grubber, but taking care of three kids has already gotten expensive. What I spend on groceries has tripled since they moved in."

"The per diem checks won't cover everything, but they'll help, anyway."

She was struck by a wonderful idea. "We should look into setting up college funds for them!"

Nick raised his eyebrows.

"I mean, every kid should have that chance, right?"

"I think you might have a pretty . . . optimistic view of our budget, Ivy."

"Really? Couldn't we set a little aside every week or something?"

"We barely have enough left over at the end of every month for our retirement. And I'm not giving that up."

Her optimism evaporated like mist in the desert. "No, I wouldn't ask you to."

"Not every kid gets a chance to go to college, Ivy. Those are just the facts of life."

"We can face that question when the time comes," she

said, unwilling to give up entirely. "Anyway, next week is about grief and loss, and discipline. You can take a nice nap through the first part, and I'll take notes for you. I sort of dread the grief part, though," she added. "I hope they're not going to make us listen to all kinds of terrible stories. I'll cry."

"I don't envy the kids who end up living with Rick and Pam. He seemed like a creep."

"You thought so too? Just imagine, if we hadn't been living next door when Lily took off, one of our kids could have been placed with someone like him."

"I never thought of that," Nick said. "I guess it was a good thing we were living next door, then."

⁂

November had arrived with a vengeance. Outside, the rain was pelting the dark windows with a vindictive sort of fury as inside, Ivy attempted to teach a reluctant DeShaun how to wash the supper dishes. Jada, sitting at the kitchen table coloring a picture, suddenly said, "What's that?"

"What's what, honey?" Ivy handed a plate back to DeShaun. "Wash the top *and* bottom. There's still spaghetti sauce underneath."

"That," Jada said. "On the radio."

Ivy cocked her head. The evening news was just starting, signaled as always by several bars of Vivaldi. "That's the news."

"No, the music."

"It's from *The Four Seasons*. This one's 'Spring.'"

136

"Not the song, the thing that's *making* the song. It sounds like crickets singing."

Ivy listened. "Crickets singing? I guess it does, sort of. Those are violins."

"What do they look like?"

"Haven't you ever seen one? I have one upstairs. I'll show it to you when DeShaun and I are done here."

Jada stared at her. "You *have* one? Can you play it?"

"I sure can. As a matter of fact, I still do every now and then. I took lessons for a lot of years."

"Play it for us!"

"All right, I will. DeShaun, you wipe down the sink and all the counters while I go upstairs and get the violin. And I'm warning you, if they're not hospital clean by the time I get back, you'll do them over again until they are."

DeShaun muttered something under his breath.

"*Excuse* me, sir?"

"Nothin'."

"That's what I thought you said. Jada, you come with me."

Her instrument lived at the back of her closet, in a case lined with midnight-blue velvet. She took it out and laid it on the bed and began to rosin the bow. Jada reached out for the violin, but Ivy said, "No, don't touch. It's only for people who know how to play, or who are learning."

Jada put both hands behind her back. "What are you doing that for?"

"I'm rubbing this stuff, called rosin, on the hairs of this, which is called the bow, so the bow will grip the strings when I play and make a nicer sound."

She finished and, raising the instrument to her chin, began to tune it. When it was ready, she said, "Shall we go to the kitchen and have a concert?"

"Yes!" Jada clattered ahead of her calling, "Hammer, Ivy's gonna play her violin!" In the kitchen, she pulled out a chair. "Sit here," she ordered, patting the seat, but Ivy said she would stand instead.

DeShaun, with a dish towel slung over one shoulder, leaned against the clean counter, trying very hard to look bored. Hammer raced in from the living room and stood beside him. The older boy automatically put his hand on his little brother's shoulder, and Hammer leaned against him.

"Wait!" Jada commanded as Ivy lifted the violin again. "Nick's not here!" She ran to the living room. "Nick! Nick, come and hear Ivy play the violin!"

"I'll listen from in here," Ivy heard her husband say.

"Come on, Nick, this is special," she heard the little girl plead.

"I've heard her play before, and I can hear her just as well from where I am."

Jada returned, looking downcast, and sat at the table. "Nick won't come," she said, "so you can start now."

"Thank you, little madam." Ivy closed her eyes and recalled the opening notes to Albinoni's "Adagio." She took a deep breath and, with her eyes still closed, began. The magic happened to her again, as it did every time she played this piece. She forgot where she was, forgot there was anyone else in the room at all, nearly forgot she was playing an instrument, the notes falling into place under her fingers and her bow as easily as the words of a well-loved poem might fall from her mouth. Alone, in her private darkness with the music, Ivy poured into the famous funeral dirge all the grief she felt for things lost, or never found. She played of mistakes made, of babies who would never be born, and of those born to mothers who abandoned them. Of children who would have given anything for a family to belong to, and of adults who regarded family so lightly that they would not love the ones they had. And she played for Nick, whose coldness she could not understand, but who surely suffered from it as much as she herself did.

She held her breath with the last note until she heard applause, then opened her eyes to see DeShaun and Hammer clapping for her, a crooked half smile on the older boy's face. Jada roused herself as though from sleep and joined in, clapping with all her strength, her eyes shining. Ivy bowed deeply.

"I want to learn to do that," Jada sighed. "Will you teach me, Ivy?"

"I don't know, sweetie," Ivy hedged. "You couldn't learn on this violin; you'd have to start on a special small one. And I'm not really a teacher."

The little girl did not press the issue, but Ivy saw the longing on her face and determined right then to look into renting a beginner-size violin. And surely Jane Darling, who had been a music teacher before she left her career to raise her children, could give Jada some lessons. She would call her mother tomorrow.

"Bath time for you two," she told the younger children, but when they clamored for her to play something else, she obliged with a quick improvisation of "Oh! Susanna." Not knowing the song, they didn't recognize how badly she played it, and when they finally went off to have their baths, she felt cheered and comforted by their admiration.

&

Laura pulled her silver Saab into a corner parking space and turned off the ignition. She extracted a tube of lipstick from her gym bag and applied it in the rearview mirror, then looked at her reflection, pursed her lips, and frowned. It was wrong; people didn't wear lipstick to the gym. She found a napkin in the glove box and wiped the lipstick off, then rummaged in her purse until she came up with a tube of cherry ChapStick. She coated her lips with this and examined the effect. Perfect. Just a hint of color, which no one would ever guess wasn't her own. She looked fresh and natural, but glamorous all the same. Calm, cool, and sophisticated. She looked, in short, like a woman who played racquetball with her married boss every day of the week. In reality, it was the first time Max had asked her, and as she took her bag from the car and headed into the Copper Cove Racquet and Fitness Club, her heart pounded as though she had run across the parking lot.

Max was waiting for her in the foyer, and his appreciative, lingering glance told her that everything had been worth it: the new aqua tracksuit, the touched-up highlights in her blonde hair, the three tanning sessions of the week before, the cherry ChapStick. At the locker rooms they parted, and when Laura had exchanged her track pants for aqua shorts that showed off the slim length of her tanned legs and had stowed her bag in a locker, they met in front of court three.

Laura had played racquetball before, but never like this. Max was a hard, fast player, and by the time he had won five points, it was clear she was outmatched. Max didn't seem to mind her ineptness in the least. On the contrary, he seemed gratified by it.

"Time-out," he called, his voice echoing in the court, which smelled of stale sweat and rubber. He came to stand behind her. "Do you mind if I give you a few pointers?"

"No, I'd love it." She flashed him a smile. She didn't mind losing when she had a feeling she was winning in the end.

"You want to hold your racquet like this." He put both arms around her and adjusted her hold.

Laura could hardly breathe.

"Your forehand swing comes from here—" he pulled her arm back slowly and moved it forward again, like a dance—"and follows through all the way to . . . here." His arms were tighter around her. "And then your backhand . . ." He closed his hands over hers on the racquet and adjusted her fingers slowly, unhurriedly. "You're automatically going to shift your grip like this—" his mouth was very close to her ear—"and bring it across your body, like so. . . . And then you connect and follow through. See?"

She nodded mutely.

He did not release his hold on her. "Think you can do it?" Again his breath, warm on her ear.

"Like . . . like this?" she said, trying not to sound as breathless as she felt. She attempted the backhand again.

"Not quite. Adjust your grip. Good." His fingers stayed on hers as she swung. "*Very* good."

There was no more reason to stand there with his arms around her, and she felt both of their reluctance as they broke apart. He served the ball, and to her own amazement, she returned it. In fact, they played for an hour, and after she found her own rhythm, Laura discovered that Max wasn't the only one who was good at this game. She wasn't as experienced as he was, and her strokes weren't as smooth, but she gave him a run for his money. By the end of the hour, there was no doubt that she could keep up with him. Anyone might even say they were well matched. Very, very well matched.

❧

In the middle of Pastor Ken's sermon, an usher touched Ivy on the shoulder. "You're needed upstairs," he whispered.

She edged her way out of the pew, past Nick's knees, wondering what in the world could be going on.

The usher pointed her to the kindergarten Sunday school room, where a tearful Hammer was waiting for her, the front of his jeans soaking wet. "I forgot to use the toilet," he whimpered. "Don't tell Miss Cooper on me."

"That's school," Ivy said, trying not to let her exasperation show. "This is church." She was trying to decide whether she should drive him home for a change of clothes and come back for Nick and the other two or just collect the whole family now and go home when Hammer's teacher said, "Ivy, don't go away. I want to talk to you for a second."

The teacher, a woman named Sherry, left the class in the charge of her teenage helper and stepped into the hall.

"Are you planning on having the kids be part of the Christmas program?" she asked.

Ivy could truthfully say she hadn't thought about it.

"Well, we can always use more shepherds and angels, so let me know. We'll definitely fit them in. Practices are Saturday and Sunday afternoons at four o'clock, starting today."

"I wanna be a shepherd!" cried Hammer, clutching at the front of his pants.

Ivy shrugged at Sherry. "See you at four o'clock."

Ivy was grateful that Vincent and Angela had registered for baby gifts at two different stores because it made the task of choosing something for them seem less personal. After work one day, she drove to Babies"R"Us in Quahog and, after consulting the registry, bought an outrageously expensive stroller that converted into a car seat. Or maybe it was a car seat that converted into a stroller. A banner across the front of the box informed her that it was the *Consumer Reports* top safety-rated model of the year. Nick would be relieved to know they were giving his sister such a *safe* gift, she thought with more than a touch of acerbity.

She spent ten dollars on the two rolls of wrapping paper that would be needed to cover the monstrous box, four dollars on an elaborate ribbon for the top, and four more on a card. It was costing her eighteen dollars just to wrap the thing. She thought of Amy, who would probably have wrapped the stroller box in recycled newspaper and handed the mother-to-be the eighteen dollars cash in an envelope. Then she smiled and corrected herself because Amy would never have bought such a contraption for a new baby in the first place. Instead, she would have hand-knit a set of cotton hats that made the baby look like she was wearing a strawberry or an acorn or a sunflower on her head.

The shower was at four o'clock on Saturday, at Tiffany's house. When Ivy arrived, she was met at the door by Angela's husband.

"Hellooooo, Ivy," he said, his standard greeting.

"Vincent. What are you doing here? I thought this was girls only," she said, following him into the kitchen and sliding the seafood quiche she had brought with her onto the counter so she could wiggle out of her coat.

He took a swig from his mug. "It is. I brought Angela over and stayed for a cup of coffee. I'm just leaving." He looked her over quickly, a not-so-subtle search to see what she had bought them.

"Nick delivered our gift here yesterday," Ivy told him. "It was too big for me to carry alone." The flash of avarice that crossed his face both gratified and irritated her. She was fairly sure Vincent and Angela had been keeping an eye on the gift registries and already knew everything they were getting anyway.

Tiffany sailed into the kitchen. "Oh. I thought I heard you."

"Hi, Tiffany. How are you?"

"Oh, you know . . . good." They looked at one another, sisters-in-law of six years who had not a thing to say to each other.

"The little girl didn't come with you?" said Tiffany at last.

"Jada is her name. No, she has Christmas pageant practice at the church."

"Oh. Did you bring this?" Tiffany had spied the quiche on the counter.

"Yes. It's seafood."

"Great. I'll just put it on the buffet." Tiffany bore the quiche out of the kitchen, it apparently not having occurred to her to lead Ivy to the party. She could hear the sounds of it emanating from some inner part of the house.

"Well, I'm out of here." Vincent dumped the remainder of his coffee into the sink and took his coat from the back of a chair.

"Going somewhere to kill time?" Ivy asked.

"Yep, Starbucks." He saluted her with his laptop case and was gone.

"Imagine that," said Ivy aloud to the empty kitchen.

❧

She had been to dozens of baby showers before, but this was the first one since the neighbor children had come to live with her, and she found herself looking at the whole process through different eyes. Vincent and Angela got an appalling amount of stuff, doubles and triples of many things, although not of the car seat/stroller set. When Angela unwrapped it, she said, "Oh, Ivy, it's just what I wanted!" as though it were some wonderful surprise that her taste and Ivy's had coincided so perfectly.

Ivy smiled and made the right response, but her mind was suddenly on something she had heard in her English comp class at college. The teacher had been talking about short fiction and had presented them with a short story that some said had been written by Hemingway. It was only six words long:

For sale: baby shoes, never worn.

The professor asked them what they thought the story meant, and the class had been divided. Some of them imagined heartbreak behind the six words: infertility, a stillbirth, sickness that had extinguished a tiny life within its first days. Other students had listened openmouthed as they debated these possibilities. Finally, one horn-rimmed freshman had summed it up for that camp. "I thought maybe the parents just got so many pairs of shoes at their baby showers that the baby outgrew them before it had a chance to wear them all."

Ivy was not sorry to leave the shower early, with the excuse that she had to pick up Jada and Hammer from the church. Pageant practice was still under way when she got there, and Ivy slipped quietly into a darkened back pew to watch. Jada was playing the part of Mary, the mother of Jesus, standing ramrod-straight in the middle of the stage and reciting her lines in a loud, carrying voice.

"The road has been long and weary, Joseph. We must find

a place to stop for the night." Her Detroit accent sounded more aggressive than weary; her dark skin and bobbled pig-tails stood out in rich and beautiful contrast to the sea of white faces around her. Ivy thought of that other Mary, two millennia ago, who had brought her child into the world without the benefit of a baby shower; of Mary's Son, who had arrived unheralded to a bed of hay, not covered with designer Beatrix Potter sheets. She watched her own girl, who surely had come to this earth in a similar way: under-privileged, unappreciated, a misfit in her world. Her heart swelled with love and pride for this sweet, earnest soul who had been entrusted to her, and tears brimmed in her eyes and spilled down her face.

❧

The week before Thanksgiving, Ivy had her hair cut and col-ored again. This time, she did not ask Nick's opinion first. When he saw her newly clipped pink locks, he only raised his eyebrows and said, "If nothing else, being married to you makes it impossible for a man to feel old."

"Yes, if nothing else, at least there's that," said Ivy.

He completely missed the irony in her tone.

8

Laura opened the front door of Ivy's house and said, "Hello?" There was no answer, so she stepped inside. "Hello?" she called again. This time, footsteps sounded overhead, and her sister's face appeared over the banister.

"Oh, hi! I didn't know you were coming over today. Or did I?" Ivy looked worried. "Lately, I have so much going on, I can't keep track."

"No, you didn't know. I didn't plan to stop, but I just got off work, and I have an hour to kill before a doctor's appointment. Where is everybody?"

Ivy came down the stairs and sat on the bottom step. She looked tired, Laura thought. "Let's see." She began ticking things off on her fingers. "Nick is working late, DeShaun is at basketball practice, and Pam Russo just picked Jada and Hammer up for Awana at the church. Do you want a cup of coffee?"

"I thought you'd never ask." Laura hung her purse on the post at the bottom of the staircase and followed Ivy into the kitchen. "Something smells good in here."

"I made turkey-shaped sugar cookies. Hammer has to bring them to his class's Thanksgiving party tomorrow."

Laura came to inspect the cookies, which were still out on cooling racks. "Wow, that's a lot of work."

"You don't know the half of it. It took me all afternoon, and I haven't even decorated them yet."

"Couldn't you have just bought cookies instead?"

Ivy rolled her eyes. "All the cool mothers *make* cookies."

"Sorry. I'm not up to date on motherhood pop culture."

Ivy started the coffee. "It's kind of late in the day for a doctor's appointment. What are you going for?"

"Yearly physical. They stay open late once a week to accommodate important career women like me." Laura wrinkled her nose. "I hate going to the doctor."

"Me too. Have a cookie; it'll make you feel better."

"No way. I have to step on the scale in an hour." Pain stabbed through Laura's right wrist, and she rubbed it. "You don't have any ibuprofen, do you?"

"I think so. What's wrong?"

"It's my wrist. I sometimes play racquetball on the weekends, and it's been bothering me."

"I didn't know you were a racquetball player. Who do you play with?"

Laura examined the fastening of her gold wristwatch. If she did not tread carefully here, Ivy would get on her high horse and start preaching again. Yet she wanted to talk to someone, to share the joy that was perpetually bubbling up in her these days, washing all the old, mundane things around her in fresh, new colors. Very casually, she said, "Usually with Max."

"I didn't realize you were still seeing him."

"It's not like you've asked me about him even once since our birthday," Laura said, trying to hold her pique in check but not quite succeeding. With Ivy, it was always all about Ivy.

"Oh." Ivy looked surprised. "I'm sorry. I just . . . I suppose I've had other things on my mind. So how's that going, with Max?"

"Fine." All at once, Laura did not want to talk about Max, not to someone who didn't really care, who was going to be judging her the whole time she talked. She changed the subject. "What about that ibuprofen?"

"Oh yeah. In the bathroom medicine chest. Help yourself."

Laura found the bottle, but it had only one pill left in it. "I need three of them and there's only one left," she called from the bathroom. "Do you have Tylenol or something?"

"I don't remember," Ivy called back. "Snoop around and see."

Laura did, then went back to the kitchen. "You're out of Tylenol, too."

Ivy wiped her hands on her jeans. "Let me look."

Laura followed her sister to the bathroom and watched

her rummage through the medicine chest, frowning. "You're right; I'm out of both." Typical Ivy, to be surprised by that. She opened the closet and dug to the very back, coming up with a prescription bottle. "If you're desperate, you could try this, I guess." She held out the bottle and Laura took it.

"Why do you have Vicodin?"

"They gave it to me when I had my wisdom teeth out. It made my head spin."

"But it's for pain?"

"Supposedly."

Laura's arm was burning now with a deep ache. "It's better than nothing," she said. "How many, just one?"

"I wouldn't take more than that. And be careful driving. Like I said, they knocked me for a loop when I tried them."

Laura swallowed one with a glass of water and shuddered. "Yuck," she said, "they're huge. How does anyone take them without gagging them back up?"

"You've got me. I think the coffee's ready."

"Oh, good. Where do you want this?" Laura shook the bottle at her.

"Just leave it there on the sink; it'll remind me to reorganize the closet before I go to bed."

Laura set the bottle on the back of the sink. "Watch out— you don't want the kids getting into something like this."

"I'll take care of it before they get home. Actually, dump that last ibuprofen in with them. I'll have to remember to get a new bottle."

"You won't remember," Laura assured her.

"O ye of little faith," Ivy said with dignity. "I *will* remember."

❧

There had been much discussion, as there was every year, about where everyone was going to celebrate Thanksgiving. At last it was decided that Nick, Ivy, and the children would spend the holiday itself with Ivy's family and would go to Jessica's house on Friday for a belated Thanksgiving dinner with the Mason clan.

There was no school on Wednesday, and Ivy spent the day in the kitchen, making apple and pumpkin pies with more help than she strictly wanted from Jada. She gave Hammer scraps of pastry and a set of miniature pie tins and let him make his own tarts, which, true to his name, he did by pounding rounds of dough flat with one end of the rolling pin and dropping them into the tins. Ivy sprinkled these with cinnamon sugar and baked them in the oven, and Hammer and Jada ate them for lunch, their delighted faces sticky and smudged with flour over glasses of apple cider.

DeShaun, who was out of sorts with a cold, lay on the living room couch all morning and flipped the channels between ESPN and cartoons, sulking because Ivy would not let him watch MTV. He cheered up at lunchtime, when she brought him a tray with two grilled cheese sandwiches and a bowl of tomato soup. As it was the day before a holiday, Nick worked only until lunchtime, and he was just backing his Volvo into the garage when Ivy glanced out the window and saw that it had started to snow.

"Look!" she said to Hammer, who was standing on a chair, turning the handle of the meat grinder, helping her grind cranberries into relish. "It's snowing!"

Jada ran to the slider door and pressed her face against it, gazing at the fat, wet flakes. "Snow! I wanna go outside and play."

Hammer jumped off the chair and joined her at the door. "Me too. I wanna play outside!"

Ivy made them go to the bathroom and wash their hands first. Hammer had made great progress with toilet training under the brilliant Miss Cooper's care, but he was still prone to wetting his pants if not reminded often. She helped them into their new boots and coats, bought at Target, and hats and mittens knit by Aunt Amy, and sent them out the back door. Nick came in, and they stood at the window together, watching the pair of them play on the swing set.

As always, Ivy's eyes were drawn to the little house next door, which sat dark and desolate in the November gloom. The For Sale sign that had been on its lawn since September was leaning forward tiredly. "I wish someone would tear that place down," she told Nick. "It's not good for the kids to have to look at it every day."

"Does it bother them?" he asked, surprised.

"I think it bothers DeShaun. He always turns his head the other way when he walks down the driveway."

They watched the children in silence for a few more minutes; then Nick said, "Is there any coffee?"

"No, but I can make a pot."

"Thanks. Where's DeShaun?"

"Watching TV on the couch. He's got a cold."

Nick went into the living room, and she heard them speaking, a brief exchange of words she couldn't hear clearly.

When she brought Nick's coffee to him, they were sitting in silence, watching a Celtics game.

"Hey," said DeShaun, looking up. "Can I have some coffee too?"

Ivy considered him. "I don't know. Are you old enough to drink responsibly?"

"What's that mean?"

"It means drinking your coffee without sugar."

"Sick! Why do I have to drink it without sugar?"

"Because coffee with sugar isn't *coffee*, it's *dessert*. It might as well be an energy drink." Energy drinks were a sore subject between the two of them. Ivy had a nearly puritan intolerance of the sugar- and caffeine-charged soft drinks and forbade them in the house, although she was pretty sure DeShaun bought them from his friends and drank them at school anyway.

"Can I have it with cream?"

"Yes."

"Okay." He turned back to the television.

"Okay what?"

"I'll try it with just cream."

"I'll try it with just cream *what*?"

He started to sigh, shot a glance at Nick, and changed his mind. "Yes, ma'am. Just cream *please*."

Nick stared blankly at the television. The game was not holding his attention. On the couch, DeShaun sipped cautiously at a cup of coffee, trying hard to like it.

The attachment Ivy had to these kids bothered him more and more. He had agreed to go through foster parenting classes with her in the hope that he would begin to feel some kind of kinship to the children. The kind of thing adoptive parents described: *"The first time I held him in my arms, I knew he was mine. . . . "* But he didn't feel that. Or anything even approaching it. To him, the three kids who lived under his roof were simply what they were: somebody else's family that he was taking care of.

Ivy was happy; he could see that. She had stopped talking about adoption. She seemed not to remember—or even to care—that they could not have their own children. He was the one left with the pain of that. Yet whose fault was it that he would never be a real father? Not his own.

The injustice was a small, sharp pebble that pricked incessantly at him. He took it out now and worried it like a talisman, mulling it over, letting the jagged unfairness of it irritate and reopen the old wound. Feeling the reassuring smooth edge of his own rightness in it. Like an inflamed tooth, he shrank from it even as the pain compelled him to keep coming back. He both loved and hated it. Resentment, he had discovered, had a comfort all its own.

❧

On Thanksgiving Day, Ivy arranged DeShaun, Jada, and Hammer, scrubbed and wearing new shirts and jeans, in the Volvo's backseat and gave them each a pie to hold. "Don't let them spill," she warned. "And, Hammer, no picking at the crust. DeShaun, make sure he doesn't pick." She sat in the front seat, holding the fourth pie on her lap, with the container of cranberry relish, two bottles of wine, and a quart of whipping cream at her feet. "We really need a bigger car," she said when Nick got in.

"There's always something we need these days," Nick muttered.

"Ain't that the truth," Ivy said with feeling.

The driveway of 14 Ladyslipper Lane was full of vehicles. Ivy did a quick count. Her parents' Subaru wagon and Amy's battered Escort would be in the double garage. Sephy had flown in from Ohio for the short break, but David's pickup was there as well as Grammie Lydia's copper-colored Audi. Laura's Saab was not in evidence.

Sephy and Amy met them at the door with kisses and cries of "Happy Thanksgiving!" Even Nick could not escape and was kissed along with the rest of them. They took the pies from Jada and DeShaun, who had carried Hammer's in for him, and Sephy said, "Hang your coats up in the closet, kids, and leave your boots here."

In the kitchen, Ivy surrendered the plastic container of cranberry relish to her mother, who went in search of a cut crystal bowl to put it in. Her grandmother was sitting in a chair in one corner. "Hi, Grammie Lydia," Ivy said, stooping to kiss the old lady's powdery-smelling cheek. "Do you remember our kids, DeShaun, Jada, and Hammer?"

Tiny Lydia Darling peered up at them. "I certainly do," she said in her clear, cheerful voice. "And my, how they've grown! This one must be near as tall as you are, Ivy." She reached for DeShaun's hand as she said it, and Ivy saw a startled look cross the boy's face. It struck her then that DeShaun was not used to being touched. Although Jada and Hammer regularly hugged and kissed their foster mother and snuggled close to her on the couch when she read to them, DeShaun never did. In fact, Ivy couldn't think of a single time she had ever touched the older boy, unless she had been feeling his forehead for a fever or brushing a piece of lint from his clothes. That was not a good way for a child—or anyone—to live. She would have to remedy it. Starting now.

She put her arm around his waist and pulled him close to her. "Look at this, Grammie; he *is* taller than me." DeShaun held himself stiffly. She felt his uneasiness.

"Going to be a basketball player, are you?" Grammie Lydia said.

DeShaun looked unsure. "Uh, yeah. Maybe. I'm on the JV team."

"Well, I'll have to come to your next home game. Make sure and tell me when it is, won't you?"

"I didn't know you liked basketball," Ivy said to her grandmother.

"I don't know's I do, but I'd come to see our boy play just the same. And you never know, I might learn a thing or two. I'm not too old for that yet."

Ivy looked sideways at DeShaun and saw that he was trying not to smile. God bless kindhearted Grammie Lydia. Pulling her arm from DeShaun's waist, Ivy gave him a gentle nudge. "I think the men are in the family room watching football. They'll be looking for you." She felt his relief too.

"Hey, Ivy." David edged his way through the crowded kitchen and paused to drop a kiss on the top of her head. "Amy, find a bowl for these shrimp, would you?" He passed a package to his sister nearest the cupboards.

Amy recoiled. "You know I don't touch fish."

"Oh, give it here; I'll do it," said Sephy, taking the bulky fish market bag from him. David sidled back out of the kitchen.

Laura arrived, looking sensational in a cashmere sweater with a fur collar, bearing champagne and a Marie Callender's pumpkin pie in a box. The kitchen was growing hot.

"All right, everybody, time to clear out." Their mother raised her voice to be heard above the chatter and the rattling of pot lids. "There's not room to breathe in here. Why don't you girls take Grammie Lydia into the living room and give us some Christmas carols?"

They coaxed Grammie Lydia, a truly accomplished musician, to play Christmas carols on the Steinway baby grand while the girls gathered around her, singing four-part harmony as they had been taught to do since childhood. They had always loved the strange, obscure carols that other families never seemed to know: "Fum, Fum, Fum," "The Boar's Head Carol," and "I Wonder as I Wander," though they rolled their eyes at each other as they sang the grammatical catastrophe of this last one:

> *"I wonder as I wander out under the sky*
> *How Jesus the Savior did come for to die*
> *For poor orn'ry creatures like you and like I . . ."*

They took turns with all the verses of "The Twelve Days of Christmas," with Amy assigned "five golden rings," as she had been since she was a toddler and it was the only part she could remember. Their grandmother joined in the singing from time to time, sparkling with animation, delighting in their foolishness. When they noticed her lagging, they found her a chair pulled close to the piano, and Sephy took over at the keyboard, changing to more mainstream songs. They sang "Ding Dong Merrily on High" as a round and "God Rest Ye Merry, Gentlemen," then unanimously insisted that Laura and Sephy, the two real vocalists of the family, sing "O Holy Night" together. They did this, Laura's clear soprano hitting the high notes flawlessly, complemented by Sephy's mellow, instinctive contralto.

When they finished, there was loud applause, and all five of them turned around in surprise. Lost in a world of music, in a way that only musicians can be, they had not noticed the rest of the family crowding into the doorway and slipping in along the edges of the room. Their mother's cheeks were wet with tears. Little Jada looked as if she had just seen a vision.

"Come, my dears," Jane Darling said to the room at large, wiping her eyes on her red apron. "Dinner is on the table."

On Friday, they celebrated Thanksgiving with Nick's family at Jessica's house in Rockport. Of all Nick's sisters, Jessica was the one Ivy liked the best. Or to be completely honest, the one she disliked the least. Jessica's children were another matter. Connor, who was thirteen, and Britney, a moody eleven, had evidently been forced by their mother to make an appearance when the family arrived.

"Connor, this is DeShaun," Ivy said, peering under her nephew's side-cocked hat. "You two are just about the same age."

Connor lifted his chin in DeShaun's direction, muttered, "Hey," and disappeared upstairs to his bedroom to play one-man video games.

"I suppose it was a dim hope that he might be hospitable," she sighed to Nick. She was glad that, based on her previous experience with Connor, she had suggested to DeShaun beforehand that he bring his iPod.

Britney disappeared into the family room to watch TV. Jada, who had less pride than DeShaun, followed her foster cousin without waiting for an invitation. Hammer tagged after them. Out of anxiety and a certain morbid curiosity, Ivy followed as well, posting herself outside the family room door to spy.

"Can we watch?" Jada asked the older girl.

Britney was picking at her chapped lower lip with one hand and manipulating the remote control with the other. She spared an apathetic look in Jada's direction, muttered, "I don't care," and did not object when Jada and Hammer climbed onto the couch to watch with her.

Ivy slipped away. Those two would be fine.

She found Jessica, Angela, and Tiffany all being very thick in the kitchen, gossiping over the sweet potato casserole and running their hands delightedly over Angela's enormous belly.

"Ah, I hate to interrupt," Ivy said from the doorway, "but is there anything I can do to help?"

Jessica looked up and cleared the smile from her face. "Oh, thanks for asking, Ivy. You could help Mumma set the table in there." She nodded in the direction of the dining room, far from where the sisters were exclaiming over Angela and her pregnancy.

Ivy smiled sweetly. "Sure. Glad to." She turned and went to the living room, where she sat on the sofa, reached into the book basket on the floor, opened the first magazine she touched, and forced herself to begin reading.

Nick and his father, Harry, were both there, along with Ruby's elderly Aunt Hilda and Uncle Merton.

"Hello, Ida," said Merton, with a vacant smile in Ivy's direction.

"Hi, Uncle Merton," said Ivy, smiling through clenched teeth. "Happy Thanksgiving."

From her position in the most comfortable armchair, Aunt Hilda regarded her with narrowed eyes. "Doesn't Jessica need help in the kitchen?" Aunt Hilda had always cherished a vision of Ivy as the ne'er-do-well hanger-on of the family, who had married Nick only in order to tie herself to the Mason clan and all the advantages it brought her.

"And a happy Thanksgiving to you, too, Aunt Hilda. Thanks for checking. Jessica has it all under control," Ivy said, gazing at a page of *Guideposts* without seeing the words.

DeShaun wandered in, his headphones in his ears, looking

lost. Ivy caught his eye and patted the couch next to her. He slouched over and sat, leaning back and closing his eyes. Alone in his world of music. Ivy envied him.

"Well, Nicholas," Aunt Hilda said, "what about these colored children you've taken on? How long is that supposed to last?"

"It . . . uh . . . it doesn't really work that way, Aunt Hilda," Nick said with a nervous glance at DeShaun, who couldn't hear them in any case.

"What do you mean, it doesn't work that way?"

Nick looked at Ivy, mutely pleading with her to intervene.

She raised her eyebrows at him, curious to hear how he would answer.

"It's not just for . . . for just a set period of time. The kids are going to stay with us, uh . . . for a while."

Hmmm. Not a *bad* answer, but still . . .

Aunt Hilda looked stern. "But how can that be, Nicholas? They belong in their own kind of family."

Nick, brave man, cast another glance in Ivy's direction and, seeing no help from that quarter, soldiered on. "Actually, that's old-fashioned thinking, Aunt Hilda. The children get along just fine with us as foster parents, and Ivy and I, uh . . . really enjoy having them live with us."

Aunt Hilda turned her gaze on DeShaun, then looked at Ivy. "But aren't you afraid in your beds at night?"

Ivy stared. The magazine slipped from her numb fingers and landed with a soft *swat* on the carpet. "You horrible woman," she whispered. "You bigoted . . . ignorant—"

Nick leaped from his chair and grabbed Ivy's arm. "Let's

go for a walk, honey," he said in a loud voice, pulling her off the couch.

It took him fully twenty minutes to defuse her, out in the garage, where there was no one to hear her rage. She did not really calm down until he said, "Look, I'll find a basketball and take DeShaun to the park to shoot hoops until dinner's ready, okay?" Only then was Ivy able to go back into the house and face the family with any kind of equanimity at all.

At dinner, she sat beside Ruby. As soon as Harry had finished offering a protracted Thanksgiving prayer, intoned as though he were reading it from the pages of a user's manual, Ruby turned to Ivy and handed her the platter of turkey.

"Janet Little tells me your foster children are going to be involved in the church Christmas pageant this year," she said. "That's just wonderful! What parts will they be playing?"

"Hammer's a shepherd, and Jada's going to play Mary," said Ivy, helping herself to turkey and passing the platter left, to Nick.

Ruby pulled back the bowl of turnips she had been about to pass. *"Who?"*

"Jada," Ivy said, reaching for the bowl and tugging it from Ruby's grip.

"No, I meant *who* is she going to play?"

"Jada's playing Mary, the mother of Jesus. The pageant's running the Friday, Saturday, and Sunday nights before Christmas. Which night are you and Harry planning to go?"

Ruby looked around the table with an expression of pure astonishment, hoping to telegraph her distress to someone. No one looked back at her, so she addressed Ivy again in a low tone, darting furtive glances at Jada, who was eating turkey with her fingers and chattering to Britney. Britney was ignoring her. "Ivy, how can a . . . a . . . How can she play the mother of Christ?"

"Well," said Ivy, "she just memorizes the lines and stands onstage and says them when it's her turn. These rolls look great. Did Jessica make them?"

Her mother-in-law, used to having people catch her unspoken meanings, was in agony. "Don't you think," she began again, "that it would be better for her to play a wise man? They came from afar. Usually one is pictured as an African."

"But Jada isn't a man, and she hasn't come from afar, and she's not African. She's American, just like you and me."

"I'm talking about her *color*, Ivy," hissed Ruby, as though they were discussing something obscene.

"Her color? Well, I imagine Mary, being an Israelite, was darker than us."

"And Joseph?"

"He was probably dark-skinned too. I mean, I'm no expert, but that's what the history books tell us."

"But there, you see!" Ruby pounced as though she had won a major point. "The real Joseph and Mary would have been *the same color*."

"So your real objection to Jada playing Mary is that she'll be part of, uh . . . a mixed marriage?"

"Well! It's not historically accurate, is it?"

Ivy had to pretend a choking fit in order to cover her laugh, which Ruby took as a sign of surrender. Pleased with the victory she had won through sheer clever logic, Nick's mother rewarded them all by being unusually good-natured for the rest of the afternoon.

CHAPTER

9

IT WAS CHRISTMAS MORNING, and Ivy was baffled. She had bought all the children's gifts herself, but someone, it seemed, had switched them on her. Surely she had never chosen anything like the real, single-seat barnstormer plane that DeShaun was unwrapping. He laughed with delight, a sound she had never heard from him before. His broad, dark face split in a delighted grin. "Thanks, Mom and Dad!" he cried and began pulling on the leather pilot's helmet and goggles.

Somewhere, a baby cried, and Jada shouted, "Help me, Ivy! What am I supposed to do?" Ivy stared in disbelief at the package the little girl had just opened. She thought she had wrapped up an American Girl doll, but it seemed she had gotten Jada a real baby instead.

And what had Nick been thinking, to give Hammer a life-size fire engine, which he was at this moment climbing into, then turning on the siren, laying on the horn. "Turn it off, Hammer!" she shouted, but he could not hear her over the siren's wail and the blast of the horn. "Get out of there; you're too little! Turn it off!"

The siren. The horn. "Get out!" The siren . . .

"Answer the phone," mumbled Nick, beside her.

Ivy came awake. Her own bed. A dream. The terror of it stayed with her as she groped for the phone that was shrilling on the bedside table. She squinted at the clock: 2:23 in the morning. "Hello?"

"Ivy! Oh, thank heaven you're there," her mother-in-law gasped down the line.

Where else would I be at this time of night? She sat up, pulling the quilt to her chin. "What's the matter, Ruby?"

Nick rolled over and looked at her, suddenly wide awake.

"It's Angela. Her water broke early. Vincent has just taken her to the hospital. I'm about to leave, but I had to call you first. I know you and Nick will want to be there."

"Wait—Ruby, is anything wrong? I mean, she's not technically early. Her due date is—" she did some rapid mental math—"eight days from now. Did something happen?"

"We don't know. We just know she was expecting to be induced on Christmas Day, and now this. Oh, my dear, I really have to go now and be with them. I've called the girls, but tell Nick for me, will you?" She hung up without waiting for an answer.

Ivy put the phone down. "Angela's in labor," she told Nick.

"Okay, so . . . ?"

"I'm not sure. It doesn't sound like there's anything wrong, just that she went a week before her due date."

"And that news couldn't have waited until seven or eight o'clock in the morning?"

She frowned. "Do you think we should go to the hospital?"

"No, I think this is the twenty-first century, and if something is wrong, they'll deal with it competently. Our being there and pacing the waiting room with my mother won't change a thing." He turned over, his back to her. "They'll call when the baby's born."

Ivy lay down and hitched herself over so her back was pressed against the warmth of his. "This isn't going to win us any popularity contests with your sisters."

"Oh, well, it'll give them something to talk about."

"Will we go to the hospital tomorrow?"

He sighed, his back moving up and down against hers. "It's my mother and Angela, Ivy. What do you think?"

Ivy thought it would be more than their lives were worth to stay away. She yawned hugely. "Good night."

"Mmph," he said in reply.

❧

Baby Rebecca arrived just after four in the afternoon on December 16, a dark, skinny scrap with wrinkled, furry skin. When Laura finished work that day, she came to stay with the children, while Ivy and Nick drove to the hospital. There, they held the baby and fussed over Angela and endured Ruby's long-winded descriptions of water breaking, of Angela being such and such a number of centimeters dilated, of contractions and pushing. When she got to the episiotomy, however, Nick left the room.

"Looks like we have to run," Ivy said hastily. "Congratulations, Ruby. And you too, Angela. Really well done." She hurried after Nick.

They headed across the hospital parking lot in search of their car. "Rebecca's a beautiful baby," she ventured. Holding her new niece minutes before, Ivy had felt a strange sense of loss that was still with her. It wasn't sadness or longing exactly, more a simple hollowness. The missing of something as a child might miss a lost tooth or a veteran soldier an amputated limb. An empty space where something should have been, but wasn't.

"Their lives are about to change big-time," said Nick.

"That's for sure. We should know, right?"

"There it is," he said, pointing to the Volvo with his keys. He unlocked it, and they got in. He sat for a moment without turning on the car. "It's been hard on you, hasn't it? Having three kids move in with us."

"Hard? Sure. But worthwhile things usually are. I wouldn't change it. Would you?"

He didn't answer until he had maneuvered the car out of the parking lot and pulled back onto the main road. At last, he said, "Sometimes I would. I'm glad we're doing some good, helping them out, but . . . they're not my kids, Ivy. They're not yours either. I just don't want you to forget that."

She looked out the window. Sometimes she did forget. Not

often, but once in a while. She felt a surge of resentment toward Nick, who could so easily compartmentalize his emotions. Turning back to him, she said, "Does that mean I shouldn't enjoy them while I have them? Shouldn't love them and pour everything I have into raising them, even if they're not *mine*?"

"I'm just saying be careful. You'll get your heart broken."

She turned away and looked out the window at the cheerless side lawn of the hospital, where last October's chrysanthemums had been allowed to wither and freeze on their stalks. "I've had my heart broken before," she told him. "I'll probably survive it this time."

❧

The week leading up to Christmas was easily the most exhausting Ivy had ever endured. There was last-minute shopping and the wrapping of gifts, which Nick refused to help with. "Save yourself time and money and just hand everyone their gifts in shopping bags" was his advice.

To Ivy, who not only wrapped every item separately but also garnished each package with ribbon and homemade tags, this idea was anathema. "I'll hand you *yours* in a shopping bag," she snapped back.

"Fine by me." He was sitting in his chair, reading the paper throughout this exchange, and his unconcern irritated Ivy.

"You're such a scrooge, Nick. You wouldn't help decorate the tree—"

"I hauled the darn thing home and put it up for you, didn't I?"

"—and instead of enjoying all the baking we did, you groused that it would ruin your cholesterol—"

"Which it will."

"Don't eat it, then."

"I haven't."

"See? Scrooge."

He peered at her over the top of the paper. "Have I uttered one word of complaint about the shopping bills, which, I remind you, have been pretty steep this year?"

Ivy had to admit that he hadn't.

"Did I say no to the Xbox, which is going to completely take over my television, or the violin, which is going to screech like a banshee while Jada learns to play it, or—?"

"All right, all right," Ivy muttered. She eyed him. "Are you done with the comics pages?"

"Why?"

"Hand them to me. I want to wrap the kids' stocking stuffers in them."

❧

There was also the church Christmas pageant, starring a strident Jada as the Virgin Mary and Hammer as a bashful shepherd. DeShaun did not like church, although Ivy and Nick required him to go every Sunday. As a compromise, they had been allowing him to sit in the sound booth during services with the technician, Larry, a patient retired school bus driver who had begun teaching the boy how to run the sound board and lights. As a result, all three of their children took part in the Christmas pageant, and Ivy left the church that night with an overflowing heart and equally overflowing eyes.

"We are blessed," she sighed to Nick, who handed her a tissue from his coat pocket as a sign of agreement.

The school holiday program followed this, just before classes ended for the break. Ivy knew that Jada was to sing a solo but had not been allowed to hear it yet. Grammie Jane, as Ivy's mother had been dubbed, knew all about it, as did Sephy, home from Ohio for the holidays.

"Just you leave her to us," Ivy had been told, first by her mother and later by Sephy. "We'll get her in shape for her solo. She'll do you proud."

And she did. After four or five rather anemic numbers by the elementary choir, Jada stepped forward and stood alone on the stage of the school gym, looking small and unsure of herself. She squinted against the spotlight shining on her, and Ivy knew she was searching for a familiar face in the sea of shadowy forms before her.

Please let her do all right.

The music began. Jada missed her cue, and the accompanist, who was one of the music students from the high school, started over. Ivy crossed her fingers and held her breath. This time, Jada nailed it.

> *"Sweet little Jesus boy,*
> *we made You be born in a manger.*
> *Sweet little holy child,*
> *we didn't know who You was."*

Ivy had never heard a voice like that from any nine-year-old child. Smoky and strong, it floated to the rafters of the auditorium with the kind of assurance that told everybody listening that she was going to hit every note.

By the second verse, the little girl had closed her eyes and was swaying as she sang, clutching unself-consciously at the sides of her skirt. Ivy, who knew the child well by now, realized she had forgotten there was anyone listening except the very baby she was singing about.

> *"The world treat You mean, Lord;*
> *Treat me mean too.*
> *But please, sir, forgive us, Lord;*
> *We didn't know it was You."*

When the last note faded, there was utter silence. Jada dropped half a curtsy and, holding her head high, marched from the stage. The auditorium erupted into wild cheers, clapping and stamping. It went on and on. Ivy, unable to help herself, jumped to her feet. The people nearest her followed suit and then the entire audience was standing, whistling and applauding what had been an extraordinary performance by any standard. A hand appeared from the curtains at stage left and pushed a dazed-looking Jada back to the center, where she curtsied again. She stood there until the noise subsided and the audience had taken their seats once again. Then she gave a small nod to the girl at the piano, who struck a single note. Jada's voice rang out unaccompanied through the quiet room.

"Silent night, holy night;
All is calm, all is bright.
Round yon virgin mother and child;
Holy infant so tender and mild;
Sleep in heavenly peace.
Sleep in heavenly peace."

Ivy's scalp tingled. Just the single verse, followed by another curtsy before Jada walked off the stage again. On one side of Ivy, the tears were flowing freely down Sephy's face. On the other side, Nick was smiling. Afterward, when Ivy had said good-bye to her parents and sisters, located Jada in the classroom assigned to the choir, and collected her coat, Mrs. Walden, the music teacher, stopped them on their way to the foyer to meet Nick.

"This young lady has a gift," she informed Ivy. "I hope you realize that."

"After tonight I do," Ivy assured her. "We'll have to make sure we do something about that. She's interested in playing the violin; has she told you that?"

"No," said the teacher, "but I have no doubt she'll be a success at any kind of music she chooses to study. You should see to training that voice of hers, though."

"I'll do that," Ivy said. She thanked the teacher, made sure Jada's coat was buttoned, and headed for the car. It was snowing—a light, lazy fall that had draped the parking lot in an airy shift of white.

DeShaun, having been allowed to start the car, was still

sitting behind the wheel while Nick and Hammer brushed off the windows. "You did a great job," Nick said, pausing in his work to look down at Jada. "I was really proud of you."

The little girl glowed and, ever generous, returned the compliment. "And you're doing a great job cleaning that snow off the car, Nick."

Laura looked at the clock on the office wall. They were closing at twelve for Christmas Eve, and it was a quarter till now. She felt despondent. Max had decided to close the office until after the New Year, which meant she wouldn't see him for nine endless days. Worse, the reason he was doing it was that he was taking his family—including the loathsome Carol—skiing in Austria over the holidays. And what was Laura supposed to do with herself during that time?

They'd only had a couple of meals together, a few late nights at the office. On several occasions, they had played racquetball, and Laura was still paying for that with an aggressive case of tendonitis in her right wrist. It had bothered her so much that she had ended up seeing a doctor about it. He was a friend of Max's from the club, so she hadn't had to bother making an appointment or going to his office and waiting, or paying, or any of the other little irritations usually involved in getting medical care. She had simply talked to Max's friend, and he had written her a prescription, also advising her to buy an elastic wrist splint and to try ice packs, and that had been that. It had been so simple and had really helped. Not for the first time, Laura thought that she could get very used to life as the wife of a rich businessman.

As though her thoughts had summoned him, her intercom buzzed and Max's voice came through. "Laura, I need to see you for a minute before you leave for home."

"Be right there." Hurriedly, she replaced a stack of files in their drawer and locked it, then straightened her desk and, with her little compact mirror, touched up her lipstick. At five minutes before twelve, she knocked on his office door and went in.

"Oh, good," he said, looking away from his computer screen. He was so impossibly handsome, the kind of man who filled a room with his presence. Laura's heart turned over.

"What can I do for you, Max?"

He got up and came around to the front of his desk. "I just wanted to wish you a merry Christmas before we go our separate ways."

"Thank you. Merry Christmas to you, too. You leave for Vienna tonight?"

"Yes. Red-eye out of Boston."

"Have a good time." She did not add, *I'll miss you.*

"I'll miss you," he said, and her heart did a kind of stutter in her chest.

Her confidence was suddenly back, and she said archly, "Will you?"

"Yes, very much. In fact, I wanted to give you a little

Christmas gift before I go. So you won't forget me." He picked up a small package from his desk and handed it to her.

Laura did not know what to say. She had the sense that her face had turned pink, and it was suddenly not very easy to breathe. "Oh . . . thank you."

"Open it."

"Now?"

"Yes, now." He sounded amused.

She removed the ribbon and slit the tape on the gold foil paper, which she pulled away to reveal a jeweler's box. She glanced at him as she lifted the lid and saw that he was watching her with an expression of great tenderness.

It was a tennis bracelet, a single strand of diamonds that sparkled against the black velvet background like white fire. "Max!"

"Since I'm responsible for that—" he touched the elastic bandage she was wearing—"I thought I could at least decorate the other wrist a little more nicely. Do you like it?"

"I *love* it. But you shouldn't—"

"Don't say I shouldn't have. I wanted to. No, don't say anything at all. I picked it out just for you, and you're going to keep it. Let me put it on."

Wordlessly, she held out her left wrist, and he fastened the strand of diamonds around it, fumbling a little with the clasp. When he was finished, he did not let go of her. "Laura," he said and pulled her to him. Then he was kissing her, and Laura could not remember how to breathe at all. The room spun away and there was nothing but her and Max, his arms warm around her and his mouth on hers.

He broke away first but did not let go of her. "I'll miss you," he whispered against her hair.

"I'll miss you too."

"I'm only going on this trip for the sake of the boys."

"I know."

"Wait for me. Please wait for me."

"I'll be right here when you get back."

"Good." He kissed her again. "Now go home, before you make me change my mind about leaving."

At the door, she looked back at him. He smiled, his eyes crinkling at the corners, twisting a blade in her stomach. "I'll miss you," she repeated.

"Me too."

She did not remember getting from the office into her car, but there she was, with her purse and her briefcase on the front seat beside her, so she supposed she must have gone through the motions of leaving the right way. She turned on the ignition and leaned her forehead against the steering wheel. At the edge of her coat cuff, the diamonds glinted at her.

Max, she thought. He had kissed her, given her jewelry. Diamonds, no less. He felt the same way about her that she felt about him. She was in love. *They* were in love.

Nine days stretched before her in a veritable desert of time. It might as well have been nine years. On the other hand, didn't they have forever? She touched the diamonds with the tip of one gloved finger. Diamonds. A symbol of eternity. *Max and Laura, together forever.*

She could live on that for nine days.

Amy turned nineteen on Christmas Eve, when it was a Darling tradition to celebrate with lobster stew at Jane and Leander's house. Amy, who had declared herself a vegetarian on her sixteenth birthday—a decision largely ignored by her mother—had made minestrone soup for herself. "It's appalling that I always have to make my own birthday dinner," she complained without rancor, and nobody paid her any attention.

Libby Hale from next door joined them for dinner, as well as Grammie Lydia. Afterward, they gathered around the piano to sing Christmas carols, as they had done on Thanksgiving. The Darling siblings and their parents did not allow the less musical guests to plead self-consciousness. Libby, Nick, and DeShaun had songbooks forced into their hands by Ivy, who informed them that anyone who did not sing, and sing loudly, would be required to give a solo.

"Oh, I can sing my solo!" cried Jada, shooting a hand into the air and jumping up and down in excitement. "I have *two* solos."

"All right," Sephy said. "Come stand here by the piano and sing for us, then." She played the introduction to "Sweet Little Jesus Boy" and Jada sang it almost as beautifully as she had at the concert.

"Now 'Silent Night,'" the little girl prompted. Sephy gave her a note, and Jada sang it flawlessly, a cappella.

"You really should have her voice trained, Ivy," said her mother, in the silence that followed.

"We're looking into that," said Ivy. "Know any good teachers? Sephy can't do it because she has to go back to school. Hey, Laura, how about you?"

Laura shook her head. "I'm no teacher."

"I'd volunteer," said Jane, "but it would take me about a month to teach her everything I know about voice, and then you'd have to find someone else anyway. Maybe Janet Little would do it. I'll give her a call after Christmas." The grandfather clock in the hall struck eleven. "Good heavens, is that the time?" she exclaimed. "You'd better get these kids home, Ivy." She looked meaningfully at Hammer, who was asleep, slack-mouthed against an arm of the sofa. "Too late and Santa won't come."

"No!" cried Jada, in real distress. "I want Santa to come!"

❧

On Christmas morning, Ivy filled her camera's memory card with pictures of the children opening their gifts. It could not have been clearer that this was another first for them.

Nick seemed to honestly like the two sweaters and the History Channel series on World War II that she had gotten him. Jada gave Ivy a batik weaving she had made in art class. Hammer's gift was a clay ashtray in the shape of his hand. DeShaun had made her a mix CD of his favorite bands.

At first, she thought Nick had not gotten her a gift, and she buried her disappointment under the business of clearing away wrapping paper and sliding the pan of cinnamon rolls and the breakfast casserole into the oven at the right moments.

But just before they sat down at the table, he coughed and said, "Ah, there's one more gift, out in the garage."

Ivy, standing at the table with a stack of plates in her arms, looked at the children. Jada was hopping up and down. Hammer was clutching at the front of his sweatpants. DeShaun wore a reluctant half smile. "What aren't you all telling me?" she asked.

"Come and see!" Jada crowed.

She went and saw. A brand-new Honda Odyssey minivan. A family car. Maroon.

"You said the Volvo's too small for all of us," Nick told her, half-apologetically.

"Nick!" The tears overflowed and spilled down her cheeks. She turned to hug him.

Stiffly, he said, "Well, it's the right time of year to buy. It'll be a good tax deduction." But he put his arms around her and patted her back. "Don't cry," he told her. "It was supposed to be a happy thing."

"It is," she sniffed into his shirtfront. "It is."

10

"Why," Ivy wondered aloud, "does real life have to start again so soon after the New Year?" She lay on the couch with her feet propped on an armrest, gazing disconsolately at the postholiday detritus of her living room. "The week's already half-over," she went on. "You'd think they'd just give us the rest of it off."

"Who do you mean," asked Nick, rattling the pages of his newspaper, "when you say *they?*"

"The world. The establishment. The people who make up school and work calendars." She wiggled her toes, waiting for him to answer this, but he merely folded the front page, laid it down, picked up the local section, and continued to read.

"Oh, well, no sense complaining, right?" Ivy said. "At least you and I have jobs to go to. At least the kids are getting an education."

DeShaun, who was slouched in a chair, absorbed in a video game, snorted at this.

Ivy sat up with a sigh. "Time to wind that thing down, DeShaun. It's your turn to clean up the kitchen, and Nick's game will be on in fifteen minutes anyway."

He looked up. "How come I gotta do the dishes again? It's Jada's turn."

"Jada washed the breakfast dishes on Monday."

"So? That means it was my turn on Monday night. Today's Tuesday."

"Monday was New Year's Eve, DeShaun. You don't remember going to a big party at my parents' house? You didn't have to wash dishes last night because there were no dishes to wash."

"So? That means I get to skip my turn."

"Come on, shut the game down, and I'll give you a hand in the kitchen."

"You *better*. It looks like a bomb went off in there," he muttered.

Nick lowered the newspaper and cleared his throat.

DeShaun slung himself off the couch and sloped, glowering, into the kitchen.

They stacked and scraped dishes together, and Ivy wiped the counters while DeShaun washed the dirty plates and silverware left over from the morning's family brunch.

"Did you like my parents' New Year's Eve party?" she asked him.

He shrugged. "It was okay."

"I didn't see much of you. Where were you all evening?"

"Mostly playing Ping-Pong with Tyler."

"Tyler . . . ," Ivy said. "Aren't his parents Dan and Cindy Cleaves, from church?"

"I don' know. I guess."

"It's hard for me to keep track of who was there and who wasn't. Mom's New Year's Eve parties get bigger every year, and everyone kept coming and going. Anyway, is this kid—Tyler—in your class?"

"Nah. He's homeschooled. Weird."

"Which is weird—Tyler or the fact that he's home-schooled?"

DeShaun considered this. "The fact that he's home-schooled. Tyler's okay, for a white kid."

Ivy put down her dishcloth. "Excuse me, sir. Do you think I'd allow other people to talk that way about you? *'DeShaun's okay, for a black kid,'*" she mimicked.

He avoided her eyes.

"Well?" she demanded.

"No."

"You're darn right *no*. It works both ways. Don't let me hear you categorize people by their skin color again, got it?"

"Yeah."

"Okay then." She picked up her cloth again and began to wipe the stove.

"Can I let this pan soak? It's nasty." DeShaun pointed to the pan that had held the farmer's strata from brunch.

"It doesn't need to soak. Try some steel wool on it."

With a hefty sigh, DeShaun began to rummage under the sink for the steel wool.

"Tell me, DeShaun, what do you want to do with your life?"

"Huh?"

"What do you want to be when you grow up? Do you want to go to college? Play sports? Have a family of your own?"

He stared at her as though she were speaking Latin. "I don' know. I never thought about it."

"Come on, you never wanted to be something when you grow up? Most boys at least dream of being a fireman or policeman or . . . or a cowboy when they're little."

He shook his head. "I'm busy taking care of Jada and Hammer. Don' have time for no daydreamin'."

She leaned against the counter. "Those days are over now, DeShaun. Nick and I are here to help you take care of the little kids; you don't have to do it all by yourself anymore. Maybe it's time for you to start having some dreams of your own."

He lifted one shoulder as though the subject were too trivial to merit a complete shrug. "Them days ain't over once they find our mama. They just startin' all over again." As always when he was on the defensive, his inner-city accent became more pronounced.

Her heart ached for this boy, forced to grow up so fast

that he had never even had time to dream for himself. She stared at the damp dish towel in her hands, unsure of what to say. She wanted it to be something magical, something that would erase the years of hurt and disillusionment, that would pave the way for happier years ahead. But the truth was, she couldn't even guess what was ahead for DeShaun and his brother and sister. She couldn't promise him anything.

She settled for telling him the truth. "I don't know what's going to happen if they find your mother. It's possible they wouldn't let you live with her again in any case. But I want you to know, DeShaun, that as long as the law allows it, you and Jada and Hammer will always have a home here with us. I hope knowing that will free you up to dream a little bit."

He did not answer or look up, only hunched his shoulders and scrubbed fiercely at the baking pan. Silently, Ivy hung up her towel to dry and left the room, touching him on the shoulder as she went.

On Monday morning, Amy called her.

"Oh, hi," Ivy said, shifting the laundry basket she was carrying to one hip. "Getting settled back in?"

There was silence on the other end. Then, "I didn't go back."

"To college?" Ivy said blankly. "Why not?"

"I couldn't stand it anymore. It was just . . . too . . . I don't know, too boring or something. Everyone just wanted to party all the time." She sounded defensive.

"Sounds like a good thing you're getting out, then. When did you decide?"

"Yesterday. I was supposed to go back last night and I just . . . couldn't."

"What will you do?"

"No idea. Try to find a job. Get my head together. Dad's driving me back to campus tomorrow to get my stuff."

"I'm sorry it didn't work out."

"Don't be sorry. It's a huge relief. You know how when you're going through something hard, you sometimes don't realize how bad it is until it's all over and you look back and think, *How did I ever do that?*"

"God's grace."

"I guess so."

"What do Mom and Dad think about it?"

"Dad would think anything I decided to do was wonderful. Mom's all like, 'God knows the plan. Ask Him.' You know how she is."

"But she's right, of course."

Silence. Then, "Yeah."

"So . . . ?"

"Okay, don't you start nagging me too."

"I wouldn't dream of it. Come over when you have time and I'll scare you up a cup of something hot and caffeine-free."

"I'll rearrange my hectic schedule and pencil you in for later this afternoon."

"Everything's going to work out just fine, Amy. Wait and see."

"I hope so." She did not sound very hopeful.

They made kissing noises and hung up. As Ivy dropped the phone into the basket of clean laundry and headed upstairs, she realized she was happy. Not just for Amy, but for herself. Sephy was in Ohio, and Laura was never around anymore. It would be good to have a sister in her life again.

The caseworker was a square, gruff woman named Willie. Hammer had been terrified of her until, at their second meeting, Willie had produced a bag of strawberry Twizzlers and two half-pint cartons of milk and showed him how to drink using a Twizzler as a straw.

"I want one!" Jada had demanded, and Willie produced another milk carton from her bag.

"You too?" she said, eyeing DeShaun.

"No way. That's sick."

The social worker ignored this and set a fourth milk carton on the table in front of him. "Look, you can blow bubbles too," she said.

After a moment's hesitation, DeShaun reached for a Twizzler and joined his brother and sister in their noisy blowing and sucking. Willie's monthly visits had been a high point ever since.

After several interviews with the children and some searches of public records, she had informed Ivy that Jada would turn ten years old on Wednesday, the ninth of January, and DeShaun would turn fifteen the day after that. Ivy, who was still trying to recover from a month of Christmas and

New Year celebrations, thought longingly of how easy it would be to simply combine the two birthday parties and call it good enough.

For the first few days of January, she struggled with her conscience. There was every reason to keep the birthday celebrations low-key. After all, she was still physically, socially, and financially exhausted from the holidays. And anything she might do to mark the children's birthdays was bound to be more than anyone had done for them before. Surely a nice family dinner with presents afterward and two cakes . . .

Yet a girl only turned ten years old once in her life, a persistent voice in her head reminded her. It was the first year of double digits. And DeShaun would be old enough to drive this year. Didn't fifteen deserve a celebration of its own? As a twin, Ivy knew what it meant to always share a birthday with someone, and this in itself was enough to give her pause. She thought about asking Nick's advice, then had to wonder why she chose not to. Instead, she resolved to call 14 Ladyslipper Lane and run the idea by the first person who answered. She punched in the number.

"Hello?"

"Oh, Amy."

"You don't have to sound so disappointed. Who were you hoping for?"

"Someone who'll make my life easier, and that's probably not going to be you."

"Good," said Amy cheerfully. "Fire away."

"Okay, here's the situation. Jada has a birthday on the ninth."

"Of January?"

"No, of August. Of *course* January. She'll be ten."

"Oh, fun! Double digits! That means last year she turned nine on the ninth. Too bad she wasn't around then. That would've been a *real* party." Amy sounded as though she were talking through a mouthful of food.

"Are you eating in my ear?" Ivy demanded.

"Yes, an almond-butter-and-raspberry sandwich. Are you jealous?"

"What, you can't just eat peanut butter and jelly like the rest of us?"

"Almond butter has more calcium. And raw berries are so much better for you than jam. The heat of processing totally destroys the vitamins. Might as well eat a big spoonful of sugar; it amounts to the same thing."

"As I was *saying*—" Ivy raised her voice—"Jada turns ten on the ninth, and DeShaun's birthday is the very next day. He'll be fifteen."

"Learner's permit year," said Amy, still chewing.

"Yes, thanks for reminding me."

"So what's the problem?"

"What am I supposed to do? I'd really rather have one party—I don't know, dinner and cake or something simple—for both of them on the same day."

"That," said Amy, "is so cheap."

Ivy sighed. "This is why I wanted to talk to Mom."

"Because Mom will tell you what you want to hear? That's moral cowardice, Ivy. Give them each a party. It's the right thing to do, and you know it."

Ivy, sagging against the kitchen counter, had a sudden inspiration and straightened up. "So . . . you'll help me, then?"

"What?" Amy sounded startled.

"You'll help me. You know—make cakes, wrap the gifts. . . . I mean, if I'm going to have a horde of fourth-grade girls at my house on Wednesday afternoon and, let's see, another of ninth-grade boys on . . . probably Friday night, I'm not going to be able to do it alone, am I?"

"I suppose it's too late for me to get Mom and pretend this conversation never happened?"

"Way too late. You're committed."

"Hmmm . . . All right, then, you can count on Auntie Amy."

"For Wednesday *and* Friday?"

"Sure. It's not like I have anything else to do. What are you going to do for the parties?"

"Jada and her friends will have to have games organized, I suppose. Or are they too old for that kind of thing?"

"Too old. Give them manicures and rent a karaoke machine."

"I am *not* renting a karaoke machine. And I was thinking of making those little hot dogs wrapped in refrigerated biscuit dough—"

"Disgusting."

"Thank you. But definitely pizza for DeShaun on Friday. He and his friends will probably just want to hang out and play Xbox. I'll tell them they can each invite five friends. We should be able to handle a round half dozen between us."

"What about Nick? Won't he be there?"

"I'm hoping Nick will take the younger ones out some-where during DeShaun's party, and take the boys out during Jada's party. Keep them all out of each other's way."

"Okay. What's my assignment?"

"I think I'll make both cakes on Wednesday morning. Want to help?"

"I should look for a job at some point that day," Amy reminded her.

"It never hurts to ask. Just having you here for the parties will be enough, I think."

"I'm happy to do it."

"You'd better be. It was your idea," Ivy said.

The parties, with Amy's help, came off better than Ivy had hoped. Afterward, when she tried to describe them to Nick, her impressions of Jada's party included lots of squealing and manicures given to all the girls by Aunt Amy, who also taught them to dance the Macarena. DeShaun's party, in contrast, was centered around his newly acquired Xbox and was char-acterized by vast quantities of pizza and Mountain Dew, by boys whose every other word seemed to be *dude*, and by a stain on the sofa that never would come out after that day. But both children, in their ways, let her know that her choice had been the right one. When Jada went to bed on the night of her party, she wrapped her arms around Ivy's neck and whispered, "This is the best day I ever had."

And DeShaun, as he drifted toward his own room around

midnight on Friday, leaving the living room littered with
pizza boxes and abandoned game controllers, said to her,
"Wow, man. That was really epic."

Ivy was in the kitchen mashing potatoes and listening to the
small evening noises of her household. Jada, who had started
violin lessons, was producing some very screechy sounds in
Ivy and Nick's bedroom, which served as the practice room
so that Ivy could be on hand to consult as needed. The
sounds were muffled through the closed door, and in spite
of all they had in common with a back-alley cat fight, Ivy
recognized the seeds of talent in what she was hearing. Jada,
given a chance to continue with her music, might one day
really shine.

From the living room came a low stream of chatter from
Hammer, punctuated by occasional remarks from Nick and
the infrequent swish of a newspaper page being turned.
Hammer had made remarkable strides in the months he
had been with them. He had nearly mastered potty training,
and they had rewarded him by signing him up for the rec
program's Saturday morning Ankle Biter Basketball League,
where he was proving to have a knack for dribbling and free
throws.

Ivy glanced at the clock. Speaking of success, it was time
to remind him to use the bathroom. She went to the living
room doorway. Hammer was doing what he called "reading the paper." Lying on his stomach on the floor, he was

absorbed in coloring the faces of all the boys and men on the comics page of the *Bangor Daily News*. He had taken to doing this every evening while Nick read the sports section. The boys he colored brown, and the men he colored in with a peach crayon. The first time he had done it, he had explained to Ivy that these men were the boys' fathers. *Zits*, *Adam@Home*, *The Family Circus*—all alike had brown sons and peach-colored fathers in the Darling-Mason version of the newspapers.

"Hammer, it's bathroom time," Ivy said, wiping her hands on a dish towel. His eyes grew wide, and he jumped up and sped bathroom-ward.

She sat on the arm of the couch, kicking one foot, and asked Nick, "How was your day?"

He shrugged, not looking up. "All right. Same old thing."

"Anything good in the news?"

"You know better than that. Good news doesn't make the paper." He turned a page.

"I-veeeeee!" Hammer's anguished howl rang out from the bathroom. "I ain't got no to'let paper!"

She stifled a sigh and stood up. "Well, I'm glad we had this little talk."

Nick shot her an annoyed glance. "There's no need to be snide. You know I like to read the paper in peace."

She ensured his peace by not answering him as she left the room.

In the bathroom, she searched the closet for a roll of toilet paper and realized she would have to open a new package. Rummaging in the back for it, she managed to knock to the ground a shoe box full of medicine, including a box of Band-Aids, which opened and scattered across the floor, and a green glass bottle of Campho-Phenique, which shattered on the tiles, filling the bathroom with an oily eucalyptus odor.

She bit back a curse, mindful of Hammer, who was sitting on the toilet kicking his feet, seeing and hearing everything. Handing him a roll of toilet paper, she said, "Finish up and go wash your hands in the kitchen sink. I don't want you in here, stepping on broken glass."

He finished his business and skipped off, and Ivy began the irksome chore of cleaning up the mess she had made. It was while she was putting everything back into the shoe box that she discovered the empty Vicodin bottle.

Not exactly empty, she corrected herself, giving the bottle a shake. There were two pills left. She squinted at the label. There had been twenty to start with, when she had filled the prescription. She had not taken more than one because it had made her feel so awful. And she had given Laura one for tendonitis in her wrist, she remembered, but that was all. So where were the rest? She did the math. Sixteen pills unaccounted for.

A sick feeling took hold of her stomach, and she sank onto the side of the bathtub, clutching the near-empty bottle. *Please, God, not DeShaun,* she prayed. But she knew there was no one else it could be.

She had begun to have some hope for the quiet boy who was so protective of his young brother and sister. He talked more than he had before. Sometimes she could make him smile. Once or twice she had nearly had a whole conversation with him before he'd clammed up again, lifting a shoulder in his characteristic half shrug, the gesture that shut her out as effectively as any brick wall. Yet there was no denying he was often sullen. He was not a particularly good student and seemed to have little ambition for anything except video games. Did all of that add up to the profile of a drug user? And if he had stolen Vicodin from her, had he stolen pills from other people? Was he drinking? Smoking pot, or worse? She had no way of knowing.

Ivy watched him covertly through dinner, scrutinizing his pupils, trying to detect any sign of drug use. She couldn't tell, didn't know what she was looking for. And she didn't know him well enough.

Jada's and Hammer's flow of chatter camouflaged her own preoccupied silence, and she let them talk on as she tried to formulate a plan. She would have to confront him about it, of course, and Nick would have to be told. She dreaded this last part most of all. It was one thing for her to think badly of DeShaun, but she felt a nearly frantic urge to protect him from Nick's low opinion. This, she realized at the same time, she could not do. Nick had a right to know what was going on under his own roof. Maybe the state would take DeShaun away from them, put him in some terrible group home that would surely only compound a drug problem, make him into a hardened criminal by the time he was old enough to get out. She pushed her tasteless food around the plate, numb with shock and dread.

When dinner was over, she said, "Nick, can I talk to you in the bedroom, please?"

She showed him the bottle with tears in her eyes. He took the news grimly and agreed that they should confront DeShaun together. "I was afraid of something like this," he said, shaking his head. "With a mother like theirs, they probably had drugs around the place all the time. It was inevitable that he would try them himself. Who knows? This may not even be the first time."

"I suppose I have to tell the social worker?"

"Of course."

"I'll call her first thing in the morning."

"You need to call her tonight, Ivy."

She began to cry in earnest then, the tears welling up and overflowing faster than she could wipe them away.

"Hey, hey. Pull it together."

Anger at his calmness surged over her. "I *can't* just pull it together. I shouldn't *have* to." With the heels of her hands, she rubbed at her eyes.

"Okay. All right." Nick reached for her and pulled her to his chest. It had been a long time since he had done that. It felt both strange and familiar. Beneath Ivy's misery, a tiny flame of hope flared.

He let go of her and fumbled in his back pocket until he found a tissue, then handed it to her. "Don't go to pieces on me now. It's going to be okay."

"I don't see how."

"Come on, blow your nose and let's go talk to him. Maybe there's an explanation." She knew he did not believe it any more than she did.

And of course, there wasn't. When they presented

DeShaun with the pill bottle, he only crossed his arms over his chest and looked past them at the wall with a blank stare. He refused to say a word, and in the end, all they could do was leave him in his room and go back downstairs, Nick angry and Ivy heartbroken.

The social worker wasn't much help. Willie told Ivy to look for proof, to keep her eyes open, to watch for changes in behavior, et cetera, et cetera. None of it was helpful. One thing was clear, though: they weren't taking DeShaun away from her. Not yet, anyway.

That night, she lay awake long after Nick had begun snoring beside her and prayed. She prayed for DeShaun, and for answers, and mostly she prayed that God would help her to somehow get it right when most of the time she felt that she was doing it all wrong.

CHAPTER

11

JANET LITTLE CALLED to say her daughter was visiting from Wichita, and could Jada come for her voice lesson a different day that week? As she talked, Ivy searched the junk drawer for a pencil to write down the date but could not find one. The drawer held everything else: emery boards, matchbooks, rubber bands, leftover nuts and bolts, and those funny angled pieces of metal from the backs of old picture frames. She answered the older lady abstractedly as she sorted through nail clippers, grocery receipts, outdated coupons, scraps of paper with odd notes on them, an empty pack of sugarless gum, a photograph of a sunset that she couldn't remember saving, six double-A batteries, an assortment of paper clips, an herbal tea bag, and three wrinkled paper coasters covered in crumbs and hair. But not one pen or pencil.

After hanging up with Janet, Ivy yanked out the drawer in disgust and began to organize it. It was then that she came across a crumpled red paper.

The Art of Short Story.
Cover the fundamentals of developing character, plot, theme, and setting. Learn to structure your short story and begin to find your own voice as you read the stories of accomplished authors and write your own.
T, Th, 6–9 p.m. 8 weeks.

She recalled the day last summer when she had picked it up from the display at Parchments. The phrase *begin to find your own voice* had resonated with her then as it did now. She still didn't consider herself a writer, but Esme had told her the class was offered through adult ed. Maybe there was more than one way to find her voice.

At Parchments the next day, she found an adult education catalog on the rack of free newspapers near the front door and looked through it during her enforced fifteen-minute break, over a cup of coffee. The classes were offered in Quahog, at the technical college. Nick had taken a class there once, she remembered. Intro to some kind of computer tax program or other. He had enjoyed it and said he learned a lot. She flipped to the "Personal Growth" section of the catalog and skimmed over descriptions of yoga classes, haiku-writing seminars, tarot card training, soap-making workshops, and small-engine repair certification. Beginner pottery caught her eye.

> Learn basic techniques of wheel throwing, hand building, electric firing, painting, and glazing in this fun and informative 12-week class.
> Taught by Jonathon Blackfeather, artist and owner of Native Feather Studio in Camden.
> April 2–June 20; T, Th, 6–8:30. 12 weeks.

Ivy read and reread the brief course description and felt a prickle over her scalp. The whole issue of DeShaun and the Vicodin was wearing her down, niggling constantly at the edges of her subconscious, a malevolent parasite that threatened to destroy the peace of mind she so carefully built up every morning over her Bible and coffee. Since she had discovered the pills missing, she had thought of little else. She dreamed about it at night. Like a hamster on a wheel, her mind ran over and over the same ground, making no progress, reaching no satisfactory conclusion. DeShaun had become nearly incommunicado, speaking only when spoken to and then with only the thinnest veneer of politeness that he could get away with. He spent most of his time at home in his room, lying on his bed listening to his iPod.

What she needed, Ivy thought, was to separate herself from home and do something just for herself for a change. Not work, which would be for Nick and the children, but something like this that would be all her own. She had no idea what "hand building" or "electric firing" were, but the words had an exciting ring to them. The promise of a new, as-yet-undiscovered world. She had always loved to buy pottery, so why not learn to make it?

She tucked the course catalog under her arm and stood up, tossing her empty coffee cup into the trash can. She would register online as soon as she got home from work.

Jane propped the telephone receiver between her ear and shoulder and took the calendar from the wall. On one of her recent birthdays, the children had all gone in together and gotten her a cell phone. She had tried to learn to use it, but it felt minuscule and ridiculous. You couldn't talk on it and use your hands at the same time, and if a person couldn't accomplish something else, like washing the dishes, during a telephone call, then it was wasted time. When she had explained this to the children, Nick had gone out and bought some attachment called a Bluetooth, though it was neither blue nor looked like a tooth, as far as Jane could see. She had tried this as well but had not been able to get used to the idea of walking around the house shouting at nothing. The cell phone was tucked inside her purse for roadside emergencies, but at home she had gone back to the wall-mounted kind she had used for more than a decade. When the children had insisted on buying her a cordless model, she had conceded graciously.

Now, she murmured, "Mm-hmm. Yes, my dear," into her

comfortable, large, old-fashioned receiver. "I think that's a fine idea—and of course I understand. I had a busy household once myself. As long as it's all right with the others."

"Thanks, Mom," Ivy said. "I know you could have family suppers without us until June, but I'm selfish, and I don't want to miss them."

"Right, then. I'll call David and Laura and tell them. Oh, and good news—Amy found a job! The music store hired her as a full-time manager."

"I know; she texted me. I told her something would turn up!"

"God always does provide, doesn't He?"

"Do you want me to call Laura and tell her about family suppers?" Ivy asked.

"No, I'll call her. I need to have a talk with her anyway."

"Okay. Bye, Mom. Thanks for being flexible. Love you."

"I love you too, dear heart. Give my love to Nick and the children." Jane made kissing noises into the phone and hung it up, scribbling on the calendar at the same time.

She dialed again.

Laura's voice. "Hi, Mom. Is everything okay?"

"How did you know—?"

"Caller ID. It's my best friend."

"I thought Ivy was your best friend."

"Ha-ha. Ivy's my twin sister."

"Isn't that the same thing?"

Laura sighed into the phone. "Mom, as much as we would all like it to be, life is not *The Brady Bunch*. What's wrong?"

"What do you mean?"

"I mean, why are you calling me?"

"Something has to be wrong in order for me to call you?"

"No. No, you're right, Mother." Jane could tell that Laura was working at sounding patient, and this irked her.

"Nothing is wrong, as a matter of fact. At least, not with me or your father. It's *you* I'm worried about."

"Oh, Mom. I'm *fine*."

"We don't see much of you these days. You hardly ever come to Thursday dinners anymore."

"Well, it's kind of hard for me to get there on weeknights. I've told you I work late a lot of the time, and I do have to get up for work the next morning."

"I have good news for you, then. Ivy just called and asked if we could change family supper to Fridays this spring. She's taking a class on Thursday nights."

She heard Laura's hesitation. "I can't come this Friday."

"Oh?" Jane kept her tone light, but dread dropped into her stomach like a lead sinker. She had the odd sense of knowing what Laura was going to say before she said it. "What've you got planned for Friday?"

"A business trip. It's a weekend-long conference in Boston."

"And your boss is going with you?"

"*I'm* going with *him*. It's his business; I'm just the assistant."

"Isn't that a little hard on both of you? I mean, to have to work all week, then spend your weekend at a conference?"

"What are you insinuating?" There was a hard edge to Laura's voice, which Jane recognized well. She sounded thirteen years old again.

Jane took her time answering. She wanted to say, *Your boss is a married man and you have no right to be going off to Boston with him for the weekend on what I know perfectly well isn't a business trip.* She knew Laura, though, and understood from long experience that such a comment would only alienate her. She would cry that her mother was judging her, that the whole family did nothing but judge her, and that they would all obviously be happier if she just stayed away from them. Months of silence and absence would ensue while Laura punished her mother for speaking the truth until, inevitably, Jane would apologize just to keep the peace, and Laura would deign to come back into the family circle. So now, Jane only sighed and dared to say, "Just remember who you are, dear." Even that, she suspected, was pushing it.

"I never have any problem remembering who I am, thank you."

"We'll miss you on Friday. Hope to see you next time."

"Okay."

"I love you, Laura."

"Right."

"Good-bye." But Laura was no longer there.

Jane put the phone down and buried her face in her hands. *Lord, don't let her self-destruct.* She could not find the words to go on and was grateful that she did not need words. God had always heard her heart without them.

She felt Leander enter the room. He came to her and wrapped his arms around her from behind. "What's the matter, Janey-girl?"

"Laura. She's going away with Max for the weekend."

"Ohhhh."

"That girl is determined to do things that are bad for her. What is it about her, Leander? She's always been this way. The kind of boys she went out with in high school, the smoking pot, the sneaking out of the house . . . She's such a bright girl. So much wasted potential."

"You know, Tolkien said, 'Not all those who wander are lost.'"

"Malarkey," Jane snapped. "She's *lost*. Or headed that way in a big hurry."

Her husband let go of her and pulled out a pair of barstools. "Let's sit down." They sat. For several moments, he said nothing. He always thought carefully before he spoke. As a result, Leander was a man of few words, but what he did say was well worth listening to. "I think Laura has always been searching out God's grace," he said at last. "No, wait." He held up a hand when Jane tried to interrupt. "Let me finish. I know there's an element of selfishness to the things she does—a willfulness and a determination to have her own way, in spite of what God says is good for her. But give her a little credit, Janey. There's more to it."

Jane made no effort to hide her skepticism.

"Hear me out, now. It seems that Laura was never really happy as a member of this family, not like the other children were. She hated the rules and the restrictions; she broke them at every turn. Our faith always rubbed at her, like a collar that was too tight."

"Were we wrong to be strict with the kids? Maybe if we'd given Laura more freedom—"

"No." He shook his head decisively. "This is not our fault. It's something Laura has to work out between herself and God. She's testing His grace, to see if there are limits to it, and if so, what they are. I believe she's looking to see how far she can go and still be loved by a God she's never really believed is loving in the first place."

Jane bit her lip. "And how far *can* she go?"

"Only God knows that. But things may get worse for her before they get better."

Jane was quiet, tracing a pattern on the countertop before her. She dreaded what was ahead for Laura, for surely it could be nothing but heartache and disillusionment. At last she said, "Well, we'd better get on our knees, then."

"You're right. But let's do it in the living room. The carpet's easier on my old joints than this hardwood floor."

THE PHONE ON Laura's desk rang, an intraoffice number lighting up. She picked up the receiver. "Yes, sir?"

"Miss Darling, could you come into my office for a moment?"

"I'll be right there."

She hung up and groped in her desk for a lipstick, which she applied and blotted before standing. She smoothed down the front of her jacket, took a deep breath, and opened Max's door.

It was dark, the lights off and the blinds pulled tight against the winter sunshine. Her heart gave a leap of excitement, sending blood singing through her veins. She slid inside the office and closed the door behind her.

In the darkness, Max's arms went around her. He spoke directly into her ear, his hot, damp whisper stealing her breath. "I found that last business trip very *profitable*. It was . . . helpful to have my assistant along."

"I . . . I learned a lot," Laura managed, slipping her own arms around him.

"I was thinking it would be a good idea for me to check out the market for doors in Greece next. I'd need someone along to take notes for me. Think you could make it?"

She barely suppressed a shriek of excitement. *"Greece?"*

"A few days on one of the islands, just the two of us. How does that sound?"

"Oh, Max!"

"Next week, then?"

She let her kiss be her answer, and it was an eloquent one.

❧

On Thursday night, Ruby called Ivy to invite them to dinner on Saturday. "It's Tiffany's birthday," she reminded Ivy. "She'll be twenty-four. Kyle's throwing that little party for her on Friday night, but I made him promise to save the big day itself for family."

Ivy, who had not heard anything about Kyle's "little party," hung up in a sour mood. Over supper that night, she asked Nick about it.

He shrugged. "Nobody said anything to me. Most likely it's just a few of their friends."

"They'll probably stand around drinking Diet Cokes and

talking about everybody who wasn't invited," said Ivy, without much conviction.

"Right. So why would either of us want to go?"

"They'll order five-dollar pizzas from Little Caesars and the men will all watch a basketball game on TV."

"Ivy, don't go on about it. You wouldn't want to go if we *had* been invited."

She had to acknowledge the truth of this. Probably, if Kyle had invited them, she and Nick would have made up an excuse to avoid the party anyway. Yet there was something about not having been asked at all that stung. It was so much easier to be the one doing the rejecting than to be the one rejected, she thought crossly.

On Friday, she went to Stone Soup, her favorite artisan shop on High Street, to search out a gift for the family party. She came out with a small, hand-thrown pottery bowl in a shade of blue exactly the color of a robin's egg. Tiffany would probably hate it, but Ivy was not one to ever bypass affordable pottery, and this had been on the clearance shelf. As she got back into her car, she imagined the expression on Tiffany's face when she unwrapped it: a *what kind of birthday gift is this supposed to be?* expression. She thought of the beautiful little bowl being relegated to the bathroom closet, living out the next decades holding bobby pins and hair elastics and other anonymous bits of cultch, and she suddenly could not bear it. She turned the car around and drove all the way to Target in Quahog, where she found a pair of white pillar candles and a set of mass-produced resin stands painted to look like wood. Now *that* was a gift Tiffany would love.

Later, at home, she wrapped up the candles and candle stands and, with great satisfaction, placed the blue pottery bowl in the center of her own coffee table. "Happy birthday to me, Tiffany," she said aloud, suddenly not caring about Kyle and his birthday party anymore.

On Saturday morning, she made a salad because Ruby had asked her to bring one to dinner. Hammer, who was sitting at the table sorting LEGOs into piles, said, "Why you cooking supper so early? We just had breakfast."

"I'm making this to take to Ruby and Harry's tonight," she informed him. "We've been invited over there for dinner because it's Tiffany's birthday."

He eyed her. "Are them big kids gonna be there?"

"Connor and Britney? I imagine so. Why?"

"DeShaun and Jada ain't gonna like that," he said, shaking his head. "I better tell 'em." He slipped out of his chair and ran off to find his brother and sister.

Jada was practicing the violin, and a few seconds later Ivy heard the half-melodious scrapings stop. There was a moment of silence, followed by a very loud, very definite curse from the little girl.

Ivy choked back a snort of laughter. "Jada!" she shouted, forcing sternness into her voice. "Come out here, Miss Priss!"

Jada came, the miniature violin still in one hand, the bow in the other. "What?"

"I don't want to hear you saying swearwords, got it?"

"I *tried* to say it quiet."

Ivy bit her lip. "I mean, I don't want you saying it at *all*."

"*You* say it."

"I—well, only when I drop something, and not very often. It's a bad habit, and I don't want you doing it, do you hear me?"

"I hear," Jada said unrepentantly. "We ain't really gotta go to Ruby's house with them snotty white kids tonight, do we?"

"And what does their color have to do with anything?"

Jada shrugged. "They just white, is all."

"I spend half my life trying to get Nick's family to look past the color of *your* skin, Jada. Don't you be guilty of the same kind of prejudice."

"Fine. Them *snotty* kids, then."

Ivy briefly considered a grammar lecture, then discarded the idea, deciding they had covered enough corrective ground for one conversation. "In answer to your question, yes, Connor and Britney will be there."

"They won't talk to us." Jada set her violin and bow on the table and slumped into a chair, resting her chin on her hands. "They don't want us there. Nobody in that family wants us there."

Ivy put down her paring knife and came to sit at the table with the little girl. "I know. If it makes you feel better, they never want me there either."

"How come?"

"Well, unfortunately, the people in Nick's family have never learned how to look outside themselves and embrace the differences between people. They only like people who are exactly the same as them. So they don't appreciate people like you and me."

Jada eyed her. "You're not different than them."

"I am on the inside. You'd be surprised how different."

"How come they don't like things that are different?"

Ivy considered this. "You know, Jada, with most things in life, there isn't just one right way of doing or being. God made us all different, and mostly those differences are good ones, right? Different skin colors, different hair colors, different ideas, different ways of worshiping God. The differences between us make the world a better and more interesting place. For instance, wouldn't it be boring if everybody drove a red minivan just like ours?"

"I guess. I never thought about it."

"If everyone drove the same kind of car, think how hard it'd be to find ours in the grocery store parking lot. We'd come out with a cart full of bags, and there'd be just this *sea* of red minivans. We'd have to go around with our keys and try every single door to see which one they opened. It would take *hours*."

Jada giggled. "Days!"

"Maybe weeks," Ivy said. "All the frozen food would melt before we found the right car. So you can see how having lots of different cars makes the world a better place, at least in grocery store parking lots. It's like that with most things. But people like Ruby and Harry and their family, they get scared by differences because they think there's only one way to be right about everything. And if something's *different*, they think that means it's *wrong*. Even worse, they're afraid it may turn out to be *right*, which would mean that *they're* the ones who are wrong. Do you understand that?"

Jada reached across the table and toyed with one of Hammer's LEGOs. "I . . . think so."

"Well, just know that their problems with you are *their* problems, not yours. You and your brothers are beautiful, bright kids, and anyone would be crazy not to want to know you better. Not to want you as their very best friends." She put her arm around the girl's shoulders and squeezed. "I'm so glad you came into our family. I wouldn't trade you for a hundred Connors and Britneys."

Jada turned in her chair and slid both arms around Ivy's waist, burying her head in Ivy's shoulder. She said nothing, but they sat there like that for a long time, rocking back and forth a little, until Ivy kissed her on the top of her fuzzy head and said, "Now how about helping me finish this salad?"

∿

At Tiffany's birthday dinner, little Rebecca was the talk of the evening. Vincent set her bouncer seat on the table while they ate, and they all watched her blink at them. When she burst forth with a baby syllable, Angela swore she had said, "Ma!"

They were eating when Ruby said, "Well, Nick and Ivy, when are we going to get some grandchildren out of *you*?"

Ivy's fork froze halfway to her mouth. Although Ruby did not know the particulars of her infertility, Ivy had been clear with her on several occasions that she and Nick did not plan to have children of their own. She glanced across the table at Nick, but he would not meet her gaze. Nor, it seemed, was he going to be the one to answer his mother. With his eyes fixed on his plate, he took a mouthful of mashed potatoes.

She put her fork down. "To be honest, Nick and I have our hands full enough right now with our foster children."

Ruby looked at her blankly. "Well, yes, but they're not your *real* children. I mean, you're not going to keep them for*ever*. And they're hardly our *grand*children."

Ivy was grateful that the children were eating at a smaller table in the kitchen, with Connor and Britney. She could hear Jada's and Hammer's unbroken chatter and hoped it had covered Ruby's thoughtless comment. "I love those children as if they were my own," she said tightly, "and I would appreciate it if you would not say anything like that in front of them. *Ever.*"

After that, she was unable to eat another bite and could hardly speak for the rest of the evening. It was as if a heavy stone had settled into her throat and blocked all passage up or down. It also seemed to be keeping any tears at bay, and for this she was grateful. Needing to escape, she offered to wash the dishes by herself after supper. While she was doing it, Tiffany opened her birthday gifts in the living room, surrounded by the rest of the family.

Nick did not seek Ivy out the rest of the time they were there and was silent on the drive home.

Later, when they were propped up against their pillows, reading, Ivy found she could not make sense of the words on the page before her. She put her book down. "That was a cruel thing for your mother to say tonight."

Nick finished the sentence he was reading before looking up. "What was?"

"To say that Jada, Hammer, and DeShaun aren't our *real* children. That they're not going to live with us for*ever*." Ivy mimicked her mother-in-law's italics.

"Ivy . . . they're *not*."

"But they're . . . they'll be welcome here as long as they need to be, right?"

He turned his attention back to the page.

"Right, Nick? Answer me!"

He marked his place in the book and set it on the nightstand, then took off his glasses and folded them on top of it. Flattening his pillows, he lay back and gazed at the ceiling. "I don't know," he said finally. "I'm still thinking about that."

"You heard what Bailey said as well as I did: that we shouldn't get into this unless we were prepared for a longterm commitment. I thought you agreed to that!" Ivy heard the half-hysterical note in her voice but could not stop. "You can't think about just . . . just sending the kids on their way when you get tired of them. Do you know how much damage that kind of rejection and instability can do to a child?"

"I didn't agree to keep a child who was a thief and a prescription drug abuser, though, did I? That's more than I bargained for, and I reserve the right to change my mind now that we know about it."

"I'm not so sure DeShaun took those pills."

Nick snorted. "Since when?"

"I've . . . I've been thinking about it. He's had friends over . . ."

"You think those three kids walk on water."

"What I told your mother is true—I do love them as if they were my own. I guess you don't."

He looked at her baldly, not bothering to hide his indifference. "No, Ivy, I don't. I don't love them. I'm not going to lie and say I do."

She stared at him. "How can you be such a heartless man, Nick Mason?"

He turned his back to her, reached out, and switched off the light. In minutes, he was breathing deeply, even as Ivy sat up against her pillows, motionless in the dark. The heavy stone in her throat dissolved, spilling a flood of hot tears down her face. There was grief in the tears, and fear, but mostly there was a blinding, jagged rage toward Nick. The sharp edge of it cut through her, opening old scars with an intensity of pain that she could not bear . . . and leaving her husband unscathed, peacefully sleeping. The injustice was like a weight on her chest, nauseating her. Suffocating her.

She gathered her pillow and a spare blanket from the bottom of the bed and went to sleep on the couch.

❧

Laura rolled over onto her back amid the snarl of covers and stared at the pattern of late-morning sunlight on the ceiling.

Greece, it turned out, was not as warm as she had expected, although the marble-green waters of the Mediterranean endlessly unfurling themselves against the sand outside her window were a vast improvement over the coast of Maine in February. At home, the ocean was always the color of iron at this time of year, and just as cold. She and Max were planning to walk on the beach later today, and the clothes she had brought with her were not going to be nearly warm enough. She mentally cataloged the contents of her suitcase, readjusting her ideas of what she would wear. The periwinkle sweater set with her leather jacket over it, she decided. The sweater set was light, but it was cashmere and would keep her warmer than anything else she'd brought. If she added the yellow scarf—

Her reverie was interrupted by a knock at the door, followed by a muffled "Room service."

Max stuck his head around the door of the bathroom, his face half-covered in shaving cream. "Get that, will you?" he said with a jerk of his head.

Laura extricated herself from the sheets and reached for her robe. "Do you have any cash for a tip?"

"Top drawer of the nightstand."

"Just a minute," she called as the knock and announcement of "Room service" were repeated. She opened the drawer and found a two-euro coin within the pile of change there. Max's wallet lay next to the change, and as she nudged it out of the way, it fell open to a photograph. She hesitated, then picked it up and looked closely. It was a picture of Max and Carol and their two boys taken, if she was any judge, in Austria at Christmas. The four of them were holding ski poles, squinting into the sun, laughing, against the broad white flank of a mountain.

The stab of pain that went through her was nearly physical, so sharp it stole her breath. She had never expected that he would still carry a picture of his wife. Dropping the wallet back into the drawer as if it had burned her, she went to answer the door.

They ate at the room's tiny table, in front of a wide window overlooking the sea. It was a blustery day, and the wind whipped the water into ragged peaks of foam. A pair of walkers on the beach below bent their heads against the wind, clutching jackets around themselves.

"Max," she said, pouring him a second cup of coffee from the metal pot, "have you told Carol about us yet?"

His fork, dripping with egg yolk, froze halfway to his mouth. "What?"

"I was just wondering if you've told Carol about us yet and, if so, how she took it."

The fork hit his plate with a clatter that made her wince. "Are you *crazy*? What man tells his wife that he's sleeping with his secretary?"

She felt the blood leave her face. "Is that all this is to you? *Sleeping* together?"

"Well . . . having a relationship, then. Call it whatever you want. It's not the kind of thing you tell your wife."

Carefully, Laura put down the coffeepot. She felt suddenly brittle, afraid to move lest something inside her crumble. She arranged her hands in her lap and looked at him. "She's going to have to know about us sooner or later. Don't you think the sooner you tell her, the easier it will be for everyone? The boys especially."

He looked bewildered. "Why in the world does she have to know about us? That's the very thing I'm trying to avoid."

"At some point, you're going to have to divorce her, though. We can't be together like this forever." She gave a flick of her hand, a movement that took in the room, Greece, the whole illicit weekend.

"I—" He frowned. "What are you talking about?"

"I'm talking about you leaving Carol so we can get married. I love you, Max. I want to spend the rest of my life with you. I thought you felt the same about me." To her mortification, her voice squeaked at the end. She took a deep breath and willed herself to calm down. To not scare him.

"Ahhhh. I see." He smiled—that slow, warm smile she loved so much. Reaching across the table, he ran one finger down her cheek and brought it to rest on her lips. "Yes, that's something you and I need to talk about. But not here. Not now. I want it to be at just the right time and place. A special place. You deserve that, Laura."

A hard, frightened knot inside her began to loosen a little. "I want to be with you all the time, Max, not just during work hours and occasional weekends away. I hate that we have to say good-bye to each other at the end of every day. It isn't fair."

"I feel the same way." He tucked a strand of hair behind her ear with infinite tenderness. "You're so beautiful, Laura. Even first thing in the morning, you're the most beautiful woman I've ever seen."

The knot dissolved completely in a surge of joy. She

reached for his hand and smiled, blinking against the sting of tears. She had so much to be happy about.

❧

It did not occur to Ivy until red construction-paper hearts began to appear among the usual end-of-school-day clutter in Hammer's and Jada's backpacks that Valentine's Day was around the corner. She was not by nature a sentimental person, so celebrating this particular holiday had always been, for her and Nick, a pragmatic matter. The years they could afford to, they went out to dinner somewhere or to the movies or, in the early years of their marriage, both. The years they were more financially strapped, they did nothing. The same guidelines governed their decisions about whether or not to give one another gifts.

She broached the subject with him one night as they were reading in bed.

"Do you want to do anything for Valentine's Day this year? It's on a weekday, which means the restaurants shouldn't be too crowded, if you want to go out."

Nick looked up from the biography of Martin Luther that he was reading. "I have a deacons' meeting that night."

"Oh . . . well, we could celebrate another night. We've talked about trying that new Indian restaurant near the beach."

He shrugged. "It's just a greeting-card holiday, Ivy. We don't have to celebrate it just because Hallmark tells us we should."

She was stung by his indifference. "I didn't suggest it

because Hallmark said I should. I'd really like to do something with you."

His eyes were back on his book. "I don't think it's going to work out this year."

She didn't intend to say it, but the question was there. Had been simmering inside her for months now, maybe even years. "Why do you hate me so much, Nick?" The words fell from her mouth like a handful of heavy coins spilling onto a table. It was as though she were listening to someone else speaking. "What have I done to make such an enemy of you?" There was both relief and terror in having said it. She had stepped off a sort of precipice and could only wait to see what was at the bottom.

He looked up from his book. "I don't hate you." His voice held no conviction.

"All right then. It doesn't feel like you *love* me. It hasn't felt like that for a long time."

"Don't be ridiculous; you're my wife."

"No, there's something not right. You . . ." She groped for the right word. "You resent me."

He said nothing.

"Why, Nick?"

There was a long silence, which she made no effort to break. At last he said, looking straight ahead at the wall, "You know why."

And then she did. Maybe she always had. "Because of . . . what happened in college?"

"Let's call it what it was, Ivy. It didn't just *happen*. It was something you *did*. You had an abortion."

Ivy felt like she'd been slapped. She had thought that was over and done with. Forgiven. Buried. "That's not fair, Nick."

"Not fair to *you* or to me?"

"It happened before you and I even started dating. And you knew about it before we got married. You promised me then that it was all in the past."

"But I didn't know back then that the doctor screwed it up and you would never be able to have a baby because of it, did I? It was three years before we figured that out."

So that was it—the thing that lay between them all the time, the wedge that was always sinking deeper, pushing them further apart. "You're punishing me," she said slowly, recognizing the truth only as she said it. "You withhold approval, affection, your friendship. . . . You're trying to make me suffer because I can't have children."

He snapped his book shut. "You're not the only one who can't have children. You can't have children; therefore *I* can't have children. And all because of the choice you made. When we decided to get married, I had no idea that your choice to have an abortion meant I would never be a father. *You* did this to us. I shouldn't have to forgive you for that."

He might as well have physically struck her, knocking the wind out of her.

It had all been the biggest mistake of her life. She had been a sophomore in college and had known the man— a boy, really; a frat boy—only two months. She had loved him. She had always been too quick to love everybody.

Ivy had grown up in the church. And the church, even in the twenty-first century, still had clear guidelines about sex. All her life, she had been taught that it was for marriage. Only for marriage. In high school, she had known she was an anomaly for clinging to this idea, yet she never questioned it. She had truly thought it was God's best plan for people. In college, when she fell in love for the first time, she still believed it. You waited. And then when you were married, you were faithful to your spouse forever. It was as simple and as difficult as that. But . . .

And there was the crux of the problem, of course. The *but*. Saying *but* to God had never yet ended happily for anyone.

But . . . at the time, love had seemed bigger than even God's best plan. The boy and her love for him were a drug like nothing she had ever experienced in her life. She was consumed with it. She rationalized away everything she believed and ended up pregnant. And then, having already cut so many of the moorings that had always anchored her, she found herself adrift, unsure anymore of what was truth and what were just old-fashioned values she had been fed. Values that seemed irrelevant in light of the way the real world did things.

Through all of it, though, two things were as clear as the mirror on her wall: The boy, who was a premed major with a bright future ahead of him, was not having any part of a baby. And she could not—could *never*—go back to Copper Cove and face everyone she loved with evidence of this moral failure. She would hurt and disappoint so many people. They would think so little of her. So she had the abortion.

At the end of the semester, she had gone home and taken a summer job at Parchments and had simply never gone back to college. She told no one what she had done. That fall, she became reacquainted with Nick Mason at Grace Chapel's college and career group and had been drawn to his seriousness and integrity. If a store clerk undercharged him for something, Nick would point out the error and insist on paying. He never ran red lights, even in the middle of the night with no traffic and no police car in sight. The first time he kissed her, he asked her permission first. She loved that he was honorable and that he made her feel safe.

That first year back home, her heart had been scored with lines of grief, weakened, bowed under at the first sign of any kind of pressure. For months, she struggled simply not to shatter. She woke every morning reminding herself to keep making the effort to breathe. She found a counselor who helped her learn to forgive herself. Only then did she have the courage to tell Nick. They were discussing marriage by then, and she wanted him to know everything about her. He had been shocked at first, then saddened. But he had supported her in her quest to heal. He had assured her that he held nothing against her, and she had believed him.

Now Ivy was appalled that she had not understood before this the depths of his pain. "I had no idea you felt this way," she said.

Nick would not look at her.

"You're right." Her voice was small as shame engulfed her all over again. "What I did before you were part of my life robbed you of the chance to ever have children of your own. I am so sorry for that, Nick. Forgive me." She laid a hand on his arm. "Please, Nick. I'm asking for your forgiveness."

Not a muscle in his face moved.

She *felt* small. "Nick? Please?"

His voice was flat. "I've tried. I thought I'd succeeded. Then every time some other happy couple announces they're having a baby, when I see a family laughing together in the mall or the park, when my mother asks me if I'm ever going to give her grandchildren, I blame you all over again." He turned his head away. "I've tried, but I can't. There's just . . . no forgiveness in me."

She felt the blood leave her head. "So you *do* hate me?"

"Sometimes." His voice cracked and he cleared his throat. "If we're being completely honest here, I guess I do sometimes. Yes."

Ivy was very conscious of the clock ticking in the hallway. *God, what do I say?*

"What's done is done. It's always been done. There's no use talking about it anymore." Nick switched off his bedside lamp with a sharp click and turned away from her in the darkness. Within minutes his breathing evened out, and she realized he was asleep.

Ivy lay down and stared at the ceiling, numb. Shocked and yet not. In the darkness, she turned her face to look at her husband, this stranger. She watched the outline of his shoulders rise and fall. Rise and fall. In the rhythm of his impassive breathing, she felt the end of hope. Sensed it wither and die quietly somewhere inside her. And then the spark of something else was kindled. The spark of hating him back. It felt good. It felt like power. Power was something she had never felt in her marriage before. But this—this was heat, light, energy. It was *something*. She would *not* be punished by him forever. That was not a marriage. That was no way to live.

Watching Nick breathe, she fanned the spark and let it flare up. Rise and fall . . . Rise and fall . . .

❧

DeShaun slid a spatula under the edge of the sandwich in the frying pan and lifted one corner to look. It was brown and crisp, just right. With a practiced motion, he flipped it over and heard the satisfying sizzle of butter meeting hot cast iron. He was trying out something new today. He had discovered a loaf of cinnamon raisin bread in the bread drawer after Ivy's shopping trip yesterday and had been unsure of what it was, how it was to be eaten. She had come into the kitchen in time to see him looking the package over and had urged him, "Try it. It makes great toast with a little butter on it or, better yet, with cream cheese."

He still wasn't sure how he felt about raisins mixed in with his food, but he had dropped two slices of the bread into the toaster, with her smiling over his shoulder, coaching him. A little afraid, he had spread cream cheese over one of the slices and, even more afraid of disappointing Ivy, had squeezed his eyes shut and bitten into it.

And he had discovered heaven.

Immediately, he had known what he must try. It had come to him as a fully formed thought, requiring no effort on his part at all. Now, alone in the kitchen because he was nervous that the experiment would fail and he didn't want anyone around to witness such a thing, he had spread a slice of raisin bread with cream cheese, topped it with a thin layer of grape jelly for extra sweetness and a second slice of bread. He had buttered the outsides of the sandwich and toasted it in the cast-iron pan he favored for making regular grilled cheese. He wasn't sure you were supposed to make a grilled cheese sandwich with cream cheese. Sure, the package said *cheese*, but it wasn't exactly cheese, the way the orange, plastic-wrapped slices of American cheese were. It was more like . . . dip. He had a furtive, shameful feeling that it wouldn't turn out, yet he felt compelled to try anyway. So far, it looked all right.

When he judged the sandwich ready, DeShaun slid it onto a plate and sat at the kitchen table, where the glass of chocolate milk he had mixed earlier stood ready and waiting. He was about to bite into it when he remembered the stove, got up and turned off the burner under the pan, and sat down again.

The first bite seared his tongue. The cream cheese was incredibly hot, and he spent half a minute whoofing and panting around a mouthful that he could not taste, just so he could swallow it. He got it down at last. The second time he was more careful, taking only a small bite. It was like taking a mouthful of happiness. Sweet and creamy, warm and satisfying. And mingled somewhere in there, among the increasingly large mouthfuls of the shrinking sandwich, there was a sense of pride that he, DeShaun Johnson, had made this recipe up himself. It had come from his own head; he had thought it up and figured out how to do it, and it had worked. It was his own, in a way that nothing else had ever been before.

He finished the sandwich and made another. He was toasting the third when Jada wandered in.

"Whatcha doin'?"

"Hey, Jada, wanna try the world's best, ultra-gourmet, one-of-a-kind, super grilled cheese sandwich? I'm the only person in this world that knows the secret recipe." He flipped the sandwich in the pan with a little flourish.

She looked impressed. "Sure."

He made her leave the sandwich alone for a few minutes after it came out of the pan. He didn't want her first taste to be spoiled by a blistered tongue.

When she bit into it, her eyes grew wide. "It tastes like cheesecake!" Jada had tried cheesecake for the first time on Valentine's Day, when Ivy had made it for supper. That was all they had eaten that night: cheesecake. Nick had been at some meeting, and the four of them had sat around the table talking and eating slice after slice. Ivy had eaten three by herself. DeShaun had eaten five.

Thinking of that happy night made him feel a strange kind of despair. He knew Ivy and Nick were still all upset about the Vicodin. He caught Ivy giving him a worried look sometimes, and Nick—well, Nick was always kind of a cold fish. You couldn't ever tell what he was thinking. You'd think he just about couldn't stand you, and then he'd come home one night with a new Xbox game for you. DeShaun could see why they blamed him for taking the pills. He only hoped they wouldn't be so mad that they kicked him out of the house. He liked it here, most of the time. He didn't like washing dishes every third night or having Ivy check his homework and ground him from playing Xbox if it wasn't all done. But he liked to see Jada learning to play the violin and Hammer getting a chance to play basketball in the rec league. The kid was really good. He liked that the house was neat and clean and kind of . . . peaceful feeling. He liked having breakfast in the morning, supper at night, and lunch money to spend in the school cafeteria in between. Already, he had outgrown the new school clothes Ivy had bought him in August; they'd had to go shopping again last month.

He looked at Jada, sitting at the table in a clean shirt, her hair shining and good-smelling, her face covered in cream cheese, and so happy, and he thought a prayer. *God, I'm not too good at praying, like they tell you in this white church here. I'm not even sure You're real. But if You are . . . please let us stay. Let them not be too mad about the pills. Let us stay here, for Hammer and for Jada. And okay, maybe a little bit for me. But mostly for them. Amen.*

CHAPTER
13

MARCH CAME IN like a lamb, as it did every year, and the weather promised spring. The air softened, the days lengthened, and the streets were wet with the runoff of melting snowbanks. On the library lawn, crocuses poked their bright-purple and yellow heads through the rough, brown grass and opened their faces to the sun. But experienced Mainers knew not to let their guard down. They might temporarily exchange winter coats for Windbreakers and begin to plan their vegetable gardens on paper, but nobody was foolish enough to actually put away the winter boots and shovels or to begin, this early on, to unearth totes of summer clothes from attics and basements. March still had to go out like a lion. That was a law as immutable as the one about death and taxes.

They were invited to Jessica's house in Rockport one night for a family meal of steak and lobster, and that morning, Ivy woke early and realized she was nervous.

"I'm just not up for exposing the kids to the unkindness of Nick's family," she confessed to Esme at work. "I mean, they would probably be fine—somehow they always are—but today *I* couldn't handle all the thoughtlessness and—" she searched for the right word—"neglect."

"So let them stay home."

"Nick will worry that it looks rude."

Esme rolled her eyes. "And we wouldn't want to be rude to the rudest people in New England."

Ivy smiled. "It's always tempting, but I mostly try to rise above it. It's not a battle you can win with that family."

"Oh, let them stay home this once. Tell your sister-in-law you're doing it for her sake, so she won't have to buy lobster and steaks for them."

"I'm pretty sure she was planning on feeding the kids hot dogs anyway."

But on her break, she called Jessica with this very excuse, which Jessica accepted with no pretense of arguing that Hammer, Jada, and DeShaun be included.

The only sticky part, Ivy realized, was it would mean leaving the children at home alone, with DeShaun in charge, and she was not entirely sure she could trust him. Did he have drugs in his possession? Three or four times, she had searched his room when he had been at school and never found a thing that wasn't supposed to be there. Was there anything even slightly illicit in the house that he could possibly get into? She tried to consult Nick on the matter, but he was distant and cool and seemed not to want to talk about it. In the end, she locked a bottle of cooking sherry in a suitcase under her bed, flushed a very old prescription for sleeping pills down the toilet, and left DeShaun in charge, praying for the entire four hours they were away that he would be trustworthy. That his brother and sister would be safe in his care.

When they got home, DeShaun was on the couch, playing video games.

"How'd it go?" Ivy asked him.

"Good." His eyes did not leave the screen.

"Where are the kids?"

"In bed."

She looked at the clock. Well, he had done that right anyway.

"Did you warm up the pizza for supper, like I said?"

"Nah. I made 'em grilled cheese."

She went upstairs and found the younger ones still awake.

"We had these really cool sandwiches for supper," Jada told her, sitting up and hugging her knees. "Me and DeShaun had bleu cheese with pears in it on those leftover croissants. Did you know you could make grilled cheese on croissants? Hammer doesn't like bleu cheese, so DeShaun made him a different kind. Why do they call it bleu cheese, Ivy, when it's really white?"

In Hammer's room, Ivy asked him, "What did you have for supper?"

"Ham and cheese."

"Was it good?"

"The best. DeShaun put mustard on it. He's a really great cook."

So it would seem, Ivy thought with a smile. *So it would seem.*

❧

A storm on the ides of March dropped eighteen inches of snow on the town, transforming the bare, corncob-colored lawns and fields into cloudscapes of brilliant, glittering white. For the most part, people were philosophical about it: winter had never yet lasted forever. Besides, the storm had started in New Hampshire and moved north, and some of the towns below Portland had gotten twenty-eight inches. Things could have been worse.

Copper Cove's children, who had an unexpected day off from school, were delighted, at least until parents handed them shovels and snow rakes and sent them to go clear the driveways and roofs.

Jane finished washing the breakfast dishes and went to the computer in the family room to check her e-mail. Now and then, she glanced up through the window, where she could see Amy, dressed in a green sweater and a red hat, shoveling a path up the front walk.

From: nursesharon1@clevelandnet.com
To: momof5@maine.cc.com

Jane,

I have bad news. Well, bad for me—maybe good for you, ha-ha. I'm sorry to
say I won't be out for my usual visit this summer. The first time I've missed
it in over 30 years!!! My blood pressure's too high, and the doc says I have
to stay put. I can't tell you how disappointed I am to miss you and Leander
and the kids (especially that handsome godson of mine). I know it's a long
shot, but if you or any of your crew happened to have a reason to come to
Ohio—maybe picking Sephy up at college or something—I'd love to have
you visit me.

XOXO,
Sharon

Sharon DeMille was Jane's best friend and former college
roommate. She lived in Cleveland, and what she wrote was
true: she hadn't missed her yearly foray to Maine since before
David was born. Sharon had never married, was David's god-
mother and "Aunt Sharon" to all the Darling children. She
was family.

Jane felt a piercing sense of disappointment. Sharon was
closer to Jane than her own sister, Ellen, who lived less than
two hours away in Freeport but never visited and rarely
returned Jane's e-mails and phone calls. Jane would miss
Sharon desperately if she could not visit.

She found Leander in his workshop, fiddling with a tiny

screw on the spit valve of a trombone. The shop was a familiar, comforting place, cluttered with band instruments waiting for repairs, the air redolent with the smells of brass polish and valve oil. "Almost finished?" she asked, leaning against the workbench to watch.

"I have some felt pads to replace on a clarinet, and then I'm through. What's up?"

She told him about the e-mail.

He looked up. "Disappointed?"

"Very. I look forward to her visits all year long."

"Why not do what she says and go see her this year? It would be good for both of you."

"Oh, Leander, it's such a long trip."

"Take Amy. She can share the driving with you."

Jane brightened. "I could do that. And I could ask Ivy to go too. She could use the time away from the children. She's been looking worn-out lately. We could go in May, when Sephy's classes are over, and she could meet us at Sharon's. Maybe Laura could join us too. It'll be a real girls' weekend!"

"Now you're talking." He set the trombone aside and picked up the clarinet. "And either Ivy or Amy could make the trip home with Sephy. Split the driving with *her*."

Jane's head was already spinning with plans. "It would be so much fun," she said. "Thank you for suggesting it, my love." She kissed her husband on the cheek. "I'm going to call Sharon right now." She turned to go.

"Is that all the thanks I get?" he called after her. "A little peck on the cheek?"

She put her head back through the door. "I'll put some thought into it and see what I can come up with later."

"I should hope so," he said, bending to his task.

Laura parked her silver Saab in a discreet corner of the Hannaford parking lot, got out, and locked it. Pulling a pair of sunglasses from her pocket and tucking her bright hair under a knit hat, she considered her reflection in the car window. With her coat collar pulled up high around her face, she would be unrecognizable to anyone who didn't look too closely. She pocketed her keys and began to walk.

It was a beautiful day for some outdoor exercise. The snow from Friday's storm was melting fast, and the scent of spring was in the air. Half a mile from the Hannaford lot, Laura turned left into a subdivision called Presidential Heights. The "heights" part was no joke, she thought as her legs began to burn with the steep climb. She walked on briskly, growing too warm as the road wound steadily upward. At last the houses began—mammoth, modern, two-story structures with elaborate windows, ells going off in all directions, and discreet, wooded lawns. She scanned the housefronts for number 35 and, glimpsing it from a distance, slowed her pace to a stroll. She reached the top of the incline, and the road flattened out, but her heart continued to pound in her ears.

And then it leaped. The double garage doors of number 35 were open wide, showing both cars parked inside.

A woman in a shapeless coat stood near the end of the driveway, sorting through a handful of mail. What would happen, Laura suddenly thought, if Carol did recognize her? On impulse, she pulled off her hat and sunglasses and stuffed them into her pocket. Laura was on the same side of the road as number 35, and as she passed by, the woman looked up. They nodded briefly at each other.

The woman did a double take and said, "Laura?"

She stopped. "Yes?" Polite. A little puzzled.

"Laura Darling! Well, hello there! Imagine seeing you out here."

Laura allowed recognition to break over her face slowly. "Oh, my goodness, Carol! I didn't realize it was you! Is this your house?"

"Yes, we moved here two years ago, when the development was built." She tucked the mail under her arm. "What in the world are you doing in this neighborhood?"

"Oh, I come here to walk all the time," Laura lied. "This hill gives me the best workout in town. What a beautiful day."

"Do you have time for a cup of coffee? I'd love to hear how the family's doing. I haven't seen your mother in an age. She missed the last library board meeting, and I missed the one before that, and I think before *that* it was the holidays."

Laura couldn't believe her sheer good luck. Surely it was a sign that things were going to work out. Yet she hesitated. Max's car was in the garage. If he were to come into the room while she was drinking coffee with his wife . . . But wouldn't it be a good thing for him to see them side by side in his home? Old, dumpy Carol with her windblown hair, half the brassy-red color grown out of it, beside his young, chic administrative assistant? The contrast would be immediate and obvious. It would help prod him in the right direction.

"I don't want to hold you up," Carol was saying, "but it would be wonderful to catch up a little."

Optimism won out over caution, and Laura feigned a glance at her watch. "I guess I could come in for a few minutes."

The kitchen was wide and modern, all shining steel appliances and butter-colored tile, with fake ferns cascading down from the tops of dropped cupboards. Through an open archway, she could see a wooden mantelpiece covered with sports trophies. She remembered that Max and Carol's two sons played nearly every sport offered at the local high school.

While Carol made them coffee, Laura sat at the counter and answered questions about the Darling family until she wanted to scream with tension. By the time they had each finished their first cup, she had been there half an hour, and there had been no sign of Max.

She had just politely refused a second cup and was gathering up her hat and gloves when he walked in. Laura saw him before Carol did. He was halfway through the kitchen when he recognized her, stopped as though he had walked into a wall, and stared, all the color draining from his face.

"Hello, Max," she said brightly. "I was out for some exercise this morning and ran into Carol. She invited me in for coffee."

"Laura." His voice had a dry, papery rasp.

"Oh, there you are, honey," said Carol, turning and holding out a hand to him. "Come have a cup of coffee with us."

"Ah—" He seemed to be fighting for breath, stranded there in the middle of the floor, unable to move his legs.

Laura began to think this had not been such a great idea. Swiftly, she stood up. "No really, Carol, I can't stay. I have to be at my mom's in fifteen minutes. I'll tell her you said hi and make sure she gives you a call." Her own voice sounded metallic and unreal in her ears, as though she were speaking inside a tin can, like that telephone game they had played as kids. "Bye, Max. See you Monday. You have a beautiful home here."

Carol walked her to the door and she escaped, half-jogging back down the hill to her car in a dreamlike haze. She was dizzy with adrenaline, disembodied. She couldn't believe her own nerve. By the time she reached her car, she was still so overwrought that she went into the store and bought a bottle of vodka, which she hid under the seat until she was far away from the parking lot.

On a deserted stretch of road, she pulled over, opened the bottle, and took a long swallow. It tasted like window cleaner and she shuddered as it went down, but she immediately felt calmer. She had not been intending to go to her parents' house at all, but now she thought it might be a good idea. Carol might ask her mother about it later. Still, Laura wasn't thrilled by the prospect of facing her parents and probably Amy, all of whom had the worst opinion of her these days.

In the side pocket of her door was half a bottle of spring water. She unscrewed the cap and poured this out the window, then half-filled the bottle with vodka. She replaced the cap and tucked the plastic bottle into the bottom of her capacious handbag, then put the large vodka bottle back under the driver's seat. It was pathetic, she thought, that the Darlings were the kind of people you couldn't face without chemical help, but that's the way it was.

❧

The work at Parchments wasn't strenuous even on a busy day, and Ivy hardly ever felt that she deserved a break by the time one rolled around. Esme insisted, however.

"It's the law," she would say, herding Ivy off the floor and into the back room. "If you don't disappear for fifteen minutes every four hours, they'll lock me up for employee abuse. Go get a coffee or something. Read a book."

"I've been reading books for the last hour and a half!" Ivy would wail, and Esme would assure her that becoming more knowledgeable about the books was all part of the job, and besides, didn't she make up for it during the summer months, when the town was just crawling with tourists looking to buy everything they could find that was written by a Maine author?

"Think of all the Stephen King you've read in the cause of this job," Esme would remind her.

"I haven't minded that part. I like Tabitha better, though—"

"Well . . . Linda Greenlaw, then. All that stuff about swordfishing and lobstering. Who could like that?"

"I can't put her books down," Ivy would confess.

"Carolyn Chute? *The Beans of Egypt, Maine*?"

"Okay, I suppose reading that one earned me fifteen minutes."

They had this conversation, or variations on it, nearly every week. Lately, however, Ivy had not had to be pressed to take a break. She felt chronically moody, contemplative, as though a heavy fog had settled on her shoulders. She could feel its weight sapping her energy, leaving her listless and grateful for someone, anyone, who would tell her what to do.

In this frame of mind, she had dragged herself to the bookstore's café to spend her allotted quarter hour one morning when she checked her phone messages and found that a stranger had called.

"Mrs. Darling," the voice mail ran, "this is Sheila, the guidance counselor at the high school, calling to remind you that we're offering driver's ed classes to all students fifteen and older this quarter. It's just five classes, and they're held after school. I notice your foster son DeShaun Johnson isn't registered yet. We can still squeeze him into a class if you like. Just give me a call."

She didn't know what to do. Surely driving was a privilege and not a right, and Nick would say that DeShaun had not earned that privilege. Had, in fact, betrayed their trust in a fundamental way. Besides, if DeShaun was using drugs, would he even be safe behind the wheel? That was another consideration altogether. Yet they had no proof that he was using drugs, or indeed any evidence to suggest it. It was very likely that he had just been curious. Experimenting. And she remembered the excitement of getting her own permit, then her license. The freedom of it. The responsibility. DeShaun, in his short life, had known little of excitement or freedom or positive responsibility. And in spite of what he had done in taking the pills, at his heart she sensed a thread of goodness. Of something she could trust. If not now, then one day.

She called the guidance counselor back and registered him for the class, then spent the rest of the afternoon at work praying she would not live to regret her decision.

CHAPTER

14

Ivy's pottery class started the first week in April, and on Tuesday night, walking into the art classroom of the adult education building in Quahog, she felt instantly at home. The air was warm with the odors of damp clay, oil paint, plaster dust, and chalk, every tabletop overlaid with a thick layer of paint smears. Canvases and odd sculptures of scrap metal lined three walls. A life-size pterodactyl made of chicken wire and milk straws hung from the ceiling in one corner.

At the front of the room, four potter's wheels had been set up. A man in clay-streaked jeans bent over one of them, adjusting something. As Ivy hesitated in the doorway of the room, he straightened and pushed a long strand of hair off his forehead. "Come on in."

She obeyed and saw that there were already three other students there besides this man, who was obviously the teacher. He shifted a block of clay from his right hand to his left, wiped his hand on his jeans, and held it out to her. "Wow, pink hair," he said. "Very cool. I'm Jonathon. And you must be Ivy because everyone else is already here."

"Oh, sorry, am I late? I usually am."

"Not at all. Have a seat, and we'll get started in just a minute."

She sat at a table beside a middle-aged woman whose long, flyaway hair was caught up in a clip on top of her head and looked none too clean. The woman glanced quickly at Ivy, then looked away. Next to this woman sat a college-age girl who was completely black-and-white: improbable black hair, black clothes, black fingernails and lipstick, and snow-white skin. The only dab of color on her entire person came from a set of violet letters tattooed across the knuckles of her left hand. The girl was drumming these fingers idly on the tabletop, and Ivy had to squint to see what the letters said.

The girl caught her looking and stopped drumming. "Whadd'r you looking at?"

The hostile tone startled Ivy, but she chose not to quail. She had always reasoned that people who did extreme things to their bodies did them because they wanted you to look. In fact, were *inviting* you to look. She nodded at the girl's hand. "I'm trying to read the letters on your fingers. What do they say?"

The girl held up her fingers so Ivy could read the Old

English letters: *Z-O-E*. Deliberately, the girl dropped her index and ring fingers, leaving her middle one sticking up.

Okay then. "Nice to meet you, Zoe," Ivy said. The middle-aged woman with the dirty hair looked frightened.

Ivy turned her back on Zoe's attitude to observe the fourth student—or, she supposed, he was actually the third one and she, as the last to arrive, was really the fourth—a twentysomething man who looked as though he might have accidentally wandered into the pottery class on the way to medical school. He nodded at her. "I'm James."

"Ivy." She offered her hand, and they shook. Might as well finish the job, she thought. "What's your name?" she asked the greasy woman.

"Madeline."

"Nice to meet you, Madeline." The woman offered a tentative smile, and Ivy saw that she had probably been beautiful a couple or three decades ago.

From the front of the room, Jonathon said, "We're all here, so why don't we get started." He lounged against a spare desk with his legs stretched out before him. He had the high cheekbones and bronzy skin of someone with Native American blood, and his black hair was tied carelessly back in a leather thong. "I'm Jonathon Blackfeather," he said. "I own the Native Feather Studio in Camden. There are a couple of brochures over there, if you're interested in taking a look at some of my work." He nodded at the windowsill, where a small littering of pamphlets shared the space with half a dozen clay pots and bowls. "I've also brought a few of my pieces to use in demonstrating the techniques we'll be talking about and practicing, so if you want to take a closer look at any of them, feel free. I just ask that you be careful with them, as you would if you were in my shop. In my last class, a student dropped one and shattered it, and that was the end of a two-hundred-dollar vase."

A two-hundred-dollar *vase?* Ivy silently vowed not to touch anything on the windowsill.

He started by demonstrating how a potter's wheel worked and walking them through the steps of throwing a basic pot. They each sat at a wheel then and tried it themselves. It was harder than it looked, but Ivy found that once she caught on to the rhythm of the wheel and got past the unpleasant feeling of having clay caked under her fingernails, there was something soothing, almost mesmerizing, about the process. Or there would have been, had she not needed to stop and start the wheel so often. She could get the lip of her bowl only so high before one side of it collapsed.

She was concentrating on her fourth attempt when Jonathon appeared at her side.

"What am I doing wrong?" she asked. "It keeps caving in on me."

"Too much pressure, I think. Try for a lighter touch. Here." His hands hovered over hers. "Do you mind?"

"No, go ahead, please. I'm hopeless on my own."

"Nobody's hopeless—Ivy, isn't it?" He placed his hands over hers and bent his head close.

"Right," she said, her throat suddenly dry.

"It's just a matter of getting a feel for it. Start your wheel now."

He guided her fingers gently as the wheel turned, pulling them back when she would have pressed harder. "Use more of your palms here," and then, "Now just with your thumbs. Can you feel it?"

She could feel it. Good heavens, could she ever feel it. Ivy nodded, afraid that if she tried to speak, her voice would come out in an incomprehensible croak.

He took his hands away, and the backs of her fingers tingled where his had rested. "Great job. See? Not hopeless at all. You've turned out a very respectable pot."

Her response to him shocked her. Never, not once in the six years she had been married to Nick, had she even noticed another man, let alone gone breathless and mute with attraction in the presence of one. The flames of romance between herself and Nick had died almost immediately after their wedding day, as Nick, having conquered and attained her, lost all interest in continuing to court her. Her own adoration, lavish and expressive in the beginning, had been so constantly strained with the effort of trying to please him, so routinely kicked down by a hundred thousand little rejections, that it had deflated like a balloon with a slow leak. Loving him had become an act of her will, an exercise in keeping her chin above water in a relationship that threatened every minute to pull her under and drown her.

She had not thought herself capable of infatuation anymore, had assumed that things like butterflies in stomachs and pounding pulses didn't happen to married people. Now, with a simple touch of fingers on fingers, she began to think she might have been wrong about that. She sneaked a glance at Jonathon, who was bent over Zoe's wheel. As if he felt her eyes on him, he turned his head and winked at her. Her heart missed a beat and she felt her cheeks go pink.

Heaven help her, she might be in trouble.

❧

Laura sat at her desk, staring at her computer screen without seeing it, and making plans. For two weeks, Max had hardly spoken to her. He had not answered her phone calls, e-mails, or texts. He had gone out of town without her two weekends in a row. In fact, since the Saturday he had found Laura in his kitchen, having coffee with his wife, Max had practically run for the cover of his office every time he'd seen her coming. His behavior simultaneously cut Laura's heart to the quick and infuriated her. She had tried to ride it out, reasoning that Max was just being cautious and that things would surely settle back to normal between the two of them.

Then this afternoon, as she'd been on her way back from lunch, she had seen him coming down the hall toward her. They had been the only two people in the corridor. Most of the offices were still empty for the lunch hour. And Max, catching sight of her, had *turned around and walked the other way.* She had recognized it as the instinctive action of a hunted creature and been stunned by it. Stunned and saddened and hurt. She did not know what was going on in his head, but she knew they could not go on like this.

Shortly before five o'clock, while Max was walking his last

client to the front door, Laura slipped inside his office. She turned off all the lights but one, undid one more button on her blouse, and sat on the sofa, crossing her long legs to show them off to their best advantage. Max loved her legs. She was there when he returned and waited until he had closed the door before she spoke.

"Max."

He started and put a hand to his heart. "Laura! Are you trying to scare a man to death?"

She unfolded herself from the couch without hurry and went to him. "I didn't mean to scare you. It's just . . . I *miss* you." She let a hint of a pout creep into her voice. "You've been avoiding me."

"Laura," he hissed, "we can't meet like this. Not right now." He shot a nervous glance at the office door. "There are still people out there."

"That's never bothered you before." She reached out to run a finger around the edge of his collar. "In fact, I remember you saying once—"

"Never mind what I said. You have to *go*."

She dropped her hand. "I'm not going anywhere until we've talked."

He sighed and, reaching over to the wall, flipped on all the lights. "All right, but make it fast. Troy has a tennis match I'm supposed to be at. And button up your shirt."

Laura obeyed, feeling small and humiliated. "Why are you avoiding me?"

"Because you showed up at *my house*, Laura. You talked to *my wife*. Are you crazy?"

"I'm not crazy," she said peevishly. "I just happened to be walking by that day, and Carol invited me in."

"Yeah, well, you know what it seemed like to me? It seemed like maybe, just a little bit, you might have been *stalking* me. And that makes me nervous."

"Don't be an idiot, Max. I was just walking by. Anyway, it only makes you nervous because you haven't told her about us yet." Laura shrugged. "So tell her."

He stared at her. "I'm not telling her about us."

"You can't hide it from her forever."

"Actually, Laura, yes. I can."

It was her turn to stare at him. "But . . . but when you leave her, when you tell her you want a divorce—"

"I'm not *leaving* my *wife*."

If he had slapped her in the face, he could not have stunned her more effectively. *"What?"*

"I said I'm not leaving Carol and the boys."

She was outraged. "You said you *loved* me. You promised me we would be *together*."

He shrugged. "We both said a lot of things. And we *were* together. For a while."

"You filthy liar! You *user*."

Silence hung between them for a few moments, and Laura's mind ricocheted, touching and abandoning every possibility, every potential avenue of fixing this.

He said, "I think you should clean out your desk."

"You're not firing me."

"I'd prefer not to have to. In fact, I'll do you a favor: I'll give you a ten-thousand-dollar bonus if you'll resign, effective today."

"You're getting *rid* of me?"

"Call it whatever you like. It'll be easier for both of us, though, if you go without a fuss."

"*No.* I'm not going *without a fuss.* In fact—in fact, I'm going to tell Carol about us." Laura kept her voice hard so that she would not break, would not dissolve into tears.

"You don't want to do that, Laura."

"I'm pretty sure I do."

He gripped her arm above the elbow, hard. "Then I'll have to press charges against you."

"For what?"

"For embezzling from the company."

The blood drained from her head, and she felt behind herself for something, any surface that would hold her up. She found the edge of his desk and slumped hard against it. He came with her, not letting go of her arm. "I *never*—" she gasped.

"I could make it look like you did. I could do that very easily."

"What . . . ?" Her throat was dry, and she had to try twice before the words would come out. "What do you want from me, Max?"

"I want you to go away quietly, to leave this company and make no trouble. I'll give you a good professional reference. I can't force you to move out of town, but I would strongly suggest that you go somewhere far away from here. It would be best if you and I never saw each other again."

She stared at him, her face hot, her hands cold, the rest of her numb with a sense that she was trapped inside a bad dream. She felt sick. Leave her job and her life here in Copper Cove? She did not want to; she wanted everything to stay as it was. She flung the question at him. "How many women have you sent away before me?"

"I'll need a letter of resignation and a list of passwords to your files before you go."

"How many, Max?"

"I want you gone within the hour."

She wrenched her arm from his grasp and straightened. "I'll leave them on your desk. You can mail me that bonus." She waited, but he did not say anything to stop her, and there was nothing else to do but to walk away. "I'd better have it within the week," she threw back over her shoulder.

Seething, Laura went straight to the copy room, where she found a box large enough to hold the personal contents of her desk. When she got back, Max was gone. His office door was locked, and the key was missing from her top desk drawer, where she always kept it. In twenty minutes, she had packed her things, and in fifteen more, had printed a letter of resignation and the list of passwords and slipped them under his door. She turned out the lights and went to her car, where she groped under the passenger's seat for the water bottle that did not contain water, which she now always kept there, and drank from it until she was sure she could make the drive home without crumbling to ashes along the way.

Driver's ed was over. DeShaun had a learner's permit. They pulled out of the driveway in the Volvo, Nick in the passenger seat and DeShaun at the wheel.

"Signal," said Nick.

"Oh yeah." DeShaun switched on his blinker and sat, watching traffic. "After that white car?" he asked.

"That's fine."

The white car passed, and DeShaun turned right onto the main road.

"You can go a little faster here; there's not much traffic," Nick said. His head jerked back, then forward again as DeShaun punched the accelerator and the Volvo's engine roared. *"Not—!"*

"Sorry," said the boy, taking his foot from the gas pedal altogether.

Nick rubbed the back of his neck. "Just a little gas at a time. Ease down on it—"

DeShaun punched the pedal again. Again, Nick's head jerked.

"Sorry."

By the time they reached the center of town, DeShaun had more or less gotten the hang of keeping the car at an even speed on a straight stretch of road. "You have a stop sign ahead," Nick reminded him. "Start to slow down now. Slow *down.* Down! The *brake,* DeShaun—*stop!*" Nick jammed both his own feet ineffectually against the floorboards of the passenger side and squeezed his eyes shut.

With a shuddering jolt and a sickening squeal of tires, the Volvo stopped, inches from a red Civic hurtling by on the cross street. Nick was flung forward and clotheslined by the seat belt strap. He raised his head just in time to see the terrified face of the old man driving the Civic as he passed.

They sat there for several moments as Nick rubbed his throat and his heartbeat slowed to normal. He looked sideways at DeShaun. He was just about the whitest black person Nick had ever seen.

"Sorry," DeShaun managed at last. "I hit the gas instead of the brake."

"Yeah." Nick's voice was none too steady.

"Should I keep going?"

Nick didn't know what else to do. The boy had to learn somehow. In typical Ivy fashion, his wife had signed their foster son up for driver's ed without consulting Nick, then flatly refused to do DeShaun's practice hours with him.

"I guess so," he said. As DeShaun looked both ways and crept out into the intersection, Nick passed a hand over his face. Didn't most parents get to ease into the teenage years? They got to teach their kids the simple things first, like how to walk and talk and eat with a spoon. They didn't have to dive in feetfirst with driving lessons during their first year of parenthood. He didn't remember signing up to risk his life like this.

The car jerked again, and again DeShaun muttered, "Sorry." A dull ache was beginning at Nick's temples. As he reached up to massage them, the car swerved hard to the right. DeShaun overcorrected and veered wildly left.

On top of it all, it looked like car sickness was going to

be part of the bargain. Nick stifled a moan and clenched his jaw. No, he had not signed up for this kind of thing at all.

∿

"Laura? Where are you? It's family supper tonight. You said you were coming." Amy frowned into the phone as Ivy, Jane, and Jada sat at the kitchen table, looking on. "You sound terrible. Did I wake you up?" Pause. "Come on, Laura. You've missed two out of three suppers all winter, and I *reminded* you of this one." She rolled her eyes at her audience. "So? Get off the couch, grab a cup of coffee at Tim Hortons, and haul yourself over here. We're waiting." She hung up the phone and addressed the anxious women. "She forgot and fell asleep on the couch. She'll be here in twenty minutes."

Twenty-seven minutes later, Laura's Saab pulled into the driveway. Ivy, who had been watching for her out the living room window, answered the door and stared at her sister. "You look terrible."

"Thanks, so do you."

"No, seriously. Your eyes are all bloodshot and puffy. You've been crying. What happened?"

"I quit my job." Laura pushed past her into the entryway. "Don't ask me any questions."

"Don't ask you any questions about what?" Amy said as Laura swept into the kitchen, followed by Ivy. "Wow, Laura, you look like you've been dragged through a hedge backward."

"It's really wonderful," Laura said with frosty disdain, "to show up at the family home and find myself surrounded by such support and comfort."

Jane reached out and patted her daughter's arm. "Sit down, honey, and don't pay any attention to them. Is everything all right?"

Laura sat. "I quit my job on Monday. It's been a rough week. So yes, I have been crying, and no, I don't feel my best. Excuse me for living."

"Why did you quit your job?" Only Amy dared to ask.

"I don't want to talk about it. I had personal reasons, and believe me, it was no hardship to be done at that place. I'm ready to move on."

The silence rang through the kitchen until Ivy ventured, "Does this have anything to do with your boss?"

"Excuse me?"

In retrospect, Ivy would realize that the ice in Laura's voice should have been a warning to back off, but she was so used to the old days, when they had talked about everything, and she had been so slow to grasp the meaning of the changes she had seen in Laura, that she rushed ahead tactlessly.

"Does this have anything to do with you sort of . . . liking Max?"

A moment of silence, then, "I do not *sort of like* Max."

"You went away to Boston with him and then to Greece."

"Those were *business* trips."

More silence. Then, "Really?"

Laura exploded. "You know what your problem is, Ivy? You know what the problem is with every one of you? You think it's your right and calling to judge the whole world!

You've looked down on me all my life. It's always been 'Ivy the perfect' and 'Laura the problem child.' Ivy, the saint who takes in foster children, and Laura, the sinner who *supposedly* has an affair with her boss." Her face had turned a hectic red, and she was breathing hard. They looked at her in shock.

"You *always* assume the worst of me. And Ivy does everything she can to elbow herself into position of family favorite. As long as *you're* happy—" she spat this in Ivy's direction—"it doesn't matter what they think of *me*. Well, I'm done being the family joke."

Ivy looked around at the faces of her family. Her mother and Amy had gone pale. Jada looked terrified. "Laura," Ivy said, reaching out a hand, "be reasonable. Nothing you're saying is true. I have never felt—"

Laura jerked away. "Right," she said coldly. "You've *never felt*. I know what I've observed my entire life. I'm tired of your superiority and self-righteousness, and I'm done putting up with it."

"Laura, please, let's talk about this." Her mother's voice was tearful. "We're *family*."

"Right, Mom. We're the enmeshed, dysfunctional, codependent Darling *family*. Only most families, in case you've never noticed, stay out of their adult children's business. They don't demand that they still come home for dinner twice a month for the rest of their lives. Has it ever occurred to you that maybe that's not healthy? Why don't you ask Nick how he feels about our *family*? I notice he never comes around, if he can help it." Her face was a remote and haughty mask. "I need some distance. From all of you."

Laura picked up her handbag from the counter, where she'd dropped it, and stalked from the kitchen.

They waited for the sound of the front door slamming and the tires chirping in the driveway before any of them dared to look at each other, and to exhale.

It was little Jada who spoke first. "How come Aunt Laura was drunk?"

"She wasn't drunk, honey. She was angry." Ivy spoke absently, her mind still reeling with Laura's accusations.

"O-oh. Okay."

Amy, more astute than her older sister at that moment, said, "What makes you think she was drunk, Jada?"

"Um." Jada looked uncertainly from Amy to Ivy. "Can I say, Ivy?"

Ivy and Amy exchanged a glance. "Of course, Jada. Say anything you want. You won't get in trouble. What makes you think Aunt Laura was drunk?"

"Because that's the way my mom talks when she's drunk. And Aunt Laura had on perfume, but you can't cover up that smell all the way."

"What smell, honey?"

Jada looked at all of them in surprise. As if it were the most obvious thing in the world. "Vodka." When no one answered her, tears welled up in her eyes. "I don't know," she whispered. "Maybe it was gin." Then she ran into the pantry and hid behind Jane's aprons, which hung there on a hook, while the others sat at the kitchen table in openmouthed astonishment.

15

IVY HAD SOMETHING on her mind, and she waited until a commercial break to make her move. "Nick," she said when the Sunday afternoon coverage of some golf match in Florida was interrupted by an ad for a family-size pickup truck, "Mom and Amy are going to Ohio to visit Aunt Sharon for a few days, and I'd like to go with them."

She could tell Nick's mind was only half on what she was saying. "Okay. Do we have any ice cream?"

"There's some vanilla and some mint chocolate chip left, I think. So . . . the trip to Ohio? I told you about it a few weeks ago."

"Oh, right. When is it?"

"We'd all drive out together Thursday and start home on Sunday."

"I don't think I can get the time off." His response was so automatic and predictable that Ivy had to fight down an intense surge of irritation.

"Actually, you're not invited. It's a girls' weekend. Sephy's going to meet us out there. I'll be gone from Thursday to Monday night."

"Would you take the kids?"

"Um, *no*, they have school."

"So . . ." She had his attention for the first time. "You're saying it'd be just me and them."

"That's right."

"Oh."

"Well?"

"And your mom wouldn't be home?"

"No, Nick. She thought she'd go along to visit her old college friend. That's the whole point of the trip." Ivy didn't bother trying to keep the sarcasm from her voice.

"And my mother . . ."

". . . isn't going to be any help with the kids. So yes, it's just you and the children for five days. But," she added sweetly, "I'll alert their caseworker and be sure you have a number handy in case you need emergency respite care to come in and take over."

"I'd still have to take time off work."

"No, actually. The kids do pretty well at getting them-selves up and ready for school in the mornings. I'll leave meals in the freezer, and DeShaun can take care of defrosting and cooking them. All you really have to do is be present within the four walls of your own home for five evenings."

He shot her a sideways glance and seemed to see that she was not really asking him. She was *telling* him. "Oh, all right," he mumbled.

She felt his relief when the golf match came back on.

❧

Nick woke at 2 a.m. to the sound of someone moaning his name. "Nick. Ni-i-i-i-ck!" There had been the impression of a ghostly figure floating beside his bed, accompanied by a very strong smell of vomit.

He'd groped for his glasses on the bedside table. Once he found them, the vague ghost materialized into Jada.

"I puked in my bed," she whimpered.

"Oh . . . oh no." He rallied himself in time to remember to ask, "Are you okay?" although what he was really thinking was *Why me, God? Why the only time of the year that Ivy's away?*

"I don't feel good."

"Did you . . . did you really throw up *in* the bed?"

"All over it."

"Oh. Okay. Okay." Rapidly, he assessed her. The white nightgown was clinging to her, soaked and vile-smelling. "Ah . . . let's . . . let's get you into the tub, and while you clean up, I'll, um . . . fix your bed." He was scrambling out of bed as he spoke, reaching for his robe and slippers, trying not to gag on the stench. He herded Jada into the bathroom and flipped on the light, which revealed her nightdress to be caked with a thick layer of something that did not bear thinking about. "Wait. Wait here." He started to leave, then turned to the forlorn little figure standing on the bath mat. "If you need to throw up again, do it there." He pointed to the toilet, turned on the hot water, stoppered the tub, and left. In the kitchen, he found an industrial-strength trash bag and brought it back to the bathroom.

"Okay, take off your nightgown and put it in here. Then climb into the tub and wash up. I'll be back in ten minutes." He left her the trash bag and went out, pausing at the door to say, "You okay? Are you going to throw up again?"

Standing there shaking, Jada tried to simultaneously nod and shake her head, and Nick spoke more softly. "You're going to be okay. I'm just going to clean up your bed." She nodded mutely.

Her bedroom smelled to high heaven, and thankful that it was a balmy night, he threw open the windows and stripped off the sheets and pillowcases, wishing for gloves but not sure where Ivy might keep such a thing, if they were even in the house. He bundled the chunk-strewn linens into a pile in the hallway and examined the blankets, which all seemed, mercifully, to have been spared.

A visit to the linen closet on the first floor yielded clean sheets, but when he got back to Jada's room, they turned out to be too big for her bed. Back downstairs he went and searched the shelves, shaking out each sheet until he found a set that looked the right size. He dashed back up and pulled on the fitted sheet, then lay the flat sheet over that, wedging it in as best he could at the bottom. The pillows seemed to be too big for their cases, but he got them stuffed in, then remembered that his mother used to lay an old towel over the pillow when he was sick. It was supposed to save the sheets. Even now, at the age of thirty-two, when he hadn't thrown up for more than twenty years, Nick could remember the clean, stiff feel of the old purple towel under his cheek. It was one of the comforting, reassuring things about being sick, that towel. He didn't know why, but it was.

Another search of the linen closet turned up an oldish-looking towel, and he tucked this in over Jada's pillow, then closed the windows. The room was chilly now, but at least it smelled better. Gathering up the pile of soiled sheets and the mattress pad, he trekked down to the bathroom and knocked on the door.

"Jada?" he called tentatively. "Are you okay? You're not sick again, are you?"

"I'm all done" came the pitiful reply, and gingerly, Nick pushed the door open. To his relief, she was sitting on the edge of the tub, wrapped in a big towel, her hair damp and falling around her face in frizzy tendrils.

He had forgotten to bring down a clean nightdress for her, but he helped her up the stairs, then found one in the top drawer of her dresser, among the underwear and socks. "Here, put this on," he said, turning his back until it was accomplished. He ushered her miserable, shivering form into the newly made bed, then realized he should have a bowl ready, in case she should do it again.

"Wait," he instructed her, "don't throw up yet." Another dash downstairs and a quick search of the cupboards turned up Ivy's biggest mixing bowl, and he brought it to Jada, confident that it would hold anything she sent its way, provided she aimed right. "Now," he said, when she had settled sleepily against the towel-covered pillow, "if you have to be sick again, try to call me first. If you can't do that, aim for the bowl. If you can't make the bowl, at least try for the towel."

"Okay," she mumbled, almost instantly asleep.

Nick trudged downstairs and stuffed the sheets into the trash bag along with the dirty nightdress. He drained and swilled out the bathtub and arrived back upstairs to hear the unmistakable sounds of retching coming from Jada's room.

"Wait!" he cried and bounded in, just in time to see her leaning over the side of the bed. She had had the foresight to aim for the bowl, but since the bowl was three feet below her on the floor, the walls and carpet were splattered with foul-smelling muck. She finished just as he reached the bedside and leaned over weakly, staring at him with huge, hollow eyes.

"I'm sorry," she whispered.

"It's okay," he whispered back, and taking the edge of the towel from her pillow, he wiped her clammy forehead and then her mouth.

She lay down again and fell asleep at once.

Nick cleaned it up, with a bucket of hot water and Lysol and half a roll of paper towels, which he added to the nearly full trash bag. After that, he couldn't think of anything to do but lie down next to her on the double bed, with the bowl on the bedside table next to him, and hope he would hear her in time to avert another catastrophe. His gamble paid off. Jada threw up twice more before dawn, and each time, he heard her in time to catch it in the big mixing bowl.

When the sky was light and the birds were in full cry outside the windows and she had not vomited in two hours, he felt it was safe to leave her. He showered and threw the trash bag of sheets and nightdress into the garage, then emptied his cleaning bucket from the night before into the bathtub and scrubbed the whole thing out, feeling inexpressibly weary. After that, he thought he should check on Jada again, and he got there not a moment too soon. She had found the bowl herself and was dry heaving into it. There was nothing he could do but sit beside her and rub her back until she finished and lay back, miserable and exhausted, to sleep again.

Watching the slow rise and fall of her shoulders, it occurred to Nick that today was Saturday. At least he wasn't missing work for this.

He tried calling Ivy but got her voice mail. No doubt she'd forgotten her charging cord and her phone was dead. He hung up without leaving a message. For a moment, he debated trying to reach her through Amy's number but decided no, if his wife couldn't be bothered to keep her phone charged, he would leave her out of the equation altogether. He called his sister Jessica instead and asked her what to do about Jada.

"Once she goes about four hours without throwing up, you can give her a little ginger ale," Jessica advised him. "You don't want her to get dehydrated. If she keeps that down, she can have some toast or saltine crackers. Later, some chicken noodle soup. Bananas, rice, applesauce, apple juice, Jell-O— only bland foods. And let her sleep as much as she wants."

Nick was writing as fast as he could with one hand and searching the refrigerator with the other. "Okay, all I have here is Diet Sprite. Is that okay?"

"No, it has to be regular soda. She needs the sugar."

"I thought sugar was bad for kids."

Jessica sighed. "Not in this case. And since it sounds like you'll be making a trip to the store, you might want to try some Gatorade with her. It'll help replace her electrolytes."

"Soda . . . Gatorade . . . soup . . . electrolytes," Nick muttered, scribbling it all down. "Does it have to be homemade soup, or can it be from a can?"

"Canned soup is fine. After she stops vomiting, try to get her to drink four ounces of fluid every hour. Soup counts."

"How much is four ounces?"

"Half a cup."

Nick's head was reeling with information. "How do you know all this stuff? Is there a website or something?"

Jessica laughed. "I know it because I'm a mother. Good luck. Call again if you need anything."

He tucked a sheet onto the couch and moved Jada downstairs with her bowl, where DeShaun could keep an eye on her while he ran to the grocery store. He left them watching cartoons and drove to Hannaford, where he bought a case of Canada Dry ginger ale, another of Campbell's chicken noodle soup, and one of Gatorade in assorted flavors. He consulted his list and added four quarts of applesauce, two boxes of saltines, three loaves of bread, and a bunch of bananas to the cart. There were microwavable cups of rice, but the only ones in stock were curry flavored. Jessica hadn't said anything about curry. He balked at the boxed rice, having no idea how to cook it, and left it on the shelves but discovered that Jell-O came premade in little cups. He cleaned out the shelf of these, hoping sixty-four of them would be enough to see him through whatever was ahead.

At home, Jada was sleeping and DeShaun said she had not been sick again. Hammer, who had been playing with his Matchbox cars on the living room floor, came into the kitchen to help Nick unpack the groceries. "I'm hungry," he said. "Can I have some Gatorade?"

"That's sick people food. How about some soup and crackers?" Nick suggested.

Hammer wrinkled his nose doubtfully. "Pancakes would be better."

Nick was inclined to agree. "Unfortunately, I don't know how to make pancakes. But I think Ivy left us plenty of cereal."

DeShaun, who had wandered in on the tail end of this exchange, said, "I could maybe make us some grilled cheese."

"Yeah!" said Hammer. "I want a grilled cheese!"

Nick started to say, "For breakfast?" but stopped himself. Why not? "Will you make me some too?"

"Sure. You want one or two?"

It had been a long night. "Two."

DeShaun pulled open a drawer and took out a spatula, giving it a practiced flip in the air and catching it neatly. "Coming right up," he said.

Afterward, they sat at the table, licking their fingers.

"You're an artist," Nick said in disbelief. "Those were the best grilled cheese sandwiches I've ever had."

DeShaun ducked his head. "That first one was pears and Gorgonzola on wheat berry bread. The other one was cheddar, tomato, red onion, and Dijon mustard on sourdough."

"I think I died and went to heaven."

"That's nothing. Later on, if you want, I can make you goat cheese and chutney on a croissant. That's my favorite."

"Do we have all that stuff in the refrigerator?"

"Sure. Ivy keeps me supplied."

"What was my sammich, DeShaun?" Hammer was not to be left out of the conversation.

"Grilled ham and American cheese on Wonder Bread."

"That's my favorite."

"I know, buddy. That's why I made it for you."

⁕

Jada spent the day alternately napping and watching Veggie Tales movies on the couch, and Nick kept her supplied with Jell-O and ginger ale and watched along with her, a little embarrassed to admit how absorbing he found the stories that starred singing cucumbers, squashes, and peas. Hammer climbed onto his lap to watch too, and after a lunch of the promised goat cheese and chutney sandwiches, they fell asleep together and didn't wake up again until suppertime.

Sometime in the night, Nick awoke to find that he was not alone in his bed. He squinted in the darkness and saw

Hammer fast asleep on Ivy's pillow. He sighed, rolled over, and went back to sleep without even looking at the clock.

They skipped church on Sunday since Nick wasn't sure how long you were supposed to keep a sick child from going out in public. Jada, however, declared that she felt just fine, and to Nick's relief, she and Hammer went into the backyard to play after breakfast (grilled Swiss and turkey on rye) while he and DeShaun watched a baseball game on ESPN. They ate grilled cheese sandwiches twice more that day, from DeShaun's seemingly endless repertoire.

In the evening, Nick eyed the kitchen, which was a shambles, and said, "Ivy comes home tomorrow. We need to get this place cleaned up."

He organized them so that DeShaun put all the food away, wiped counters, and swept the floor; Jada and Hammer dried and put away dishes while he himself took care of the washing. By the time it was done, he was longing for bed. Jada informed him in no uncertain terms, however, that *nobody* went to bed at seven thirty.

"What do you usually do on Sunday night, then?" he asked her, genuinely interested in the answer.

"We watch the Sunday night movie on the Disney Channel."

Nick watched it with them. It was a musical about a group of high school students who were auditioning for a play, rife with all the relational drama that was supposed to go along with being a teenager. Nick could not have vouched for any of that, as he had been a fairly straightforward kid back in the day: an athlete, a good student who got along with his family, involved in youth group, only mildly and occasionally interested in girls. He found the story line mindless, the music mediocre, and observed Jada's obvious infatuation with the characters uneasily. Ivy had mentioned that the little girl seemed to have some musical talent, but as he looked from her to the television screen and back again, he thought that there was "talent" and then there was *talent*. He considered ordering her to turn off the TV and go practice her violin instead but was astute enough to realize that such an idea might be a recipe for mutiny.

Instead he waited it out, then per the long list of instructions left by Ivy, ordered Hammer into the bathtub. He was supposed to have done this Saturday night but had forgotten all about it. He was again informed—being informed by a ten-year-old girl was rapidly becoming one of his least favorite modes of communication—that he was supposed to read them a bedtime story. They each got to pick one. Hammer chose a library book about Sesame Street characters, and Jada chose a horse book with multiple chapters, of which Nick firmly agreed to read only one.

After what seemed an eternity of toothbrushing, water drinking, and bathroom going, he at last tucked the younger children into bed and said good night to DeShaun with a sense of gratitude that tomorrow was a regular workday and school day, a return to normalcy, and that by bedtime tomorrow night, Ivy would be home. A weekend of parenting hadn't turned out to be so bad, but it was without a doubt the most exhausting thing he had ever done.

CHAPTER

16

By now in her pottery class, Ivy was capable of turning out basic pots and bowls that she was actually proud of and was learning about glazing, painting, and firing. She was no longer bothered by the feel of clay under her fingernails and had come to like Madeline and James and even the prickly Zoe.

Madeline had an enviable gift for mixing colors. She was a painter, she told them shyly one evening, and her watercolor landscapes sold well in the tourist shops along the beach in the summer. Ivy, on hearing this, went home and examined the little watercolor that Nick had given her on her birthday, discovering that Madeline was the artist. She brought the painting to the next class, told Madeline how much she treasured it, and made a friend for life.

On the next-to-last week of class, as she was centering a block of clay on her wheel, Jonathon stopped by and said, "Feel like grabbing a cup of coffee somewhere after class?"

Ivy looked at him, too astonished to speak. Had he just asked her on a *date*? She blurted the first thing that came to mind. "I'm married."

"I figured," he said easily, nodding at her left hand, where her wedding ring gleamed dully under a fine film of clay. "I meant it as just a friendly thing. I thought I'd ask Madeline, too."

"Oh. Okay, sure." Ivy wanted to crawl under the potter's wheel and hide. What an idiot she was.

"So . . . maybe the Rasta Coffeehouse? I have to stay after class to clean up, but we could all just meet there. Say, at nine o'clock?"

"Great. Nine o'clock." She did not add, *It's a date*, but she could not stop the thought from flitting through her head all the same.

Madeline, however, could not join them. "I have to pick my grandson up on the way home," she said. "He always sleeps over at my house on Tuesdays."

Ivy got into her car after class and sat there, debating whether or not to meet Jonathon by herself. Something about it seemed not quite right. Would Nick mind her going out for coffee with a good-looking man? She tried reversing the circumstances in her mind. How would she feel if Nick went out for coffee with an attractive coworker on his way home from the bank? She examined her gut reaction to such a scenario and discovered that she wouldn't mind at all. She would not be jealous; she would not really care. She might even be glad.

She drove to the coffeehouse.

The newspaper was open in front of him, but Nick could not concentrate on the words. Something was going on with Ivy. She had talked about her pottery teacher all through dinner. Last night she had not come home from her class until well after eleven o'clock. He was pretty sure she had been losing weight.

Beyond the edge of the newspaper, a flash of blue caught his eye. It was a little pottery bowl on the coffee table. Something he had seen before but never paid attention to. He put the paper down and stared at it, overcome by the intense impression that there was an intruder in his house. Yet it was only a small blue bowl. He felt suddenly cold, although the air through the open window was warm and heavy with the scent of early summer.

For Nick's birthday, Ivy made him a coffee mug in pottery class and renewed his membership to the racquet and fitness club.

"What?" he teased when he opened his presents. "No book of poetry this year?"

She did not smile. "It took me long enough, but I finally got the hint."

He felt like he had kicked a dog that had only been trying to lick his hand.

Mid-June meant the end of the school year, and DeShaun found a job washing dishes at the Silver Star Diner. Ivy and Nick bought him a bike so he could get back and forth on his own, and suddenly it seemed that he worked so many evenings and weekends that they never saw him anymore. Jada and Hammer enrolled in day camp, and Ivy's pottery class ended.

"I'd really like to keep learning," she said to Nick after her last night of class, when she was showing him the things she had made. "Jonathon gives lessons at his studio, and he's offered me a discount."

"Why did he offer you a discount?"

"How should I know? Because I'm a former student?"

"Just you?" The hostility in his tone did and didn't surprise her. Mostly, it made her feel tired.

"Just me what?"

"Did he offer just you a discount, or does he give it to all his students?"

"Uh . . . I'm not sure. To all his students, I think."

"But these would be private lessons?"

"Yes. Do you mind if I spend the money? It wouldn't be expensive."

"I guess I'd feel better if they weren't *private* lessons."

"He doesn't offer group lessons," she said.

Nick was silent, running a finger around the glazed lip of a bright-yellow bowl. At last, he said, "Do what you want."

"Thanks," Ivy said coldly. "I will."

Ivy was trying to take a rare nap when, under the pillow, her phone vibrated. Irritated, she fished it out and looked at the caller ID. Jessica. Great—just what she needed right now. But Jessica was notoriously persistent, so it was either deal with her now or deal with her later. The nap was probably a lost cause anyway.

She sat up and answered. "Hello?"

"Oh, Ivy. Jessica here. How *are* you?"

"Fine, thanks. How are you?"

"I'm well." Jessica cleared her throat and got right to the point. "As you know, it's Mumma and Daddy's thirty-fifth anniversary in two weeks."

Was it? "I'd forgotten, although I must have it written down around here somewhere," said Ivy, knowing it would never have occurred to her to write it down.

"Yes, well," Jessica went on, "the point is that we're thinking of doing something special for them."

"Oh. Special like . . . ?"

"Like a big family dinner at the Four Winds hotel in Quahog."

In the ensuing silence, Ivy tried to imagine such an evening.

Ruby would wear an enormous corsage on her best dress and introduce each of her children to the waiters. She would monopolize Nick all evening, talking loudly so that everyone in the dining room would see that she was the guest of honor. Harry would be dour and silent, understanding nothing on the menu and disliking everything he ate. Jessica, Angela, and Tiffany would huddle together at one end of the table and whisper. When one had to get up to use the bathroom, all three of them would go together, like a pack of middle school girls. Connor and Britney would be as charmless as ever. Ivy and her children would sit in silence all evening, invisible and ignored by her in-laws. Nick's family didn't drink, so there would be no hope of a glass of wine to help the evening along, and she was pretty sure none of them would even conceive of dancing to the five-piece combo the hotel was locally famous for. If there were a more miserable way to spend an evening and several hundred dollars, Ivy did not know what it might be.

A way out occurred to her. "Ummm . . . I don't mean to be insensitive here, but isn't the big celebration usually saved for the fortieth anniversary?"

"Yes, that's true, Ivy. I hear what you're saying. Only, shouldn't every year of marriage be a cause for celebration? And besides—" Jessica gave a delicate cough—"with Daddy's health being what it is, we can't take it for granted that he'll be here in five years to celebrate their fortieth."

This was the first Ivy had heard of her father-in-law having any health problems. "What's wrong with Harry?"

"It's his cholesterol. At his last appointment, the doctor put him on one of those, oh, what do you call them . . . ?

Statins. I googled them. They're *terrible.* The side effects alone can kill you. Who knows what kind of fight is ahead for Daddy. That's why we thought, let's celebrate now. Let's live every day like it's our last."

Ivy could think of nothing to say to this piece of utter nonsense. She only knew that she could not bear the thought of such an evening. If Nick wanted to go, let him do it without her and the children. She had no illusions that they would be missed in any way. "Sorry, I can't make it," she said.

"What's that?"

"I said sorry, I can't make it to your parents' anniversary dinner."

"What? Why not?"

"I'm doing something really important that day. It was already scheduled in advance."

"But . . . but I haven't even *told* you the date yet."

Ivy forced herself to sound very serious. "So what's the date?"

"The twenty-eighth."

"Oh, darn. That's just the date I have that important thing planned. Sorry, Jessica. I'm sure you'll have a great time without me. I'll mention it to Nick and see if he wants to go. Bye now."

Ivy pushed End and sat looking at her phone. She had given up hoping that she would ever belong in Nick's family. She was no longer going to bend over backward to try. She didn't know how Nick would feel about it, nor did she care. She only knew it felt good to stand up for herself. She should have done it years ago.

Ivy was hanging a cooking pot on its hook as Nick came into the kitchen.

"What are you doing?" he asked. He felt nervous, as though he were about to ask a girl on a date for the first time.

She draped her damp dish towel over the oven door. "Just finishing up the dishes."

"Feel like playing rummy?"

"I have a pottery lesson in half an hour."

"Oh." A silence lay between them that Ivy did not break. She turned back to the sink, rinsed out the dishcloth, and began to wipe the counters.

Nick cleared his throat. "Is dinner still on at your parents' tomorrow night?"

"Yes, as usual."

"I thought I'd go along."

"Don't you have a deacons' meeting or something?"

"I can skip it just this once."

She shrugged. "If that's what you want to do."

"What time do we leave?"

"Five thirty-ish."

"Fine. I'll make sure I'm home from work in time."

"Okay. Whatever you want." She stepped around him to wipe the stove top, then rinsed out her cloth again and hung it up to dry. "I need to get ready for my class now."

He put a hand on her arm. "Ivy, are you okay?"

The smile she gave him was brittle. "Actually, I've never been better."

He watched her leave the room with the sensation that a piece of formerly solid ground had begun to shift beneath his feet.

❧

It was close to midnight and Nick was still awake. A copy of *Courting Your Wife for Life* lay open across his chest. He wondered where Ivy was. Technically, he didn't wonder where she *was*, since she had told him she was going to a pottery lesson. One of those private lessons with What's-his-name Indianfeather at his studio. But what was she *doing* out this late?

Ivy had changed, and it scared Nick. All their married life, she had lavished attention on him, sought him out, tried eagerly to please him. But that part of her had vanished now. She was cool and distant. Polite as a stranger.

Okay, maybe he *had* been trying, all these years, to make her pay because she could not give him children. But he hadn't meant to push her away; it was just . . .

He thought hard, trying to dig deep and figure out what it was he had been aiming for. It was just that if somebody hurt you, and you could make that person hurt just a little bit too, you expected that it would somehow lessen your own pain. Only it never seemed to really work that way. The bottom line was he had always known at some gut level just how he was treating her, and why. He had taken matters of punishment and vindication into his own hands. And he had badly overplayed it.

Now, in a stroke of human nature as old as the Garden of Eden, Nick found that the thing he could not have was the very thing he wanted most. He wanted his wife to love him. To seek him out and pay attention to him like she'd always done. He wanted a relationship with her. But Ivy, it seemed, did not care anymore.

Who made pots and vases at eleven thirty at night anyway?

The clock showed just after midnight, but Ivy was not asleep. Her mind kept playing over the evening's pottery lesson with Jonathon. It had not actually turned out to be a lesson. In fact, they had not done any work with clay at all. They had intended to, but when Ivy got to the studio, which was really just a small addition on the side of the old farmhouse he lived in, he had offered her coffee, and she had accepted.

They had sat at the counter in his kitchen and, mesmerized by the play of summer evening light across the wide pine boards, she had begun to tell him about everything. She talked about her decaying marriage, about her past bad decisions and her husband who refused to forgive her for them. She told him about the foster children she was growing so attached to that she had begun to wonder how in the world she would ever give them up if the day came when she had to. She told him about Laura, who had once been her closest friend but now seemed to blame her for everything that had gone wrong in her life.

Jonathon had listened. Not just with his ears; he had

watched her face, really heard and seen what she was saying. Then he told her about his divorce from the wife who had run away with another man, about the daughter who lived somewhere in California but wanted nothing to do with him. She listened in her turn, at times with tears in her eyes. They talked for three hours, without once touching each other, yet Ivy had never before felt so close to a man. When she said she had to get home, he refused to let her pay for the scheduled lesson time. "This was just an evening between friends," he said.

Ivy left him, feeling, for the first time in many years, not lonely in the company of a man.

She lay awake, preoccupied with all they had said and not said, but mostly feeling astonishment and gratification and profound relief at finding herself simply appreciated. She had forgotten that she had anything to offer that was worthy of appreciation—had become convinced, in fact, that she did not. At the same time, she felt the danger in the direction she was headed. It was a danger that both frightened and beckoned her. At last, she moved out to the couch with *The History of Love*, hoping to read her way through to daylight and a sense of perspective.

She was still reading when the ringing of the phone startled her. She glanced at the display—2:58 in the morning. And it was Amy.

"Why are you calling this late?" she asked without bothering to say hello.

"I'm at the emergency room in Quahog," Amy said, just as abruptly. "It's Laura. Someone found her unconscious in the courtyard of her apartment building. They're saying it's alcohol poisoning."

Ivy couldn't speak.

"They did a CT scan of her brain, and they've got her on an IV with some kind of yellow vitamins in it. They're going to admit her to SCU."

"What does *skew* mean?" Ivy tried to swallow the choking fear that rose up around her throat.

"Special care unit. Intensive care. Can you come?"

"I'm leaving in five minutes." She hung up and went to wake Nick. As she dressed, she told him what she knew. To her surprise, he threw back the covers and sat up.

"I'll go with you."

"You don't have to do that."

"You're upset, and I don't want you driving to Quahog alone."

She suddenly wanted to cry. "Thank you."

"You go wake up DeShaun and tell him while I get dressed."

She shook the groggy boy awake and told him where they were going. Then, not trusting him to remember what she had said, she scribbled a hurried note and left it on the kitchen table.

The streets were empty, and they made the thirty-minute drive to the hospital without speaking. Nick dropped her off at the emergency department door and went to park the car.

At the visitor information desk, Ivy found an earnest-looking young man reading a college textbook. "My sister Laura Darling—"

"Oh yes," he said with a neutral smile. Apparently he had been cued for her arrival. Probably by Amy. "Special care unit, second floor. Follow this corridor to the end and take the elevators on your right."

"Thank you. My husband's right behind me. Will you send him up?"

"Yes, ma'am."

She backtracked long enough to say, "His name is Nick Mason."

"Yes, ma'am."

Nick caught up with her at the elevators. On the second floor, they found the tiny visitors' lounge, which, to her relief, seemed to be overflowing with family. Her parents were there, along with David, Sephy, and Amy. "What happened?" she said at once.

It was David who answered. "A neighbor found her unconscious in the courtyard of her apartment complex and called 911. When she got to the ER, her blood alcohol level was point-three-five."

"That's bad?"

"Very. But it looks like she'll be okay, as long as she doesn't have a seizure in the next few hours."

"A seizure?"

"The nurse said it can be a complication."

Ivy sat down, hard, in the nearest chair. Her mother was weeping.

Amy pulled several tissues from a box on the magazine-strewn table. "Here, Mom, blow your nose. She's going to be all right. She's in good hands."

"What will happen to her next?" Ivy addressed her question to Amy, who seemed to be in charge at the moment.

"The hospital has a two-week inpatient recovery program. The ER doctor thinks she should do that, once she's out of SCU, but that'll be up to her and her primary care doctor."

"Recovery?" Jane sounded fearful.

"From alcohol, Mom."

"Are you saying she's an . . . an . . . ?" It seemed the word would not come out of their mother's mouth.

Amy's voice was uncharacteristically gentle. "The nurse said that to have a blood alcohol level that high, you have to be used to some pretty hard drinking. If not, you'd pass out before you ever got there."

"Pretty hard drinking? What does that mean?" To Jane, who had never drunk more than one glass of wine at a time in her life, this was a foreign language.

Sephy spoke up. "Point-three-five is a level you see in college kids who've binged all night. It's pretty dangerous."

They sat in silence for several minutes, digesting this. Trying to fit their sister and daughter into the picture the ER nurse had painted for them.

"I want to see her," Jane said at last.

"Let me ask if they have her settled yet. I think we can go in one or two at a time." At her mother's nod, Amy left them. They sat without speaking, each of them holding hands with someone else, until Amy reappeared in the doorway. "Okay, they said two at a time, and no more than two or three minutes. She's asleep, and she probably won't even know we're there, but there's a whiteboard on the wall we can leave messages on. She'll see them when she wakes up."

Ivy went in after her parents. Laura lay pallid and still in the bed with the side rails up like a cage around her, tubes running into her nose and arm. Even with her puffy face and lank hair, she managed to be prettier than all the rest of them put together, Ivy thought.

"Laura," she said, feeling for her sister's hand. "Laura, it's Ivy. Can you hear me?" Her twin's eyelids fluttered open and the dry lips moved ineffectually. Ivy bent her head close. The sour smells of alcohol and vomit still hung on her sister's breath. "Laura?"

A long sigh escaped Laura, and she turned her head away and closed her eyes again.

In the waiting room the family joined hands once more.

"Lord," Leander said, "take care of our girl in there. Now, when she's weak and sick, and also later, when she's strong again and likely to be fighting You. We pray for the hands that will be caring for her in the next hours: the doctors and nurses and aides and everyone else. Bless them and give them wisdom and kindness toward Laura. You are the Great Physician, and we ask that in the days and weeks to come, You'll heal her in the places she needs to be healed. Show us how to help, and give us the wisdom to stay out of her way when it's time to do that too. In Jesus' name, amen."

After that, there seemed nothing to do but go home. On her way out, Ivy squeezed Amy's and Sephy's hands. "Thanks, you guys. I don't think Mom and Dad would be able to do this without you."

Her sisters smiled grimly and squeezed back.

At home, Ivy drew a cup of water at the kitchen sink and drank it, looking at her own reflection in the window.

Nick came and stood behind her, not touching her. She spoke to him in the glass. "Have I really made her feel inferior all this time? Is that why she did this?"

"You know better than that."

"I guess." She couldn't muster any conviction.

"Ivy, taking in these foster children . . ."

She glared at his reflection. "What about it?"

"There are always going to be people who put a bad spin on the good things you do. You're going to have to get used to it."

"But *why*? Don't we all want the same thing—a good life for these abandoned children?"

"Maybe Laura used to see you two as being on equal footing. And then, just when she was living in a way she knew wasn't right, you set the bar higher."

"Come on, Nick. Nobody's that small. They're *children*. Who needed a *home*. Anyone would have done it."

"Not necessarily."

She was unconvinced. "But surely she doesn't think I'd do it just to make her look bad."

"Maybe villainizing you is the only way she can soothe her own conscience."

"I would *never* do that to someone."

"Don't be too hard on her. I doubt she's doing it on purpose."

"I don't care. It's despicable."

"Oh, come on. Haven't you ever looked at a woman you thought was prettier or thinner or more successful than yourself and said something critical about her?"

"Who hasn't?"

"Well, it's the same thing, isn't it?"

She considered this for a moment, then said, "Thank you for coming with me tonight."

"That's my job."

Ivy felt a weariness that had nothing to do with her lack of sleep. "Your job. Right. Everything is a duty to you, isn't it, Nick?"

He opened his mouth to speak, but she silenced him with a wave of her hand. "Don't bother. I'm going to bed."

17

JANE DARLING PULLED a pan of barbecued beans from the oven and set them on the stove top. Her movements were automatic, her mind disengaged. The kitchen was empty for the moment, with the crowd gathered for Thursday night dinner mostly outside, taking advantage of the early evening shade on the lawn. She hung up her oven mitts, turned off the oven, and went to the slider door.

Laura, of course, was not there. She was approaching the end of her stay at the inpatient recovery program. During the nearly two weeks she had been there, none of them had been allowed to visit. There were confidentiality issues, apparently, all kinds of new laws about that. Even Sephy, who was working as a nurse's aide at the hospital for the summer, could not see her. Jane had talked with Laura twice on the phone, and then only because Laura had called her. Both times, her daughter had been vague and distant. She seemed embarrassed about what had happened and changed the subject every time Jane tried to talk about it. But Laura did say that in two days she would be moving back to her apartment and continuing the program as an outpatient. Jane and Leander had tried to convince her to move in with them for those months. It was what the doctor and counselors recommended, but Laura had been adamant about going back to her own home. She had agreed that they could pick her up from the hospital and drive her back to her apartment, but that was all.

They had talked to their pastor at length about the guilt, the conviction that they had done something to push their daughter into this lifestyle. Pastor Ken, whose own son had lost his battle with drugs and died from an overdose when he was just nineteen, kept telling them not to blame themselves, that Laura had not made the choices she had because they were bad parents. If anyone could say this with authority, surely it was Ken, and they tried to believe him. At heart, though, neither of them really did.

Laura said she was doing just fine. *You never know, though, do you?* Jane tried to keep thoughts like these at bay, not to be gripped and ruled by fear. But they slipped through once in a while, reminding her how thin was her hold on serenity these days. She was nearly overwhelmed all the time now by a compulsive need to have her children close to her, to keep them within sight, so that she could make sure they were safe.

Her beautiful blonde daughter had always had a devious streak to her. As a teenager, her willfulness had manifested itself in sneakiness. For instance, if the girls had felt their curfew was too early, Amy would have been the one to debate and reason with her parents until they saw things her way and let her stay out an hour later. Ivy and Sephy would have abided by the rules. Laura would have waited until everyone else had gone to bed, then climbed out her bedroom window to go and do exactly as she pleased. So now, when she said she was doing fine, how could they know whether to believe her or not?

Ivy, too, had turned into something of a puzzle. She had been a steady, responsible child and teenager, with a remarkably even temperament in spite of her creative bent. Steadiness and creativity, Jane had observed in her years as a musician, did not always go hand in hand. But somewhere along the line—in college, she thought—something had changed in Ivy. That year she had come home from Orono to stay, it had been as though a great sadness had permeated her soul like a fog rolling in off the ocean and settled there for good. It was not that Ivy herself had turned sad. In fact, she laughed as much and was as fun-loving as ever. But somehow, Jane had never been able to shake the notion that Ivy's heart had broken while she was away at college and had never fully healed. She had found Nick after that and fitted herself to him like a broken limb to a rigid cast, in the hope that something in her would mend.

Jane never learned what that something was, and she was not so sure anything had been fixed by her daughter's marrying Nick Mason. But it was good to see Nick with her tonight. And he had come last time too, so maybe something was thawing there. He was throwing the basketball into the net at the end of the driveway with DeShaun. "Shooting hoops," she thought they still called it. The sight of the two of them doing this together felt like relief. Maybe she didn't have to worry about them after all.

The thought brought her up short. No one ever had to worry about anything, she reminded herself with a stern mental shake. *"Do not be anxious about anything, but in every situation, by prayer and petition, with thanksgiving, present your requests to God. And the peace of God, which transcends all understanding, will guard your hearts and your minds in Christ Jesus."* She had memorized those verses three decades ago, as a young mother, and she had clung to them, testing them nearly every day of her life and finding them true. Surely this crisis with Laura would be no different; her heavenly Father had never let her down yet, and He was not about to start.

The memory of Pastor Ken's son passed over her thoughts like a cloud over the sun. What if . . . ? She could not make herself form that worst of all possibilities into a complete thought. *Peace, Jane,* she reminded herself. *It doesn't promise happy endings, only peace.* She hoped she would never have to find out what it meant to have one without the other.

✑

Ivy was folding laundry when her cell phone buzzed. She glanced at it and saw a number she didn't recognize.

Hey you. How's your day?

She keyed in a reply. Who is this?

The phone vibrated again. Jonathon

A thrill of electricity shot through her. How'd you get my #?

Adult ed records. Do you mind?

You're stalking me?

Maybe. Ha-ha. Just wanted to say hi.

She punched in: Hi.

Hi.

That's all?

Just thinking about you. How are you?

He was thinking about her? Although she was alone, she felt her face flush.

Jada wandered out of the bedroom, her violin in one hand, her bow in the other. "What does 'dance on the ashes' mean?" the little girl asked.

Ivy nearly dropped the phone but managed to type, Gotta go, before slipping it under a folded towel. She looked up, trying to collect her thoughts. "Dance on the ashes? Where in the world did you hear such a thing?"

"It's words to a song. Mikhaila has it on her iPod," her foster daughter said vaguely. "What's it mean?"

The phone vibrated again. Ivy pulled it from under the towel and tried to glance at it discreetly. I get it. Urgent stuff. Have a good night.

"Well, uh . . ." She had no idea who Mikhaila might be. "I guess it means to celebrate over . . ." Her mind was only half on what she was saying. "Over the end of something bad because it means the beginning of something good."

"Oh. Okay." Jada turned and went back into the bedroom, shutting the door behind her. In a moment, the strains of a G scale drifted through the wall.

Ivy picked up her phone and quickly keyed in, Night!

She waited a minute or two, but there was no reply. She looked down at the basket of clean clothes. Dancing on the ashes. Jonathon had texted her. Warmth spread through her in a joyous, golden glow, seeping from the corners of her mouth in a smile. She'd dance right now, at this moment, if anyone would ask her.

"Peewee soccer tryouts are next week," Ivy told Nick. "Although they're not exactly tryouts because every kid makes the team." She reached over the pan of cheese sauce she was whisking for the letter on the counter.

He took it without looking at it. "Why bother, then?"

"I guess going through the motions gives them a sense of accomplishment. Or helps the coaches see which kid should play which position. Or something like that." She started whisking again. "That letter came from the rec department this morning."

"Hammer wants to play, does he? I thought he would."

Ivy nodded at the sheet of paper. "Read it."

As he read, his face took on a hunted look. "Oh, come on, Ivy."

She shrugged. "I'm not telling you what to do. I only thought you might be interested. If you're not, it's no big deal."

"I've never coached soccer!"

"You've *played* soccer. You know the rules."

"I'm no good with little kids."

"You," she said firmly, "are just fine with little kids. Hammer and Jada are crazy about you."

"But other people's kids? Hundreds of them at once?" His voice was plaintive.

"Not hundreds, only dozens. But suit yourself. Nobody's pressuring you." She reached for the letter, but he snatched it back, turned, and headed for the living room with a hangdog slouch.

A moment later, she heard him talking and realized he was on the phone. "Glenn Prout, please. . . . Oh, hello. This is Nick Mason. My . . . er . . . foster son Hammer Hernandez is going to be trying out for peewee soccer next week. . . . Right, I understand they're not exactly tryouts. That's good. I think every kid should get a chance to play. Teaches them good sportsmanship and the rules of the game." His voice sounded strained and falsely hearty. "Anyway, we got this letter that says you need parent coaches. . . ."

Ivy smiled and kept whisking.

❧

Laura sat in the therapy circle and reminded herself not to cross her arms or legs. They were always on the lookout here for what they called "defensive posturing," body language that screamed, *Get out of my business. I didn't ask to be here.* Which was exactly how she felt. She must be very careful not to convey that message, though, so she sat with her knees apart, her elbows resting loosely on them, palms facing upward in a receptive pose, and gazed down at the frayed hems of her jeans. From time to time she nodded thoughtfully or let a wry half smile slip across her face as though she really related to, really *agreed* with the stupid girl on the other side of the circle who was rambling on about why she liked to cut herself with razor blades.

It was ludicrous how self-absorbed these people were. Every one of them ran around inside their problems like a hamster in an exercise ball, running, running, working, working, talking, talking, but never getting any further away from their baggage than they had been when they started. Their problems defined the little worlds they lived in. *My father did this to me; my mother never did that for me; so-and-so died when I was a child and it ruined my life forever.* Laura was so tired of their stories, she could have screamed out loud. At first she had listened to them with a sick sort of fascination. Some of these people were walking train wrecks. She had never had much patience with overt, messy displays of emotion, however, and she had quickly grown bored. *Deal with it,* she wanted to say. *Quit whining about the hand life has dealt you and just get on with playing it.*

As for herself, today was her last day of inpatient, as they called it around here. This, in fact, was her last session. In thirty-five minutes, her parents were arriving to spring her from this place, and she would be free. For this last half hour, she was playing it safe, doing nothing that might mess up her chance of release. She was thinking of her apartment—of the houseplants that would have died of thirst after two weeks without water, the mail that would be piled up in her box, the expired milk in the fridge. And all the while she was nodding at her sandals with little, thoughtful frowns and making sympathetic noises at the girl across the circle.

She had little enough to pack, but as soon as group was over, she went back to her room to retrieve the plastic bag of books and pamphlets and self-tests they had piled on her over the last fourteen days. Until yesterday she, like all the drunks and addicts in the program, had worn hospital scrubs and slippers. She had been issued a hospital comb and toothbrush, and nothing more. Last night, Sephy had been allowed to bring her a change of clothes—all things borrowed from Ivy, since no one but Laura had a key to her apartment—and a bag of toiletries. No razor, though. It had been fourteen days since she had seen a blow-dryer or shaved her legs. Her underarms itched from the unaccustomed growth of stubble, and she wasn't wearing a stitch of makeup, but Sephy had thoughtfully included a baseball cap in the bag of clothes, and Laura, having stuffed her shapeless hair under this, felt marginally more equipped to show her face in public.

In her room, she gave a quick, insincere hug to her roommate, Glenda, a heroin addict who was on her third time through the program, and wished her luck.

"Here's my number," Glenda said, holding out a scrap of paper. "If you ever need anything, don't hesitate to give me a call."

"Oh, thank you!" Laura nailed a smile to her face. "If I ever *do* need anything, you'll be the first one I'll call." She made no reciprocating offer but snatched up her bag, saying, "My parents are waiting," and made her escape.

In the elevator, on the way down, she rehearsed her story one last time. The night she had been brought to the emergency room, she had been out at a girlfriend's bachelorette party, and since it was a hot night, she had drunk several cups of punch, plus a glass of wine. Only after she had started feeling strange had one of the girls confessed that the punch was spiked. Laura, shocked and by then very, very dizzy, had taken a cab home and apparently passed out in the courtyard of her apartment building. In no way did she have a drinking problem. Blah-blah-blah.

It was a good story. Who knew? It might even be true. To be honest, Laura couldn't remember how she had ended up in the courtyard that night.

Her parents, who met her in the lobby, were subdued. Laura suspected that either Ivy or Amy had coached their mother before the pickup, because Jane did not weep or show any emotion at all beyond hugging her briefly and asking, "Are these all your things?" before they headed for the car. Her father's hug was a little longer, and he asked, "How are you, sweetie?" before letting her go. Her parents spoke little on the way home except to ask, "Do you need to stop at the store?"

At Hannaford, Laura bought a cartful of groceries. Her mother and father did not volunteer either to come into the store with her or to pay for the groceries. There were no tears, no attempts to coddle her or treat her like she was sick. They simply dropped her and her bags at the front of the apartment complex, said, "Call if you need anything," and drove away.

Watching their car disappear around the end of the block, Laura felt abandoned. With a twinge of annoyance, she considered the six bags of groceries on the sidewalk at her feet. They could have at least offered to walk her up to the front door. It would take her three trips to get it all inside. And she hadn't gotten to tell her version of what had happened to her. They hadn't even asked.

18

THE SUN WAS HOT, making Hammer's face sweat as he ran drills up and down the field, stopping and starting at the sound of the coach's whistle. It was Saturday morning, and it was going to get a lot hotter by afternoon. Ivy had said they could go to the beach after practice. The sweat just *dripped* off him. Hammer loved that feeling. It made him feel like a professional soccer player. He loved the burn in his legs and the harshness in his lungs as he pushed himself to get to the end of the field first, before the other boys. He almost always did it too. He was the fastest runner on the team.

He reached the end ahead of the pack and leaned against a goalpost, gasping, wiping the sweat out of his eyes with his arm. Around him, the other guys were flopping onto the grass, groaning. He flopped next to them.

"Our last coach never made us run this much," said Sam, who was fat and red-haired. Sam was always whining about something. He volunteered to play goalie so he wouldn't have to run as much as everyone else.

"How you gonna get faster if you don't practice running?" Hammer said.

"Our old coach was better. This coach sucks."

"You shut your face about Coach," Hammer snapped. "That's my dad. He's the greatest coach this soccer team ever had."

Sam was scornful. "He's not your *dad*. White dads have white kids, not black ones. You're just a *foster* child. It's not the same thing."

With a howl, Hammer hurtled up off the ground and leaped on top of Sam. His fists flew on their own, pummeling the freckled white face. It felt good to see the other boy's surprise turn to fear, to feel the solid crunch as his fists connected with bone until the white face was smeared pink with blood. His vision narrowed until he was looking down a black tunnel with only that broad, ugly, bloody face at the end. His back burned, his arms burned, and it felt *good*.

"Ow! Ow! Quit it!" Under him, Sam twisted and thrashed, trying to get away, but Hammer held on, digging his knees into the boy's soft sides. Sam tried to cover his face with his hands, but Hammer got in enough punches under and over them to keep the blood flowing.

All around them, boys had jumped to their feet. "Fight!"

someone yelled. The rest of them took up the chant. "Fight! Fight! Fight! Fight!"

Dimly, Hammer heard the shrilling of the coach's whistle and felt a hand yank him up by the back of the shirt. As he was pulled away, he aimed a last solid kick at Sam and caught him in the leg.

He spent the rest of the practice sitting on the bench. It made him feel only a little bit better that Sam was also on the bench, scooted way down to the other end, as far away from Hammer as he could get and looking at him in a nervous way. Plus, Sam was bleeding. Hammer didn't even have a scratch.

He figured Nick would yell at him on the way home, but he had forgotten that Nick and Ivy weren't much for yelling at any time. Instead, when they had pulled out of the rec center parking lot and onto the main street, Nick just said, "Why don't you tell me your version of what happened?"

"Sam said you sucked as a coach."

"Oh. And . . . do I?"

"No. You're a *great* coach. Sam's just lazy. He don't like to run."

"Well, everyone's entitled to their own opinion. It's okay with me if Sam thinks I'm a bad coach, as long as you think I'm a good one."

Hammer was quiet for a while, trying to decide whether or not to tell Nick the other thing. The mean thing. It was fighting to get out of him, like it *had* to be said out loud. "He said you weren't my dad." He said it so quietly he wasn't sure at first that Nick had heard.

"I see. Well . . . I'm your foster father. Did you tell him that?"

"He said it wasn't the same thing."

For a long time, Nick didn't answer. Then he said, "Do *you* think it's the same thing?"

Hammer shrugged. "I dunno. I ain't never had a dad before."

Nick just kept driving along and neither of them said anything. Hammer thought he'd forgotten about it and was just starting to feel better when Nick slowed down, put on his blinker light, and turned right onto a strange road.

He leaned forward. "Where we goin'?"

Nick looked at him seriously. "Sometimes dads take their sons for ice cream after soccer practice. I thought we could get a cone."

Hammer couldn't help it—the smile burst out of him like fireworks on the Fourth of July.

They pulled into the parking lot of Beals, and Nick turned off the car. "Listen to me, Hammer. People are going to say stupid things to you all your life. You can't solve the problem by hitting them."

"Sure I can. Everybody hits each other when they get mad."

"Not true. Do Ivy and I hit each other?"

He considered this. "Not really."

"Not *really?*"

"I mean no. You don't hit each other."

"Do we hit you kids?"

"No."

"The truth is, most people *don't* hit each other when they get upset. There are better ways of solving problems. And when you're older, hitting people can get you thrown in jail. For now, if you do it again, it'll get you kicked off the team. Understand?"

Hammer nodded, looking at his knees. They were covered with grass stains, which meant Ivy would make him take a bath when he got home.

"And one more thing?"

He dreaded to hear it. "What?"

"Don't tell Ivy I let you have ice cream before lunch, okay?"

He grinned. "Okay, Dad."

Ivy swirled the last bit of chocolate frosting onto the cake and handed both spreader and bowl to Hammer. "Keep it out of your hair, please," she reminded him, knowing she had already lost that battle but feeling compelled to say it anyway.

"Me too!" Jada was practically jumping up and down in her excitement over the three-layer cake on the counter.

"Be patient!" Ivy laughed at her. "We agreed that Hammer could lick the bowl of chocolate frosting and you could lick *this* one." She dipped her finger into the bowl of strawberry frosting and smeared a dab of it onto the girl's nose.

Jada giggled and tried, but failed, to reach the frosting with her tongue. "Can I help with it?"

Ivy set the finished chocolate cake to one side, next to a

carrot cake with cream cheese frosting and, pulling the final cake toward herself, began to smear pink frosting on it. "No, silly, the guest of honor can't help make her own cake."

"My own cake!" Jada put her arms out, flapped them like a bird, and began to twirl in the middle of the kitchen. "Three cakes!"

"Three cakes!" echoed Hammer, dropping the spreader and bowl onto the countertop. He too began to twirl. "Three cakes! Three cakes!"

"Three cakes!" Ivy crowed, still spreading frosting.

The kitchen door opened. "Anybody home?"

Ivy recognized her mother's voice.

"Yeah," called Amy above the racket, coming in behind Jane. "It's so quiet, we weren't sure anyone was here."

Jada and Hammer hurled themselves at the guests. "We have three cakes, Aunt Amy!" Jada shouted, hugging Amy's waist.

"We're havin' our own party!" Hammer informed Jane and Leander.

"You are?" Jane said in mock surprise, despite the pile of wrapped gifts she held. "What's the occasion?"

"It's our anni*ver*sary. We've been here one year!"

"One year, one year!" Both children broke away from the adults and began to twirl in the middle of the kitchen again. "One year! One year!"

"Quiet!" Nick materialized in the kitchen doorway. "Either quiet down or take the racket outside! Here, Jane, I'll take those." He moved to relieve his mother-in-law of her presents.

"Hammer," Ivy said, "go tell DeShaun that Grammie and Grampie are here." The little boy obeyed, running full tilt for the stairs.

"Hi!" called Sephy from the doorway. She held a pair of gift bags, which she handed to Jada. "Happy anniversary, sweetie," she told the excited girl, giving her a kiss. "The purple one's for you, and the green one's for Hammer." She dropped her voice to a confidential whisper. "I got DeShaun money because that's all boring teenagers ever want. Don't tell!" As Jada ran to the streamer-decked dining room to put the gifts on the table, Sephy said in a markedly different tone, "Is Laura coming?"

"Not sure," Ivy said. "I called and left an invitation on her voice mail, but I haven't heard from her since she got out of rehab."

The question was answered a second later when Laura breezed in. "Hi, all," she said, leaning around Sephy to drop a kiss on her mother's cheek. DeShaun and Hammer entered the kitchen at that moment, and with utmost cheerfulness, Laura said, "Hi there, boys! Happy . . . what is it? Anniversary?"

Both boys mumbled something that sounded like a cross between "hi" and "thanks," but hung back. They did not know Laura as well as their other "aunts" and in any case were always a little overawed by her glamorous air and her silver Saab.

David arrived with Grammie Lydia, and the party, now complete, moved to the dining room.

When the gifts had been opened and everyone was

thoroughly "sugared up," as Amy said, with three kinds of cake and three kinds of ice cream, Ivy said, "Jada, Hammer, DeShaun, why don't you put in the new movie Aunt Sephy brought you? I'll make another pot of coffee." Standing up, she caught her mother's eye and said pointedly, "You could give me a hand, Mom."

When they were alone in the kitchen with the door closed, Jane said at once, "What is it?"

Ivy began, "Bailey called today—"

The kitchen door burst open and Amy and Sephy both barged through.

"We like secrets too!" Amy proclaimed.

"Yeah, no fair whispering without us!" Sephy added.

Laura followed close behind. "Don't be talking behind my back in here!"

"Honestly!" Ivy said in exasperation. "This family has *no* sense of boundaries. I'm trying to talk to Mom *alone*."

"Boundaries schmoundaries," Amy said. "Methinks this is about the kids, and we want to know what's going on."

"Yeah, we love them too," Sephy put in.

Ivy raised her eyebrows. "How do you know it's about the kids?"

"Because *ob*viously Bailey called Mom this morning to say she'd been trying to reach you for two days and ask why you hadn't called her back. Mom told her it was because you never bother to check your voice mail or cell phone for missed calls, and *ob*viously I happened to be in the kitchen when she did. Why would she be looking for you, unless she was—*ob*viously—calling about the kids?"

"Not bad," Ivy said. "You're right; it was about them."

Sephy took a coffee filter from the cupboard and began measuring grounds into it while Ivy talked.

"They found Lily. She's in prison in Alabama under a different name. I mean, under her real name, which is Linda Adams. Apparently Lily Allen is only one of several aliases she uses."

"The children didn't know her real name?" Jane asked.

Ivy shrugged. "I guess not. They knew her as Mom."

There was a general appalled silence; then Laura asked, "What's she in prison for?"

"Felony drug trafficking and prostitution. Not for the first time. She's a drug addict, with no interest in getting clean. The state of Maine has started the procedure to terminate her parental rights. Bailey said when they told Lily that, she just shrugged and said, 'I can't even remember what my kids look like.'"

With tears in her eyes, Jane asked, "Do the children know?"

"No. I'm trying to figure out how to tell them without . . . well, without destroying them."

"What does that mean—that her parental rights are going to be terminated?"

"For now, it means the kids will be made wards of the state, and as long as things continue to work out, they can keep living here. It takes away the uncertainty that one day they might be snatched away from us."

"Would they be available for adoption?" Laura asked.

"Technically, yes."

"Technically?"

"Nick and I have talked about it. He won't adopt them." She hesitated. "There's another thing." She told them about DeShaun and the Vicodin. "It's hard for Nick to think about adopting him when he wonders if this is just the start of bigger problems, you know?"

"Oh, honey," Jane said, putting her arm around her daughter's shoulders and giving her a squeeze.

"It's sad," said Laura, "but I think Nick has a point."

There was silence again. Then, "Well, it's good news," Amy pointed out. "Even if they're only your foster children, it means stability for them."

"They couldn't ask for a better home." This from Sephy.

"And they know you love them," Jane added.

Ivy took a shaky breath and swiped at her eyes. "I know it's good news. It's just . . . I dread telling them. Even if she's a complete loser, she's still their *mother*."

"Dear Lord," Jane said, "give Ivy and Nick wisdom as they tell the children this hard truth about their mother. Work ahead of time in each child's heart so that they will be ready to hear the news. Most of all, thank You for bringing Hammer, Jada, and DeShaun into our lives. We know You have a special plan for each one of them, and we are grateful to be a part of that. Thank You for this opportunity to provide a more stable life for them. We pray for Lily in prison right now, Lord. Please heal her there. Bring someone into her life who can introduce her to You. Amen."

"Amen," they all echoed. They looked at each other, smiling through their tears.

"Dry your eyes," Sephy said at last, to the room in general. She gave a great, noisy sniff. "The coffee's ready, and if we don't get out there, the men will be breaking down the door to find it."

❧

"That was a nice party." Nick came into the kitchen and picked up a dish towel. "Want me to dry?"

Ivy turned from the sink, where she was up to her elbows in soapsuds, and raised her eyebrows at him. "It was noisy, chaotic, and the house was stuffed to the rafters with Darlings. Dinner was three kinds of cake and three kinds of ice cream, which you don't approve of. Hammer spent the last hour bouncing off the walls, and you think the party was *nice*?"

He began to dry a coffee cup. "That's not what I meant. I mean it was nice that you gave the kids an anniversary party at all."

"Oh. Well, it was fun for me." They washed and dried in silence.

Nick tried again. "At this time last year, you had just dyed your hair pink, remember?"

She snorted. "How could I forget?"

"No, it's . . . cute."

She shot him an arch, disbelieving look. "You didn't think so a year ago."

"Sure I did."

"You must have forgotten to tell me."

Nick was foundering. He was trying with Ivy, but she

wasn't being much help. "Want to play rummy when we're done here?"

She gave an enormous yawn. "I couldn't keep my eyes open long enough. And you don't have to help me with the dishes."

"It's okay; I want to."

She handed him the last plate and drained the sink, yawning again. "It's been a long day and we have to be up early tomorrow. Thanks for drying." She turned and left him holding the plate alone in the kitchen.

He felt that something had not gone right here. This was not what the book had promised. He wished he knew what to do about it.

❧

At four thirty in the morning, DeShaun woke Ivy to say it was pouring rain and he couldn't ride his bike to the diner, where he was expected to open for the breakfast shift at five o'clock. Ivy managed to drive him to work and make her way home through the dim, wet dawn without coming fully awake. In her room once more, she kicked off her damp flip-flops and crawled into the still-warm bed beside Nick, who was sleeping so soundly he hadn't even realized she was gone. She sank back into the blissful haze of sleep, letting the tide roll over and pull her down . . .

Shirts!

She came wide awake in a cold instant. Nick had no clean shirts left for work. She had intended to throw a load in the washer before bed, but the cakes and the party had pushed it out of her mind.

Swearing just the tiniest bit under her breath, Ivy threw back the covers, ignoring Nick's protests, and stormed down to the basement. By the time the shirts were in the washer, she knew that going back to sleep was a distant fantasy. She went upstairs and turned on the coffeepot. The familiar morning scent of it against the sound of the pouring rain outside the window cheered her, and she curled up on the corner of the sofa with her coffee cup and Bible, feeling very cozy. She had gotten out of the habit of starting her day like this. She ought to do it more often, she reflected. It was what her mother had always done, and still did, every day of her life. Ivy had grown up watching her do it.

She spent some time praying for the kids—another thing she didn't do enough of. They were so good. How many other fifteen-year-old boys in this town got themselves out of bed at four thirty every morning, rode their bikes to work, and never uttered a word of complaint? She was willing to bet there weren't many. Hammer was becoming a real athlete: peewee striker extraordinaire and the star of his soccer team. Jada thrived in the atmosphere of the summer theater workshops Ivy had signed her up for. She was taking a singing class on Mondays and Wednesdays, a drama class on Tuesdays and Thursdays, and had skit camp on Fridays. They were each finding a voice, something they liked and were good at.

They had their issues, of course: DeShaun was still remote and hard to reach. Hammer was a whirling dervish most of the time, and his teacher had pointed out with some concern that he had trouble focusing and concentrating.

Ivy prayed for Laura, and as it happened every time, remembering the things her twin had said to her was like ripping a scab off a wound. *"You've looked down on me all my life. . . . You* always *assume the worst of me. . . . Ivy does everything she can to elbow herself into position of family favorite."* She knew, with an absolutely clean conscience, that none of these things were true, but it didn't make the fact that her sister would think them any less hurtful.

She tried to pray for Nick, but it was like running up against a brick wall. She couldn't form the thoughts to ask God for good things for him. In the end, all she could do was be honest. *Lord, there's been too little love for too long in this marriage. Something has died. I can't even muster up the hope that things might change. I just don't care anymore.*

❧

Ivy told the children about their mother at supper one night, being as brief and as gentle as possible. They accepted it silently, with Hammer only saying, "Does this mean she's not coming back anymore?"

"That's right, honey."

Jada's eyes were fixed on her plate. In a small voice, she asked, "What will happen to us?"

"You'll keep on living here, just like you have been. The truth is, Nick and I love having you all around so much, we don't know what we'd do without you."

"So . . . I can keep my violin, then?"

"Oh yes, sweetheart, you can keep your violin."

Two days later, Nick came home to report that all the windows in the little house next door had been broken. "Someone's been throwing rocks at it," he told her.

She felt the sick, dizzy drop of her stomach. "DeShaun?"

"There's no way to know for sure, but I would bet on it."

"What do we do?"

"Ivy, I'm as new at this as you are," he said, exasperated. "I have no idea what to do."

Before supper, they pulled DeShaun into their bedroom and asked him about it. DeShaun, stone-faced and unrepentant, readily admitted that he had broken the windows. "I hate that old house," he ground out.

It always surprised Ivy to glimpse the depth of this boy's wounds. Of the three children, their mother's betrayal seemed hardest for him to bear. "Oh, DeShaun." She reached out a hand to him, but he drew back.

"One of these days, I might just burn it right to the ground," he said, his voice savage.

From the door, which was open a crack, came an unexpected voice. "I would dance on the ashes." Jada's voice broke with a sob.

Ivy pushed the door open to find two small eavesdroppers kneeling there. Hammer's face wore a look of fear. Ivy could think of no words that would be enough, so she said nothing, only held out her arms and let the younger children run into them.

19

THE FIRST OF SEPTEMBER was cool and rainy, as if the weather were conceding to the calendar and admitting that it was time to think of fall. The kids still needed one or two things for school, and Ivy needed to pick up a birthday present for Laura, so when Nick got home from work, she left him in charge of the kids and headed for the mall in Quahog.

She was in the food court, standing in line at Au Bon Pain, when she heard her name. Turning, she saw Jonathon standing there and could not suppress the rush of pleasure she felt.

"What are you doing here?" she asked. "You don't seem like a mall kind of person."

"I'm not. But my iPod finally bit the dust, so I thought I'd come down and see what's new in the world of electronics. What are you doing?"

She told him, and he said, "Why don't you get your food and come sit with me?"

"That would be nice."

She ordered a salad and made her way over to where he was sitting, eyeing his tray as she sat. "Mall sushi? Is it good?"

"Not particularly. But it's probably the healthiest choice here."

"How's the pottery business?" she asked, opening her salad and sticking a straw into her Diet Coke.

"Going well. I just placed some things on consignment in a shop in Freeport and one in Portland. If they sell, it'll help get my name out there. Expand the business."

"Do you want to expand? I mean, do you have the time for more work?"

He considered this. "What I want is for people to buy my pottery and put it on their coffee tables and have a sense of joy every time they look at it. Knowing that someone owns something I made and treasures and loves it like I would—that's the greatest high I've ever experienced. Expanding the business means that more people will discover my work and love it. So that's my goal, I guess. Can you understand that?"

She could. "In a small way, I guess I feel like that about my flower garden. Knowing that people can look at it and have that—" she searched to put words to what she meant—"that inner need for order and beauty met. That's really satisfying to me. I even feel that way when I wrap a gift or cook a meal. Is that weird?"

"No. I think it means you have the soul of an artist."

"I miss taking pottery lessons."

"Why don't you start again?"

"I just don't have the time right now. The kids are starting school again. Maybe after the holidays."

They took their time eating, and when they had finished, Jonathon bought her a coffee and they sat and talked for another hour. At last, she looked at her watch. "I have to get going. I still need to buy a gift for my sister. Our birthday is in two days."

"How old will you be?"

"Never ask a lady her age, sirrah," she said with mock severity. "But as it happens, I'll be twenty-nine and proud of it, thank you very much."

"You should be proud of it. You don't look twenty-nine."

"Thank you, I think."

"What are you getting your sister?"

"Perfume, probably, or maybe a sweater. Something that will suit her caviar taste on my tuna-fish budget."

"Want some company?"

"What, shopping for her gift?"

"Sure, why not? I can give you my objective male opinion."

She did not want their time together to end. When she talked to him, she felt . . . intelligent. Interesting. Even attractive. All the things she never felt at home. "I would really like that," she said, meaning it.

He helped her pick out a hand-painted scarf of vivid

cobalt-blue silk for Laura, two packs of athletic socks for Hammer, and a bag of assorted notebooks, pens, and pencils. Afterward, she went to Best Buy with him and looked at MP3 players, but the mall closed before he had time to make up his mind.

He walked her to her car. "That was fun," he said, smiling down at her. "I'm glad we ran into each other."

"Me too. Normally I hate shopping, but doing it together made it much less of a chore."

"Do you have time to get some dessert with me somewhere?"

Yes! Her unconscious mind leaped at the suggestion, but she hesitated. Until now, their evening could be justified as simply two friends who had bumped into each other at the mall and done their shopping together. But going to a café now seemed almost like . . . like a date.

"We don't have to stay long," he said, misinterpreting her hesitation. "Look, there's a Cold Stone over there. We could have a quick ice cream or coffee, and you can be on your way home in twenty minutes."

She let him think that time was the issue. "Well," she said, giving in to what she really wanted, "I guess I could spare twenty minutes."

❧

"I thought summer was busy," Ivy told her mother and sisters on Thursday night, "but then school started and I realized I didn't even know what busy was." A rainstorm had driven them into the kitchen, where Ivy was counting out silverware to set the table for dinner. "Jada is still taking voice lessons—"

"I'm glad she's continuing her music," said Jane. "She has real talent."

"What about the boys?" Amy wanted to know. She was mashing potatoes by hand at the counter, scowling as she bore down on them.

"You could use the electric mixer for those," Ivy told her. "It would be quicker and easier."

"But not nearly as good, right?"

"If you say so. Anyway, peewee football starts next week, and of course Hammer wants to play."

"Is Nick coaching again?"

"No. He says he paid his dues this summer. He's earned the rest of the year off from any kind of involvement with kids' sports teams."

"DeShaun must be done working at the diner now that school's started." This from Jane, who had pulled four roasting chickens out of the oven and was basting them.

"No, he wants to keep working weekends. I've never known a teenage boy to be so crazy about his job."

"Maybe there's a girl," Amy suggested. "A cute waitress or dishwasher."

"I don't think so. There's just his friend Milo, who's a busboy. The two of them are developing a whole menu of specialty grilled cheese sandwiches. The owner said he'll let them do a trial run some weekend. If people like them, he might put one or two on the menu permanently."

"Wow, an entrepreneur!" said Amy, with pride.

Ivy laughed. "I'm pretty sure DeShaun doesn't even know what the word means, but that's what he is all the same."

"Ivy, get me the ice cubes from the freezer, will you?" Laura was at the island, mixing sugar into a pitcher of iced tea. "Mom, do you have any fresh mint?"

"I don't like mint in my iced tea," Ivy objected, passing two ice cube trays over Amy's head. "I hope you're making a pitcher without it."

"No, I'm not," Laura told her.

"You'll have to," said Jane. "I don't have any mint."

"No sugar!" said Amy. "I don't drink sugar in my tea."

"Too late. I already added it."

"Good, because I *only* drink it with sugar," said David, who had come in for a glass of water.

Amy looked over Laura's shoulder. "You're making some herbal too, right? You know I don't do caffeine."

"Mom!" Laura said, exasperated. "Tell them to leave me alone!"

"It's a case of too many cooks in the kitchen," Jane said wisely.

༄

JONATHON

Did your sister like b-day scarf?

LOVED it. Thanks for remembering.

Remembering? I picked it out! Glad
your sister likes my taste.

> Hey, I get some of the credit for such
> a great gift! Are you still stalking me?

Maybe. Do you mind?

Ivy? Do you mind?

> I don't mind. :)

Nick called his wife at lunchtime and did not think to wonder until after he had punched in the number and was waiting for her to answer whether she would be home or not. He realized he had very little idea of what Ivy did on her days off.

She picked up on the fifth ring, sounding breathless. "Hello?"

"What are you doing?"

"I'm mucking out the attic. Why?" She sounded peevish, and no wonder. To Ivy, the attic, reached by a ladder that pulled down from a trapdoor in the ceiling, was a formidable black hole that you opened once a season only if you absolutely had to. The last time Nick had climbed the ladder, he had been appalled to find himself looking at walls of boxes, twelve inches from his face on every side. Beyond them, he could see three hundred square feet of bare floor. There were totes labeled *Summer Clothes, Hats and Mittens, Christmas Deco, Sheet Music* . . . and all wedged just as close to the door as they could get.

"You really should clean that out," he had told Ivy, to which she had replied, "I have a system."

"What system? Everything's just shoved into the opening."

"Right. That way, I can stand on the ladder and, by turning in any direction, find exactly what I'm looking for."

"But why not organize the boxes neatly along the walls? I built all those shelves for you when we first moved in. There's plenty of space up there."

"This way minimizes my actual in-attic time. In fact, I have the system perfected to the point where I haven't set foot on the attic floor in two years."

"But why?"

Her answer had been summed up in two words: "Spiders. Mice."

Which was why he was surprised now to hear what she was doing.

"Why did you decide to clean out the attic?" he asked.

He heard her sigh. "DeShaun was up there poking around yesterday. He took a liking to it and asked if he could move his bedroom up there."

"What was he doing in the attic yesterday?"

"Looking for the waffle iron. Don't ask me why."

"Why would he want to sleep up there?"

"Well, he wants his own room, for one thing. But I think it also has something to do with the charm of having a bedroom you can only reach by ladder. Plus, it's a pretty big area."

"So you're cleaning it out for him."

"The things we do for love."

"Speaking of love, what are we doing the weekend of our anniversary?"

"No idea. I haven't thought beyond Halloween, which is a whole two days before that. Why?"

"I was thinking we could go away somewhere. Just the two of us."

She did not answer. In fact, she was silent for so long that Nick began to wonder if they'd been disconnected.

"Ivy?"

"Go away somewhere?" she said at last. "Where? And who would watch the kids?"

"There's this little bed-and-breakfast outside of Manchester that I heard about. It's on a working sheep farm. Your mom can watch the kids for two days; you know she'd be glad to."

"Manchester, Maine?"

"New Hampshire."

"Oh." Silence again.

"You don't want to do it?"

"Nick, I'm so busy. . . . Going away for a weekend would feel like just one more thing to do."

His throat felt thick with disappointment. His wife did not want to spend time with him; he could hear the reluctance in her voice.

She sighed again. "I don't mean to be a wet blanket. I'll think about it, okay?"

"No, I don't want you to go if you don't want to. I just thought it would be fun."

"Another time, it might be. Just . . . not now."

When? he wanted to say. But he was afraid he already knew the answer: *Never again.*

❧

Laura pulled her Saab to the side of the road and turned off the lights. She kept it running because the evening was chilly, but the engine was almost silent, and the early nightfall covered her in a protective cloak of darkness.

Twenty minutes earlier, she had watched Carol leave the house with one of the boys. Max had kissed his wife and son and stowed two suitcases in the trunk, then stood in the driveway waving as they pulled away. She had guessed they were going to visit Carol's mother in New Hampshire for the long holiday weekend. She knew the other boy was away at college. Max would be alone.

He had turned and gone back inside, and now, through the kitchen windows, Laura caught glimpses of him. Probably mixing himself a drink. She took a long swallow of her own drink—vodka and cranberry juice, light on the cranberry juice—from a one-quart Ocean Spray bottle on the console beside her.

Max, she thought. *Max, Max, Max.* Just the thought of his name ripped at something inside her that was still raw and tender, though it should have healed by now. She had been so good. She had not chased him or followed him or even gone looking for him at all since she had come out of the hospital. But she missed him so much, and tonight had been especially hard. She was lonely. And she had remembered that Carol usually went to New Hampshire for Columbus Day weekend because it was her mother's birthday or something. At this time last year, Laura had been working for Max, and he had taken her out to dinner, saying his wife was away so he didn't need to be home at any particular time. They had drunk champagne together for no special reason, and she had been so in love with him, even then.

Laura took another swallow and wondered if she had the courage to go knock on his door. If she did, would he let her in or send her away?

She sat in the car and watched the house until her bottle was empty. Then, pulling down the visor and giving her reflection a quick check in the mirror, she turned off the car and got out. The slam of the door echoed like a gunshot in the still, cold night. She shivered and pulled her wool peacoat closer around herself.

When he answered the door, his face went slack with shock. "Laura! You're the last person I expected to see."

"I was just driving by," she began. She heard the slur in her words and spoke more carefully. "I thought I'd stop to say hello."

He frowned. "Have you been drinking?"

"I went to dinner with a friend and had a glass of wine." She enunciated carefully to prove the truth of her words.

"Just a glass of wine?"

"Yes. I—It's cold out here. Could I come in?"

He considered this for a moment, then smiled at her, that familiar slow smile that turned her insides to warmed oil. "Sure, come on in. I was just about to open a bottle of wine myself. Maybe you'd join me for another glass?"

"That sounds wonderful."

He looked past her, into the night. "Where's your car?"

"I parked across the road and down the hill a little."

He craned his neck. "I can't see it."

"Should I go get it and park in the driveway?"

"No, leave it. It's perfect right where it is." He reached for her hand and pulled her through, into the warmth, closing the door on the dark and the chill of the world outside.

❧

Ruby called on Saturday afternoon. "Wonderful news!" she said breathlessly.

Ivy braced herself. Ruby's definition of *wonderful* didn't always jibe with her own.

"You'll never guess!"

Angela's pregnant again, Ivy thought. Aloud, she said, "I can't guess. What?"

"Tiffany's pregnant!" Ruby crowed. "Due in June. She just found out this morning."

"Oh, that's . . . that's . . ." Ivy did some rapid soul-searching and found that she could say with all honesty, "I'm so happy for her."

"That's all three of the girls," Ruby said, as though having fecund daughters were something she, personally, had accomplished. "Now we're just waiting for you and Nick to take the plunge, my dear."

"Nick and I have already taken the plunge," Ivy said sweetly. "Last I checked, we had three beautiful children."

Ruby made a noise like a creaking door.

"I have to run, Ruby. Give my best to Harry. I'll call Tiffany tomorrow and congratulate her myself." She hung up and stuck her tongue out at the telephone.

❧

JONATHON

Do you have in-laws?

I used to. How are yours?

The worst ever.

Anything in particular?

Too much. Wouldn't know where to start. What are you doing?

Working @ home. Want to meet for coffee so you can tell me about it?

Ivy?

It's tempting, but . . . better not. Have a great day!

❧

"Laura! Laura, wake up!" Someone was slapping her face and none too gently.

"Mmmmph!" She turned and tried to bury her face in the pillow, but it disappeared from under her head.

"Wake up!"

"What time is it?" she mumbled.

"Seven o'clock. Time for you to go home."

She opened one eye and gave Max a grumpy pout. "Too early."

"No, you have to go now. Carol will be home tomorrow, and I need to get the sheets changed and the house cleaned up."

She opened her other eye. "You're kicking me out? That's mean!"

"You didn't think you could stay forever, did you?"

She closed both eyes against the small wave of pain that washed through her. *I hoped.*

"Come on. I'll walk you to your car."

"No coffee first? No shower?"

"Laura."

It was so unfair of him. Peevishly, she pulled herself up to a sitting position in the bed. Her head spun.

Friday night and all of Saturday had been wonderful. They had left the bedroom only to make trips to the kitchen, where they had fortified themselves with a wedge of brie, some slightly stale French rolls, and half a Sara Lee tiramisu from the freezer. Once she had made him an omelet, and another time, Max had searched the refrigerator and come up with a jar of black caviar, which they had eaten with sour cream and more French rolls. Close to midnight on Saturday, she and Max had shared a last bottle of wine. It was still standing, along with their empty glasses, on his dresser.

But at three o'clock Laura had awoken and, unable to get back to sleep, wandered down to the kitchen, where she found half a bottle of Scotch in the liquor cabinet. She had finished it off and stashed the empty bottle in the back, behind the vermouth and crème de menthe. With any luck, when Carol discovered it, she would think one of the boys had drunk it. Laura would let that be their problem.

Hardly feeling the Scotch, she'd remembered that Max was the only person she knew who actually had a wine cellar. He'd often mentioned it back when they worked together. She supposed that was where the wine they'd been drinking all weekend had sprung from, although she hadn't paid attention. Feeling melancholy, she had found the basement stairs and stumbled down them. There, she hit pay dirt. Max's "wine cellar" consisted of three dozen dusty bottles in racks outside the laundry room. There were enough left that one more would not be missed. Careful not to disturb the dust, she'd chosen a Madeira, then put the others back, arranging them so the space left by the missing bottle would not show, before heading upstairs in search of a corkscrew.

Now, hardly two hours later, Max was slapping her face and kicking her out. It was incredibly cold and unfeeling of him.

"Fine," she muttered. "Let me go to the bathroom and clean up first." She reached for her purse on the floor by the bed and found her pill case.

"What's that?" Max wanted to know.

"Something for a headache."

"They're kind of big for aspirin."

"They're not aspirin."

"What are they?"

She stalked to the bathroom, her head held high. "None of your business."

Mutely, she handed them over, and he unlocked the door and helped her in. The cold morning air helped revive her a little, but she felt very unsteady nevertheless. He waited until she had the car started and the windows defogged, leaning against the open door, drumming his fingers irritatingly on the roof until she was ready to pull away.

"Good-bye, Max. It was really great."

Suddenly he grinned at her, his impatience gone. "Yeah, it was, wasn't it?" He leaned down to kiss her. "Drive carefully."

Laura tried to drive carefully. She did. But somehow, half a mile from home, the trees that lined the quiet street did not seem to be staying in their usual places. They were standing in her way. Why were trees growing in the middle of the road?

She swerved to avoid one and immediately there was another one. She swerved again, confused, beleaguered. The trees were trying to get her. She spun the wheel, lurching out of their way, but they reached out to her. She felt a shattering jolt. Her head snapped back and her face exploded in pain.

❧

Ivy got the call from Amy as they were on the way out the door to church.

"Laura's had a car accident. We're on our way to the emergency room right now."

"Is she okay?"

"They think so, but they're doing tests to be sure. X-rays and things."

"I'll be right there."

She hung up and told Nick.

"Do you want me to go with you?" he asked.

She nodded mutely.

"All right, you guys," he said to the three kids, who were standing by the front door, Bibles in hand. "I guess it's Sunday morning cartoons for you."

All three faces brightened, but remembering the reason for their reprieve, they lowered their eyes and murmured, "Okay."

"Make them lunch, okay, DeShaun?" Ivy said.

"I'll make 'em grilled cheese."

"I thought you probably would."

⁎

The emergency room doctor was maddeningly closemouthed about the whole thing. For reasons of privacy, he said, he could not disclose anything about Laura's condition other than that she would be all right. She had suffered no head trauma, only some bruising to her face when the air bag had deployed.

It was Sephy, home for Columbus Day weekend, who found out the truth. For three years, Sephy had spent her vacations working as a nurse's aide at the hospital, and when the doctor continued to stonewall them, she sent David down the street to Dunkin' Donuts, whence he returned with a steaming-hot Box O' Joe and a dozen assorted pastries.

"Thank you," said his red-haired sister, taking it all from him and gliding off toward the nurses' station. "I'll be right back with information."

When she returned, she was grim. "Her blood alcohol level was point-two-three."

"That's not as bad as last time, though, right?" David said.

"No, but it's still almost three times the legal limit. She was definitely driving drunk. Her urine drug screen isn't back yet."

"*Drug* screen?" their mother half whispered.

"Looks like it. They found prescription painkillers in her purse."

"Why was she taking painkillers?" Amy wanted to know.

"Tendonitis in her wrist, or so she told the nurse."

"But . . . you don't believe that?"

Sephy shrugged. "You don't usually take opioids for tendonitis. Ibuprofen maybe, but not Vicodin."

Ivy felt all the air leave her body. "The pills from my bathroom closet!" She turned to Nick and saw comprehension on his face. "I gave her a Vicodin once, when her arm was bothering her." She told them about the missing pills, adding, "We blamed DeShaun." She looked at Sephy. "Is that what they're testing her for?"

"Exactly. How long ago did you give them to her?"

"Months ago. Last year, I think."

"Obviously she's still taking them. And not from your

supply." Sephy looked grim. "I'd guess she blew through that a long time ago."

$$\backsim$$

"I can't believe she would do something like this," Ivy said for the twentieth time. The Volvo's dashboard clock said 4:38 in the afternoon.

"I mean," she continued, as though Nick had answered her, "stealing my pills is bad enough, but to let DeShaun take the blame for it all these months? He could have gone to jail. I just can't believe it."

"What part can't you believe?" Nick sounded tired. "If you think Laura's above letting a kid she hardly knows and doesn't care about be slandered, then you don't know your sister very well."

She turned to stare at him. "What do you mean?"

"I mean Laura's always been all about taking care of Laura, and a little thing like concern for the reputation of a teenage boy would never stand in the way of her getting what she wants."

"Nick! Laura's not like that."

"*Yes*, Ivy. Unfortunately, she is."

Such an assessment of the sister who had always been her best friend was too cold at a time like this. It was like kicking Laura when she was down. "Give me an example," she demanded.

"When's the last time she went to a Thursday night dinner at your parents' house?"

"You don't usually go either," she pointed out.

"No, but I don't promise and then not show up. Every week Laura tells your mother she'll be there, and something always comes up at the last minute."

She considered whether or not this was a fair statement and decided reluctantly that it was.

After a moment, he said, "Want to talk about our wedding?"

Ivy flinched. It had been almost seven years, and she still felt a stab of humiliation at the memory. "Not really."

"I'll talk about it then. You asked her to be your maid of honor; she said yes, then ended up floating off to Europe and didn't even *come* to the wedding."

"She bought the tickets for Spain before she knew the wedding date." Even as she said it, Ivy wondered why she continued to justify something that was still, after all these years, inexcusable.

"You love her and need her far more than she loves and needs you."

"That's not true. She's my best friend!"

"Really? How often does she call you?"

"We talk . . . we *used to* talk on the phone nearly every day."

"And now?"

"She's busy."

"She doesn't even have a job right now! And still, no one's ever as busy as Laura. You, with three needy kids, a part-time job, a church you're involved with, and a husband, never have as many urgent demands on your time as she does."

Ivy was silent, staring out the window, watching the

CARRE ARMSTRONG GARDNER

familiar buildings of the town slip by the pane of glass. At last she said, "Was this my fault, Nick? Because I gave her that pill last fall?"

He made a noise of disgust. "Did you give her pills the second time, and the third, and the thirtieth?"

"No."

"This is not your fault. If it hadn't been the Vicodin, it would have been something else."

She tried to believe him.

"DeShaun will be happy, anyway," Nick said.

"Yeah, he will. He's a good kid, isn't he?"

"He really is."

"Are you sorry we took them in?"

He took his time in answering. "I can truthfully say I don't regret it."

"Even though we thought DeShaun stole the pills?"

"I'll admit I was nervous for a while, thinking we might have a drug addict on our hands, but no, I'm glad we have them."

❧

Laura spent the night on a medical floor and in the morning was admitted directly to the inpatient rehab unit, where once again, the family would have no contact with her for two weeks. There was nothing to do but wait it out.

Ivy and Nick talked to DeShaun together that evening, after the younger children had gone to bed.

"I'm sorry we assumed it was you," Nick told him. "That was unfair of us."

DeShaun, sitting on the couch with his elbows on his knees, merely looked at the floor and nodded.

"Or one of your friends," Ivy put in. "We thought it could have been one of your friends too. Will you forgive us for that, DeShaun? For mistrusting you when you really hadn't given us any reason to?"

"Yeah," the boy muttered. "All right."

Watching him, his dark head bowed, his shoulders hunched in his characteristic half-defensive posture, Ivy felt a surge of protectiveness that surprised her with its ferocity. She hadn't fully realized what a great burden it was to think him guilty all this time. She would so much rather be in the position of his advocate and defender. His simple acceptance of their apology humbled her, and she had to blink away tears. "Thank you, DeShaun."

"Yes, thank you," Nick said.

DeShaun looked up at them then, his mouth quirked in a half smile. "It's okay," he said. "I guess if I was you, I'da thought it was me too."

Seeing that smile brought a wave of relief that was almost physical. *Thank You,* Ivy told God. *Thank You for giving us this boy.*

"Do you want me to invite your family over to celebrate our anniversary on Saturday?" Ivy asked. "We could have lobster and steak."

Nick was not insensible of the sacrifice this offer represented for his wife. "To tell you the truth, I'd rather go out to dinner with just you," he told her.

"Oh . . . but what about the kids? They'll be disappointed not to celebrate with us."

"We can celebrate with them on Friday night. Or Sunday. Whenever. Have lobster and steak then, and forget about inviting my parents and everybody else."

"Can we afford to do both? I mean, that could get expensive."

Nick was losing patience. He did not appreciate that he had to beg for a date with his own wife. "Do you not *want* to go out to dinner with me?"

"It's not that," she said, although he knew it was. "It's just . . . it's going to be a busy week, with Halloween and all."

He raised his eyebrows.

"Okay, okay. Where?"

"Nonna Mia's," he said flatly. "Saturday night at six."

"Fine." She did not look happy about it.

⸙

"Stand still, Hammer, or you'll have greasepaint on your nose!" Ivy knelt before the little boy in her bedroom, smearing black paint below his eyes as he hopped from foot to foot, his outsize shoulder pads jiggling on his thin shoulders. He was going trick-or-treating dressed as a football player, and he couldn't wait to get started. Ivy suspected he was more excited about showing off his costume than he was about the prospect of candy.

Jada, on the other hand, was sitting on Ivy's vanity stool with her head in her arms, sobbing with abandon. Ivy was ignoring her.

"All done," she told Hammer, making a last, futile attempt to straighten the shoulder pads. "Take your helmet to Nick and ask him to put it on for you. Jada, your turn."

The little girl did not lift her head but let out a loud wail of anguish.

"Stop sulking!" Ivy told her crossly. "I warned you it was

going to be cold tonight. This is Maine and it's twenty-five degrees outside. You're not trick-or-treating without a coat."

"Ballerinas don't wear coats!"

Ivy closed her eyes and prayed for patience. "Your pink tutu will still show underneath, and Aunt Amy lent you those beautiful leg warmers. All ballerinas wear leg warmers."

"I don't *want* leg warmers!"

In the kitchen, the phone rang.

"Somebody get the phone!" Ivy called. To Jada, she said, "I'm not going to argue with you all night. Hammer and I are going trick-or-treating, and we're leaving in twenty minutes. If you want to go, get dressed. If you're quick enough, we'll even have time to paint some glitter around your eyes like we talked about."

Jada made what Ivy classified as a "spoiled-brat sound" and aimed a kick at the vanity table leg.

Ivy shrugged. "Suit yourself. And stop kicking the furniture."

DeShaun appeared in the doorway. "Uh, Ivy?"

"What?"

"That was Milo on the phone. His mother's sick, so we can't work on our grilled cheese menu at his house like we planned. Is it okay if he comes here instead? I could show him my new room."

"Does he have a ride?"

"Yeah, he has his license."

"It's fine with me. But you know the rules."

"Clean up whatever mess we make. I know; we will."

"And let me know if you use anything up—cheese, bread, whatever—so I can buy more."

"Okay." He disappeared again, presumably to call Milo back. A second later, his head reappeared around the doorway. "Thanks," he said gruffly.

Will wonders never cease! Ivy thought. She cast a last look at Jada, who was still sniffling, facedown on the vanity table, and went to find her camera.

Ten minutes later, a subdued Jada found her in the living room. She was dressed in her pink leotard, tutu, and leg warmers and carrying the glittery eye pencils Ivy had bought for the occasion.

"You look very pretty," Ivy told her. "Just like a real ballerina."

"Thank you," the little girl said in a small voice. But by the time Ivy had drawn elaborate butterfly wings around her eyes in silver glitter, she had forgotten her unhappiness and was posing and preening for the camera like the prima donna she was at heart.

"Grab your coats and pillowcases and let's hit the street!" Ivy called when the photo session was done.

"Bring me lots of candy," Nick said, looking over the top of his newspaper.

"What kind?" Hammer asked seriously.

"Ummm . . . Reese's Peanut Butter Cups."

As they pulled on their coats, amid many assurances that they would bring him some of *everything* they got, the doorbell rang.

Ivy thought it might be trick-or-treaters, but it was

only Milo. She stepped aside and let him pass as DeShaun appeared in the doorway.

"Hey, Milo." DeShaun must have outweighed the other boy two to one, and Milo came no higher than his shoulder. In the dim light of the entryway, beside DeShaun's darkness, Milo's pale skin seemed to glow faintly. The two boys headed for the kitchen. Milo, Ivy saw, was carrying a leather briefcase.

"Have fun," Ivy called after them.

DeShaun looked over his shoulder. "We will," he said. "Milo's teaching me how to cook kosher."

Will wonders never cease, indeed.

21

JONATHON

Are you there?

Here. What's up?

I need to go to the mall. Feel like
coffee with an old friend tonite?

Um . . . it's my anniversary, actually.

Oops. Awkward.

Yeah.

Another time, then.

Definitely another time :)

The lights at Nonna Mia's were low, the waiter discreet, the wine excellent, the music Vivaldi, but Nick felt as though he were on a blind date with a stranger who had turned out not to like him very much. It wasn't that they had nothing to talk about, but there was a distance, a restraint that had been there for months. Maybe it had really been there for years, and it was only months ago that he had begun to notice it. He was trying everything to cross the desert that lay between them, but he was making no progress.

They had eaten their way through fried calamari, lobster ravioli, and veal scaloppine, now having coffee and sharing a plate of tiramisu. And conversation was lagging. All at once, he felt nearly overcome with despair.

He laid down his fork. "Ivy."

"What?"

"Do you still love me?"

Stark silence.

"Why don't you love me anymore?"

She put her own fork down and rested her face in her hands. He did not press her. He was oddly grateful for this moment of respite before he would know—and then could never unknow—the truth.

At last she looked up. "Why should I love you, Nick?"

"I—because I'm your husband."

"So being my husband entitles you to my love; is that right?"

Wasn't it?

"Tell me this: has being your wife entitled me to *your* love for the last seven years?"

"Of course. Yes. I *do* love you." He felt foolishly close to tears.

"I don't think you even know what love is."

He opened his mouth, feeling trapped, and closed it again.

"Why don't I give you the textbook definition of love?" she said, looking not at him but into the depths of her coffee cup. "It goes like this: the textbook says that love is *patient*. Love is *kind*. It is not proud. It is not rude."

She was quoting the Bible—1 Corinthians 13, the love chapter. He knew it well. Something inside him shriveled with shame.

Ivy went on. "Love keeps no record of wrongs. It always *protects*; always *trusts*; always *hopes*; always *perseveres*. At least—according to the textbook—that's what God says love is.

"But how have you 'loved' me for the past seven years, Nick?" She held up a hand and began to tick her sentences off on her fingers. "You have been impatient and irritable. You have been unkind. Yes, I made bad choices and mistakes that changed both our lives forever. I've been the first to admit that. I've asked for your forgiveness. But you've decided that your high moral ground gives you the right to slight me and belittle the things that are important to me." Her eyes held a hard glitter that was not tears. "You have held my past wrongs against me. You have left me to bear my burdens alone. You have given up on me."

He was silenced by her words. Sickened by the naked truth of them.

"Don't ask me if I love you when you're the one who has refused to love me."

That was before. He wanted to howl it. *I've changed!* But she would never believe him. Why should she? He had so far proven nothing to her, except that every word of what she said was true. He looked at his hands, clenched on the tablecloth, and tried anyway. "You're right. And . . . and I know there's no way I can begin to—"

She interrupted him. "Save your breath. My love for you died of neglect a long time ago."

Nick felt the blood drain from his face. He had suspected that her love had cooled off a bit, that maybe it would take some rekindling, a little courting of her in order to get back to where they had once been. He had not expected this.

Across the table from him, Ivy was expressionless, detached. Her absence of emotion chilled him. "What now?" He forced out the words, his voice hoarse.

She picked up the check the waiter had laid on the tablecloth and examined it. "I honestly don't know, Nick. I'm still thinking about that part."

❧

The following Saturday morning, Jane, Leander, and Amy met them at the school for Hammer's first basketball game.

Hammer was the star of the team, as Ivy had suspected he would be. It wasn't a particularly fast-paced game, and being peewee league, it was short, only eight-minute quarters. But to her surprise, Nick was on the edge of his seat for all of it. Afterward, while they waited for Hammer to gather his water bottle and gear bag, he said, "He handles the ball like a much older kid. I think he has talent."

"*All* my kids have talent," Ivy informed him.

They went to the Silver Star for lunch, where they ordered from the new Grilled Cheese Special menu. They had hoped to see DeShaun, but he and Milo were busy cooking in the back and, from the look of things, doing a stiff trade. Ivy chose the grilled Brie and pear with walnut pesto on a croissant. Nick had the grilled Philly cheesesteak on sourdough. Hammer and Jada each had the "classic"—processed American cheese on Wonder Bread. Amy had spinach, artichoke, and Asiago on focaccia, and Jane and Leander split the "loaded"—cheddar, onions, tomatoes, and mustard on chewy peasant bread. Two bites in, Leander beckoned the waitress over. "This is too good to share with my wife," he declared. "Bring us another."

All around them, Ivy saw people ordering her boy's creations: cheese quesadillas with cilantro and black beans; chicken and Emmentaler hot pockets; toasted brioche with cream cheese and cherry jam. Everywhere, she saw smiles, nods of approval, and exclamations of pleased surprise as people ate. She thought her heart would burst from pride and gratitude.

Nick was nervous. Ivy sensed his eyes on her as she moved around the house; she could feel the anxious weight of his unasked questions. She tried to summon the emotional energy to care as much as he did, but could not. Mostly, she was indifferent to him. Indifference fueled by attention from someone else, she was discovering, could be a heady mix.

No, she was in no hurry at all to alleviate Nick's anxiety. Let him stew.

22

Ivy hung up the phone. "That was Mom. Laura's coming home the day before Thanksgiving." This time, Laura had gone directly from the hospital's two-week inpatient program to a twenty-eight-day rehab program in Bangor. This was the first news of her they had had in a month.

Nick looked up from the newspaper. "Do you want to spend Thanksgiving with your family this year? I'm sure my family would understand."

"I'm sure they *wouldn't*. I can't even imagine trying to explain that to your mother. No, let's just go ahead as planned."

"Are you sure?"

"Yes. The world has stopped enough for Laura lately without disrupting the Mason family's Thanksgiving plans too. We're invited over to Mom's for leftovers on Friday, though; is that okay?"

"Fine with me."

"Thanks. What time is your mom expecting us on Thursday?"

"I'm not sure. Want me to call her?"

"No, I will. But I'd better do it now, while my courage is high."

❧

Thanksgiving at the Masons' this year was a marked improvement over the last one. DeShaun had thought to bring a basketball, with the intention of going down the street to the park. "Take my phone," Ivy said, handing it to him. "I'll call you when it's time to come back for dinner."

To her surprise and gratification, Jessica's son, Connor, sidled down the stairs with his hat on backward just then and muttered, "Dude, I'll go with you."

"Oh, Ivy—" Ruby caught her arm—"there's something I want to show you."

Ivy let herself be steered into the kitchen, where Ruby's kitchen television sat on a corner of the countertop. It was turned on by a timer every morning at the same time as the coffeepot and not turned off again until the last of the lights in the house were extinguished at bedtime.

Ruby picked up a remote control. "It's the most wonderful

clock. I DVR'd it so I could show you." She flipped through the menu until she found what she was looking for: a saved infomercial about a clock that played a different birdcall every hour. "It only costs $19.99," she said. "I was thinking it would look lovely on the kitchen wall, over the microwave."

Ivy recognized a hint when she heard one. As the infomercial played on, she was a little appalled by the gadget but was happy enough to know that if she bought it, she would be giving her mother-in-law something she actually wanted for Christmas. She glanced at the space above Ruby's microwave. It was occupied by a Thomas Kinkade print of a thatch-roofed cottage with glowing windows. Ivy assumed that could easily be moved. "You're right," she said. "It would look lovely over the microwave. Thanks for showing me, Ruby. And just in time for Christmas."

Jessica's daughter, Britney, came in, followed by Jada, and peered over their shoulders. "What are you watching?"

The salesman on the screen was demonstrating the sounds of the clock at three, six, and nine: a cardinal, a sparrow, and a titmouse.

"A *tit*mouse?" Britney said in disbelief. "That's not a mouse."

"It's the name of a bird," Ivy told her.

"Sounds like a mouse with big you-know-whats." She cackled loudly.

Being a year older had not improved Britney.

Ruby frowned. "That's enough of that kind of talk."

Britney was unfazed. "Nana, can I watch *The Walking Dead* in the family room?"

"You'll have to ask your mother."

Britney took a deep breath and howled, "M-o-o-o-o-o-o-m!"

Ruby and Ivy both flinched.

"Don't shout. Go *find* her," Ruby said.

Britney ignored her. "M-o-o-o-o-o-o-m!" Louder this time, with the added twist of a whine.

Jessica hurried into the kitchen with Tiffany and Angela squeezing through the doorway behind her, like a single three-headed entity. "*What*, Brit?"

"Can I watch *The Walking Dead*? Nana DVR'd it for me."

"*Mother!* That show is not appropriate for a twelve-year-old girl," Jessica said primly.

Ruby threw her hands up. "How was I supposed to know? She asked me, and I recorded it. I thought I was doing the right thing."

Britney's face scrunched into a frightening scowl and she wailed, "Mo-om! How do you *know*? You've never even *seen* it!"

"I saw a segment about it on *Entertainment Tonight*," Jessica said. "I know what it's about. No, Brit, you may *not* watch it."

Britney stamped her designer sneaker–clad foot and shouted at her mother, "*Every*body watches that show! You never let me do *any*thing fun!"

"I hear your frustration, Brit—"

"No, you don't! You don't understand *anything* except your stupid, old-fashioned ideas. You're mean to me on purpose because you *hate* me!"

Jessica's smile began to look strained at the edges. "Now, sweetheart, listen—"

Britney abruptly switched to a sweet, wheedling tone. "*Please*, Mom? Please, please, pleeeeease?" She was joggling up and down so desperately that Ivy was tempted to ask her if she needed to use the bathroom. The girl clasped her hands against her heart. "Please, please, pleeeeease? Just this once, so I can know what everyone's talking about? I'll fast-forward through any inappropriate parts, I *promise*."

Jessica gazed at her daughter, and a look of indulgent affection overtook her face. "Well . . . maybe just this once. But you have to fast-forward the inappropriate parts like you said, agreed? I'm trusting you on this."

"Agreed! Oh, you are the best mom *ever*!" Britney flung herself at her mother's waist, gave it a quick hug, and raced off for the family room.

Jessica shook her head at the room in general. "Preteen girls. What are you going to do?"

Jada made as if to follow her foster cousin.

"Uh, Jada?" Ivy said quietly. "I think Ruby has a cupboard full of puzzles in the living room. Let's go see if we can find one you like."

"But I want to watch with Britney!"

Ivy shook her head. "Puzzles for you, sweetie."

"Please?" Jada cried, in a fair imitation of Britney. "Please, please, pleeeeease?"

Ivy raised her eyebrows and stared her foster daughter in the eye until Jada looked away. As the little girl moped toward the living room cupboard, Ivy shot a glance at Jessica. Her expression of amused tolerance said it all. Later, the sisters would talk among themselves about how well Jessica had handled her daughter and how unreasonably strict Ivy had been.

Half an hour later, she made a detour by the family room and looked in. A rapt Britney did not even notice her. And judging by what was happening on the screen at that moment, there was very little fast-forwarding going on in there.

⟍⟋

Dinner itself was civil. Baby Rebecca was nearly a year old and as engaging a baby as Ivy had ever seen. She was beautiful, too, with her combination of Angela's blonde, curly hair and Vincent's olive skin and brown eyes. Angela was full of pregnancy advice for Tiffany, who couldn't eat a thing and spent a good deal of the afternoon in the bathroom, throwing up.

"We're thinking of trying again in four months," Angela confided to Ivy, who happened to be sitting next to her. "That way, Rebecca will be exactly two years old when the new baby's born, and I'm sure she'll be potty trained by then. She's already starting to train herself!"

Ivy, who had no idea at what age normal children potty trained, gathered that Rebecca was considered some sort of prodigy. She congratulated Angela with all the heartiness she could muster.

Harry asked Jessica's husband, Allen, to say the blessing, which he did, keeping it short, sweet, and articulate so that the food was mostly still hot by the time they started eating. Best of all, Ruby refrained from any racial comments except to say, "Jada's hair is so sweet, the way you've put it up in all those little pigtails. I've heard that *their* hair can be very hard to handle."

"Thank you," Ivy said and was able to truly recognize the good intent behind her mother-in-law's words. It was a mark of progress, she realized, that she chose to chew up the meat of this comment and spit out the bone.

On the Monday after Thanksgiving, Jane came home from the grocery store to see the light blinking on her answering machine. Her children laughed at her for still using one, but she had never quite been able to get the hang of voice mail. It was so comforting to be able to *see* the place where your messages were stored. She set a gallon of milk and a bag of vegetables on the counter and pushed the Play button.

"Hi, Mom and Dad, it's Laura. I have some good news."

Jane heard her daughter take a deep breath, and all at once, ice water began to trickle into the space between her shoulder blades. She forced herself to begin unpacking vegetables from the bag.

"I found a new job," Laura's voice went on. "It's in Phoenix, Arizona. It's, um . . . it's an accounting job. For a grocery store chain. Lots of room for growth, that kind of thing. And I'm, um . . . I'm kind of thinking it would be good for me to get away from Maine for a while. One of the girls I was at rehab with has friends out there. She helped me find the job, actually. So . . . so, anyway, just give me a call back when you get time. They want me to start in a week, so I'm going to be moving pretty soon. Just, ah, wanted to tell you. So . . . bye."

Jane held a head of lettuce in her hand and stared at the answering machine. She felt numb. Automatically, from a lifetime of habit, her heart groped for the hand of God. *She can't go. This is the worst possible time. She needs her family.*

She waited for that old familiar peace to seep into her heart, the assurance that everything was going to turn out for the best.

All she felt was silence.

CHAPTER

23

THE LINE AT STARBUCKS inched ahead, but at last it was Nick's turn. He ordered a tall dark roast, black. The cashier was a gum-popping college student who asked in a rapid monotone if he wanted to buy a muffin the size of a softball to go with his coffee. Fending off this suggestion as well as another that he donate his change to United Way, he collected his cardboard cup, turned away, and scanned the room for a place to sit.

Even in the middle of the afternoon on a Wednesday, the mall was packed with Christmas shoppers. Nick felt harassed, stressed, unable to think clearly. He was shopping for Ivy's Christmas present with absolutely no success, and he was beginning to panic. His lunch hour had stretched to two, and at last he did something he had never in his working life done before: he called the bank and told them he was taking the afternoon off.

He spotted an empty seat at the counter along the wall and slipped onto the high, uncomfortable barstool. On one side of him, a twentysomething with white wires spouting from his ears hunched, unblinking, over the screen of a laptop. On the other side, a woman texted on a cell phone while simultaneously checking her e-mail on a tablet. He was surrounded by people—beleaguered, crushed, and jostled by them. Communication was happening on all sides, inescapable, its very ubiquity robbing it of value. And he was as alone as he had ever been in his life.

Alone in his marriage.

He had no idea what to get for Ivy. He had looked at sweaters and leather jackets, at electronics and scented candles. In desperation, he had even briefly considered a puppy. At the bookstore, he bought her a journal of handmade paper, and at the Lindt store, two pounds of her favorite dark chocolate. It was all he had been able to come up with. Granted, there were still three weeks to shop before Christmas, but Nick was starting to realize that the problem did not lie in a shortage of available things to buy.

He was on the brink of losing her. It was foolish to even think that finding the perfect Christmas present might unravel the mess he had made of his marriage. That a mere gift might be able to save them. And yet he hoped. He buried his face in his hands and began to pray.

JONATHON

Done xmas shopping yet?

Not even close. You?

Easy for me, I just give pottery. Hey,
you could come to the studio one day
& look around for ideas. Big discount
for friends.

You have no idea how appealing that
sounds.

So it's a date?

. . . bad choice of words, maybe.

. . . or . . . good choice, maybe.

You still there?

Just trying to get my head together.
Give me time.

Take as much time as you need.
I'll be here.

David leaned against a wardrobe in the bedroom of Laura's apartment. "Are you sure you can carry this all the way down to the truck?" he asked her. "That last one was heavier than we thought. Don't go hurting yourself."

"I can do it," said Laura. "Come on." Together they

crouched and each grasped an end. "One, two, three." They lifted it, her end much lower than his.

"Come on, Laura! Put your back into it!"

"Shut up," she gasped and began to shuffle forward. Somehow, they maneuvered the mammoth piece of furniture through the living room and front door, to the head of the stairs.

"Put it down," he said.

Laura obeyed with a groan and stood up, rubbing her lower back.

"Look, this is too much for you. Let me call George." George was David's roommate.

"No. I can do this."

"I know you can. The point is, you don't *have* to. George would be more than glad—"

"This is the last heavy piece. Three flights of stairs and we're home free. Come on."

He sighed. "Suit yourself." Flight by flight, stopping to rest at the landings, they wrestled the wardrobe down the stairs and up the ramp of the moving truck, where they set it down between her coffee table and a set of box springs. Laura sagged against the wall of the truck and wiped her forehead with the heel of a hand.

"I hate to see you go, you know," David told her. "The whole family does. We all wish you'd stay in Copper Cove."

"Oh, David, you're sweet, but I just . . . can't."

"Why can't you? You'd find another job around here, easy."

She regarded him with pity. "David, don't you ever feel like maybe the Darling family is sort of . . . the *source* of your problems in life?"

He scuffed the toe of a work boot against a bolt in the moving truck's floor and considered the question. "I guess I'm not complicated enough to think like that. I'm actually pretty high on Mom and Dad and all you girls." He shook his head. "If you're looking for psychotherapy, I'm not going to be much help."

"Hmmm. You're all brawn and no brain, is that it?"

"That's it. I'm good for manual labor and not much else."

"Good, because muscle is what I need right now, not another lecture on the error of my ways. Come on, there's that pair of end tables left, then all those boxes. I'll buy you a pizza when we're done."

He sighed. "Laura . . . I mean it when I say we're all going to miss you."

She straightened and headed down the truck's ramp. "End tables," she said over her shoulder.

David shook his head and followed.

❧

Ivy was writing out a stack of Christmas cards one evening when the phone rang. She heard Nick pick it up in the living room. A moment later he came into the dining room, where she sat at the table, surrounded by cards, envelopes, and a long list of addresses.

"Angela," he mouthed.

Ivy frowned. "Your sister?"

He nodded.

"She wants to talk to *me*?"

He held out the phone to her.

Ivy drew back as though he were trying to hand her a live spider. "What does she want to talk to me for?" she whispered.

"No idea. She definitely asked for you, though."

Ivy eyed the phone. She could not remember Angela ever once having called her. "Maybe she wants me to watch the baby?"

He shook the phone in her direction. "Just *talk* to her."

Gingerly, she took it from him and held it to her ear. "Hello?"

"Hello, Ivy, this is Angela."

"Hi, Angela. What's up?"

"I'm calling about Mumma and Daddy's Christmas gift."

"Their gift?" Ivy and Nick had already bought his parents the clock that played different birdcalls on the hour.

"We were thinking we could all chip in and buy them a TV."

Ivy was confused. "I thought they had a TV already. Actually, they have two, right? The kitchen television and one in the family room."

"This one would be for their bedroom."

"Ah."

"I already bought it. I stood in line outside Best Buy for three hours on Black Friday because it was such a good sale."

Ivy tried to imagine standing outside a store in the freezing predawn for three hours, on the day after Thanksgiving, in a line that stretched around the building, just to buy a gift for someone who already had two of the exact thing you were about to pay hundreds of dollars for. She shuddered. "Better you than me, Angela."

"Oh, it's fun," her sister-in-law assured her. "I love Black Friday."

"Well . . . a TV's a great idea," Ivy lied, "but Nick and I have already gotten them something."

"Oh?"

Out of sheer perversity, Ivy was not going to tell Angela about the clock. "Yes. Already bought and wrapped. So better not count on us for the TV."

Angela was silent. Then, "You know, you could try a little harder to be a member of this family, Ivy."

"What's that supposed to mean?"

"It means that Jessica and Tiffany and I are trying to make sure you and Nick are included, but you won't let us."

As long as she had known Nick's sisters, Ivy had never known them to be concerned with including her. She felt tired. "And we really appreciate it, Angela. But like I told you, we've already bought them a gift."

"Fine. Suit yourselves. But it's a little unfair, don't you think, to stick the three of us and our families with the whole cost of the TV? We were counting on splitting it four ways."

Now it came out. Ivy bit her lip to keep herself from saying this very thing. Irritating as Angela might be, she was still Nick's sister. Shallow, rude, shamelessly self-centered, but family all the same. "Of course, Angela. I didn't even think of that. How much do you need from us?" If she didn't have high blood pressure already, she was bound to have it by the time she got through this phone call, she thought.

"It was $500. We're each chipping in $125." Angela sounded pleased with herself. "I got a really good deal."

If $500 was a really good deal, Ivy thought, the thing had better be the size of a movie screen. So much for giving her mother-in-law a birdcall clock that had only set her back $19.99. "I'll have Nick send you a check," she said.

"Actually, I'd rather you paid me in cash. It would save me a trip to the bank."

Ivy had her limits. "But if I pay you in cash, that means *I'll* have to make a trip to the bank," she said. "Nick will put the check in the mail tomorrow."

Angela sighed noisily.

"Good-bye," Ivy said, but her sister-in-law was no longer there.

❧

JONATHON

Merry xmas a week early.

> Merry Christmas to you too.

All your shopping done?

> Yep. And wrapped. Go ahead, admire me.

You have no idea how much I admire you. Sorry you didn't come to my shop, though.

It's complicated.

I know. Just wanted to let you know
I'm here.

Thanks.

◦ゝ

They celebrated Christmas with Nick's family on the twenty-second. When Ruby and Harry opened the box containing the Black Friday television, Ruby clapped both hands to her face in astonished joy and began to cry. Ivy was suddenly glad Angela had strong-armed her and Nick into contributing. Never mind that a third television wasn't something she ever, in a million years, would have chosen to buy for someone. That wasn't the point of giving a gift, after all. Giving was not about what the giver wanted to give. It was about knowing someone and putting some thought into what would make the other person happy. It was worth $125—worth the whole $500, in fact—to see her mother-in-law so overjoyed.

She was doubly glad she had gone along with Angela's plan when she unwrapped her own gift from Nick's parents: a singing bird clock. "I don't care for them myself, but I remember how much you liked it when you saw it on TV at Thanksgiving," Ruby said, proud of herself. "I thought it would look just right in your kitchen, above the microwave."

Above the microwave indeed. "I love it," Ivy told her mother-in-law. An outright lie, but a kind one.

"Ivy, could I talk to you in the bedroom?" Nick stood in the doorway of the kitchen, where she was finishing putting together a salad. The collar of his dress shirt was unbuttoned and his tie hung, unknotted, around his neck. It was Christmas Eve, Amy's birthday. They were going, as they always did, to her parents' house for lobster stew and carols.

"Now?" she said, attempting to tear off a sheet of plastic wrap to cover the salad. She succeeded only in twisting it into an unusable tangle. Disgusted, she wadded it up and started again.

"If it's convenient."

Her pulse gave a skip of apprehension. She put down the plastic wrap and followed him.

In the bedroom, he closed the door. Automatically she stepped back.

"I'm not going to bite you," he said, his voice sad. "I just wanted to give you your Christmas gift."

Ivy bit back her impatience. Hammer had spilled orange juice on his shirt not ten minutes before, and she needed to find him another one. "We'll be late for dinner. Christmas is tomorrow; you can give it to me then."

"It's something I don't want to give you in front of the kids."

She hoped it was not going to be a sentimental piece of jewelry or some kind of lingerie. Anything that would force her to pretend more intimacy with Nick than she felt. She blew out a breath. "All right."

He lifted the pillow on his side of the bed and brought out a cylinder-shaped package, wrapped in garish red paper covered with Santa Clauses. He handed it to her.

It was light. She gave it a little shake. Nothing. "What is it?"

"You always ask that, and I never tell you."

She loosened the paper and pulled it away. It was the cardboard tube from a roll of paper towels. "What—?"

"Inside."

She fished around and extracted a thin sheaf of papers. They were stapled at one corner, crowded with fading print from an old-fashioned typewriter. The papers had taken on the shape of the tube, and she had to hold them flat with both hands in order to read them. It took her twice through the tangle of unfamiliar words before she understood what she was reading.

It was the deed to the house next door.

"What . . . ? Did you *buy* this?"

"Yes."

She was bewildered. "How? We can't afford a second mortgage."

"We don't have to. I cashed in my 401(k)."

His precious retirement fund. Ivy felt suddenly dizzy. "Why?"

Nick sat on the edge of the bed and stared at his hands, clasped between his knees. At last, he said, "I don't know what's going to happen with us, Ivy. Every day I wake up expecting you to say you're leaving. And . . . and I wouldn't blame you if you did." He looked up. His eyes were red and bright with tears.

In all the years she had known Nick Mason, she had never seen him cry. The sight of it distressed her, and in spite of herself, she reached out a hand. He grasped it and held on so tightly it hurt.

"Please don't leave me," he whispered. "I am so sorry." His voice was thick, and he let go of her hand to fish in his pocket for a tissue. He blew his nose. Wiped his eyes. "Sorry," he said with a shaky laugh. "I didn't intend to go to pieces on you."

"It's okay."

He went on, though his voice was not quite steady. "I know you don't love me anymore, and I have no right to ask you for a second chance. I promised myself I wouldn't. And I . . . I'll try not to. At least, not again.

"But I want you to have the house next door because I know it's hard on the kids to see it there every day. I know you'd like it to be gone. I . . . I thought that maybe after the New Year, we could do what the kids said: burn it to the ground and . . . and dance on the ashes. Maybe plant a garden on that spot in the spring. Whatever you and the kids want."

She did not know what to say. Laying the deed on top of the bureau, she went to him and put her arms around his head. He clung to her like a drowning man, buried his face in her belly, and sobbed.

Ivy looked down on the head of this stranger, her husband. His brokenness, which had been so long in coming, did not move her like she had imagined it would.

She felt gratitude, but that was all. And gratitude alone just wasn't enough.

Dinner was over at 14 Ladyslipper Lane, and the carols had been sung. David's roommate, George, and Libby Hale and her parents from next door had come for coffee and dessert. Sephy sat tinkling at the piano in an absentminded way while she and Libby caught up. Grammie Lydia sat in a chair in one corner, talking to Amy. They were all there except Laura.

Ivy wondered where her twin was, whether she was thinking of all of them tonight. No one had heard from her since she'd moved.

"Ivy, take this to the kitchen and refill it, would you?" Her mother handed her a plate of Christmas cookies that had been heartily attacked by Hammer and Jada and looked the worse for it. She was alone in the kitchen when her phone vibrated with a text.

JONATHON

> Hope I'm not waking you up. Just thinking about that cup of coffee you promised me & wishing we were drinking it together right now.

Ivy stared at the screen as though the writing were made of hieroglyphs. There was nothing about this message that was different from any of the others, yet all at once, she was flooded with shame. The phone in her hand felt dirty. She fought an urge to drop it into the trash can and bury it beneath the greasy napkins and broken lobster shells. What had she been thinking by encouraging Jonathon? Who had she become? A few attentions from a good-looking man and her head had been completely turned. And how did that make her any better than Laura, who had so freely helped herself to another woman's husband?

Ivy put down the phone and sat on one of her mother's barstools. She felt nauseated at the realization of what she had been doing.

She was a married woman, for heaven's sake. The thought of it made her limp with despair. What hope was there for them? So much damage had been done on both sides. Nick had held her past against her. And she . . . in return, she had hardened her heart against him. Had flirted with unfaithfulness. When Nick had been unloving, she had reciprocated in kind. She had flung God's words about love into his face but had not held herself to the same standard. So sure that she was on the side of right, she had ended up getting it all wrong.

So what was the answer? She knew already that it was not justice. She had tried hurting Nick back, had inflicted some retaliatory wounds, but the sweet taste of victory she had expected was not there. There was only more bitterness. She could hold out till kingdom come for all the wrongs to be righted, and it would not be enough. It would never heal anything.

It came to her like a commandment spoken into her heart: *Forgive.*

She gave a defeated little laugh. If only it were that easy.

Didn't God *know* she wanted to forgive Nick? *It's not that easy. You don't know what he's like.* Even as her heart formed the words, she realized how ridiculous they were. Of course God knew what Nick was like. Hadn't He created the man? She sat, staring at the countertop.

It came again: *Forgive him.*

No! She prayed it forcefully. *How he's treated me—it isn't fair.* The bald truth, she realized, was that she did *not* want to forgive Nick Mason. To forgive was to surrender your weapons. Give up your strength. Abandon what armor you had and lay yourself open to being hurt again. It was not fair of God, or anybody, to ask that of her. She could not do it. She should not *have* to. Tears stung her eyes and began to run down her face. It was not *right*. But even as her soul railed, she could do nothing more than sit there, her face wet and her nose running, and keep listening.

You will never be free until you forgive him.

I am perfectly free, thank You. But there was no conviction in the thought. For the first time, she felt the weight of her own injuries and resentments binding and pulling her down, like manacles around her soul. And freedom, which she had not even known she was missing, was suddenly what she wanted more than anything.

I wouldn't even know where to start.

Again, the quiet, compelling reply. *Decide to.*

It dropped into place, the final missing piece of a puzzle. She couldn't force herself to feel forgiveness; she knew because she had already tried. Like an ill-fitting coat, the feeling of forgiveness just wouldn't stay on her. It kept slipping off, leaving her clad only in the chill garments of righteous anger and bitterness.

Maybe there was no other way to forgive than to start with a decision. To make it an act of your will, and then— here, her thoughts gained momentum and she felt the first, quick stirrings of something exciting. It might have been the beginning of hope.

And then, once you decided, to keep on deciding, minute by minute, day by day, and then maybe, one day, you would wake up and discover that forgiveness was no longer an act of the will and of habit, but that it had really taken root, and you had just *forgiven*. You might realize that all the mistakes and injustices and deliberate wrongs just didn't matter anymore. Was such a thing possible?

She knew it was the right answer, as surely as she had ever known anything in her life. And at the same time, there was something else she knew: Nick wasn't the only one who needed to be forgiven. She had been only too glad to let herself lose sight of her marriage. To avoid what was difficult by losing herself in what was gratifying. She needed to ask Nick's forgiveness.

And not only his.

Ivy reached for a napkin and blew her nose, then rested her elbows on the counter. "Forgive me," she whispered. She heard the music and laughter from the living room, but in the kitchen, she felt cocooned in a kind of stillness, as though time there had slowed to a different pace. "Please. Forgive me."

She stayed like that for a long time, head in her hands,

pulse beating in her ears, looking down at the blue-flecked countertop between her elbows. The refrigerator hummed. A dish shifted in the sink. Outside, a car horn sounded. In the living room, the family laughed and talked. And gradually, in the quiet of the unquiet kitchen, she had the sensation that a kind of carapace had loosened and fallen away from her heart. What was beneath was raw and tender. Exposed and sore. But it felt like promise. Like a new birth.

Gratitude flooded her, saturated her. It shot through to her skin and emanated from her very pores. It buoyed her up. Lightened and amazed her. What a grace forgiveness was, both to give and to get. How meager and ineffectual was justice in comparison.

Awed, she whispered, "Thank You." And then she was astonished that five words of a prayer—*Please. Forgive me. Thank You*—could so utterly change everything. Could turn a heart of stone to one of raw, vulnerable, malleable flesh. Surely there was no greater miracle than that.

She stood and moved to the living room door, looking at them all. The most important things in the world were all right here in this room. There was DeShaun, standing by the bookshelves, in serious conversation with David. Hammer was sitting on her father's lap, his head against Leander's shoulder, face sanded with cookie crumbs. Jada sat on the piano bench beside Sephy, plinking out a simple duet with her.

Nick was talking, or rather listening, to her mother. Ivy was startled, from this distance, to see how much gray was in his hair. In spite of his height and broad shoulders, there seemed a frailty to him tonight. She thought of the ways he had learned to bend, in order to help her make a home for the children. The Xbox that had taken over his TV. The minivan. The noise and the mess he had quietly absorbed into his formerly placid life. The house next door that he had bought for all of them. The retirement fund that no longer existed. Nick Mason was never going to set the town on fire, but he was a good man. He was learning to be kind. It was a start.

୧

She texted Jonathon.

> I'm not up for coffee, thanks. I'm pretty busy with my family these days. In fact, I'm always going to be busy with them.

Oh?

> All the best to you, Jonathon.

Does this mean what I think it means?

> It means good-bye.

The phone did not vibrate again.

୧

In an apartment in Phoenix, Laura reclined on her sofa and watched on TV as the ball dropped in Times Square. For a moment she felt a stab of nostalgia, remembering other New

Year's Eves from the past. As long as she could remember, she had welcomed the New Year by singing around the baby grand piano at her parents' party. They would be having shrimp cocktail, she guessed, and tiny beef Wellingtons and crab puffs. It was a far cry from this city, where she knew nobody unless they worked at the grocery store where she did the bookkeeping. And most of them she only knew by first name.

Still, she had this apartment, even if it wasn't in the greatest part of town. At least it was affordable. And it had secure parking, so her Saab's hubcaps wouldn't get jacked in the middle of the night. And it was the New Year, a time for resolutions. For starting over on a clean, blank page in the journal of life.

Laura raised her champagne bottle high in the air and toasted herself. "To new beginnings!" she said aloud, although there was no one to hear.

She took a long swallow, straight from the bottle, and resolved that tomorrow would be a fresh beginning. In the morning, everything would be better. She was absolutely certain of it.

❧

On New Year's Day, Ivy was putting laundry away when she realized that Nick's top drawer was an uncharacteristic mess. Had it been her own, she would have left it as it was, she not being nearly as bothered by disorganized drawers as he. But this was Nick's side of the dresser, so she opened it wide and began clearing out socks and underwear, determined to do the job right. In the very back, she felt the crinkle of paper and pulled out a thick manila envelope, stuffed with folded sheets of paper, all addressed to Nick at his bank. She frowned and sat down on the edge of the bed to snoop.

At first, she could make nothing of the papers, but eventually she recognized a pattern. There were three bank accounts, one in each of the children's names. Each with a balance of several thousand dollars. She was bewildered. Where on earth had the money come from? The statements were easy enough to read because every single deposit was for the same odd amount, down to the cent. One deposit per child per month, for the last thirteen months. She let the papers fall from her hands and stared at the wall, baffled.

All at once, she clapped a hand to her mouth. *Of course.* Their stipend checks from the state of Maine. The money they got each month for taking care of the children's basic needs. She picked up one of the statements again and added up the numbers. It was the right amount.

Nick did all the bookkeeping in their family. In truth, Ivy could hardly have said what they paid for utilities each month. She had assumed that whenever the checks came, he was depositing them into their account, as he was intended to, and that the money was going toward the cost of raising the children, as *it* was intended to. Clearly that wasn't the case. For some reason he had instead been depositing it all into accounts in the children's names.

College, she thought, and the instant the word passed through her mind, she knew she was right. She was equally certain that the children knew nothing about this. She wondered when he was intending to tell them. And in the same instant, she knew that she would not ask him. Whatever his reasons and his plan, she knew that they were honorable because everything Nick ever did was honorable. She would wait, even if she had to wait for years, and see what happened.

Ivy arranged all the papers as she had found them, then carelessly tossed socks and underwear back on top of the envelope and closed the drawer.

That evening, she told him, "I was putting laundry away today and noticed your top drawer's kind of a mess. It's hard to fit anything else in there. Want me to organize it for you?"

And just as casually, without looking up from his newspaper, he said, "Don't bother. I'll do it tonight before I go to bed, thanks."

Why, Nick Mason, who would ever have thought it.

She went to him and kissed the top of his head.

He looked up. "What was that for?"

"No reason. Just because I love you."

"Well, if you love me so much, why don't you get down here and give me a real kiss?" And Nick, who had never before done such a thing, put aside his paper, pulled her into his lap, and kissed her so long and so thoroughly that when DeShaun wandered into the living room a minute later and cried, "Aw, sick, man!" Ivy hardly heard him at all.

ACKNOWLEDGMENTS

A HUGE THANK-YOU TO the experts at Maine's Department of Health and Human Services, and especially to Rana O'Connor, resource coordinator; Spurwink Treatment Foster Care; and to Leslie Kelly, trainer and foster mom extraordinaire, who patiently and thoroughly answered my questions. This book is in no way meant as a how-to manual for foster parenting, and there are instances when, aiming for readability, I may have sacrificed accuracy. Any mistakes or blurring of realism are solely my responsibility.

I am grateful for the under-twenty experts who fine-tuned my understanding of teenage language and culture as well: Mark Gardner, Miles Gardner, and Caleb Balser (for his particular expertise in gaming systems). My thanks to fellow writer Carey Christian, who helped me research the details of rosining a bow. It is always handy to have a contact in law enforcement, so thank you to my husband, Tim Gardner, for helping me sort out the legalities of Lily Allen's situation, and for just generally thinking that everything I do is wonderful.

I am filled with awe at my editor, Sarah Mason, who thinks of *everything* and is the only other person in the world who will ever care to know this story as well as I do.

Finally, thank you to my gracious family, who cheerfully do their own laundry, live for weeks at a time in a dirty house, and fend for themselves at mealtimes so that I can sit on the couch in my yoga pants and write books.

About the Author

Carre Armstrong Gardner was raised in the Adirondack Mountains of New York—the most beautiful of all possible settings—where she spent countless hours rambling through woods and beside streams, making up stories, usually with herself as the heroine. In fact, it wasn't until well into adulthood that she realized not everyone in the world sat at traffic lights or passed the time in doctors' waiting rooms creating plots and characters in their heads. It was that realization that first gave her permission to think of herself as a writer.

Carre's favorite stories have always been those about the ordinary lives of ordinary people. She believes every life is a fascinating drama, every person is the hero of his or her own story, and Carre's desire is to tell those kinds of stories in a way that makes readers love her characters.

As a teenager, she was a pianist, and a teacher encouraged her to attend conservatory as a performance major. But in a fit of altruism she decided to become a nurse instead—a career that had the double benefit of assuring a paycheck while allowing her to pursue music and writing in her spare time.

From 2007 to 2010, Carre lived and worked in Russia with her husband and children. Now she lives in Portland, Maine, where she works as a nurse at a local hospital. She has three teenagers and two rescue dogs, which is far too many. (Dogs, not teenagers.)

Discussion Questions

1. Jane recalls that when Ivy came home from college, "she found Nick and fitted herself to him like a broken limb to a rigid cast, in the hope that something in her would mend." What does Jane mean? What are other situations in which you've seen people cope this way? Do you think it's effective?

2. Ivy remembers the romance between herself and her husband dying soon after their wedding "as Nick, having conquered and attained her, lost all interest in continuing to court her." Do you think this happens to many couples in real life? Why or why not?

3. Jane reminds herself that God doesn't promise happy endings, only peace, and hopes that "she would never have to find out what it meant to have one without the other." Have you ever experienced a happy ending without peace or found a sense of peace even when the ending wasn't so happy? Describe what it was like.

4. When Leander tells Jane that Laura is "looking to see how far she can go and still be loved by a God she's never really believed is loving in the first place," Jane asks, "And how far *can* she go?" How would you have answered that question?

5. Laura asks David, "Don't you ever feel like maybe the Darling family is sort of . . . the *source* of your problems in life?" In what way does Laura blame her family for her problems? Do you think there is any truth to her complaints about the family?

6. Nick suggests to Ivy that "maybe villainizing you is the only way [Laura] can soothe her own conscience." What does he mean? Do you think it's human nature to do this? If so, what do you think motivates this kind of response?

7. Describe how Nick eventually comes to accept the children. What are some of the turning points for him? What does he have to give up in order to do this?

8. When Nick is worried about losing Ivy, we read, "Now, in a stroke of human nature as old as the Garden of Eden, Nick found that the thing he could not have was the very thing he wanted most." Has this ever been true in your own life?

9. Do you think Ivy crosses a line she shouldn't cross by texting back and forth with Jonathon when it's clear that he's interested in her? How does this make you

feel about the lecture she delivers to Nick on their anniversary about the 1 Corinthians 13 version of love? Is she in a position to be saying these things to him? Why or why not?

10. In the final chapter, Ivy is flooded with shame at a text from Jonathon, even though it's no different from others she has received. What do you think prompts her change of heart there?

11. How does Ivy grow or regress in her relationship with Nick's family? By the end of the book, where might there still be room for improvement in her attitude toward them?

12. Do you think Ivy grows in her faith throughout the story? Does Nick? How?

RETURN TO MAINE'S ROCKY
SHORES FOR THE NEXT

Darling Family novel

IN BOOKSTORES
AND ONLINE

Fall 2015